Enter Kit

Pendleton felt as if he had suddenly stumbled into a Frank Capra movie, replete with a cast of the usual suspects. The only thing missing was the madcap heiress, a perky redhead in a gold lamé gown, who had an equally perky little name. Like Pepper, Dody or Annabelle or—

"Kit!"

Yeah, that too.

At McClellan, Sr.'s outburst, Pendleton turned to greet what he assumed could only be the mysterious, toothsome Miss McClellan. But instead of a redhead, he found himself staring at what his mother referred to as a dishwater blonde. And in place of the gold lamé gown was a little black dress that fairly shrieked *Va-va-va-voom*. Miss McClellan herself, however, wasn't particularly little.

Nor, he noted with some trepidation, did she appear to be in any way perky.

MY MAN
PENDLETON

ELIZABETH BEVARLY

AVON BOOKS  NEW YORK

AVON BOOKS, INC.
1350 Avenue of the Americas
New York, New York 10019

Copyright © 1998 by Elizabeth Bevarly
Inside cover author photo by Chuck King
Published by arrangement with the author
Visit our website at **http://www.AvonBooks.com**
Library of Congress Catalog Card Number: 98-92768
ISBN: 0-380-80019-5

First Avon Books Printing: October 1998

AVON TRADEMARK REG. U.S. PAT. OFF. AND IN OTHER COUNTRIES, MARCA REGISTRADA, HECHO EN U.S.A.

Printed in the U.S.A.

WCD   10 9 8 7 6 5 4 3 2 1

This book is dedicated
with much affection and gratitude
to Marty Sussman,
who, once upon a time,
brought magic to my hometown
and inspiration to my young life
in the form of the Vogue Theatre.

Thanks for the memories.

Acknowledgments

I have a few people I need to thank on this one. Thanks first to Laura Bevarly and Maria South of Seiller & Handmaker, UP in Louisville, for making Lena Hensley McClellan's last will and testament "legal" for me. And thanks to Dan(ny) Bevarly, who answers all of my wine (and baseball) questions. Thanks to Jim(my) Bevarly for being there for my car and driver inquiries. And thanks also to my Colombian connection, Maritza Bevarly, who spells exotic words like *merengue* for me.

Thanks go, too, to Squirrel Nut Zippers, an incredibly talented group of people, whose album *Hot* provided exactly the kind of music I needed for this book. You all are truly an inspiration.

I'd also like to thank my editor, Lucia Macro, who's been there for just about every milestone of my writing career (and who's been responsible for a good many of them). Thank you for taking a chance on me blind and inviting me into the Avon family (and thanks to Carrie Feron for letting her do it), and for being such a fabulous editor and all-around wonderful human being.

Most of all, though, I want to acknowledge and

thank my husband, David Beard, who put his dreams on hold so that I could pursue mine. There isn't a romantic hero alive or dead, in fact or fiction, who is more heroic or romantic than you are. Thank you, David. I love you.

MY MAN PENDLETON

Prologue

Oh, Mama, what have you gone and done now?

Kit McClellan clapped a hand over her open mouth and marveled at what her mother's attorney was telling the family she had left behind. Although the reading of a will wasn't usually performed these days with the formality it once was, Hatton Abernathy had gathered the remaining McClellans together to do so, thereby fulfilling the late Lena Hensley McClellan's final wishes.

And, evidently, to let fly a couple of the late Lena Hensley McClellan's final zingers, too.

"The entire estate is to be placed in trust for two years," Mr. Abernathy repeated, directing his words toward Kit's father, Holt McClellan, Sr. "No one—neither you nor your children, nor anyone else for that matter—will be receiving an inheritance any time soon."

To Kit, the announcement was immaterial. Frankly, she couldn't care less about her mother's money, and would gladly surrender every nickel if it meant bringing Mama back. Being rich had never made any of them particularly happy, anyway. Except, maybe, her father. She turned her attention to him to see how he was handling the news.

Oooh. Not well. She'd never seen his face turn quite that color before.

"I'm afraid I don't understand," he told Mr. Abernathy. "Why would she put the entire estate into trust?"

"She never stated a reason," the lawyer said blandly, "and I never asked for one. But at the end of that two years, she indicated that one of two things should happen."

Kit's father narrowed his eyes but said nothing, waiting for the attorney to continue.

"Mrs. McClellan had a rather strong fondness for six local charities, and she expressed a desire for those charities to inherit the entirety of her estate."

"*What?*"

Kit flinched at the sound of the word, thundering throughout the room as it was when shouted by her four brothers in addition to her father. She glanced down the row of chairs to her left, to see how the rest of the McClellans were handling the news.

About as well as her father was, she decided. Bart, the youngest of her older brothers, looked dazed and stiff. Dirk, next up the line, looked dazed and surly. Mick, the second born, looked dazed and distracted. And Holt, Jr., the oldest, looked dazed and drunk. Yep. All of them seemed to be handling this pretty much the way she would have expected them to.

Mr. Abernathy went on as if no one had spoken. "One possible scenario of your wife's wishes would be that, at the trust's expiration, the business would be sold, the holdings would be dissolved, the assets would be liquidated, and all of it would be distributed to the organizations Mrs. McClellan indicated. One donation in your name, Mr. Mc-Clellan, and one in the names of each of your children."

Kit's father paled. "We, uh, we're talking about a hundred million dollars here, Abernathy."

"Ninety-nine-point-four, actually," the attorney corrected him.

No one said another word. In fact, the silence was so profound that Kit could scarcely hear a thing. Even the surly April wind outside seemed to have stopped blowing in light of the attorney's announcement.

Her father finally interrupted the silence, voicing, Kit was sure, what was of utmost importance in his life. "I was under the impression that Lena's money would come directly to me," he told Mr. Abernathy. "Why would she change her will this way?"

The attorney eyed her father coolly as he offered, "She never said."

"Well, when did she do it?"

"Almost three years ago."

"*Three years ago?*" Holt, Sr. roared. "My wife changed her entire will, stripped her family of everything, and no one bothered to inform me for *three years?*"

"Mrs. McClellan asked me to keep the change confidential," Mr. Abernathy said smoothly. "And frankly, Mr. McClellan, it was none of your business."

"None of my business."

Uh-oh, Kit thought. Her father was getting way too calm now. Then again, so was Mr. Abernathy. He actually appeared to dislike her father, which was very surprising. Not the part about him disliking her father—that was no surprise at all. There weren't that many people who *did* like her father. But it *was* surprising that Mr. Abernathy would make no secret of his animosity. People always at least *pretended* to like her father.

"I don't think I need to remind you, Mr. McClellan," the attorney said, "that the money was never yours to begin with."

A muscle in her father's jaw twitched. Hoo-boy, was he mad.

"No. You don't need to remind me. My father-in-law, God rest his miserable soul, always made it clear that I would never get my hands on the Hensley fortune as long as he—and his daughter— were alive. But after he died, Lena agreed that if she went before I did, I was to inherit the bulk of the estate. And I made damned sure things were in order."

Mr. Abernathy's mouth tightened into a thin line. "Yes, well, the money was still hers to do with as she pleased until she died. And it pleased her to give it to charity."

Holt, Sr. emitted a derisive snort. "And she never gave you a reason for why she wanted the change?" he asked again.

"None." Mr. Abernathy seemed to weigh his options for a moment, then added, "Although she appeared to be quite angry about something at the time."

"Angry?" her father echoed. "What the hell did Lena ever have to be angry about? She had a perfect life."

Oh, now *that*, Kit thought, was open to debate. Naturally, her father would think her mother's life was perfect. Hey, what had he ever bothered to learn about Mama's experiences, anyway? Jack, that's what. Although to all outward appearances, the McClellans of Louisville, Kentucky, certainly seemed to have it all—wealth, prominence, education, fame, you name it—Mama would've had a thing or two to say about the actual quality of life in the McClellan household. Starting with the quality of her own.

What on earth could have happened between her parents "almost three years ago" that would have made Mama do something like this? Knowing her parents, it could have been anything.

Only four days had passed since her mother's death, but Kit felt an emptiness inside herself that seemed to go on forever. She felt lost without her mother. Mama had always been the one stable force in her life. She'd been the only person who had ever stood up for Kit, the only one who had ever even tried to understand her. The only person who'd ever really loved her. And her only advocate during that whole Michael Derringer thing almost three years—

Like an iridescent bubble, realization popped in Kit's head, and suddenly she understood. Almost three years ago. Her mother quite angry. Thinking back now, Mama had been more furious than Kit had ever seen her in her life the night Daddy had paid off Michael Derringer in exchange for abandoning his only daughter.

"The second scenario of your wife's final wishes," Mr. Abernathy continued then, stirring Kit from her thoughts, "would, at the trust's expiration in two years, have the family inheriting the entirety of Mrs. McClellan's estate."

Six McClellan heads snapped up at the announcement.

"Well, hell, Abernathy," Holt, Sr. said, "why didn't you say so in the first place?"

Ignoring the question, the attorney continued, "For the family to inherit, one criterion must be met before the trust's expiration."

"Name it," Holt, Sr. stated emphatically.

"Miss McClellan," Mr. Abernathy said, dipping his head toward Kit, "must be married."

"*What?*" This time the exclamation came from Kit.

The attorney glanced over at her and smiled warmly in spite of the bombshell he had just dropped. "If you are legally married within two years' time, Miss McClellan, then your family will inherit your mother's estate, in full. However, should you choose to remain single, then the estate—every last penny—will go to charity. It's that simple."

He turned his attention back to the McClellan men and added, "Mrs. McClellan also indicated that no one in the family should marry until her daughter does. Should one of the boys—or you, Mr. McClellan, for that matter—marry before Miss McClellan does, then the estate would go to charity."

"But—" Kit started to object. Unfortunately, no other words emerged to join that one. Because she had absolutely no idea what to say.

Interpreting her silence as understanding, instead of the total confusion it really was, Mr. Abernathy continued. "For two years, the business and holdings shall continue on as usual, but they and the other assets will be managed by me and my firm, as Mrs. McClellan indicated they should be. The family will continue to reside here at Cherrywood, and all will receive their normal allowances. Really, your lifestyles will remain virtually unchanged. At least, until the trust's expiration. After that, well . . . What happens then will be entirely up to Miss McClellan.''

Somehow, the words sank into Kit's muddled brain until she understood what her mother had done. Whether her family kept or lost their fortune was entirely up to Kit, and no one would be getting married until she did herself. When she glanced up, she wasn't surprised to find every set of eyes in the room directed her way, and she could only imagine what they were all thinking.

Holt, Jr. was probably wondering how prudent he'd been to let his wife divorce him last year. Mick, on the other hand, had always made it clear that he preferred adventure to matrimony anyway. And Dirk was far too morose for dating. Bart was going to be upset, though—he'd gotten pretty tight with Donna lately.

All of them, however, doubtless had one thought circling in their heads over all the others. There was no question that they were all wishing they hadn't chased off Kit's date for prom night. Or for the Spring Fling. Or homecoming. Or Dorian Asquith's twenty-first birthday party. Or on any of the other aborted attempts she'd made to have a social life.

Her father's thoughts, however, were the ones that Kit found most interesting. Mainly because she pretty much knew what was going through his head.

"Gee, Daddy," she said, her voice emerging as little more than a croak. "Guess you're feeling pretty silly now about paying off Michael Derringer the night before my wedding, aren't you?"

Her father said nothing, just turned that odd shade of purple once again.

"But you know what's *really* ironic in all this?" she ventured further, amazed at her nerve. "Michael's happily married now with a baby on the way, and the business he started with the money you gave him is absolutely *booming*. I'm not sure I could *ever* find another man like him. Even if I had two whole years to look."

Chapter 1

Almost two years later . . .

His life fit very nicely into seven boxes. Three of those boxes contained books. Two held his music collection. One housed the sort of small appliances that made a single man's life complete—digital alarm clock, coffee maker, wet/dry razor, portable CD player. And one box—the biggest one—held all the designer suits and pointy-toed Italian shoes a man could ever use in one lifetime. All in all, he had everything he needed to start a new life. New city. New house. New job. New wardrobe.

He was a new man.

Restlessly, he scrubbed a hand over his nape, still not quite comfortable feeling the brush of frigid February air on a part of his body that hadn't been exposed for almost half a decade. The heat and electricity were working fine in the house in Old Louisville on which he had closed three days before. But thanks to the ice and wind of his first Kentucky winter that currently pelted his new home, the radiators in the old brick Victorian were taking their time warming up the roomy three-story structure. And because he hadn't yet bought any new furniture to furnish his new life, save a mattress and box springs to sleep on, there were no lamps for him to light to keep the darkness at bay.

A chill wound through him in spite of the leather jacket hugging his shoulders, so he puffed briefly on his bare hands and shoved them deep into the pockets of his blue jeans. Then, unable to tolerate the darkness any longer, he crossed the empty living room, continued without slowing through the dining room, and entered the kitchen, where he flipped on the overhead light. The sputter of the bare fluorescent bulb spilled a perfect bluish-white rectangle of illumination into the dining room, creating at least the illusion of warmth. And in spite of all the misgivings eating him up inside, he sighed with much satisfaction.

Tomorrow he would start his new job as executive vice president in charge of finances at Hensley's Distilleries, Inc., Kentucky's premiere producer of fine Bourbon whiskey. Frankly, he'd never much planned on becoming a high-powered corporate suit again. But, at thirty-two, he needed a change. And he had something to prove. Hey, it wasn't like his new position was something he couldn't handle, right? He'd been in a far more demanding position before. Granted, it had been one that had nearly destroyed him as a human being, but still . . .

Things would be different this time. Holt McClellan, Sr., the CEO of Hensley's, and the head of the family that had run the distillery for more than a century, was crazy about him. Although he had been a bit surprised to find himself seated across from the Big Guy himself when he'd interviewed for the position, he was fully confident he'd won the old man's approval. And although he didn't kid himself that someday he'd take over as CEO himself—Hensley's was, after all, a family-run business, and McClellan had five kids, one of whom was a VP himself—he knew he could be happy there for some time. Or, at least, until he had proved his point.

His new home was the land of Bourbon, tobacco, and thoroughbred horses, the greatest trio to come along since wine, women, and song. What wasn't there to like here?

Pushing away from the kitchen doorjamb, he sauntered slowly back toward his living room. His boot heels scuffed softly over the hardwood floors, and his nose filled with the combined fragrances of old dust and neglected fireplace. He absorbed the quiet, the solitude, the darkness. And he felt very, very good inside.

A new life in a new place for a new man. Nothing but blue skies and smooth sailing ahead, he promised himself. He decided to overlook the fact that the sky had been gray since his arrival and that he'd never sailed anywhere in his life. Because hey, what could possibly go wrong?

Something was very, very wrong.

As he folded himself into one of thirteen chairs that surrounded the long, mahogany table bisecting the boardroom of Hensley's Distilleries, Inc., the hair on his nape leaped to attention. And it had nothing to do with the haircut on which he'd spent more than he normally paid for a good lube job. There was definitely something strange about the entire collection of Hensley's executives, something that bothered him significantly. He just couldn't quite say what it was.

He watched as Holt McClellan, Sr., CEO, seated himself at the head of the table beside his son, Holt McClellan, Jr. "Gentlemen," he said, clearly unconcerned that his greeting excluded the solitary female who sat at the other end. "Good morning."

"Good morning, sir," the executives replied with all the precision of a Broadway chorus line.

McClellan, Sr. sifted through a small stack of papers before him as he announced, "I assume you've all heard by now that we've filled Riordan's position. Pendleton is our new VP in charge of finances. I hope you'll all make him feel welcome."

Pendleton, he repeated to himself. Corporate America, he recalled now, had an Ellis Island–like habit of changing the names of its citizens. Simply put, no one had a first name in this particular country. Only a last name, a career label, a personnel number, and a tee time. Pendleton, he supposed, he would be from now on.

"Thank you, sir," he said to his new employer.

McClellan, Sr., who most closely resembled a white-haired Burt Lancaster playing his most eccentric role to the hilt, bowed his head in silent acknowledgment of Pendleton's gratitude. Pendleton tried not to throw up.

The other executives nodded and welcomed him quietly, but somehow their greetings seemed a bit strained. Pendleton shrugged off his odd feeling to new-kid nerves, greeted them quietly as a group, then turned his attention back to his employer.

"We have a lot to cover today," McClellan, Sr. continued. "We're launching our new ad campaign next month, and with this new FCC ruling, we may very well be returning to television. Carmichael is handling that and will give us her report shortly."

He nodded toward his sole female executive, who nodded back in silence, each of their expressions somber and intent. Suddenly, Pendleton wondered if there was some kind of secret handshake or something that he should have learned in training.

"Also," the CEO went on, "as much as I hate to give in to the annoying little buggers, I honestly don't think we can ignore the Louisville Temperance League any longer. Though what those people think they're going to accomplish in this day and age, I can't begin to imagine."

Beside him, McClellan, Jr. grunted something that Pendleton assumed was an agreement. And he had to confess himself that he couldn't recall hearing the word *temperance* uttered by anyone anywhere in oh, say . . . his entire lifetime.

"For now, though, I've decided to let Holt, Jr. here handle them," McClellan, Sr. continued.

Much, evidently, to his son's surprise. Because McClellan, Jr. turned to face his father as the other man was making the announcement, his face etched in obvious surprise and consternation.

In profile, Pendleton noted, the two men looked almost exactly alike, save the evidence of the twenty-five or thirty years separating them that McClellan, Sr. clearly wore with honor. McClellan, Jr., even sitting, was as tall as his father, as good-looking, as blond as the senior had probably been in his youth. He also appeared to be every bit as capable, as self-assured, and as intimidating as his old man was now.

"Hold on," he said to his father without a trace of deference, something that went a long way toward putting him on Pendleton's list of people to be admired, a list that was none too lengthy. "Just when were you planning on telling me about this?"

The elder McClellan eyed his son with much impatience. "I'm telling you now."

"Oh, well, thank you so much for the warning," the younger man said sarcastically.

"I had to tell you sooner or later, Holt," his father retorted with equal sarcasm. "Otherwise, you wouldn't know what the hell you were doing."

McClellan, Jr. ignored the jab. "And do you think it's wise to put me in charge of something like that?"

McClellan, Sr. shot his gaze abruptly—anxiously—around the table before pinning it back on his son. "And why the hell *wouldn't* it be wise, son?"

McClellan, Jr. narrowed his eyes at his father, and a single muscle twitched in his jaw as he clenched his teeth. Hard. My, my, my, Pendleton thought, but this was getting rather interesting. He'd never worked in a family-run corporation before, though he'd heard tales from colleagues in like positions. He'd always wondered how true to life TV shows like *Dynasty* and *Dallas* had been. Not very, evidently, he thought now. Because the weighted responses of the two McClellans were proving to be *far* more entertaining than either of those TV shows had been.

McClellan, Jr. was the one to break the standoff, though when he did, his words were in no way successful in cooling the antipathy burning up the air between the two men. "In light of the, uh . . ." He suddenly seemed to remember that the room was full of people—people who were focused *very* carefully on the byplay—because he quickly arced his gaze around the table, much in the same way his father had, before glancing back at the elder McClellan and lowering his voice a bit. "In light of the . . . *situation* . . ." he said meaningfully. At least, Pendleton assumed it was meaningful to *some*body. "Don't you think it might be more . . . appropriate . . . for someone else to handle this?"

His father shook his head slowly. "I think the *situation* being what it is, you're without question the perfect candidate for the job."

"But—"

"But nothing," his father interrupted him. "You handle the temperance people. Now let's move on."

McClellan, Jr. obviously wanted to say more, but must have decided to do it elsewhere, because he only ground his teeth together and turned back toward the others without a further word.

So McClellan, Sr. continued. "We also need to address the asinine new law the boys in Frankfort have enacted against the tobacco companies," he said, "because I think we can safely assume that those joyless little bastards will be coming after the distillers next. We need to start planning our counterattack now. I've asked Novak and Martin to prepare a presentation, and I understand they're ready to proceed. Novak? Martin?"

Two men rose from the middle of the massive table, one bearing a big cardboard tube, the other with a collapsible easel tucked under one arm.

Oh, yeah, Pendleton recalled from some dusty, cobwebbed corner of his mind. The corporate presentation. He'd almost forgotten what those were like. Looked like his first day on the job was going to be a nice, long, boring one indeed. But then, was that really surprising?

The two men launched into an inflated dialogue

about cost overrun and capital-intensive, punctuated with excessive use of the words *parlay* and *utilize,* and with frequent emphasis on *impact* as a verb. Pendleton took that as his cue to ignore the pie charts and bell curves and view graphs and study his coworkers instead, quizzing himself in an effort to remember their names. He'd been introduced to each of them during training, and although his memory was exceptional, it never hurt to practice.

Rutledge, he recalled, eyeing the man directly opposite him, was VP in charge of public relations. To Rutledge's right was Hayes, VP in charge of research and development. Carmichael, the solitary woman at the table, headed up advertising.

One by one, Pendleton took in his colleagues, trying to note distinguishing characteristics of each of them that would help him keep names linked to faces. And that was when it hit him, what had initially bothered him when he first sat down at the table, what it was that seemed so wrong. Except for Carmichael, whose obvious lack of a Y chromosome, not to mention truly spectacular legs, would make her easy to remember, none of Hensley's VPs *had* any distinguishing characteristics. Except for McClellan, Jr., who was blond, all the executives looked exactly alike.

Like Pendleton, they were all dark-haired and appeared to have brown eyes. Seated as they were, the male contingent seemed to have heights, weights, and builds that were virtually identical. Even Chang, Bahadoori, Redhawk, Washington and Ramirez, whose clear ethnic backgrounds at least offered them some measure of individuality, all bore a marked resemblance in coloring and body type to every man present. Carmichael, too, was a brown-eyed brunette, tall and solidly built.

Good God, Pendleton thought, he was a Stepford Executive.

Certainly dark coloring was dominant over light, he tried to reassure himself, but still . . . Eleven people of nearly identical appearance kind of skewed the odds a bit. Surely there should be one or two blonds at least in the group. A Knutson or Wilhelm or Johannes or something. Of course, Pendleton was no expert on genetics—hey, who was?—but even he doubted that the odds of this kind of thing occurring were very—

"Pendleton!"

He flinched at the sound of his name thundering from McClellan, Sr.'s end of the table. "Sir?" he responded.

"I asked what you thought about Novak's suggestion."

Pendleton bit the inside of his jaw and pretended to give the matter great thought. "I think, sir, that utilizing such a parlay might potentially impact productivity with a dynamic we can't possibly leverage at this time."

Oh, now *that* had been truly inspired, he congratulated himself. Man, it was amazing how this corporate stuff just never left you. One quick flick of a mental switch, and it was all coming back to him.

McClellan, Sr.'s snowy eyebrows shot up at his statement. "Do you?"

Pendleton nodded sagely, steepled his fingers on the table before him, and strove for a grim expression. "Yes, sir, I'm afraid I do. Not only that," he added, hoping he wasn't taking the training wheels off too soon, "but channeling such a core strategy that way could decentralize market-driven revenues." He paused for a meaningful moment before adding, "And if I may speak frankly, sir?"

"By all means, Pendleton. You seem to be on a roll."

"Thank you, sir. But I wonder if Novak and Martin have fully considered the fact that the implementation of such a trend might rouse the concern of the AFL-CIO, the NLRB and the TUC, not to mention the FCC and ATF. Furthermore, in my opinion, a discussion of P and L, PPI, GNP, and AGI wouldn't be out of place here."

Now McClellan, Sr. nodded as he gave lengthy consideration to the weight of Pendleton's argument. Finally, he said, "Yes, I think I see what you mean. And you may be on to something."

Pendleton leaned back in his chair. "Of course, sir, ultimately the decision is yours to make."

"Yes, it is." He turned to the two men at the front of the room. "Novak, Martin, I think you need to go back and expand your presentation to include all the concerns that Pendleton just raised."

The two men glared venomously at Pendleton.

"And you can pitch it again on Thursday. That's three full days. Surely you can implement the data by then."

A sudden tic assaulted Novak's eye as he said, "Yes, sir."

McClellan, Sr. turned back to Pendleton. "I think you're going to be a fine asset to Hensley's, Pendleton. A fine asset indeed. Come around to the house tonight, will you?"

This time Pendleton was the one to arch his eyebrows. "Sir?"

"Cherrywood. It's where I live. In Glenview. See Margie for my address. I'll expect you for drinks at six. Dinner will be at seven." Then, without missing a beat, he directed his words once more to the others present. "I don't think we're going to have time for Carmichael's input today, so we'll postpone that until Thursday, along with anything else anyone wanted to discuss. It's getting late, and you all have work to do. Now get out."

The first to follow his own instructions, McClellan, Sr. rose from his chair, turned his back on his executives, and disappeared through a door behind him. Then, with a brief nod toward the other VPs, McClellan, Jr. followed immediately behind, closing the door with a soft *click*.

"Oh, way to go, Pendleton."

He looked up to find Novak smiling at him now, with what appeared to be heartfelt delight. As was Martin. Before he could comment, however, a chuckle greeted him from the other side of the table. When he turned, he saw that every other VP present was smiling the same sort of smile.

"What?" he asked.

In response, the others only chuckled some more.

Finally Rutledge stood, casually buttoning his double-breasted blazer as he did so. "You, uh, you might want to make sure you're armed when you go to the old man's house tonight, Pendleton. An Uzi ought to cover you just fine, though you might want to hide a little something extra in your sock, too."

Redhawk nodded. "Yeah, like a bazooka."

Chang concurred. "And Kevlar under your Hugo Boss wouldn't be out of place."

"The boys are relatively harmless," Carmichael said with an odd smirk.

"But watch out for the girl," Bahadoori added.

Dizzy from his confusion, all Pendleton could ask was, "The girl?"

"She bites," Washington clarified, gnashing his teeth for illustration.

Pendleton, too, finally stood, gathering up his portfolio in the process. "I'm afraid I have no idea what you guys are talking about."

They all chuckled even harder at that. "Yeah, we know," Ramirez said gleefully, obviously speaking for everyone present.

"But you will," Carmichael told him, winking. She was halfway to the door before she turned around, a thoughtful expression on her face. As she scanned Pendleton quickly from head to toe, she nodded with what he could only assume was approval. Then she added, "Just between you and me, Pendleton, you might be exactly the man for the job."

Chapter 2

Cherrywood, the McClellan home, was a majestic brick Georgian monstrosity perched high on a majestic green hill in majestic Glenview, an enclave for the way too rich just outside Louisville. The house was nestled amid huge, majestic trees— probably oaks and maples that were doubtless even more majestic when they weren't stripped of foliage by the winter chill. Because the sun had just set, the house was awash in soft, golden, majestic light, thanks to majestic outdoor illumination hidden in the majestic landscaping.

All in all, it was very majestic.

Pendleton rolled his car to a stop in the cobbled court in front of Cherrywood and simply sat behind the wheel, staring. A house with a name. God. He didn't begrudge anyone the material rewards that came with success. Hell, he planned to buy a few of his own once his paychecks from Hensley's started kicking in. But no one should be allowed to have as much money as the McClellans obviously had. There was just something very unbalanced about it.

Nevertheless, he supposed it wasn't his role in

life to decide who got what and how much. So he pushed the thought away, opened the door of his brand new BMW roadster—okay, so he'd already bought himself a material reward—and unfolded himself from inside. The winter wind whipped around him again, and he tugged the collar of his Ungaro overcoat—okay, *two* material rewards—up over his bare neck. Then he approached the Mc-Clellans' front door as he checked the time on his Breitling watch.

All right, all right. *Three* material rewards. But that was it.

Noting that he was a few minutes early, he lifted leather-clad fingers to the brass door knocker, an art deco sun with an expression on its face Pendleton could only liken to completely soused. After four quick falls of the knocker, he stepped back to await a response. Within seconds, the door opened, and he was met by a slender, white-haired woman with a very nice smile.

"Mrs. McClellan?" he asked.

She shook her head slightly. "Mrs. McClellan passed away almost two years ago. I'm Mrs. Mason, the McClellans' housekeeper. You must be Mr. Pendleton."

The *Mr.* part surprised him for a moment. Even having been employed at Hensley's for such a short time, he had already begun to think of himself as just *Pendleton*. "Yes, ma'am," he returned with a smile of his own.

"Please come in," Mrs. Mason told him, stepping to the side of the door. She swept an arm toward the interior, seemingly oblivious to the fact that it felt like it was about forty-two below zero outside.

As he entered and watched her close the door softly behind him, Pendleton noted that she wore the traditional livery of a housemaid—a plain black dress with white collar and cuffs. She lifted her hands at shoulder level, and for a moment, he wondered why she was surrendering. Then he realized she was waiting for him to remove his coat so she could hang it up for him. Feeling a little self-conscious, he unbuttoned himself, turned around, and let the woman who was his mother's age help him out of his coat.

And he made a mental note to remember that if he ever rose to the status of filthy, stinkin' rich, he'd never hire anyone to undress him.

Pendleton found himself standing in a foyer bigger than most suburban living rooms. It opened onto an ivory-colored, softly lit hallway that extended a good fifty feet before ending in a staircase that wound up to the next story. The hardwood floor was buffed to honey-colored perfection, and topped with the biggest Oriental rug he'd ever seen, woven of the softest colors he could ever imagine—apricot, ivory, pale blue. Along the walls, flowered loveseats beckoned to visitors, while marble-topped tables boasted a variety of knickknacks and family photographs, antiques, and fresh-cut flowers. Above the furnishings hung massive oil paintings of hunt scenes that—just a shot in the dark here—must have cost a small fortune.

Halfway down the hall were two large entryways facing each other beneath elaborate molding, the French doors of both thrown open wide in welcome. Muffled voices emerged from one of the rooms, though Pendleton couldn't have said which. He glanced at Mrs. Mason in silent question.

"Mr. McClellan and the boys are in the library,"

she told him. "Miss McClellan hasn't yet come down."

The girl. Pendleton recalled Washington gritting his teeth and decided that Miss McClellan must be the one with the overbite that he was supposed to watch out for.

"The library?" he asked, pointing first to one entryway and then the other.

Mrs. Mason smiled benignly, and Pendleton couldn't help but wonder if she really, really hated her job. "On the right," she told him with a quick gesture.

"Thank you."

She dipped her head forward in silent acknowledgment, and Pendleton stiffened a bit, uncomfortable with her display of deference. He wasn't much one for being deferred to, mainly because he wasn't much one for deferring. Unless, of course, his paycheck depended on it, and even then, it stuck in his craw. He gazed toward the door the housekeeper had indicated, but paused before taking a step.

He hadn't bothered with the Kevlar that Chang had suggested, but he had opted for his Hugo Boss. Now he ran a hand quickly over the finely woven, charcoal-colored wool, nudged a little tighter the Valentino necktie knotted expertly at his throat, and made his way toward the room Mrs. Mason had indicated. The sweet aroma of old books and cigars met him first. Then he entered a room furnished in Early Rich Guy, occupied by four of the more contemporary versions.

The library was small when compared to the brief sample he'd seen of the rest of the house, but it was still bigger than the studio apartment Pendleton had occupied while he was in college. Nevertheless, intimacy prevailed here. The ceiling was low and decorated with ornate molding, and the walls on three sides were covered with shelves— most of them crammed full of books in every color and texture available. Interspersed with the books were more knickknacks, more family photographs, more antiques. Another massive Oriental rug, this one spattered with rich jewel tones of emerald, ruby, sapphire, and topaz, spanned much of the floor, while illumination came from twin torchieres of brass and milk glass that stood sentry on opposite sides of the room.

"Pendleton!" McClellan, Sr. greeted him the moment he rounded the entry. "There you are, at last."

"Am I late, sir?"

McClellan, Sr. waved a cigar gregariously through the air. "Not at all. You're right on time. Cigar?"

Pendleton had actually always preferred Marlboros, but he'd quit smoking almost five years ago. So naturally, he now nodded enthusiastically at his employer's offer. "Thank you, sir."

"They're Cohibas," his host stated, as if Pendleton should know what that meant. "Would you prefer a Churchill or a robusto?"

"Uh . . ."

Now this was going to be tricky. The Cult of the Cigar was something that had flourished in the years that Pendleton had been away from high-powered corporate life. Although he recalled that Churchill was a rather prominent figure from twentieth-century British history, he couldn't imagine smoking the man. And, of course, he had absolutely no idea what a robusto was.

Finally, he replied, "Why don't you choose for me, sir?"

McClellan, Sr. nodded his approval as he headed for a small wooden box that sat alone on a table near an oxblood leather chair. "All right. You seem like the robusto type to me. And these are very mild. You'll love them," he added as he deftly snipped the end off the cigar with a tiny pair of strangely shaped scissors.

"Thank you, sir," Pendleton said as he took the proffered cigar.

He rolled it between his thumb and forefinger as McClellan, Sr. had done upon removing it from the box, then, because he'd seen James Bond perform the gesture in movies, he lifted it to his nose for an idle sniff. What exactly he was sniffing for, he couldn't have possibly said. But the cigar did have a rather pleasing, bittersweet aroma.

Holt McClellan, Jr. stepped in with a flick of what appeared to be—and doubtless was—a solid gold lighter, and Pendleton puffed robustly on his robusto with what he hoped was acceptable relish.

McClellan, Jr. was the oldest of four sons, Pendleton knew, and, judging by the little scene with his father earlier in the day, the younger McClellan seemed to be agreeable enough. Probably in his mid-thirties, the junior was clearly planning to take over the reins of Hensley's upon the senior's retirement. Likewise, it was clear that the senior McClellan was grooming his namesake for just such a scenario.

"What do you think?" McClellan, Jr. asked after Pendleton had enjoyed a good half-dozen puffs.

As fluent as Pendleton was in corporate speak, he'd received absolutely no education at all in cigarese, so he had no idea how to answer. So he casually expelled a stream of fragrant white smoke and replied, "That, McClellan, is one fine cigar."

"Pendleton, I'd like you to meet my other sons," McClellan, Sr. interrupted. "Holt, as you probably know, is the oldest. Mick, my second, is currently unavailable."

"Unavailable sir?"

"Last we heard, he was hugging the side of some mountain in Tibet. That was a good month ago. God only knows where he is now. Transylvania, maybe."

"Transylvania, sir?"

"He's working his way around the world in alphabetical order," McClellan, Sr. said.

Pendleton arched his brows in surprise. "Wouldn't it be more prudent to go around the world in a more, shall we say, geographical manner? East to west? North to south? That kind of thing?"

"Well, Mick never did like doing things the easy way," his employer stated negligently. "Says it's not manly."

"Ah."

McClellan, Sr. moved toward a sandy-haired son who appeared to be about Pendleton's age. But instead of the corporate uniform of suit and tie, this younger McClellan was dressed in a pair of baggy, cognac-colored corduroys and an even baggier, burgundy-colored sweater. Chic tortoiseshell glasses were perched on his nose, and his dark blond hair was bound fashionably—or perhaps rebelliously, if one was a McClellan—in a shoulder-length ponytail. Like his father and brothers, he was armed with a cigar, and he was clearly not afraid to use it.

"Dirk, here," McClellan, Sr. continued as he

clapped a hand over his son's shoulder, "is a professor of men's studies at U of L."

"Men's studies, sir?" Belatedly, Pendleton realized he had asked the question of his host, and not of the man who could more accurately answer it, thereby dismissing young Dirk in a manner that showed Very Bad Form. After voicing the question, Pendleton sensed instinctively that he had committed a grave faux pas.

He also sensed it by the way Dirk stiffened and clutched his drink with enough force to whiten his knuckles. And also by the snippy little tone in the other man's voice when he assured Pendleton, "Men's studies is an *extremely* important part of the liberal arts curriculum at U of L. It's an area of scholarship that's been sadly neglected for far too long, on campuses across the country."

In comment, all Pendleton could manage was, "Ah." In no way did he mean for the remark to be encouraging. Unfortunately, Dirk took it in exactly that way.

"Proponents of men's studies," he continued, still rather snippily, "delve far more deeply into the realm of manhood than the unfortunate stereotype that lingers from the genesis of the men's movement."

"Ah," Pendleton murmured again.

And again, Dirk misunderstood. "The fur-wearing, drum-beating, poetry-spouting stereotype, I mean," he continued. "The one that people have come to associate with anyone who has the temerity to suggest that a man's experience in the world is every bit as important as a woman's. God forbid we should let men have their say in this the late twentieth century. Oh, no."

Pendleton nodded, hopefully sympathetically, and reiterated, "Ah."

"The father-son relationship alone," Dirk went on, evidently anxious to don his own metaphorical fur and beat his own proverbial drum, "is an area rife for scholarly study. Do you realize how many perfectly good men have been ruined by a total lack of fathering?" he demanded, arcing his cigar through the air for emphasis.

"Ah . . . no."

"Or worse still, by shoddy fathering? Do you realize how many men have fathers who were never even present in their lives? Fathers who spent their weekends working instead of tending to their sons' needs? Who left the entire shaping of the male experience to their sons' *mothers*, for God's sake? Who selfishly thought it more important to carve a niche for *themselves* in the world, instead of helping their sons form some kind of cohesive—"

"Dirk."

McClellan, Sr.'s single-syllable interruption put an effective—and immediate—stop to Dirk's meandering, though, Pendleton had to admit, compelling, thesis.

"Anyway," the younger McClellan concluded, glancing down at his Hush Puppies. "My work is very, *very* important."

"Ah," Pendleton said again. Then he expanded his response by adding, "I see."

"And this," McClellan, Sr. said as he moved on to the fourth son, "is my youngest boy, Bart. We're fortunate that he could be with us tonight. Normally, he makes his home in Camp Lejeune, but he's visiting on leave. Marines."

Actually, Pendleton probably could have guessed that part, seeing as how young Bart was wearing his dress blues, complete with sword, in spite of the fact that the occasion was dinner with his family. Then again, he thought, recalling his colleagues' warnings of that morning, maybe keeping a sharp object within reach at all times wasn't such a bad idea.

By way of a greeting, Bart snapped to attention and saluted Pendleton. Actually saluted him. How very off-putting.

"Captain Bartholomew McClellan, *sir*," he corrected his father's introduction and avoided Pendleton's gaze.

"Uh," Pendleton replied eloquently, suddenly unsure what to do with his hands. So he only clutched his cigar more tightly. "*Semper paratus?*"

Bart's hands sprang to the small of his back, then he spread his legs and assumed a new position Pendleton supposed was meant to look more relaxed, but not really. Still avoiding his gaze, Bart replied formally, "*Semper fidelis. Semper paratus* is the Coast Guard."

"Ah. Well. *Semper fidelis* to you, too."

Bart nodded once, then turned to his father. "Request permission to speak with you about a private matter, sir?"

"Of course, Bart." McClellan, Sr. puffed his cigar a few times, then eyed his youngest son warily. "This isn't about that Donna person again, is it?"

Bart's face suddenly flamed fuschia, a color that did nothing to complement his uniform. His gaze flickered once to Pendleton, then back to his father. "Da-a-ad. I told you it's *private*," he whined softly.

As McClellan, Sr. and Captain McClellan moved to the other side of the room in quiet conversation, Pendleton considered McClellan, Jr. and Professor McClellan again. For a moment, he wondered where the three sons' wives were. Then he decided quickly that the McClellan testosterone level being what it was, the little women were probably all at home skinning fresh kill, and wondering what to do about the waxy yellow buildup on their husbands' pedestals.

The McClellans were, to say the least, a colorful family. For some reason, Pendleton felt as if he had suddenly stumbled into a Preston Sturges movie circa 1930ish, replete with a cast of the usual suspects. The only thing missing was the madcap heiress, a perky little redhead in a gold lamé gown, who had an equally perky little name. Like Pepper or Dody or Annabelle or—

"Kit!"

Yeah, that'd do.

At McClellan, Sr.'s outburst, Pendleton turned to greet what he assumed could only be the mysterious, toothsome Miss McClellan. But instead of a redhead, he found himself staring at what his mother referred to as a dishwater blond. And in place of the gold lamé gown was a little black dress that fairly shrieked, *Va-va-va-voooooom*. Miss McClellan herself, however, wasn't particularly little. Nor, he noted with some trepidation, did she appear to be in any way perky.

What she was in her black high heels was close to Pendleton's own six-feet-plus, and every inch of her seemed to crackle with energy. She wasn't by any means beautiful—her features were too angular, too strong, too striking, to be labeled *beautiful*. Nevertheless, there was something very compelling about her. The smile she wore held a hint of mischief, and her blue eyes fairly sparkled with anticipation. What she might possibly have been anticipating, however, Pendleton was hesitant to ponder.

"You must be Pendleton," she greeted him easily as she drew near.

He tipped his head forward. "If I must be, then I suppose I am."

She threw her head back, giving her dark blond, chin-length curls a dramatic shake. Then she sighed with all the melodrama of a madcap heiress, and announced, "I'm Katherine Atherton McClellan. My friends call me Kit. You, however, may call me Miss McClellan."

"Kit," her father called from the other side of the room, his voice edged with warning. "Play nice."

She chuckled, her smile dazzling, and her gaze never left Pendleton's as she asked, "Who says I'm not playing nice?"

Oh, yeah. He could see her taking a bite out of Washington. Easy. Probably from his butt.

McClellan, Sr. cut a quick swath across the library and stepped between him and Kit, though whether to make introductions or read them the rules of the fight, Pendleton couldn't have said.

"Pendleton," he began, his voice level and smooth, offering absolutely no clue as to what he might be thinking, "This is my daughter, Katherine. Call her whatever you want to. In my opinion, the list of possibilities is endless."

Something strangely melancholy shot through her expression at her father's words, but she recovered herself admirably. "Can I fix you a drink, Pendleton?" she asked.

"Yes, thank you." Automatically, he began to request his usual Scotch and water, completely forgetting for a moment who his new employer was. "Sco—uh, Bourbon and water," he hastily corrected himself when every eye in the room snapped toward him. "Or just, um . . . Bourbon straight over ice?"

"Good choice," Kit said smoothly. "After all, the only hard liquor we keep on hand is Hensley's. Duh."

It was then that Pendleton decided he would have to be on his guard around the sole McClellan female. Not just because she was impossible to gauge, but because she didn't keep Scotch in the house. He didn't care how well she filled out her little va-va-voom dress. Or that her long, long legs looked even longer thanks to the black silk hugging them. Or that her family had millions and millions and *millions* of dollars, not to mention a house with a name. They had no Scotch. And a man had to draw the line somewhere.

He watched her graceful movements as she plopped ice cubes into a cut crystal tumbler, then splashed a generous two fingers of Hensley's over them. When she returned to Pendleton's side, she was carrying another drink identical to the first, and was still wearing the same expression on her face—one that resembled a cat's, when it has one paw on a mouse's tail and the other on a catnip salad.

"So, Pendleton, tell me about yourself," she said as she handed him his drink.

He shrugged off the request, sipped his drink and tried not to gag. God, he hated Bourbon. "What's there to tell?"

"You big-wheeling corporate types," she said with a nonchalant wave of her hand. "Always so unwilling to talk about yourselves. Why is that, I wonder? Is it because you have absolutely no life outside the workplace? And because having to talk about yourself would just make you face the fact once and for all that, gosh, your life is just a big fat zero when it comes to leisurely enjoyment?"

Pendleton pretended to consider the suggestion as he sipped his drink again, then he shook his head slowly as he swallowed. "Nah. I'm pretty sure that's not it."

She shifted her weight to one foot and eyed him speculatively. "Okay, fine," she said. "Then let me just give you a little quiz I developed to better understand the people who work for my father."

"Oh, now wait a minute," he interjected, feigning concern. "No one told me there was going to be a test. I didn't have a chance to study."

"Oh, don't worry," she cooed. "I'll take it easy on you. Only multiple choice and true or false."

"I don't know," he hedged. "I was never very good at pop quizzes. Will there be math?"

"Maybe for extra credit. Question number one," she continued before he had a chance to stop her. "I, Pendleton, received my MBA from (A) Harvard, (B) Stanford, or (C) Bob's School of Big Business."

He felt a smile threatening, so quickly bit it back as he replied, "A."

She nodded. "Question number two. I've always envisioned myself (A) as the ruthless, sadistic CEO of my own corporation, (B) retiring before I turn forty to sail around the world, or (C) following Jerry Springer's lead and hosting my own daytime talk show so I can meet lots of dysfunctional strippers with big hooters."

He gave some serious thought to that one, then replied, "D."

She narrowed her eyes. "D?"

"All of the above."

She considered his response, then evidently decided to allow him credit. "Okay. Final multiple choice, then we'll move on to the true or false portion of our exam."

Pendleton filled his mouth with a generous, fortifying sip of his drink, remembered belatedly that it was Bourbon, and somehow managed not to spit the entire mouthful on his examiner. "Shoot," he managed after swallowing, the word a bit strangled.

Kit smiled coquettishly, and for the briefest of moments, something inside Pendleton went zing.

"If I could be anywhere in the world right at this moment," she said, "I'd like to be (A) at home watching *Xena Warrior Princess* and hoping it was an episode where she got wet at least once, (B) in the eye of a hurricane on a kayak with a broken paddle, or (C) why, right here with you, Miss McClellan—where else would I want to be?"

"Oh, now that's an easy one," Pendleton said smoothly. "I wouldn't think of insulting your intelligence by even bothering to answer that one."

She tilted her head to the side and eyed him with much interest, but gave no hint as to what she might be thinking. Instead, she straightened again and quickly launched into part two of what he supposed was the KMAT—the Kit McClellan Aptitude Test.

"True or false," she began. "I only receive the Victoria's Secret catalog by accident—I have never actually ordered anything from it."

"True."

She nodded, though whether she believed him, he couldn't have said.

"True or false," she went on. "When I'm flipping through my Victoria's Secret catalog, I always look at the faces of the models, too."

He started to fudge a bit on that one, then decided, What the hell, and told the truth. "Mmm . . . false."

She actually did chuckle at that one. But all she said was, "Final question. True or false. If given a choice between spending an evening with Mahatma Gandhi and Golda Meir, or two Victoria's Secret models, I would choose the models."

He didn't have to think about that one at all. "Absolutely true."

Kit smiled at him again before turning toward her father, who had moved to the other side of the room, where he appeared to be caught up in a very important conversation with McClellan, Jr.

"Hey, Daddy!" she sang out. When her father's head snapped up at the summons, she called further, "Gosh, he's really cute and everything, and he seems to be more intelligent than the last two you got me, but I couldn't possibly keep him. Thanks, anyway."

Her father inhaled a deep breath, excused himself from the company of his oldest son, and strode across the room as if nothing in the world was wrong. Then he completely ignored his daughter and said, "Pendleton, would you mind joining me and Holt? We're discussing the new trade agreement with Canada."

And before Pendleton had a chance to comment—or to say goodbye to the enigmatic Miss McClellan and her gorgeous legs—his boss was leading him away.

Chapter 3

All things considered, dinner didn't go nearly as well as happy hour, Kit decided. She drummed her perfectly manicured, coral-lacquered fingernails silently on the linen tablecloth, gazed at Pendleton sitting on the other side of the wisteria centerpiece, and pondered the benefits of lobbing a dinner roll at him. Ultimately, she decided it would have been frightfully impolite. Plus, she hadn't gotten a rise out of her father when she'd thrown summer squash at Novak last month, so why should a dinner roll make any difference tonight?

She sighed heavily, poked a fork into her ratatouille and guided the eggplant from one side of her plate to the other for aesthetic purposes. Seated on her left was the youngest of her older brothers, and on her right was a vacant chair. That was where she sat in the McClellan hierarchy. Just below Bart, right above the furniture.

She supposed it was something.

She snuck another peek at Pendleton from beneath her lowered lashes, and wondered why he intrigued her so much more than the others had. Probably because he was the first one who had actually passed her test, she told herself. He'd answered her questions honestly, and now she wasn't sure what to make of him.

Although he appeared to be exactly like every other man her father had paraded before her in the last two years—each of them bearing an uncanny resemblance to Michael Derringer—there was still something very unsettling about Pendleton. Worse, he unsettled her in a way that she hadn't been unsettled for a very long time now.

She hadn't been lying when she'd told her father that his new VP was really cute. Although, now that she thought about it, maybe *cute* didn't exactly suit this particular suit. *Cute* suggested a certain boyishness, and there was nothing boyish about the man seated opposite her now. On the contrary, he seemed to possess a maturity that even her father lacked.

Then again, that wasn't necessarily a compliment.

With a quick mental shove Kit swept the thoughts out of her mind. Pendleton, for all his cuteness and maturity was corporate. Simply put, ick. And he was Hensley's corporate, at that. Double ick. Like she was really going to fall for one of *them*.

She would have thought by now that, in spite of his desperation, her father would have learned his lesson and stopped dragging her out to meet his latest acquisition. But *nooooo*. Holt McClellan, Sr. would stop at nothing to save the family fortune, even if it meant *finally* marrying off his daughter after years of chasing off—or paying off—every man that had ever dared to come near her. And he wasn't even holding out for the highest bidder these days. He was entertaining any and all offers for his only daughter's hand in marriage.

Too bad for him that Kit wouldn't entertain even one.

Hey, her father had had his chance years ago, and he'd blown it. All of them had. If the McClellan men had just left her alone to marry Michael Derringer, none of this would be happening now. Hensley's would be well in her father's hand, her brothers wouldn't be starving for female companionship, and Kit would be as happily married as she was ever likely to be.

Instead of sitting here at her father's dinner table, wondering if a big ol' marinara stain would come out of a one-hundred-dollar necktie, or if Pendleton would just have to toss the expensive accessory in the garbage.

"So, Pendleton," she said as she fingered her spoon with idle interest, "have you gotten all settled in?"

He leaned easily back in his chair. "Actually, Miss McClellan, no. I've barely had a chance to unpack."

Telling herself that her curiosity about her father's new VP was no different from her curiosity about oh, say, the molecular structure of boron, she asked, "Where did you find a place to live?"

He met her gaze levelly, looking far too confident for her comfort. "I bought a house in Old Louisville."

Kit nodded, thinking the neighborhood suited him for some reason. The East End and Oldham County, where most of the suits settled, were too new, too hip, too happening for someone like Pendleton. Old Louisville, with its big brick Victorians and big, inner-city trees somehow seemed a more likely choice. She could somehow see him fitting into an old, urban setting far better than a shiny, new suburban one.

"St. James Court?" she guessed.

He shook his head. "Two blocks over."

She uttered a soft *tsk*. "Newcomer. Ah, well, it's something you can work on."

"Actually, it is," he agreed with a broad smile that went way beyond boyish, and right into the realm of *hubba-hubba*. But he said nothing more to clarify his remark.

So she steered the conversation down a new route. "You're not from Louisville originally, are you?"

He chuckled, a rough, masculine sound reminiscent of a wind-swept canyon, and all Kit could think was, *Ooooh, wow*. "Is it that obvious?" he asked.

"No," she told him honestly. "But Daddy hasn't hired anyone local for almost a year." She thought for a moment. "In fact, I think he's pretty much ruled out the entire Midwest now, haven't you, Daddy?"

At the head of the table, her father wiped his mouth with a linen napkin, glared at his daughter, and ignored her question by taking a sip of his wine.

So Kit returned her attention to the man seated across from her, and lowered her voice to a stage whisper before confessing, "I have a reputation for being rather . . . oh, unpredictable, shall we say? By now, it's reached as far as Chicago, Cincinnati, and Atlanta, thereby diminishing significantly the potential pool for Daddy to choose from."

To his credit, Pendleton offered no discernible reaction whatever. "Do you? I have a cousin who has a reputation like that."

Kit returned to her regular voice as she asked sweetly, "And is she an embarrassment to her family, too?"

Pendleton shook his head. "Not at all. We just love her to pieces on the weekends they let her out of the home."

Kit drummed her fingers more restlessly on the table. This wasn't going at all the way she had planned. "So where *are* you from?" she asked.

He hesitated only a moment, but it was long enough for her to see that he was stalling. "Before coming to Hensley's, I worked in Philadelphia," he told her.

"Doing what?"

He shrugged, but she got the impression the gesture was anything but negligent. "Pretty much the same thing I'm doing now."

"Oh. You were making some rich, greedy corporation richer and greedier?"

He smiled as he nodded, obviously proud of his accomplishments. "Something like that, yes."

"So are you from Philadelphia originally?"

"No."

She waited for him to elaborate, but he showed no sign that he would do so. She had opened her mouth to ask for more details when, for some reason, she turned her gaze to the head of the table. Her father was leaning back in his chair, his arms crossed over his chest, his attention utterly fixed on the byplay between her and Pendleton. He was watching her reaction to his new VP with great interest, a smug little smile playing about his lips. He looked to Kit very much like a man who was about to get exactly what he wanted. Like maybe ninety-nine-point-four million bucks in his name, and his daughter living under someone else's roof.

Ah, ah, ah, Daddy, she thought. *Not . . . so . . . fast.*

But as she thought further, a truly masterful idea began to take seed in the darkest corner of her brain. No, she told herself quickly, even as the idea took root. She couldn't do *that.* Not to her family. Even if her family *had* bushwhacked every opportunity she'd had to put a little romance into her life. Even if they *had* chased off—or paid off—every guy who had ever taken an interest in her. Even if they *had* messed up any and every chance she'd ever had to find happiness with a man . . .

She still couldn't do *that* to them.

Could she?

But bit by bit, as she considered her father's satisfaction with the way his little tableau was proceeding, the idea in Kit's head began to blossom. And slowly, she began to think that yes, maybe she *could* do that to them. Maybe . . .

This situation with her father's new VP could work very well to her advantage. But she was going to have to make sure she played her role *juuuuust riiiiight.*

She smiled, the first genuine smile she'd felt in some time. And she asked, "So, Daddy . . . what's for dessert?"

"What's this all about?"

Pendleton's question diverted Kit's attention from the plotting that had kept her busy throughout dinner. When she turned, she found him gazing at the photograph that hung above the fireplace in the living room. The dinner party had retired here with the three C's—coffee, cognac, and cigars—to wind up the evening. Except that in the McClellans' case, the cognac was really Bourbon, because they didn't keep any other hard liquor in the house.

Like every other room in Cherrywood, the main living room was filled with old things—old furniture, old rugs, old smells, old memories. And an old black-and-white photograph blown up to poster size, which hung where most people would post a portrait of the family patriarch. Though, in essence, she supposed that was exactly what the photograph was.

"That's my great-great-grandfather, Noble Hensley," Kit told Pendleton.

"What's that big, um, machine he's standing next to?"

She smiled proudly. "That would be his still."

"Ah."

"He was a moonshiner."

Pendleton nodded. "How fortunate for him to have had the opportunity to make his living working out in the sunshine and fresh air like that."

"I assume you've never been within smelling distance of a still, have you, Pendleton?"

"No, I can't say that I have been."

"I could tell."

Before she could elaborate, he gestured again toward the photograph and asked further, "And who are all those men surrounding your great-great-grandfather?"

"The ones with the guns?" she asked benignly.

"Yes, those."

"Those would be his VPs."

"Ah."

"They were always on the lookout for revenuers. Back then, Hensley's Distilleries, Inc. was known as 'Old Noble's still up in Hoot Owl Hollow." She pronounced "Hollow" as "Holler," as the locals would, giving her Appalachian heritage, of which she was extremely proud, its due. "Instead of things like research and development and public relations, Noble's boys handled things like corn acquisition and midnight distribution."

"Ah."

"The distilling business was much more romantic back then."

"And more dangerous, I'll wager."

Kit eyed him blandly. "Is there a difference?"

Pendleton eyed her back. "Between romantic and dangerous?"

She nodded.

"Don't you think there is?"

Now she shook her head.

"Ah."

He was driving Kit crazy with his total lack of reaction, especially when she'd been doing her best all evening to be annoying. And the complete absence of animosity on his part was starting to get her really steamed.

"It was your great-grandfather, Amon Hensley, who legitimized the Bourbon-making process, though, wasn't it?"

Pendleton's question roused Kit from her thoughts. "I don't know that I'd say he *legitimized* it," she replied.

"He wasn't the one who made it legal?"

"Oh, *that*. Yes. He did, eventually. Except during Prohibition, when they went back to the old-fashioned way of doing things. But a lot of people said the Bourbon tasted better when Noble was stirring it up out in the woods. God only knows what kind of woodland creatures found their way into it."

That, if nothing else, seemed to get a reaction

from Pendleton. Not a big one. Just a funny little kind of squinting. But it was a reaction nonetheless, and Kit gave herself a point for it.

"You mean wild animals drinking from the mixture allegedly made it taste better?" he asked.

She shook her head. "No. I mean little critters falling into the mixture, drowning and dying in it made it taste better."

He hesitated only a moment this time before remarking, "Ah."

"After Amon, came my grandfather, Beaumont Hensley," she continued, "who was really the one to turn the company into a big success."

"Excuse me," her father cut in from his position on the sofa. "I think you could include me in that equation."

She cast a quick glance over her shoulder at her father. "Well it *is* called Hensley's Bourbon, and not McClellan's, isn't it, Daddy?"

"That's beside the point. The product was established under the name Hensley's. It would have been foolish to change it to McClellan's, just because the power shifted on Beaumont's retirement."

Kit feigned surprise. "Did the power shift then? Really?"

"You know it did."

Instead of acknowledging her father's remark, Kit turned back to Pendleton. "Did you know Granddaddy asked Daddy to change his name when he married Mama?"

"Katherine," her father growled in warning.

She could see Pendleton hiding a smile. "No, I didn't know that," he said.

"It's true," she assured him.

"Katherine," her father tried again.

But she hurried on, "Granddaddy didn't have any sons, just my mother, and he wanted Daddy to be Holt Hensley, so that when he became the figurehead, there would still be a Hensley cutting through the surf, instead of a McClellan. Can you imagine? Asking a man back in 1959 to change his last name to his wife's?"

"*Katherine.*"

"Anyway," she continued blithely, "I suppose calling it 'McClellan's' would make it sound like Scotch, and it might potentially confuse the consumer. Not to mention make Noble spin in the ol' grave, if you know what I mean."

She was just starting to warm to the subject of the more colorful aspects of the Hensley's history when her father rose from the sofa and stubbed out his cigar.

"The show's over for tonight," he announced resolutely, his voice still tinted with his irritation. "Maybe this weekend we can hold a matinee for Pendleton, but I think you've exhausted your repertoire for now, Katherine. See Pendleton out, will you?"

Without awaiting her reply, he bid farewell to his newest executive, then waved his sons out of the room behind him. And then Kit was left alone in the living room with Pendleton and a cold sensation of empty accomplishment.

Her gaze lingered on the vacant doorway as she asked quietly, "You can find your own way out, can't you, Pendleton?"

A moment passed in silence before she realized that he hadn't answered her. When she turned to face him, she found him standing as if he hadn't heard her, a snifter of Bourbon cradled in one hand, a smoldering cigar in the other. If she hadn't known better, she would have thought he looked like he felt sorry for her. But hey, why would anyone feel sorry for her? She was a member of one of the wealthiest, most prominent families in the state. Obviously, it was just a trick of the light.

"Pendleton, can you find your own way out?" she asked again, a bit more softly this time.

He hesitated before answering, and she wondered for a moment if he had a problem with his hearing. And his eyesight, too, for that matter. He seemed to be spending an extraordinary amount of time staring at her, as if he couldn't quite bring her into focus.

"I don't know," he finally said. "It's a big house. I'm not quite sure how I got here."

Join the club, she thought. "It's this way," she said halfheartedly, jabbing a thumb over her shoulder.

She watched with veiled interest as he swallowed the last of his Bourbon and stubbed out his cigar. And she tried not to notice how easily he completed the gestures. For some reason, it bothered her that the good life seemed to suit him so well, and that he wore the mantle of wealth and luxury so comfortably. Why couldn't he be just an ordinary guy?

And why, suddenly, did she wish that he was?

She knew he didn't deserve the reception he'd gotten from her all night. Really, none of her father's executives did. Well, except maybe Novak. But Pendleton, like those other men, was a symbol of something she would just as soon forget. And even though she tried to keep a rein on her feelings, there were times when she just couldn't quite keep herself from striking out, in spite of the fact that nothing she did would ever completely erase the wrong. Or the memories. Or the hurt.

Restlessly, Kit shifted her weight from one foot to the other, watching as Pendleton rebuttoned his suit jacket. Then she hastily straightened when he swept his hand forward in a silent indication that she should precede him. When they came to the front door, she opened the foyer closet to retrieve his coat. She started to hold it up for him, but he deftly claimed it himself and shrugged into it, unfolding the collar around his neck before reaching for the buttons.

He really was very handsome, she had to admit. And there was something about him that was different from most men. If the situation were different, she might possibly be able to like him. But he was working for her father, and that meant money mattered to him more than anything else in the world. It was a shame. But then, she supposed, nobody was perfect.

"Good night, Pendleton," she said as she opened the door. "It's been real."

"Thank you for dinner," he said as he took a step forward.

She shook her head slightly. "You don't have to thank *me*."

"Thank your father then. For dinner, at least."

She crossed her bare arms over her midsection as the wintry wind whipped into the house, and she wondered at the merriment that danced in his dark eyes. "What does that mean?"

"Just that there was more to like tonight than the ratatouille, that's all."

Oh, right, she thought. Like she was supposed to believe *that*. "Good night, Pendleton," she said again, more vigorously this time.

He smiled at her, what appeared to be an honest-to-goodness smile of pleasure. But all he said was,

"Good night, Miss McClellan." Then he passed through the door and out into the chilly night.

And as Kit watched him go, all she could do was stand there with the cold wind swirling around her, and puzzle over why she suddenly felt so warm inside.

In the library, Holt McClellan, Jr. sipped his third cup of post-dinner coffee and resigned himself to working through the night at the home computer. Again. Because he knew there was no way his system was going to be shutting down anytime soon. Not because of the caffeine that was currently rampaging through his bloodstream—that was a nice, however inaccurate, excuse—but because sleep had been eluding him for a while now. To be exact, for twenty-one months, fourteen days, six hours and . . . He glanced at his watch. And forty-two minutes.

Ah, well. He was finally starting to get used to it. He'd been learning all kinds of things about the nighttime hours that he'd never known before. Problem was, he was learning all kinds of things about himself, too. And that could only lead to trouble.

As could his father's latest assignment for him, he thought, recalling the elder McClellan's insistence that morning that Holt be the one to handle the temperance people. "What the hell were you thinking to pass off the Louisville Temperance League to me?" he demanded, voicing his apprehension out loud.

His father glanced up from his seat opposite Holt and frowned. "What do you mean, what was I thinking? It makes perfect sense for you to be the one who deals with them."

"What if they find out about . . ." Holt dropped his gaze down toward his coffee again. "About my . . . history?" At his father's rough chuckle, he snapped his head back up again. "I'm serious, Dad. You might think it's no big deal that the second-in-command of one of Kentucky's biggest distilleries is a recovering alcoholic, but there are other people who might use the information in a way that is, shall we say, not sporting? And that could affect us all."

His father grimaced. "Nobody knows better than I do what your . . . condition . . . has caused this family."

This time Holt was the one to chuckle, but there wasn't an ounce of good humor in the sound. "No, Dad, I think I can safely say that I do know better than you."

His father glared at him. "I'm no more anxious for anyone to learn about your past than you are. All I'm saying is that, your perception of *temperance* being what it is, you can keep an open mind better than I could, and you'll certainly be more tolerant of these people than anyone else would be."

"Don't count on it."

His father uttered an exasperated sound. "Just take care of it, all right? And don't screw up."

"Yeah, right." Holt shook his head and sipped his coffee and wondered what he'd done lately to piss his father off. Hell, usually Kit was the one who was the focus of all of the senior McClellan's miscreant tendencies.

As if reading his mind, his father said, "So. What did you think of Pendleton?"

The quick change of subject jerked Holt out of his reverie, and he was thankful for the interruption. "He's all right. But I don't know why you think you'll have success with him when none of the others have worked out."

His father sipped his Bourbon slowly. "Pendleton's different."

"In what way? Other than the fact that he left the house tonight without a food stain on some part of his person."

"I'm not sure. I can just feel it. When I interviewed him to take over for Riordan, Pendleton came across as smart. Hungry. Plainspoken. The type to go after what he wants, but who doesn't put up with any nonsense." The older man glanced at his son with a knowing smile. "And did you see the way Kit was looking at him all through dinner?"

"Yeah. Like she wanted to strangle him."

His father smiled. "Exactly."

"And you think that's good?"

The elder McClellan nodded. "Damned right it's good. The way Kit was looking at Pendleton was just the way your mother used to look at me."

Holt shook his head. "I'm not sure that's such a good thing, Dad. By the time she died, Mama'd had it with you."

McClellan, Sr. waved off his son's concern. "She'd had it with all of us. That doesn't mean she didn't love us."

Holt glanced down into his coffee and said softly, "But she loved Kit best. She always loved Kit best."

"Kit was Lena's only daughter," his father replied softly. "Women always look out for each other."

"To the exclusion of the rest of the family?" Holt asked, unable to quite mask the bitterness he felt.

"Dad, we only have a little over two months to find someone to—"

"Pendleton is going to work out," his father insisted. "He's the man for Kit."

Holt wished he could feel as certain. "You know, we wouldn't be in this boat now if you'd just left her alone to marry Michael Derringer."

His father spat out an angry sound. "Michael Derringer was a self-serving, egotistical, gold-digging sonofabitch."

Takes one to know one, Holt thought.

"He would have made Kit miserable," his father concluded.

And since when did you ever give a damn about Kit's happiness? Holt wanted to ask. But aloud, he only said, "She seemed happy enough to me when she was with him."

His father waved him off again as he crossed to refill his glass. "Oh, what the hell do you know about it? Back then everyone seemed happy to you."

Instead of rising to the bait, Holt steered the conversation back to the task at hand. "Mama changed her will because of what you did."

"Lena changed her will because of what we *all* did. You can't hold me alone responsible. I seem to recall you and your brothers chasing off more than your fair share of Kit's boyfriends over the years."

"Yeah, at your insistence," he pointed out. "And because they were all creeps who couldn't care less about her. Kit deserves somebody who loves her. Not some jerk who's only after her money."

Only problem was, Holt thought now, that kind of somebody had never materialized in Kit's life. Or if he had, he'd never been given a chance by any of the McClellan men. And now, thanks to that, the McClellan women were having the last word.

"Do you think Mama really thought this was the best way to get us to leave Kit alone so her daughter could get married?" Holt asked his father. "Or do you think she just wanted to get even?"

That seemed to surprise the elder McClellan. "Get even? For the Michael Derringer thing you mean?"

Holt shrugged. "Or something else."

"What else could Lena have wanted to get even for?"

For starters, how about the fact that you never loved her? Holt thought. And then, of course, there was the fact that, where his father was concerned, family had always come second to wealth. And on those rare occasions when he *had* taken notice of the family, the old man had always had an obvious pecking order of preference. Even as the clear favorite, Holt had never felt quite comfortable with that. He could only imagine how his mother and Kit—at the opposite end of the spectrum—must have felt.

Not too great, obviously.

"Kit's not going to go for it," Holt said. "And I sure as hell hope you have someone else waiting in the wings. Because in two months—"

"Don't worry about it," his father interrupted him. "Pendleton is the man for Kit. Bank on it."

As was invariably the case whenever her father and oldest brother segregated themselves to talk, Kit overheard every word they said. Not by accident, of course. But because she deliberately sought them out to eavesdrop on the conversation. It was a habit she had acquired as an eight-year-old, when she'd overheard—by accident, that time—her father discussing her performance at Louisville Collegiate Elementary compared to Holt's performance at Louisville Collegiate High.

Holt had been a senior that year, and his grades had begun to fall drastically, in direct relation to the rise in his drinking. Kit, on the other hand, was, as always, making straight A's. And on that day nineteen years ago, her father had held her up as an example for her brother to follow, had expressed his pride in her as a student.

It was the first time she had ever heard her father praise her or her accomplishments in any way. And because of that, she had sought out every opportunity to hear him do it again, whenever he and Holt separated themselves to talk.

Unfortunately, that was also the last time she ever heard her father's praise. Because as hard as she'd worked to overhear even the smallest tidbit of approval, he'd never spoken of her again. Instead, his conversations with Holt had always centered first around Holt's work at Hensley's, then about Holt's excessive behavior, then about Holt's failing marriage, then about Holt's return to the fold.

Holt, Holt, Holt. It had always been about Holt.

Until tonight. Tonight, Kit's father had talked about her again. But nothing he'd said was good. Nothing he'd said was exactly a surprise, she conceded, but none of it was good, either.

She pushed herself away from the wall outside the library and headed slowly for the stairs. There had been one thing her father had said, however, that Kit couldn't deny. Pendleton was definitely different from the other men he'd thrown at her over the last two years. Where the others had blithered and fawned over her in an effort to curry her favor—and her mother's fortune—Pendleton had had the nerve to be forthright and honest. Kit had been totally unprepared for that. Forthrightness and honesty were unnatural in a man. Despite their presence in Pendleton, however, and for all her father's conviction to the contrary, he was *not* the man for her.

Still, she thought as she closed her bedroom door behind her, that didn't mean she couldn't have a little fun in the meantime.

Chapter 4

The Thursday morning version of the Novak-Martin Variety Hour went much better than Monday's had. Best of all, the addition of even more visuals, like the productivity report and the strategy graph, provided Pendleton with something to look at while his brain had the opportunity to wander at will.

Unfortunately, the path his brain seemed most intent on wandering down ended with the not quite completed puzzle of Miss Katherine Atherton McClellan. Oddly, it was exactly the same route his brain had taken for nearly every one of the sixty-three hours and change—both conscious and unconscious—that had passed since he had first made her acquaintance. And *that*, he had decided quickly, was terrain no sane man should explore.

Just what the hell had Monday night been about anyway? he wondered yet again. For all the McClellans' dubious civil behavior, there had been a tension in the air thick enough to hack with a meat cleaver. Pendleton had felt like a dead fly in the soup of family politics all evening long.

"Pendleton!"

Damn. Caught again.

"Sir?" he replied halfheartedly.

"I'd like your opinion," McClellan, Sr. announced. "What do you think of the modifications Novak and Martin have made to their presentation?"

Pendleton pretended to study all the visual aids—and, my, how they'd grown in the time he'd been thinking about the enigmatic Miss McClellan—then leaned forward and propped his elbows on the table. Entwining his fingers thoughtfully, he said, "In my opinion, sir, the implementation of such a visionary objective does seem to impact our mission statement, but I wonder if it won't be more productive in segmenting our quality group."

McClellan, Sr. studied him through narrowed eyes. "In what way?"

This time Pendleton leaned back in his seat, exuding far more confidence than he felt. "Well, sir, reengineering uncompetitive criteria can't possibly achieve a strategic trend. I think we should focus instead on data compilation, the performance track, quality assurance, and a dynamic paradigm. And let's not forget core competency."

"Oh, I could never forget that."

"Then I think we're in agreement."

McClellan, Sr. nodded. "I think we are." He turned to Novak and Martin, who stood amid charts, graphs, what appeared to be a chemical equation of some kind, and a big blowup of something that somehow resembled a map of downtown Trenton. "Men," he stated, "good work."

The two VPs twitched a bit, clear indications of their relief. "Thank you, sir," they chorused as one.

"Now then," McClellan, Sr. continued as Novak and Martin returned to their seats. "There's one final, little matter on our agenda that we need to address this morning. Kit's run off again."

Well, that certainly caught Pendleton's attention. Not just because it wasn't often that a CEO's daughter's activities made it onto the corporate agenda, but also because every single one of the executives present began to squirm and avert his or her gaze steadfastly away from their fearless leader.

"Who went after her last time?" McClellan, Sr. asked, considering each of his executives one by one as they began to fidget even more restlessly.

"Come on, come on," he cajoled. "Be a man about it." Then, when still no one came forward, he added, "I can check the files, you know."

Across the table and to the left of Pendleton, Ramirez, with clear reluctance, raised a hand—a hand, he noted further, that was encased in a plaster cast that disappeared into the sleeve of his pinstriped blazer. McClellan, Sr. seemed to notice, too, because he squinted more closely at his VP.

"Did Kit do that to you?" he asked, indicating the cast.

Ramirez glanced at his hand, then back at his boss. "Oh, no, sir. This happened while I was playing squash. Miss McClellan only sprained my wrist. Novak was the one who got a broken arm."

"Actually, it was just a hairline fracture," Novak said. "It was Bahadoori who got something broken, wasn't it, Bahadoori?"

The other executive nodded. "Ankle," he replied, as if that explained everything.

"That's right," McClellan, Sr. recalled with a faint nod. "And, of course, we all know about Washington's, um, posterior."

Washington shifted a bit awkwardly in his chair,

but remained noncommittal otherwise. Oh, wow, so she *did* bite him on the butt, Pendleton thought with some small measure of triumph . . . right before he realized just how bizarre the conversation had become.

"Carmichael was the one who escaped without incident," Bahadoori added.

Carmichael lifted a hand to her close-cropped hair. "Well, except for the hair," she said. Hastily, she qualified, "But I'd been thinking about going short with it anyway."

As Pendleton catalogued each of the other executives' experiences with the boss's daughter, he once again received the sensation of having entered an alternate plane of existence. What on earth was going on? Surely Kit hadn't been responsible for all those injuries. Washington, after all, topped six feet, and in no way seemed like the kind of man who would put himself in the position of . . . of . . . well, of being bitten on the butt. Not even by Kit McClellan.

"Pendleton, you're up."

As always, his boss's announcement snapped him right out of what had promised to be a very good preoccupation. And, as always, all he could say in response was, "Sir?"

His employer eyed him impatiently. "Go get Kit," he reiterated. "Bring her home."

"But—"

"Beaches," McClellan, Sr. elaborated. "She likes beaches, Pendleton. Try the beaches."

Well, gee, that certainly narrowed it down. That is, Pendleton thought further, it would have narrowed it down. If he'd had any intention of going after the boss's daughter. Which, of course, he didn't. Hey, it wasn't in his job description.

But all he could manage by way of an objection was, "Beaches, sir?"

Instead of answering him, McClellan, Sr. turned to Rutledge. "Where did you find her, Rutledge?"

"St. Lucia," the other man replied.

McClellan, Sr. nodded, then eyed the next executive in the group. "Hayes, where was she when you went after her?"

"Antigua, sir."

"Washington?"

"I found her in Jamaica."

"Redhawk?"

"St. Croix, sir."

"Bahadoori?"

"Montserrat."

And so it went, all around the table, until McClellan, Sr. had quizzed each of his VPs as to his runaway daughter's various destinations. Clearly, running away from home was a habit of Kit's. And clearly, sending his executives after her was the way McClellan, Sr. handled it. What wasn't clear was why the Hensley's executives would go along with such a thing.

"It would appear, Pendleton," his boss said, "that she rather likes the Caribbean. You might want to begin your search there."

"*My* search, sir?"

McClellan, Sr.'s expression probably would have been the same if Pendleton had just hopped up onto the table, whipped open his pants, and introduced everyone in the room to Mr. Happy. "Of course, Pendleton," he said evenly. "I thought I made that clear. It's *your* turn to go after Kit."

"But, sir," he continued, already feeling defeated, "is that really necessary? After all, your daughter is an adult who's free to do as she—"

"You can have a week off," his boss interrupted him before he could finish. "I'll look forward to Kit's return to the house by Thursday night, next week. Put all your expenses on the company credit card. Oh, and, Pendleton."

"Sir?"

"Don't forget to pack your sunscreen. That sun down there in the Caribbean . . . it's merciless."

For one long moment, Pendleton only sat in his chair, pinching his nose harder, squeezing his eyes shut tighter, willing himself to please, in the name of God, wake up from whatever bizarre dream he had tumbled into. Unfortunately, with the passage of every second, it became crystal clear that what he had been hoping was nothing more than the surreal, was, in reality . . . well, reality.

"Um, sir?" he finally managed to say.

"Yes, Pendleton."

He forced his eyes open, willed his hand back down to the table, and somehow managed to meet his employer's gaze. "This, um . . . That is, sir . . . What I mean to say is . . ."

"Spit it out, Pendleton."

He pressed his tongue to the back of his teeth for a moment, searching for the right words. "It's just that . . . well, going after your daughter isn't exactly in my job description, sir."

"Yes, it is."

"Sir?"

"Have you read your job description all the way through yet, Pendleton?"

He hedged. "Well, it is a bit longer than the average job description, and getting settled in my office has taken a lot more time than I thought it would, and—"

"Read it," McClellan, Sr. interrupted him.

"Yes, sir."

"And pay special attention to page four, paragraph six, subheading . . . subheading . . ."

"Subheading A, sir," each of the executives offered as one.

"Subheading A," McClellan, Sr. continued without missing a beat. "It's perfectly self-explanatory. Anything else?"

Actually, there were quite a few anything elses on Pendleton's mind, but for the life of him, he couldn't find it in himself to utter even one.

So McClellan, Sr. gave his executives the final once-over, rose from his chair, and announced, "I think that's everything. Now get out."

Then, as was his habit, he disappeared through the door to his office, his son following in his wake. And no sooner had the door clicked shut behind them did the rest of the executives leap up from their chairs, descend upon Pendleton like a plague of pinstripes, and begin to speak in a single, solitary roar.

"Forget about packing sunscreen," Martin began. "You go after that girl, you better be packing a piece. The sun down there in the Caribbean isn't the only thing that's merciless."

"And forget about watching the beaches," Ramirez told him. "You watch your back, man."

Not more than an hour later, someone thrust a legal pad toward him with what appeared to be the names of several travel agencies.

"These are the agencies Miss McClellan has used in the past," he heard Novak say. "Though you probably won't have any luck there. She never uses the same one twice."

"And she always travels under an assumed

name," Washington added, "but it'll be one you can probably identify if you try hard enough. Like Gertrude Stein, for instance."

"Or Betty Crocker," Carmichael said.

"Ida Lupino," Rutledge added.

"Dr. Denton," Ramirez continued.

"Che Guevera," Bahadoori offered.

Pendleton studied each of his colleagues in turn. "I'm sorry, but I don't see a pattern here."

"Exactly," Novak said, as the others nodded sagely.

He waited for a more complete explanation, but wasn't quite surprised when none was forthcoming. So, with a sigh of resignation, he asked, "Then you think I should contact one of these travel agencies?"

"*No!*" the entire group chorused.

"You should absolutely *not* contact *any* of them," Rutledge stated adamantly. "Miss McClellan's reputation definitely precedes her."

Hadn't Pendleton heard that already from someone? Oh, right, he immediately recalled. He'd heard about Kit's reputation from Kit herself. Hmmm . . . "So I should try a new one then?" he wondered aloud.

"Preferably in another city," Bahadoori told him.

"Another state," Carmichael added.

"Another country," Washington threw in. "They might not of heard about her in Abu Dhabi."

This was ridiculous, Pendleton thought. No human being could possibly wreak the single-handed havoc that everyone ascribed to Kit McClellan. Certainly she came across as a handful, sharpedged, sharp-witted, sharp-tongued.

Sharp-shooter?

Stop it, he ordered himself. No way would he

believe she was anywhere near as destructive as these people made her out to be. "She can't be as bad as all that," he voiced his thoughts aloud.

A ripple of anxious chuckles was his only reply.

"Okay, then can I just ask one last question?"

The others nodded.

"If Miss McClellan is so awful, then why doesn't McClellan, Sr. just let her stay wherever she runs off to? And why do you guys keep going after her, job description or no job description?"

"That's two questions, Pendleton," Novak pointed out.

"Okay, two last questions then."

For a long moment, none of the other VPs responded. Then Carmichael, evidently the least fearful of the repercussions, smiled a little grimly. "McClellan, Sr. needs her back, Pendleton, because Kit McClellan, for all her questionable tendencies, is far too valuable a possession for the McClellans to let her stray far."

"And why do you all keep going after her?"

Novak answered this time. "Same reason."

As answers went, Pendleton thought, those left a lot to be desired. "Valuable in what way?" he asked further.

"Sorry, Pendleton," Carmichael told him. "But any more questions you have, you'll need to run by one of the McClellans." Her grim smile returned as she added, "And I think you know which one would be most likely to give you the most accurate answer."

Pendleton nodded silently. That, he thought, was exactly what he'd been afraid of.

"Well, I'll be damned."

Pendleton shook his head in disbelief as he

slumped back in his chair. He tossed his job description back down onto his desk, his gaze pinned to the bottom of page four. Page four, paragraph six, to be specific. Right underneath subheading A.

Good God, it really was in his job description. Right there, in black and white, Times New Roman on Fine Linen Southworth, it stated quite clearly that should Miss Katherine Atherton McClellan ever take off for parts unknown, at any time during the period of his employment, he might indeed be called upon to travel to those parts and fetch her back to the bosom of her loving family.

Well, my, my, my. They certainly did things differently in this part of the country.

He expelled an exasperated sigh and spun around in his chair, focusing on the inky sky outside his window. Below him, Main Street was alive with the hum and honk of cars headed home for the evening. Across from him, the assortment of shapes and sizes known as the Center for the Arts was awash with glitzy light. Beyond that, the dark ribbon of the Ohio River rambled languidly on its way, emptying into rivers, gulfs and oceans beyond. And somewhere amid one of those oceans was a madcap heiress he was professionally obligated to find.

One week. That's how long he'd been granted to locate Kit McClellan, to bring her home to a father who demanded her return, yet clearly did not want her. For all the McClellan clan's wealth and prominence and opportunity, Pendleton thanked his lucky stars that his own family was one hundred and eighty degrees away from them.

The legal pad that his colleagues had so thoughtfully provided mocked him from atop his desk. Unwilling to tolerate the reminder of his duty, he ripped off the top sheet, folded it in half, then in quarters, then eighths, then sixteenths, and he stuffed it into his shirt pocket. Then he stood and straightened his tie, crossed to collect his blazer and overcoat from the coat stand near the door, and shrugged into the rest of his corporate uniform.

If McClellan, Sr. wanted his daughter returned, then Pendleton would retrieve her. It was, after all, in his job description. And bottom line, he needed his job. He needed the money his salary provided, the prestige his position afforded, the opportunity it offered him to show a certain person of his acquaintance that, hey, he could, too, hack it, so who's laughing now, huh? Therefore, resigned to his fate, he wrapped his fingers around the doorknob and prepared to face his destiny head on.

But his destiny was interrupted just then by a quick series of soft raps that greeted him from the other side of the door. "Mr. Pendleton?" Beatrice, his secretary, called out. "Are you still here?"

He opened the door to find her standing on the other side, her own coat buttoned up to her numerous chins, obviously on her way out, too. Beatrice had come with his office, having worked for Hensley's for longer than he himself had been alive. In spite of that, she left quite a lot to be desired in a secretary. He'd discovered that on his first day of work, when she couldn't seem to remember even the most rudimentary of company policies. Like, for instance, where they kept the microwave popcorn.

"I really apologize," she said, "but this arrived for you this morning while you were in your meeting with Mr. McClellan, and I just now realized I forgot to give it to you." She extended a cardboard overnight mailer. "I am so sorry. I hope it wasn't anything too important."

Actually, he thought, one might assume that the words EXTREMELY URGENT, in big red capital letters, emblazoned on both the front and back of the envelope, might have alerted her that there was some degree of importance attached to its delivery. But then, hey, that was just Pendleton—always assuming the obvious.

So all he said was, "Thank you, Beatrice. I'm sure it will be fine."

She smiled feebly, surrendered the overnight mailer, then spun around and fled without another word. When he glanced down to open it, he noted that instead of having a fancy, embossed label, the mailer had been addressed by hand and embellished by the word CONFIDENTIAL. Addressed by a bold, feminine hand, too, if he wasn't mistaken, he noted further, something that made a strange feeling of dread shimmy right down his spine.

Hastily, he tugged the plastic thread on the back and pulled the sides of the mailer open wide. For a moment, he thought it was empty. Then he tipped it upside down and shook it once, and a tiny bit of cardboard color came fluttering out, tumbling end over end to land on the pale peach carpet. He bent over to inspect it, for some reason reluctant to pick it up. Especially when he realized it was a postcard.

Of a beach.

Probably the Caribbean.

Dread filled him again as he snatched it up and flipped it over, only to find on the other side the same bold feminine handwriting that had appeared on the mailer.

Hi, Pendleton! the words inscribed there read.

Having a great time! Wish you were here! Love, Kit.

For long moments he only stared at those words, reading them over and over and over. And then his gaze fell on the fine print in the lower left-hand corner of the postcard. *Sunset at Veranda Bay. St. John, U.S. Virgin Islands.*

And all he could think was, *Oh, no. Don't make it easy. Please, whatever you do, don't make this easy for me.*

Just to reassure himself, Pendleton turned the overnight mailer to the address side and checked the postmark. Veranda Bay. St. John. U.S. Virgin Islands.

Well, my goodness, hadn't Kit been just too, too clever to realize in advance that her father would be sending him to retrieve her from her current tropical locale. Why did he suddenly get the feeling that he was some pinstriped amoeba under a big, karmic microscope, and that McClellan, Sr. was the one rolling him in and out of focus?

"Dammit," he hissed under his breath.

He tucked the postcard into the breast pocket of his suit jacket, and withdrew the much-folded list of travel agencies from his shirt pocket. Then he forced his feet to move forward, tossing the latter into Beatrice's trash can as he passed it. Hey, he could make his own travel arrangements. He only wished he knew exactly what he was headed into.

Chapter 5

Holt McClellan, Jr. folded himself into the big, executive chair behind his big, executive desk and gazed morosely at the big, executive pile of papers that required his immediate attention. Another day, another fifty-five hundred dollars, he thought blandly. In gross profit, anyway. All in all, life didn't get much better than this, right?

Of course, if Kit stayed in a snit, Hensley's Distilleries, Inc. and the rest of the McClellan legacy would be nothing but a sweet memory in a couple of months, and then he'd be lucky to pull in fifty-five hundred a month in salary. But hey, he reminded himself halfheartedly, they still had two whole months to find Mr. Right for his kid sister, and then they could marry her off like a good little heiress, right under the wire, and still be solvent. Otherwise . . .

He let the thought go. He couldn't even imagine his life otherwise. Holt braced his elbows on his desk and knifed his fingers restlessly through his dark blond hair. Hell, you'd think Kit would have been grateful to have Michael Derringer—her intended *husband*, for God's sake—exposed for the money-grubbing, gold-digging sonofabitch that he was. But *nooooo*. Not Kit. No way. She would have been perfectly content to live the rest of her life as a lie, as long as it meant that she didn't have to be alone.

Just as Holt began to reach for the collection of pink telephone memos fanned out across his blotter, the intercom on his desk beeped discreetly. "Yes, Jeanette?" he responded absently, already feeling weary in spite of the early hour.

"Mr. McClellan, a woman who says she's a representative from the Louisville Temperance League is here to see you." After a slight, but significant, pause, she added, "Again."

Oh, great, he thought. Just what he needed to make a cold, rainy morning even more frigid and forbidding.

"Does she have an appointment?" he asked, even though he was already certain of the answer.

"No, she doesn't. Again."

Of course she didn't have an appointment. What distiller in his right mind would make an appointment with someone whose single-minded goal in life was to put him out of business?

For months now, the Louisville Temperance League had been after all the area manufacturers of spirits, hammering them mercilessly—however ineffectually—with petitions, surveys, press releases, flyers, and other various and sundry promotional materials. They'd hosted everything from bonfires to prayer vigils to walk-a-thons, had done everything within their power to raise money, hackles, and public awareness. All in the name of sobriety.

Like any normal person would want that.

Nevertheless, representatives from the organization had been turning up at all the local distillers' doors, pretty much weekly, since well before the holidays. They never had an appointment, but they always had an agenda. Holt supposed his father was right. Sooner or later, they were going to have to let the group's members vent their respective spleens—spleens untouched by the poisonous presence of liquor, he was sure. He might as well get it over with.

"Her name?" he asked his secretary with a sigh of resignation.

"It's a Ms. Ivory," Jeanette replied.

Naturally, he thought. Naturally such a woman would have a wholesome, uncorrupted name like Ivory.

"Ms. Faith Ivory," his secretary elaborated further.

Naturally. "Faith Ivory," he repeated, the woman's moniker feeling stiff and unpleasant on his tongue. Relenting some, he asked, "Do I have any other appointments this morning?"

"Not until ten," Jeanette told him.

He sighed again. "All right. I suppose it's inevitable. Show her in."

Expecting a hatchet-wielding grandma trussed up in black like Carrie Nation, Holt was almost pleasantly surprised by the woman Jeanette led into his office. Instead of black, she wore a suit the color of champagne—good, pale golden champagne, not the cheap, yellowy stuff. What didn't surprise him, though, was the fact that the hem of her skirt fell modestly below her knees, and that her snowy shirt was buttoned to the neck, then pinned closed even more tightly by what appeared to be an antique brooch.

Even from the other side of the room, he could

see that her creamy complexion was flawless, touched by a blush of peach riding high on each cheek. Her hair, almost the same pale gold color as her suit, was also bound up snugly, her eyes were green, clear, almost bottomless, and framed by lush, dark gold lashes. And her mouth . . .

Good God. Holt swallowed hard, feeling a part of himself swell and grow warm that had no business swelling or warming in public. Her mouth, that generous, erotic mouth, made it impossible for Faith Ivory to *ever* appear temperate.

Clearly nervous about their meeting, she transferred the coat folded neatly over one arm to the other, then back to its original position, then back over the other arm again, all the while looking at him as if she wished he were someone else.

"Ms. Ivory," he greeted her, tamping down his irritation. He rose to his full six-foot-four, rebuttoning his dark suit jacket as he went, then moved easily around to the front of his desk.

"*Mrs.* Ivory," she corrected him immediately, taking a step backward for each one that he took forward.

At her designation of her title, he quickly dropped his gaze to her left hand, but he saw no sign of a ring on its fourth finger. Strange, that. Stranger still was the little twist of disappointment that wound through him at the recognition of her married state.

What difference did it make? he asked himself. The last thing he needed to do was involve himself with the Louisville Temperance League in any way, shape or form. Even if Mrs. Ivory's shape and form were too tempting to pass up.

"*Mrs.* Ivory," he conceded reluctantly, emphasizing her title more for his own benefit than for hers.

He swept his hand toward a chair that sat vacant opposite his desk. "Can I offer you a seat?"

She nodded, the motion jerky and anxious. Then she fled for the chair he had indicated and fairly collapsed into it, her entire body seeming to shrink into the upholstery the moment she was settled. She clutched her coat and purse on her lap as if she might need them later, to use them as a shield to ward him off. And it hit him then that she was genuinely frightened of him.

With no small amount of discomfort, Holt shrugged off her reaction, chalking it up to another extremist behaving, well, extremely. He returned to his chair and sat forward, steepling his fingers on his desk. With the big piece of furniture between them, the delectable Mrs. Ivory seemed to relax some.

"Now then," he tried again. "How can I help you?"

She inhaled deeply, her gaze darting everywhere in the room except to him. "As your secretary told you, Mr. McClellan," she began, her voice soft, well modulated, and a bit huskier than he would have expected, "I'm here as a representative of the Louisville Temperance League."

He nodded. "I'm aware of your position. But I can't imagine how Hensley's could possibly be of service to you."

"Well, you can't be of service to us," she told him frankly, her gaze finally skidding toward his for a moment before ricocheting away again. "That's the point. Your company, and the product you manufacture, aren't of service to anyone."

He hoped his smile wasn't as brittle as it felt. "On that matter, Mrs. Ivory, I beg to differ with you. As would millions of Bourbon drinkers world-wide. Hensley's is one of the best, if not *the* best Bourbon available. Our product—and our service—are of impeccable quality and have been for generations. We take great pride in that.''

At his pronouncement, she fixed her gaze levelly on his without flinching. ''Your *product*,'' she said, virtually spitting out the word, ''has been responsible for the suffering, the sickness, the *death* of millions of people over the years. I don't know how you can possibly take pride in something like that. In fact, I don't know how you can sleep at night.''

This time Holt didn't even bother to fake a smile. Instead, he leaned back in his chair, all pretense of civility gone. ''Cutting right to the chase, are we, Mrs. Ivory?''

''Well, I know you're a busy man, Mr. McClellan.''

Her outburst had clearly provided her with the needed boost for battle, because she suddenly didn't seem to be at all intimidated by him. Ignoring her remark about him not sleeping at night—frankly, it was none of her damned business why he had trouble sleeping—he backpedaled to address her other remarks instead.

''It isn't Bourbon that's been responsible for the things you like to blame it for,'' he said. ''It's irresponsible people who have caused those things.''

''The old 'Guns don't kill people' line, Mr. McClellan? I'm disappointed. I would have thought you could be more creative than that when making excuses for your role in ruining countless lives.''

He frowned. ''As much as I abhor the presence of handguns in our society, and regardless of the cliché, the reasoning is appropriate. It's not the product that the Louisville Temperance League should be going after, Mrs. Ivory. It's the people who misuse it that you should be directing your attentions to."

He sat forward now, linking his fingers loosely on his desk. "Will you be going after Hillerich and Bradsby when you're finished with Hensley's?"

She looked a bit puzzled, but only said, "The baseball bat manufacturers? Why on earth would we do that?"

He shrugged. "Hey, one good blow to the head with a Louisville Slugger could kill someone."

"Mr. McClellan," Faith Ivory interjected mildly, "I don't think—"

"And don't forget the Ford plant," he continued, ignoring her as he warmed to his argument. "Automobile accidents have maimed and killed a lot more people than Bourbon has."

"Mr. McClellan, you're being—"

"And General Electric. My God. I don't think I need to remind you that one fork in a toaster and you're . . ." He shrugged again, philosophically this time. "Well, you're toast."

She gazed at him in silence for a moment before asking, "Are you finished?"

"I don't know. Have I made my point?"

"Repeatedly."

"Then I guess I'm finished."

She hesitated, not seeming to know exactly how to proceed. Finally, she began again, "Few people can dispute the fact that drinking alcohol is dangerous. Drunk drivers have killed thousands of innocent people. And alcoholism is responsible for everything from domestic violence to birth defects to heart disease to—"

Beautiful mouth or no, Holt was losing patience with Faith Ivory. Her arguments were the same ones he'd been hearing for years, and frankly, he didn't want to hear them again. "Alcoholism and the enjoyment of spirits," he interrupted her, "are two entirely unrelated things, Mrs. Ivory."

"They're not at all unrelated," she countered.

"They are *completely* unrelated," Holt insisted. He inhaled a deep breath to clear his thoughts, then continued, as levelly as he could manage, "Alcoholism is a serious illness. The enjoyment of a cocktail after work or a glass of wine with dinner isn't."

"One leads directly to the other," she retorted.

"Not necessarily, though irresponsible behavior can contribute to it," he volleyed.

Faith Ivory studied him in silence, as if she'd known they would reach such an impasse, and she was just gearing up to drive home her next point. Oddly enough, Holt found himself looking forward to her argument. Strangely enough, somewhere along the line, this little sparring match with Faith Ivory had become diverting. Almost enjoyable. So he waited. But, surprisingly, Faith Ivory's luscious mouth remained firmly shut on the subject.

"Mrs. Ivory?" he finally spurred her, still unsure why he would try to prolong such a dialogue.

With some distraction, she answered, "Yes?"

"Aren't you going to respond to my comment that alcoholism is a serious illness?"

Very quietly, she said, "Alcoholism *is* a serious illness."

He nodded. "Well, my gracious goodness. We actually agree on something." When she still offered no comment to set them off again, he continued, "How about the irresponsible behavior part? Don't you want to say something about that?"

She shook her head slowly, her mind obviously still elsewhere. "No. Irresponsible behavior definitely contributes to alcoholism. I'll grant you that, too."

Well, golly, Holt thought. If she kept this up, she was going to take all the fun out of it. "So your point would be . . . ?" he tried again.

The steam she had been gathering evaporated, and whatever argument Faith Ivory had been about to make evidently disappeared with it, because she simply sat there and said nothing.

"Mrs. Ivory?" he tried again.

"My point, Mr. McClellan, would be . . ." Abruptly, she stood, slinging the strap of her purse tightly over her shoulder, folding her coat back over her arm. "I have no point, Mr. McClellan. Obviously, it was a mistake for me to come here. I apologize for taking up so much of your time."

Holt jerked to attention. Suddenly, he was desperate to do something to keep her from going. What had begun as an odious task to deal with as quickly as possible had turned into a strangely enjoyable little interlude with a woman full of mysteries he somehow wanted to solve.

It had been a long time since Holt had been drawn to a woman, especially with the immediacy and ferocity for which he'd become ensnared by Faith Ivory. Of all the women he could find himself attracted to, she was the last type he needed. Yet somehow he got the feeling that there were layers under her brittleness that she didn't allow others to see. And now he found himself wanting to flake away that thin shell of her exterior and find out what kind of motor was revving up beneath.

Because Faith Ivory was definitely revving up. Holt wasn't sure where she intended to go once her motor was at full throttle—he wasn't even sure *she* knew where she wanted to go—but there was definitely some destination on her horizon.

And just what made him so philosophical on a rainy Friday morning, he couldn't possibly have said. Unless maybe it was a beautiful woman with hair the color of champagne and eyes as deep as the ocean. A woman of mystery. A woman of intrigue.

A woman who called herself *Mrs.*

Faith didn't dare stop running until she'd made it through the Humana Building's Main Street entrance and stood in front of the fountain outside. Only with the knowledge that fourteen floors and countless feet of pink marble and steel I-beams separated her from Holt McClellan could she even begin to breathe again. And only out in the frigid air, with the cold rain pelting her, surrounded by strangers, could she at last feel safe.

Safe, she thought hollowly. Like she would ever feel that again in this lifetime.

In no way could she have anticipated Holt McClellan. He had just been so . . . so . . . Her breath caught in her throat at the memory of him rising from behind his desk. And rising, and rising, and rising. She'd been afraid he would keep rising until his head brushed the ceiling, and he reached across his desk to pluck her off the carpet and consume her whole. She squeezed her eyes shut at the recollection, pressed her hands to her cheeks and tried to steady her breathing. Holt McClellan had been, in a word . . .

Well, in a word, he'd been *awesome.*

She opened her eyes and spun away from the passing throngs of people to face the fountain, focusing her attention on the gentle stream of water that rippled poetically down the flat black marble.

Best not to think about it, she told herself.

Unfortunately, she knew that wasn't likely. Because now she was going to have to face the members of the Louisville Temperance League and tell them what a miserable failure she was.

She'd been so sure that her contribution to the cause would be her superior debating and argumentative skills. And under other circumstances, she knew she would have made a difference. She'd been an incredible criminal justice attorney once, had brought juries and judges to their knees. Of course, it had been years since she'd performed in the courtroom, but still . . . Some things never left you, in spite of the tests and obstacles you put them through. Some things were just inbred. Some things . . .

She cut off her own little pep talk, knowing it was pointless. She had failed at her task—just as she'd failed at so many other things—and now, as always, she was going to have to make reparations. The Temperance League could let someone else take over the Hensley's maneuvers. Maybe they could give her Maker's Mark or Brown-Forman or Heaven Hill instead. That way, she wouldn't have to deal with Holt McClellan again.

Because there was no question in her mind that *he* was the reason she hadn't been able to continue with her duties that morning. He was just too big, too handsome, too blond, too self-assured. Just like Stephen had been.

Don't think about him, Faith commanded herself. *Don't even think about Stephen Ivory.*

But the admonishment was as ineffective as always. Nothing would ever be able to make her stop thinking about her late, but hardly lamented, husband.

Forcing the thoughts away before they could turn into memories, she shrugged into her coat. Miriam was going to be disappointed that Faith had finally managed to breach the fortress of Hensley's Distilleries, Inc. only to surrender at the first sign of combat. What a coward she was.

Faith shoved her hand into her coat pocket to retrieve her car keys, only to find herself grasping a fingerful of lint where her keys should have been. She tried the other pocket, but it, too, was empty, save for a stray gum wrapper. Her purse provided her with little more than the basic paraphernalia necessary for feminine upkeep—hairbrush, lipstick, compact . . . a ball-point pen of questionable effectiveness, a half-full box of Tic-Tacs. But no keys.

When she realized what she'd done, she dropped her hands to her sides and threw back her head in defeat. Considering the way she'd been manhandling her coat in Holt McClellan's office—not to mention the velocity of her flight—it was a good bet that she'd dropped her keys in there on his lush-pile carpet.

Great. Now she was going to have to walk back to the Temperance League offices. Because there was no way she would go back into Holt McClellan's lair. Now she'd have to take a bus all the way to her sister's house in Fern Creek, for the spare set of keys Stephanie kept in case of emergency.

Faith eyed the slate sky overhead and felt the sting of ice-cold rain patter against her face. The Temperance League offices were on Chestnut Street and down some, a walk of nearly a dozen blocks from her present position. No way could she afford a taxi, and she had no idea which bus to take, or the time to figure it out. And her umbrella was in the backseat of her car. Her *locked* car.

Just as the realization materialized, the rain began to fall more resolutely, and Faith sighed as she stepped from beneath the meager protection of the Humana Building's generous overhang.

Was there anything, she wondered, that could possibly make this day worse?

It was only a matter of hours until Faith had the answer to that question. Yes. As a matter of fact, the day could get much, *much* worse.

Not because Miriam Dodd, the director of the Louisville Temperance League, had pontificated with even more vigor than usual about Faith's inability to achieve her goal where Hensley's Distilleries was concerned. And not because Faith's car dealer had told her that it would be at least twenty-four hours before he could get her a new set of keys. Nor was it because she'd been notified that her car was towed away, due to its being parked illegally during rush hour. And not because she'd had to sit on her sister's back porch for forty-five minutes—in the pouring, icy rain—waiting for Stephanie to arrive home from work.

No, Faith's day didn't really get much, *much* worse until after Stephanie had driven her back to her Highlands apartment. Until after she was safe and sound at home, had towel-dried her hair and slipped into her favorite flannel pajamas, had brewed a cup of hot chamomile tea, and had settled down to enjoy a rented copy of *My Man Godfrey*. Just as the credits for the film began to roll, there was a soft knock at her front door.

And that was a sound she seldom heard. Although she had plenty of acquaintances, people with whom she could pass the time pleasantly enough, there really wasn't anyone Faith considered a friend. Certainly there was no one who would pop in for an impromptu visit. She'd gradually abandoned all her friends after she'd married Stephen, and she'd been too embarrassed to look up any of them again after his death. She didn't want to have to explain things. It was just easier to be alone.

Carefully, she set her mug of tea on the coffee table and rose from the sofa. Quietly, she padded in her stocking feet to the front door. Cautiously, she peeked through the peephole. And crestfallen, she saw Holt McClellan standing on the other side.

She should have just gone back for her keys when she'd had the chance, she thought. Gee, hindsight really was twenty-twenty.

"Yes?" she called through the door, keeping her eye pressed to the peephole.

"Mrs. Ivory?" he asked.

"Yes?"

"It's Holt McClellan. Of Hensley's Distilleries?"

"What do you want?"

Belatedly, she realized how rude the question must have sounded. But really, what difference did it make? She had no reason to be polite to the man. Their exchange earlier in the day had made clear their feelings for each other's outlooks on life—and for each other—and they were scarcely on the same side when it came to their personal and professional philosophies. What did Faith care if she offended the man? Strangely, however, she found that she *did* care.

"You, uh, you left something in my office this morning," he told her. "But I imagine you've already discovered that."

"My keys," she said unnecessarily.

"Your keys," he concurred.

As was always the case when Faith was home, the chain was in place on the door. So she braved twisting the key in the lock, braved loosing the deadbolt, and even braved edging the door open a scant few inches to look beyond it.

The peephole had distorted him more than she'd realized. Only when she saw Holt McClellan standing there in the flesh did she recall how handsome he was, how blond, how large. How much like Stephen. Faith swallowed hard and tried not to panic. But when he began to lift his hand, her fear—her irrational, irrepressible fear—betrayed her. Automatically, she closed her eyes and waited in arrested silence for him to—

"Mrs. Ivory?"

She snapped her eyes open again. Holt McClellan stood exactly as he had before, except that now, he was extending a ring of keys toward her and he was looking at her as if she had lost her mind. Of course, who could blame him? There were times when she looked at herself in the mirror in exactly that same way.

Pushing the sensation away, she reached beyond the door for her keys, only to watch them be withdrawn again. When she glanced up at Holt McClellan's face, he was smiling. Softly, sweetly, seductively.

Oh, my.

"Can I come in?" he asked.

Oh, no, no, no, no, no, she thought. *Absolutely not.* But her voice betrayed her conviction when she stammered, "Wh-what for?"

"Because our conversation today was interrupted before we could finish it," he said easily.

"I know," she replied. "I was the one who interrupted it."

"So you were. I can only wonder why you did."

"I-I just didn't see any reason to continue our discussion."

"Why not? Things were just starting to heat up."

That was the problem. Faith bit her lip to keep the rash words from spilling out of her mouth. "I just . . . That is, we didn't seem to be . . . I mean, the whole conversation was just . . ."

"What?"

She licked her lips against the dryness that had overtaken her mouth and forced herself to look away from his eyes. His beautiful midnight-blue eyes. The eyes that had created no small amount of turbulence in her midsection the moment she had entered his office. The eyes that continued to dazzle her now.

"We both, um . . ." she tried again. "We both seem to be pretty strong in our convictions, that's all."

"Is that surprising?"

"Well, no, but . . . but . . ."

"But what?" he asked.

She raked a hand restlessly through her unbound, still-damp hair and pretended she knew where she was going with her thoughts. "Look, if we're going to start this thing up again, can I at least change out of my pajamas?"

He arched his eyebrows in surprise. "You're already in your pajamas? But it's barely seven-thirty."

"Yeah, well . . . somewhere in the world, it's bed-time."

He quirked a smile at that. "Somewhere in the

world it's mambo time, too, but you don't see me putting on my ruffled shirt, do you?"

She narrowed her eyes at him. "I'm afraid I don't quite follow you."

He chuckled, a sound that was more nervous than humorous, and she was amazed to witness the blush that crept over his features. "I'm sorry. I guess that didn't make much sense, did it? You make me say dumb things, that's all."

"*I* make *you* say dumb things?" Oh, now *that* was an interesting development, seeing as how she'd been thinking the same thing about herself. "But I hardly know you."

"That's the problem," he responded. "Beautiful women always make me nervous until I get to know them better." He paused a brief, but telling, moment before adding, "And even then, I always seem to make a mess of things."

A little burst of heat exploded in Faith's belly and quickly spread outward to warm the rest of her. "M-Mr. McClellan," she stammered. "I-I'm not sure it's appropriate for us to—"

"You're absolutely right," he interjected, taking a step backward, clearly knowing he'd overstepped the bounds of . . . of whatever it was that had them bound. "I apologize," he continued hastily. "Like I said, beautiful women make me say dumb things. And you're just very—" He halted abruptly, then cleared his throat with some difficulty. "Here—" He extended the keys out to her again. "I'm sorry I bothered you. I'll go."

Faith reached for her keys, but no sooner had she closed her fingers over them than she discovered that she didn't really want Holt McClellan to leave. Yet she had no idea what to say to make him stay, now that she'd made him feel uncomfortable. So she only retrieved her keys and thanked him quietly and began to close her front door. But almost as if they had a mind of their own, her fingers, instead of turning the deadbolt and key in the lock, unhooked the chain and opened the door wider.

"You didn't have to come all this way to bring them back," she said. "You could have just mailed them to me."

He had turned around to make his way toward the stairs, but at her quietly uttered statement, he spun around again. His wool, charcoal-colored overcoat swung open with the action, to reveal an obviously expensive suit of the same hue beneath. He was very, very handsome. And he was clearly surprised that she was continuing their interaction. Perhaps as surprised as Faith was herself.

"No, I couldn't," he told her.

"Why not?"

"You're not in the phone book. I couldn't find your address."

Oh, yeah. She'd forgotten about that. So if that was the case, then—"Then how did you find out where I live?" she asked him.

He smiled apologetically. "I, uh, I have a friend who's highly placed at the phone company. He owed me a favor. Actually, it was more like I blackmailed him," he confided. "He gave me your address."

She wasn't sure if she should be angry about that or not. Strangely, she found that she wasn't. "Then, once you got my address, you could have mailed my keys to me," she pointed out.

He met her gaze levelly. "No, I couldn't."

"Why not?"

"Because then I wouldn't have been able to see you."

"Oh."

The soft, single syllable was all she could manage, because the fire in her midsection began to burn hotter. It nearly exploded when she glanced down and remembered that she was standing there in her pajamas. She felt heat seep into her face as she fingered the collar of her shirt ineffectually. "I, um . . ." she said eloquently. "Uh . . ."

He laughed when he understood her train of thought. "I guess I should have phoned you before I came over. But your apartment was on my way home, so it just seemed easier to . . . But now that I'm here, it's not easy at all to . . . What I mean is . . ." He laughed again. "We both seem to be having a little trouble with the English language tonight, don't we? Funny. It wasn't a problem this morning."

Faith gripped the door harder and forced herself not to invite him inside. Their encounter this morning had been entirely different from the one they were having now. For one thing, they'd both had their guards up. Now, however . . .

"Yeah, about that," she said. "I'm sorry I left so abruptly."

"So am I," he murmured. "Why did you?"

"You . . . you weren't what I was expecting."

"That makes two of us," he concurred. "You weren't what I was expecting, either."

She told herself not to ask, but heard herself say anyway, "Is that good?"

The smile he gave her this time was cryptic. "I haven't decided yet."

"Oh."

"What were *you* expecting?" he asked, deftly turning the tables.

"I'm not sure. Just not . . . you."

"Is that good?" he echoed her earlier question.

Faith bit her lip, wondering just how honest she should be. Then she decided that there was no harm in speaking the truth. Not anymore. "Not really," she said softly.

Her response seemed to surprise him. "Why not?"

"You remind me of someone. Someone I'd rather not be reminded of. Seeing you this morning . . . It sort of knocked me off-kilter, that's all."

"I'd apologize, but there's not much I can do about the way I look."

And Faith wouldn't ask him to change his appearance if he could. Even if he did evoke way too many memories of Stephen, there was no reason in the world to alter Holt McClellan's looks. Why mess with perfection, after all?

"No, there's no need for you to apologize," she said softly. "No harm done." *Not yet anyway.* "Well, thank you for bringing my keys," she hurried on. "It was nice of you to come all this way."

"Like I said. It was on my way home."

Everyone in Louisville knew the McClellan family lived in Glenview. As Faith knew, Holt worked downtown on Main Street. It was one block north, then a straight shot out River Road for him to drive home at night. Faith, on the other hand, lived south of downtown, in the Highlands. Deep in the Highlands, in the gridwork of Cherokee Triangle, a few blocks off notoriously congested Bardstown Road, right by the difficult-to-navigate circle surrounding the statue of Daniel Boone.

Her apartment wasn't *anywhere* near his way home. Holt had gone to a lot of trouble to bring her keys to her. Why? She had no idea. Although he'd told her he thought she was a beautiful woman, she had little reason to believe he meant anything by the comment. Men said things. Women knew that. It was all part of the game, the one rule with which Faith was definitely familiar. But Holt McClellan seemed to be using a playbook she'd never glimpsed before.

Rich, handsome, successful distiller, versus woman of meager means whose professional and personal goal is to put him out of business. The odds on that one were simply too weird for her to fathom, the outcome too shadowy to ponder.

"Well, thanks again, Mr. McClellan," she said, forcing her hand to start pushing the door closed, as much as she hated to do it. "Good night."

He lifted a hand in silent farewell, but didn't turn away. She watched the space between her front door and the doorjamb grow smaller and smaller, watched as Holt McClellan disappeared bit by handsome bit. She had just about matched bolt to latch when he called out her name again from the other side.

"Mrs. Ivory?"

Slowly, she opened the door again.

"I, um, I couldn't help but notice that *Mr.* Ivory doesn't seem to be home."

She supposed she should have expected his observation. It never worked for long when she identified herself as a married woman. Not having a husband around rather ruined the image.

"No, he's not home. He's . . ." She took a deep breath and concluded quickly, "He's dead."

Something darkened in Holt McClellan's eyes as he took a step forward, then stopped. "Oh. I . . . I'm sorry. I . . . I didn't know."

"It happened about six months ago."

"I see. I'm sorry," he repeated.

"Thank you." It was all she could manage. She never knew what to say when people spoke of Stephen. So she simply said nothing at all. "Good night, Mr. McClellan. And thanks again."

He dipped his head in farewell. "Good night, Mrs. Ivory. And you're welcome."

Once more, as she closed the front door, Holt McClellan only stood there and watched her do it, something that made it nearly impossible for Faith to complete the action. When she heard the click of the latch catching, she quickly spun the deadbolt to a locked position and hooked the chain into place. Then she pressed her eye against the peephole to watch him leave.

But he didn't leave. Not right away. He stared at her front door, as if he were lost in thought. At one point, she thought he was about to lift his hand to knock again, but he only shoved it deep into his coat pocket. Then, slowly, he spun around and began to make his way up the hall, toward the stairway at the end. Twice he halted and turned around, and twice she thought he would come back. But he didn't come back. At the end of the hall, he turned left, and exited into the stairwell.

Even after he was gone, Faith continued to gaze through the peephole, staring at her empty hallway. For fifteen full minutes, she watched. For fifteen full minutes, she waited. For fifteen full minutes, she wished.

And for fifteen full minutes, she somehow managed to keep her tears from falling.

Chapter 6

The weather in Veranda Bay, St. John, U.S. Virgin Islands, was quite extraordinary, Pendleton had to admit. Beneath a perfect, pale blue sky, the seventy-six degrees surrounding him were made even more enjoyable by a warm, restive breeze redolent of the salty sea, the rich jungle soil, Hawaiian Tropic suntan lotion, and a wide variety of red and yellow rum drinks that dotted the bar around him.

Kit had chosen well, he thought grudgingly. The Veranda Bay Resort was a primo bit of real estate. It was also the solitary structure on Veranda Bay, something that had narrowed considerably his search for her exact whereabouts. Of course, the massive resort did lay claim to roughly two hundred rooms, fourteen luxury suites, twenty private bungalows, five restaurants, two cafés, a bistro, and nearly a dozen bars, but that was beside the point. Kit was here. Somewhere. And he would find her.

His current position seated at the bar by the pool afforded him panoramic views of both the lush hotel grounds and the ribbon of white beach beyond—not to mention the incredible turquoise expanse of the Caribbean. It was undoubtedly the best seat in the house for spying runaway madcap heiresses. Unless, of course, the runaway madcap heiress in question happened to be Kit McClellan, in which case, Pendleton was fairly certain she'd have to *want* to be spotted before he would be able to spot her.

But she obviously did want to be found, he told himself confidently. Of that, he was absolutely certain. Pretty certain, anyway. In a way.

The unruly breeze pushed a lock of his dark hair down over his forehead, and when he carefully nudged it back into place, the wind returned to fondle the open collar of his white linen shirt. Baggy khaki trousers and buff-colored loafers—sans socks, natch—completed his attire, suggesting to a casual passerby that he was simply a vacationing corporate executive of generous means, instead of a boss's spineless lackey sent to recover a rebellious daughter.

Thankfully, his thoughts were interrupted then by the arrival of a very large, very pink drink on the bar beside him. When he glanced up, it was to find a gorgeous, curvaceous bartender with elegant Latina looks, wearing a skin-tight sarong, smiling at him. "Compliments of the house," she said. "Welcome to Veranda Bay."

He returned her salacious smile with one of his own, automatically curling his fingers around the cool, slender glass. The drink was really far too pretty for anyone of the masculine persuasion to be caught dead possessing, but it had been a nice gesture. "Thank you," he said. "Do you do this for all the guests?"

She shook her head, her smile broadening. "No.

Only the attractive ones I'd like to get to know better."

Well, well, well. Maybe this trip wouldn't be a total washout after all. "Oh, yeah?"

She touched the tip of her tongue to the corner of her mouth. "Oh, yeah."

And then she was gone, glancing over her naked shoulder as she went, the warm sun gilding the dark, bare skin of her back that was revealed by the brief sarong uniform. And as he watched her go, Pendleton found himself wondering why he'd never visited the Caribbean before. Balmy weather, picture-perfect beach, beautiful women, free drinks . . . What could be better?

His question was answered almost immediately by a brief slash of feedback from a microphone, followed by an overloud, nervous chuckle, and the arrival of a large man poolside. He was dressed in the biggest pair of shorts and the most obnoxious Hawaiian shirt Pendleton had ever seen, and he brought with him tidings of great joy.

"Sorry about that, folks," he said with another anxious chuckle. "But if you'd all like to turn your attention poolside, we're about to begin the swimwear fashion show."

Pendleton nearly dropped the drink he had begun to lift to his mouth. Good God, the day *could* honestly get better.

"And that," the man continued, "will be followed immediately by the lingerie fashion show."

Pendleton's voice nearly lifted in song as his libido jumped up to do the macarena. What next? he wondered. Swimwear/lingerie mud wrestling? Would his most excellent fortune never end?

"Hi, Pendleton! I didn't know you already had

some vacation time coming. I'm going to have to ask Daddy about his new policy."

Jinx.

He sighed as a murky fog that was becoming way too familiar began to roll into his brain. He halted just shy of his lips the progress of the beautiful drink that the beautiful woman had given him only a few beautiful moments ago.

"Miss McClellan," he greeted her as he slowly spun around on his stool. Reluctantly, he set his drink down on the bar and said, "Well, my, my, my. What a surprise to find you here."

She stood on the opposite side of the bar, wearing the same kind of tiny sarong that the other bartender had been wearing. But where the other woman's had been bright pink and burgeoning in all the nice, soft places that men liked to see a sarong burgeon, Kit McClellan's was pale yellow, sleek, and . . . He sighed again. And hardly burgeoning at all.

"What're you drinking?" she asked further, her smile dazzling. Before he had a chance to answer, she rushed on, "No, wait—let me guess. Not Bourbon."

"No," he agreed mildly. "Not Bourbon."

"I had a feeling."

"I bet you did." When she only smiled in response, he added, "Thank you for the lovely postcard."

She rocked back on her heels and gazed at him through laughing eyes. "Don't mention it."

"Oh, of course I should mention it. It would have broken your heart if I hadn't."

"Would it?"

"Sure, it would. It's all part of the game, after all, isn't it?"

She studied him in what was clearly feigned bewilderment. "Game? What game?"

He chuckled as he wrapped his fingers more tightly around his drink, thumbing the condensation that trickled down its sides. When he looked up at Kit, he noted that she was watching the subtle movement of his hands quite closely.

"See, now that's the two-dollar-and-sixty-eight-cent question, isn't it?" he asked her.

For a moment, she didn't answer him, but only continued to watch with much fascination the leisure motion of his thumb stroking up . . . and . . . down, up . . . and . . . down the side of the glass. Then, quietly, slowly, as if her mind was a million miles away, she asked, "Is it?"

Just to see how closely she was paying attention, Pendleton suddenly altered the movement of his fingers, and began rotating his thumb in a slow spiral, around and around and around in the moisture streaking the side of the glass. A flush of pale pink stained Kit's cheeks, and her mouth opened slightly, as if she suddenly needed more air.

And for some reason, he felt a very wicked, thoroughly unwanted heat wind through his own body. "You know," he continued, his voice suddenly sounding a bit ragged, "I'm going to have to ask you to go over the specific rules of the game before long. Frankly, I'm having a hell of a time keeping up."

He halted the movement of his hand and gripped his drink tightly, and only then was the mysterious spell broken. Kit glanced up at him again, but her wide blue eyes revealed nothing of what she might be thinking, in spite of the tell-tale blush that still stained her cheeks.

"I don't know why you're making such a big

deal out of this," she said, her voice sounding almost as rough as his own had. "It was just a postcard."

"Overnighted to me," he pointed out.

She lifted one—naked—shoulder in a shrug, and somehow made the gesture seem very erotic. "I just wanted to make sure you got it. You never know with the mail down here."

"Yeah, well, you really shouldn't have."

She waved her hand negligently through the air. "Are you kidding? It took Novak almost a month to find me. And Daddy's getting more impatient all the time. How long did he give you to bring me back? Two weeks?"

"One."

"He really *is* getting impatient. He still has more than two months. I wouldn't think he'd become quite so desperate just yet."

As always happened when Pendleton came within hailing distance of any member of the McClellan family, his head began to spin. "Two months?" he echoed. "Before what? You succumb to melanoma from overexposure to the Caribbean sun?"

"Nah," she replied readily. "No chance of that. I'm always careful. I never go out without an SPF of at least forty-five, which is basically the equivalent of lying under a Mack truck. I'd spontaneously combust, if I did." She settled an elbow on the bar, cupped her jaw negligently in her palm, and leaned forward. Then she whispered conspiratorially, "I'm cursed with the fair Hensley complexion, you know."

No, Pendleton hadn't known. And somehow, gaining the knowledge at this point clarified the situation not at all.

"I suppose, however," she continued, not altering her pose, "that we've put you through enough. Since you've come all the way down here to find me, the least I can do is let you know what you're doing here."

"That," he said, "would endear you to me forever."

She pushed herself away from the bar and muttered, "Well, gee, Pendleton. Don't go getting all mushy on me." Her fair Hensley complexion suddenly turned a bit pink again. "I just hate to see a guy like you with a look like that on his face, that's all."

"A look like what?" he asked.

"Like someone just gave you a good, solid blow to the back of the head."

"Ah."

He began to lift his pink, frilly drink to his lips again, but before he could complete the action, Kit snatched the glass away from him.

"I knew you wouldn't be drinking Bourbon, but good God, Pendleton, don't drink this," she commanded. "Drinks like this will mess with a man's testosterone level bigtime. Even a guy like you, who clearly has buckets to spare, could potentially turn into a flaming parfait eater."

Without further comment—and before he had a chance to ask her to elaborate on the buckets-full state of his testosterone—she set a shorter glass on the bar and spun around to a veritable pyramid of liquor behind her.

Pendleton's heart sank a bit as he watched her fingers hover over a bottle of Hensley's Bourbon that was situated on the top row. But after a moment of consideration—not to mention a sly little smile that she tossed over her shoulder—she opted instead for a single malt Scotch for which he had always embraced a *very* fond affection. In one single, fluid maneuver, she uncorked it, spun around, and waved it over his glass, until it was half-full of the dark amber liquid.

"Thank you," he said.

"No problem," she assured him. "That'll be ten bucks. And don't forget to tip your bartender at least fifteen percent. You want I should just charge it to your room?"

He had begun to reach for the glass, but now his fingers hesitated. "Ten dollars?" he echoed incredulously. "For one drink?"

She shook her head as she returned the bottle to its shelf. "Pendleton. Honey, sweetie, baby, cookie. That's Abelour Scotch. You wanna play the resort game, big guy, you gotta pay the resort prices. Don't you get around much? I mean, where were you brought up? A barn?"

"No, New Jersey," he responded before thinking.

She emitted a sound that was a mixture of disbelief and delight, and he knew at once that Kit McClellan was almost certainly envisioning him as the product of a Bruce Springsteen video, complete with vacant lots, crumbling rowhouses, factory smokestacks, and Lady Liberty's backside in the background.

"*South* Jersey," he felt compelled to clarify.

But all she said in response was, "New Jersey? Really?"

"Yes, really."

She eyed him with much speculation. "Funny, but I don't picture you as coming from New Jersey."

He sipped his Scotch, enjoyed the smoky, mellow flavor, and felt his testosterone levels surging mightily. "Why is that?" he asked.

As she considered him in silence, it occurred to Pendleton that for a woman who wasn't beautiful, Kit McClellan was certainly very attractive.

"I don't know," she finally admitted. "You just don't seem . . ."

"What?" he asked.

Her—naked—shoulders lifted and dipped again, but she only shook her head slowly in silence.

So he sipped his drink once more, rolling the warm liquid around in his mouth, and focused on Kit McClellan's striking face as she watched him. Her lips parted softly as he relished the dusky flavor of the liquor on his tongue, and her eyes darkened dangerously when he took his time to swallow it.

And a hot splash of lightning ignited in his belly, long before the Scotch ever got there.

"Actually," he said, the word coming out a bit strangled for some reason, "the part of New Jersey I come from isn't much different from your part of the country."

Except, of course, he amended to himself, for the funny way of talking people had in Kentucky. For instance, no one in New Jersey had ever asked him if he was brought up in a barn. And he still wasn't sure which of the half-dozen different pronunciations for "Louisville" he'd heard was correct, although the garbled, incomprehensible version seemed to be the one used most frequently.

For a long, intriguing moment, Kit only continued to stare at him with dreamy eyes, as if she were thinking of something totally unrelated to the conversation at hand. Finally, however, she said,

"Funny, but I have trouble seeing you as a product of my part of the country, too."

This time Pendleton was the one to remain quiet and thoughtful for a bit too long. He gazed down into the depths of the liquid he swirled nonchalantly in his glass, and wondered if he should even bother to clarify any conclusions—whether accurate or not—that the boss's daughter might be drawing about him.

Ultimately, his curiosity—and surely it was nothing more than that—got the better of him, and he heard himself ask, "Well, then, Miss McClellan, just where do you picture me as coming from?"

That mystified expression cluttered her face once more, and she expelled another nervous chuckle. "I don't know," she repeated.

She continued to scrutinize him, and it occurred to Pendleton that she was expending an inordinate amount of energy trying to figure him out. It seemed to bother her that she couldn't easily peg him and send him on his merry way. And for some reason, it irritated the hell out of him that she *was* trying so hard to peg him, because he knew he shouldn't care one way or another what Kit McClellan thought about him. But oddly enough, he found that he did care. A lot.

"I believe you were going to tell me my reason for being here."

She nodded. "Right. I almost forgot. Buy me dinner tonight. La Belle Mer, the restaurant here, does a fabulous buffet. You'll love it."

The quickness of subject change dizzied him for a moment. "My reason for being here is to buy you dinner?"

She smiled. "No, Pendleton. Buy me dinner tonight, and I'll tell you what you're doing here. I can't right now. I'm working. Sheesh."

She folded her elbows on the bar, leaned forward again, and smiled a very tempting little smile. Though why exactly it was tempting, Pendleton couldn't have said. It was her mouth, he finally decided. The sight of her mouth was what kept blurring his thoughts and making him forget the things he knew he should be remembering. For all the planes and angles of her face, Kit's mouth was red and ripe and rich with curves, full and lush and sexy. It distracted him, her mouth, because he kept wondering what it was going to do next. She was as quick to smile as she was to frown, and she had a habit of snagging her slightly crooked eyetooth at one end of her lower lip whenever she was lost in thought. Like right now.

And God help him, he really, really, *really* liked it when she did that. He kept thinking about that mouth—and that eyetooth—nibbling on other body parts besides her lip. And not necessarily *her* body parts, either.

"The meaning of your life, Pendleton, for the price of a seafood buffet," she said, interrupting his thoughts. "It's the deal of the century."

The warm breeze kicked up again, but they only gazed at each other in silence, each oblivious to the beauty and tranquillity of the sunny, tropical afternoon surrounding them. Not far away, a steel drum band began to warm up, the soft trilling of felt against metal singing through the air. A squawky bird cried out from a palm tree above them, and a woman on the other side of the bar called for another sloe gin fizz.

And finally, finally, Pendleton broke the silence. He had no idea what spurred the question in his brain, but, out of nowhere, he asked, "Will you wear your sarong?"

As questions went, that one clearly wasn't at the top of Kit's "Things Pendleton Will Be Most Likely To Ask Me" list. And as a result of her surprise, she lost her momentum a bit. "Wh-what?" she stammered.

And just like that, he felt the upper hand slip comfortably back into his grasp.

"I'll meet you in the hotel lobby at six o'clock," he said, "in front of the concierge desk." Then, without further ado—or further adieu, for that matter—he spun on his heel and walked away.

The strangest thing happened to Kit as she was readying herself for dinner. The dull thump of melancholy that normally settled in her belly at the arrival of one of her father's emissaries wasn't there. Usually, an encounter with one of the Hensley's VPs only acted as a reminder to her that her worth to the McClellans, although substantial— ninety-nine-point-four million bucks, to be exact— was strictly financial in nature. Had it not been for her mother's will, Kit's father would have gleefully left her to rot in the tropical paradise of her choosing, wasting neither time nor effort to retrieve her. So naturally, whenever she found herself face to face with one of his minions, who had strict orders to bring her back to the fold, Kit felt a bit down.

But not tonight.

Tonight, in place of the cool feelings of dejection and abandonment, there was a warm fizzy sensation bubbling up inside her. It was a sensation so alien, so unfamiliar, that she almost didn't recognize it. Yet it had been her companion ever since she'd seen Pendleton that afternoon. For some reason, the sight of him sitting at the bar, looking so unbelievably attractive with the breeze ruffling his dark hair, the sun dappling his gentleman-vacationer duds, and laughter brightening his espresso-colored eyes when he'd asked her to wear her sarong . . .

She bit back a wistful sigh. Well, the whole thing had just started to generate a very odd reaction inside her, one that felt strangely like . . . happiness? She wasn't quite sure. It had been so long since she had experienced such a thing that she'd almost forgotten what it felt like.

In spite of Pendleton's request, Kit didn't wear her sarong that night. However, taking pity on the poor boy—he would, after all, be saddled with her for an entire evening—she donned something only marginally less revealing: a brief, snug little turquoise miniskirt and an even briefer, even snugger, little cropped halter top to go with.

And heels. High heels. Really high heels that she'd bought that afternoon for just this meeting—she hesitated to call it a date—with Pendleton. For some reason, she wanted to be as tall as she possibly could be, despite the fact that, all her life, her accelerated height had made her feel like such a great, hulking ogre. Above all else, she wanted to make certain that she was sexy as all get-out tonight.

Why? Well, usually, when she donned such sexy little outfits, it was because she wanted to maintain control over the whole man-woman thing. And she knew she couldn't accomplish such a feat with her beauty alone, simply because she didn't *have* any real beauty. She did, however, claim truly phenomenal gams, and not a bad torso, in spite of its being bereft of any real bosom action.

As long as she could keep a man's interest lingering below her neck, Kit was fairly confident that she could eventually draw him in, lull him into a false sense of security, and then reveal him for what he was—an emissary of her father's whose sole purpose in life was to corral her into matrimony and collect a fat little reward for his trouble.

Pendleton, however, was threatening to be a bit more elusive than usual. For one thing, he spent far more time than other men did gazing at her face. And that, Kit decided, was something she simply could not have him doing. If she had any hope of exposing him, then she was going to have to direct his attentions elsewhere.

Hence, the little blue ensemble, tiny enough to bring even the most uncooperative man's eyes to the place a woman wanted to keep them. Away from the face. Always away from the face. As singular an impression as Pendleton made, she was certain that deep down he was no different from any other man. Shallow. Superficial. Greedy.

My, but she was looking forward to the evening.

She glanced at her watch long enough to see that she was running the required fifteen minutes late and smiled. By now, Pendleton would be in the lobby, pacing like a caged animal, wondering where she was. Why, she could almost feel his sweaty palms and the anxious wrinkling of his brow from here. Men were just *so* predictable.

She spritzed perfume on her arms and neck and down the front of her top—well, you just never knew—gave her gold bangle bracelets an affectionate jingle, grabbed her tiny purse, and headed for the door. Thanks to the luminous full moon—which she simply *had* to pause to appreciate for a few moments when she exited her bungalow—she was running twenty minutes late by the time she reached the lobby.

But that was okay. Her date—or rather, Pendleton—would, of course, be waiting for her. His financial future depended on her, after all. So she fluffed up her dark blond curls—well, as much as she could fluff the unruly, chin-length mass—threw back her shoulders, and sauntered forward, immediately darting her gaze to the concierge desk. And, just as she'd expected, she found Pendleton—

Not there.

Wait a minute. She squeezed her eyes shut for a moment, then opened them again, fixing her gaze on the concierge desk. That *was* the concierge desk, wasn't it? C-o-n-c-i-e-r-g-e. Yep, that was how you spelled *concierge*. She could have gotten that one even without four years of high school French. But there was no pacing, sweaty-palmed, furrowed-browed Pendleton in sight.

Okay, so maybe she'd misunderstood. Maybe he'd said he would meet her at the reservations desk. But there was no Pendleton there, either, sweaty, furrowed, or otherwise. Kit spun around in a full circle, taking in the entire lobby, from its polished pink marble floor to the skylights opening on the star-studded night above, scanning all the lush potted palm trees and tastefully arranged rattan furniture. There were lots of people milling about, but none of them was Pendleton.

The men's room, she thought then, reluctant to acknowledge the bubble of relief that burst in her belly. She gave her forehead a mental smack. Of course. He was probably in there throwing up because he thought he'd lost the boss's daughter, and his job was sure to be next on the list. Poor guy.

She hadn't meant for him to become so over-wrought as all that. She'd have to find some way to make it up to him.

With a contented sigh, she fluffed up her dark blond curls again, threw back her shoulders again, and sauntered forward again, halting only when she stood outside the men's room. Then, as discreetly as she could, she leaned forward and cupped an ear to the closed door. Unfortunately, she detected not a murmur of ghastly retching, nor even the rush of a faucet to tell her Pendleton was cleaning up the aftermath.

Just as she was taking a step closer, the door flew open, and a man—not Pendleton—emerged, casting her a look of censure.

"Do you mind?" he asked when she didn't move out of his way.

"Not at all," she replied. Before he could make a clean break, however, she added, "Was there anyone else in there? A tall, dark-haired man? Wearing some expensive, though understated, vacation wear? And, oh, say . . . losing his lunch, perhaps?"

The man's expression would have been the same if he had just found something really disgusting on the bottom of one of his huaraches. "No," he said. "There was no one. Only the attendant."

Bewilderment—surely it wasn't disappointment—welled up inside her at the news. "Oh. Thank you."

All right, so if Pendleton wasn't in the lobby waiting for her, or in the men's room getting sick all over himself on her account, then where was he? Slowly, oh, so slowly, a strange suspicion flickered to life at the back of her brain, a suspicion that was really quite unthinkable. Yet no matter how hard she tried to tell herself that such a development was impossible, Kit found herself striding back across the lobby in the direction of La Belle Mer, the restaurant that was to have been her ultimate destination with Pendleton.

But surely he wouldn't have . . . ? Not without . . . ? He wouldn't dare think of . . . ? Would he . . . ?

Before she even realized her intention, she found herself standing in front of the maitre d's stand, waiting patiently until he glanced up with an obsequious smile. "Yes?" he asked. "May I help you?"

She smiled as becomingly as she could and said, "Although I know you must be frightfully busy, could you be so kind as to tell me if you have a reservation under the name Pendleton?"

The maitre d' scanned the list of names before him and, without glancing up, told her, "Yes. Mr. Pendleton arrived right on time—at six-fifteen."

He'd only waited fifteen minutes? Kit thought. How incredibly gauche. "Could you take me to him, please?"

"I'm sorry, miss," he said as if he were addressing a small child or cocker spaniel. "But our policy is to leave our guests to their meals unless they request otherwise. And Mr. Pendleton made no mention of a guest. It would be against hotel policy—not to mention grossly impolite—for me to interrupt Mr. Pendleton's dinner."

"Oh, I wouldn't want you to be impolite or go against hotel policy," Kit assured him.

Fortunately, she had no such problem with doing so herself and moved easily past him.

When he realized her intention, however, he called out and abandoned his post in hot pursuit. But she had the element of surprise on her side—

not to mention a much longer stride—and continued confidently on her way.

He still hadn't caught up with her when she cleared the bar and caught sight of Pendleton. He was seated alone in the corner of the restaurant at an intimate little table for two, chatting amiably with his waitress, an auburn-haired woman whose sarong-clad—or rather, sarong-bare—back was turned to Kit.

Kit fluffed up her hair *again*, threw back her shoulders *again*, and sauntered forward *again*. She *would* make an entrance, just as she had planned. Katherine Atherton McClellan *always* made an entrance. And she wasn't about to let Pendleton ruin her record.

Unfortunately, as entrances went, it wasn't one of her better efforts. Because Pendleton glanced up as she made her approach, smiled benignly, and waved a fork-impaled shrimp at her, as if she were a passing sous chef and he was showing his approval for the fare.

"Miss McClellan," he greeted her warmly as she drew nearer. "How fortunate that you made it after all."

As she came to a halt by the table, he replaced his fork on his plate, settled his linen napkin beside it, and rose formally from his chair, hand extended.

She forced a smile, ignored his gesture, and was about to speak when the maitre d'—who was, by now, understandably agitated—clamped a hand over her upper arm.

"Excuse me, miss," he said, a little breathlessly. "But you'll have to come with me."

"It's all right, Orlando," Pendleton assured the man. "I was expecting Miss McClellan. Quite some time ago, as a matter of fact."

Clearly reluctant to do so, Pendleton's new best buddy, Orlando, released her arm, and, with an awkward dip of his chin, he scurried off. Kit watched him go, her irritation at the maitre d' evaporating as her annoyance with her father's emissary compounded.

"Pendleton," she greeted him stiffly. "I thought we were supposed to meet in the lobby."

Without missing a beat, he said, "I thought so, too."

"Then why aren't you there waiting for me?"

His smile never wavered, but something darkened his eyes. "Because when you didn't show up on time, I assumed you had changed your mind. Fortunately, Stacie here has been keeping me company in your absence."

Kit glanced at the other woman and clenched her jaw tight. Oh, fine. Stacie, of the huge green eyes and fiery mane and an orange sarong that was only about six sizes too small, had made the supreme sacrifice of keeping Pendleton company in Kit's absence. Well, wasn't that just dandy?

"Go away," she said eloquently to Pendleton's server.

Frankly, the terse edict was all Kit could manage. Because for the first time in two years, she had no idea what to say or how to act. She could scarcely believe what was happening. Pendleton had blown her off. And no one, absolutely no one—no one unrelated by blood anyway—had dared do something like that. Just who did Pendleton think he was? She was Katherine Atherton McClellan, heiress to a fortune. Well, potential heiress to a fortune, anyway. Depending on her mood.

Stacie opened her mouth to offer a commentary on Kit's command, but one look at Kit, and she must have decided it would be more prudent to keep her response to herself. Instead, she only leaned *waaaaay* in toward Pendleton and purred something to him about dessert. Then, with a throaty chuckle and a toss of enough hair to suit two voluptuous, squishy women, she departed.

Kit stifled a growl as she sat down, focusing her attention on the man who occupied the chair opposite. "Pendleton," she began, surprised at how steady she managed to keep her voice. "I don't think you quite grasp the . . . the . . . oh, shall we say . . . the *sine qua non* of this situation."

He arched his eyebrows in mild surprise as he replaced his napkin in his lap. "Why, Miss McClellan, I didn't know you spoke Latin."

She expelled an exasperated sound and cut right to the meat of it. "You're supposed to be having dinner with *me*."

"It would appear that I *am* having dinner with you, Miss McClellan. Or will be, once you order something. However, seeing as how you chased away our server, it could be lean cuisine for you tonight." He reached toward the little crustaceans hung like pink pearls around the lip of the glass sitting before him. "Here," he added generously, "you can have one of my shrimps."

"No thank you," she muttered. She'd rather have his head. On a platter.

He shrugged as he reached for his wine. "I'm so glad you were able to make it," he said.

She managed a chuckle for that. "Oh, I bet you are."

He halted his glass just shy of his lips. "You don't sound convinced of my sincerity."

She placed an elbow on the table and cupped her chin in her hand. "Gee, I wonder why."

"I can't imagine. Oh, there's Stacie," he added, hailing the waitress. Upon her return, he took the liberty of ordering for Kit, a repeat of what he was having himself—lobster Newberry, arugula and goat cheese salad and, hey, what the heck, a bottle of 1989 Haut-Brion blanc to go with.

Before Kit could ask, he snapped the menu shut and explained, "They're the most expensive items on the menu. I knew that would be what you'd want. It is, after all, going on the company credit card."

Stacie jiggled off again, returning moments later with an additional wineglass, a bottle of wine, and another place setting. And all Kit could do was watch in silence as Pendleton poured her a generous helping of wine.

Well, that, and ponder the fact that the evening wasn't starting off at all the way she had planned.

Chapter 7

All things said and done, Pendleton had enjoyed one or two better dinner dates in his life. Thinking back, he supposed it had been foolish for him to be so surprised when Kit hadn't shown up on time. Just because she'd slipped up a little when he'd asked her to wear her sarong, and just because she'd looked so warm and rosy that afternoon, and just because, dammit, he had started actually to *like* her for some reason—

He sighed and watched her face as he filled her glass with wine. Just because of all that, there was no reason for him to think she might treat him a little differently than she did anyone else, was there? Nevertheless, he had thought she would treat him differently. And for all her coolness during the episode that had just transpired, she still seemed strangely fragile somehow. And that made no sense at all.

It was just that he'd expected better of Kit. Yeah, she was a spoiled, pampered brat. Hey, he'd noticed that about her almost immediately. But all this time, he had suspected her rich bitch act was just that—an act. An attitude she adopted as a weapon of self-defense, a wall she erected whenever someone threatened to tear her down—which, thinking back on his dinner at the McClellan home, probably happened to her pretty frequently.

Now, however, he was beginning to wonder if it was an act at all. Maybe she really was as bad as the other Hensley's VPs made her out to be. Maybe she really was a man-eater. Maybe she really did intend to do him grave damage. Maybe, in addition to his sunscreen, he really should have packed a piece.

"Did you really break Novak's arm?"

The question erupted from his mouth before he could stop it, and when he looked at Kit, she was staring at him as if he'd lost his mind. "Oh please. It was just a hairline fracture."

"But did you do it?" he persisted, still unwilling to believe the worst of her.

She shook her head. "A cab driver in the Caymans did. When Novak tried to stuff me into the backseat of the cab. He thought Novak was attacking me."

Something hot and heavy tightened in Pendleton's midsection. "And *was* Novak attacking you?"

"Oh, God, no," she was quick to assure him. "Novak is a pussycat. He was only trying to take me home. I was just putting up a more, um, energetic fight than usual."

"And Bahadoori's ankle?" he asked further.

She twirled her wineglass by the stem, watching the pale yellow liquid sheet up one side and down the other. "Um, he sort of fell down."

"*Sort of* fell down?"

"Yeah. Well, actually, it was more like he fell off the side of a volcano."

"A . . . volcano?"

This time she nodded. "See, there was this virgin sacrifice going on for Carnival—all mock, I assure you—and . . . well, it's kind of a long story. But it wasn't my fault," she hastened to add.

Pendleton decided he didn't want to know the details of that one. So he only asked, "And Ramirez's wrist?"

"He fell, too. Over the side of El Morro."

"El Morro?"

"It's a popular tourist attraction in Puerto Rico. A big fort. Looks more like a castle. Ramirez went right over one of the battlements. It was only a drop of about twenty feet, though. Nothing major."

Nothing major? "And on this fall, did he, oh . . . have any help?" Pendleton asked.

She gaped at him, clearly outraged at his suggestion. "Oh, please. Pendleton, what are you thinking? I would *never* help a man over the side of a battlement. I might chip a nail."

Of course. "What about Carmichael's hair?"

She smiled, the first genuine smile he'd seen from her all evening. "Oh, now *that* was a fun night. Carmichael and I actually hit it off really well, and after dinner—and oh, six or seven mai tais, I guess—I talked her into letting me give her a home perm. Unfortunately, it didn't take very well. In fact, she wound up looking kind of like a giant Q-Tip. So she got it cut out."

"Oh. And Washington's, uh . . . derriere?" he concluded halfheartedly. "If it wasn't you who bit him on the . . . If it wasn't you who bit him, then who did?"

She blushed a bit, her gaze skittering away. "Well, actually . . ."

This time Pendleton was the one to gape. "You

bit Washington on the butt?'' he asked. ''Are you serious?''

''It was an accident,'' she said. ''A terrible mix-up. It's a long story, too, but the gist of it was that I didn't realize it was Washington's, um, tushie that I was biting.''

''Whose, um, tushie did you think it was?''

She stalled, tracing her thumb over a damask rose on the tablecloth. ''I thought it was, uh . . . Well, see, there was this, ah . . . Actually, with his back to me like that, and wearing that purple Speedo of his, I thought he was this perfectly nice scuba instructor named Julian, whom I was hoping to get to know better.''

Pendleton bit his lip to keep from asking anything more. If the way Kit got to know men better was to bite them on the tushie, then he had no choice but to drag her back to the States and lock her up in Cherrywood as soon as was humanly possible. He owed it to the men of the global dating community.

''Miss McClellan,'' he began again.

''Look, Pendleton,'' she cut him off. ''I know I owe you an apology—''

''Only one?'' he interrupted.

She glanced up to acknowledge his interjection. ''Okay, I owe you several. And I'd like to offer them in the form of an explanation.'' When he opened his mouth to say something more, she rushed on, ''But don't start with all that 'endearing' stuff again, okay. It makes me nauseous. No offense.''

''Oh, none taken, Miss McClellan. It doesn't bother me at all when a woman tells me I make her sick.''

"That's not what I . . ." She sighed impatiently. "Never mind."

He remained silent as she enjoyed deep swallow of her wine. Then, almost immediately, she downed a second of comparable size. Somehow, Pendleton thought she was doing it because she needed the false courage that alcohol brought on in some people. Either that, or she just really liked the wine a lot.

"Okay," she finally said as she set her empty glass on the table. "Here's the deal. I suspect that, unlike some of his other VPs, Daddy sent you to fetch me without filling you in on all the particulars."

"Gee, what makes you think that?"

She smiled. "Because you've been way too tolerant, and not at all obsequious."

"Ah. Then again, fetching you *is* in my job description."

"Yeah, well, you'll forgive me if I say that you don't seem like the kind of guy who takes his job description all that seriously."

He wasn't sure, but he thought he should be offended by that. "Are you saying I'm not a good VP?"

"No, Pendleton, I'm saying you're not a doormat."

"Ah."

"But the reason paragraph six, subheading A exists on page four of your job description is because it's essential for Daddy's executives to be the ones who come after me. It's the main reason he's hired them, after all."

"I'm afraid I don't follow you," Pendleton said, studying her with interest. "Why can't he send one of your brothers after you?"

She smiled again, but this time the expression wasn't exactly happy. "Because I can't marry one of my brothers. It's against the law. Even in Kentucky."

"Excuse me?"

"It's true," she said. "Not many people believe it, but it really is illegal to marry your own brother or sister in Kentucky. It has been for, oh, gosh . . . years now, I guess."

He made a face at her. "I meant why would your father find it necessary to hire men to marry you?"

"So that he can collect my mother's fortune."

"Excuse me?" Pendleton was hopelessly lost. What was it about the McClellans that turned his brain into pudding?

But instead of answering his question, Kit posed one of her own. And not some idle, oh-by-the-way question, either. No, when she opened her mouth again, the oddest thing came out.

"Pendleton? Have you ever been in love?"

As questions went, it wasn't one he heard often. Nevertheless, he replied honestly, "Yes. Once."

Her eyes widened in what was obvious surprise at his revelation. "Really?"

He nodded.

"Wow." She gazed at him with what he could only liken to awe, then asked further, "Was she in love with you?"

Now that one was difficult to answer with the truth, simply because he didn't know the truth. So he replied, "She told me she loved me. Many times, in fact."

Kit continued to gaze at him as if he were some mythic creature that had just risen from the surf amid fanfare and fire. Then, as he'd known she would, she asked the one question that he really, really hated to answer.

"What happened to her?"

And, as always, he answered anyway. "She left me."

That didn't seem to surprise Kit at all, because she only nodded as if she completely understood.

He had no idea why he would want to prolong such a discussion, but somehow, he heard himself ask in return, "How about you? Have you ever been in love?"

Evidently, she didn't have to think about her response, because, immediately, she shook her head. Then she reached for her empty wineglass and held it out to Pendleton in a silent request for a refill. So he plucked the bottle out of the ice bucket and obeyed her command.

As he was pouring, she qualified, "But I was engaged once, if that counts for anything."

Oh, it counted, he thought as the wine poured over the rim of her glass and cascaded onto the tablecloth. He jerked the bottle back and met her gaze levelly, but had no idea what to say.

All he could manage by way of a response was an echo of her earlier sentiment. "Really?"

She wiped her hand on her napkin, then sipped carefully from her over-filled glass. "Really."

"But you didn't get married?"

Still not looking at him, she replied, "Nope."

He knew it was none of his business, and probably a bad idea to boot, but he asked, "Did you get cold feet at the last minute?"

She turned her head to stare out the window, and inevitably, he repeated the gesture. The black ocean beyond stretched to infinity, linking with the black sky at some point on the horizon. But since both were spattered with starlight, it was impossible for him to see exactly where that line between air and water lay. In the nighttime, both mingled and joined, becoming one. Only at daybreak would they part again.

"Nope," she said again, her voice insubstantial, as if coming from a great distance. "I didn't get cold feet. He did."

Pendleton felt a twist of regret turn inside him, and he wished he hadn't asked her to elaborate. He was about to say something about how the two of them had actually managed to find something in common, when she opened her mouth and, to his even greater regret, she elaborated some more.

"Actually, he didn't get cold feet," she said softly. "What he got was cold cash."

Thinking he'd misunderstood, Pendleton asked, "I beg your pardon?"

"Actually, that's not quite right, either," she said, finally turning to look at him again. "What Michael got was a check. From my father. Daddy gave him one for a quarter-million dollars at the rehearsal dinner as kind of a ditch-the-wedding present. But Michael cashed it the next day, so I guess that makes it close enough to cold cash, don't you think? It certainly made for cold feet. Michael couldn't get out of the restaurant fast enough."

"Your father paid your fiancé a quarter of a million dollars to leave you?" he asked. "The night before your wedding?"

Kit dropped her gaze to her wine again. "Yeah. Pretty tacky, huh?"

"And your fiancé actually *took* it?"

The chuckle that emerged from her mouth was obviously forced and false. "Gee, Pendleton. You almost sound surprised."

"Well of *course* I'm surprised. That's outrageous."

"Yeah, I guess a guy like you would have held out for a cool million. But Michael came from humble beginnings and all that. He'd never seen that many numbers in front of a decimal point in his whole life."

"That's not what I—"

"In fact," she interrupted him again, "Michael was so eager to take the money, that Daddy figured later he probably could have gotten off with a hundred gees instead of two hundred and fifty. But then, hey, that's my dad. Always overdoing things."

When she *finally* seemed to be through talking, Pendleton tried to jump into the conversation again. "What I meant was, it was outrageous for your fiancé to take *any* amount of money in exchange for abandoning you."

She glanced up again, her eyes dark and troubled and sad. "Why was that so outrageous?" she asked. "Any other guy would have done the same thing."

Pendleton refused to dignify the latter part of her objection with a comment. Instead, he said, "It was outrageous, because in the long run, he could have had the money *and* you."

For a long moment, she only observed him through narrowed eyes, as if she wasn't quite sure what to think of him. Then, slowly, she began to smile. It wasn't a big smile. But it wasn't bad. "Why, Pendleton," she said. "I'm not sure, but I think you just paid me a compliment."

He was as surprised by the realization as she seemed to be, but said nothing to retract his statement.

"At any rate," Kit hurried on, her gaze skittering away again, "my father's now paying about ninety-nine-point-four million more for that bribe than he thought he would."

"Excuse me?"

The question seemed to be Pendleton's response to everything that night, but honestly, he couldn't help but excuse himself. He'd never been more bewitched, more bothered, more bewildered in his entire life. Unfortunately, when Kit spoke again, he realized that he was nowhere near as befuddled as he was going to be.

"Unless I'm married in two months," she told him, "my family will lose everything."

"Excuse me?"

Kit chuckled at Pendleton's echo of bewilderment. Dearie dear. What to tell the poor boy that wouldn't overwhelm him. Maybe she should do something different for a change and tell him all about it. Obviously, no one else had. She twisted her wineglass by the stem and decided, What the hey? If nothing else, maybe it would make her feel better to finally talk about it.

"As you know," she began, "my family is very wealthy."

"I did rather notice that the night I was at your house."

She nodded. "What you may *not* know, however, is that the McClellan wealth comes entirely from my mother's side of the family."

"No, I assumed your father—"

"Daddy started off as a laborer for Hensley's, working in the bottling plant for union wages. He and my mother met at some big function that Granddaddy threw for the workers one summer. Mama was immediately smitten. And Daddy knew a good opportunity when he saw it. They got married six months later. Mama was pregnant with Holt at the time."

"Whoa."

Kit smiled at Pendleton's slip into the vernacular, then continued. "For what it's worth, Daddy was a relatively decent husband to her. To the best of my knowledge, he was never unfaithful, and he always came straight home from work. But he never loved her."

"How do you know?"

"I just do," she said quickly before hurrying on. "And so did Mama. And I guess Granddaddy did, too, because he made my father sign a pre-nup, back in 1959, when such things were unheard of."

"No way."

Kit smiled again at his second lapse. "Way, Pendleton. Granddaddy wasn't about to condone the marriage, bastard child or no, unless Daddy agreed to enjoy the Hensley lifestyle without getting his grubby hands on the Hensley money. Daddy lived at Cherrywood, drove the cars, wore the clothes, walked the walk, talked the talk. But he never owned any of it. Mama did. He was groomed to take over the company, but the company—and everything else—always belonged to my mother."

"Get out."

This time, Kit chuckled out loud at Pendleton's exclamation. For some reason, telling the story tonight didn't make her feel quite so empty inside as it usually did. "It's true," she assured him. "It wasn't the outcome Daddy had expected when he'd deliberately knocked up the boss's daughter. But, in the long run, he realized he could do a lot worse. So he agreed to play by Granddaddy's rules."

"He married your mother for her money, even though it would never be his."

"Not while Granddaddy and my mother were alive. Granddaddy made sure of that."

The wheels of thought seemed to be turning in Pendleton's brain, so Kit waited before continuing. "But since your mother passed away," he finally began again, "your father must have ultimately come into her fortune, right?"

She shook her head. "Mama changed her will a while back without telling any of us. We didn't find out the details until after she died."

"Why would she change it?"

Kit would have thought by now that voicing the next part wouldn't be quite so painful these days as it used to be. Funny, though, how the prospect of revealing it to Pendleton now hurt even more than usual. "Because Mama knew it was the only way I would ever snag a husband."

"I'm sorry, but I'm still not following you."

A band kicked up in another room then, a lively, lovely number rich with horns and piano that roused her from what was fast becoming a sullen mood. So, seeking to put an end to their conversation as quickly as possible, Kit concluded her story in a rush of words.

"In order for my father to get his hands on the Hensley millions, he has to make sure I'm married within two months. That's what it says in my mother's will. At this point, Daddy figures any available guy has son-in-law potential, and you're unfortunate enough to be his latest acquisition. For that, as much as anything else, I apologize. But don't worry. You're not my type, so there's absolutely no reason why we can't just be friends. Now, with all that said, dance with me."

He gazed at her, nonplussed. "Excuse me?"

"Dance with me, Pendleton. The band is playing a marimba. It's my favorite. Don't they marimba in New Jersey?"

He laughed low. "Not in the neighborhood where I grew up. Do they do a lot of marimba-ing in Louisville?"

She wiggled her eyebrows playfully. "They do at Arthur Murray. Come on. Dance with me."

She laughed, too, as she stood, the ripple of sound bubbling up unbidden, effervescing in her chest with an explosion of warmth. It was a nice feeling, she thought. One she hadn't experienced for some time. Funny, it coming out of nowhere like that.

When Pendleton made no move to accompany her, she extended her hand across the table. "Please?" she asked softly.

He shook his head. "I'm sorry, Miss McClellan, but my job description is quite specific. And nowhere on page four, paragraph six, subheading A does it say that I am required to marimba with the boss's daughter."

She settled her hands on her hips and smiled the most winning smile she could rouse. "I'll give you a dollar."

He twirled his wineglass by the stem and avoided her gaze. "I think I've had enough excitement for one evening. I think that, as soon as we finish with our dinner, I should take you home."

"One dance, Pendleton. That's all I ask. Pretty please?"

He glanced up with a look of put-upon patience. "Oh, all right. But don't forget—you owe me a dollar."

He stood and buttoned his suit jacket, then

closed his hand over hers. And when he did, that explosion of warmth in Kit's chest suddenly fireballed, shooting heat throughout her entire system. His dark eyes glittered with something she didn't dare ponder, and his mouth was set in a smile that she found simply irresistible. So she wove her fingers with his and tugged gently, then guided him in the direction of the festive music.

But by the time they reached the room where the band was playing—which actually wasn't a room at all, but an open-air patio—the marimba had segued into something softer and slower and more suited to the sultry night. When she felt Pendleton hesitating behind her, she spun around to look at him.

"Marimba's over," he pointed out unnecessarily. "Guess you don't owe me that dollar after all."

Instead of answering, Kit tugged playfully on his arm, pulling him forward until his body brushed up and down hers. "Not so fast," she said. "You promised you'd dance with me. Marimba, mambo, rumba, samba . . . it's all the same to me."

"It's all the same to me, too," he told her. "I don't know what any of those are."

"Then I'll teach you."

Pendleton gazed down at Kit and tried to pinpoint the exact moment when the balance of power had shifted. Until just a few seconds ago—right around the same time her body had come moseying on up to his—he'd been thinking he had things under control. Now, suddenly, he found himself looping his arms loosely around Kit McClellan's waist—and quite a nice waist it was, too—as she danced him backward onto the dance floor.

Dammit, she would want to lead.

Then again, seeing as how he suddenly had no

idea what he was doing, maybe he should just surrender to her. The thought of surrendering to Kit
took on a way too erotic connotation then, so he
set the thought aside and tried to concentrate on
something else.

Unfortunately, his concentration seemed to be intent on erotic thoughts this evening, and they kept
zeroing in on things they had no business target-
ing. Like how warm and silky was the bare flesh
above Kit's skirt that his fingertips encountered
when he settled his hands on her hips. Like how
good she smelled all up close this way, sweet and
decadent and tempting. Like how fluid and natural
her movements were when she propelled her body
forward into his again. Like how unspeakably
lovely her eyes were when she glanced up to see
how he was doing.

Like how he wondered what she would do if he
kissed her.

"Getting the hang of things, Pendleton?" she
asked as she executed a stunning pirouette that offered him quite a nice view of her bare back.

"Oh, yeah," he replied, the words coming out a
bit rougher than he had intended. "I'm getting the
hang of things really well."

"It's all in the hips," she told him.

"It certainly is."

"And the legs."

"I noticed that, too."

She laughed with genuine delight, oblivious to
the fact that the two of them were talking about
entirely different things. "I knew you'd be a good
dancer," she said, spinning closer still.

"How did you know that?"

She smiled. "You got good moves."

"Why, Miss McClellan, I didn't think you'd noticed."

"I notice more than you think, Pendleton."

"I don't doubt that for a moment. Something tells me you miss very little."

"And something tells me *you* don't miss a thing."

The music changed again, and he found that he couldn't comment to her statement, because he was too busy trying to figure out where the hell she was going. The pace had quickened riotously, the piano player's fingers tripping up and down the keys, stopping and starting without warning. Kit kept up effortlessly, reeling and darting around Pendleton with the grace of a summer breeze, chuckling good-naturedly at his obvious and total confusion. Before he realized his own intentions, he snaked an arm out to halt her, pulling her to him until her body was flush against his.

And then the strangest thing happened. Although the music kept playing, faster and faster, and the dancers surrounding them still pranced and staggered merrily about, the world enclosing them gradually slowed down to a halt. So Pendleton slowed down with it, spinning Kit in a gradually more languid circle, pulling her closer with every turn, until the two of them stood utterly still at the center of the dance floor.

And then, although he never planned to do it, he kissed her.

As he dipped his head forward, Kit tipped hers back, and oh, so slowly, he covered her mouth with his. Her lips opened easily beneath his, and the taste of her filled him, nourished him, intoxicated him. But it didn't quite satisfy him. Instead, the kiss only inflamed his appetite, making him hunger for more of her than he could ever hope to have. Despite that, he deepened the kiss, cupping her face in his hands, tilting her head back further, plundering her mouth at will.

And Kit acquiesced through all of it, curling one hand around his nape, knifing the fingers of her other through his hair with much affection. She returned his kisses with equal fervor, equal finesse, equal fire. And for the life of him, he simply could not let her go.

He wasn't sure how long they stood there so entwined—perhaps seconds, perhaps centuries—but when the music changed again, slowing down this time, the enchanted moment was lost. He pulled his head back from hers and opened his eyes, only to find her gazing steadily back at him. But she never said a word about what had happened. Instead, she dropped her hands to his shoulders, retreated one step, and began to move her body in time to the beat once again.

"Now this is a merengue, Pendleton," she said, the unsteadiness of her voice belying her composure. "It's a bit trickier. You might have trouble keeping up, so I'll go slow. Maybe you should go slow, too, okay?"

Slow. Right. He'd forgotten.

"On second thought," she said, interrupting both his thoughts and their dancing, "maybe you're right. Maybe it would be better if you just took me home. I'm really not all that hungry. And I'm staying here at the hotel, so it's not far to go."

It took a moment for her words to sink in, because he was too focused on the flush of pink that stained the creamy flesh above her breasts. When he finally realized what she had said, he told her, "No, Kit, when I said that earlier, I meant I should take you *home* home. Back to Louisville."

He didn't realize he'd called her by her first name until her blue eyes turned almost midnight, and her lips parted in surprise. But she didn't protest the familiarity. The wind kicked up again and nudged a single, stray curl down over her forehead. Kit reached up to push it back into place at exactly the same time he did, and as a result, he found himself curling his fingers over hers. For one long moment, neither of them moved. Then she dropped her hand back down to her side, and he deftly tucked the strand of hair back into place.

"That, um, that sounds like a good idea," she said softly. "Maybe you should take me home. I'll just get my purse, and you can settle up with our server while I give my notice to the bar manager."

"Is that going to be a problem?" he asked, not certain whether he was talking about her job or something else entirely.

She shook her head. "Nah. Bartenders are a dime a dozen down here." She turned to go, tossing over her shoulder, "Then again, so are marimbas. I'll meet you at the maitre d's stand, okay? And then you can take me home. To Louisville."

Pendleton watched in silence as she retreated, his mind a flurry of impressions that refused to connect. All he could do was wonder why, suddenly, the last thing he wanted to do was take Kit back to the McClellan home in Glenview. Because in spite of his earlier convictions to the contrary, Cherrywood seemed like the last place for her to be. Somehow, she deserved something more than a multimillion dollar estate with a name.

Though what, exactly, she did deserve, Pendleton couldn't yet quite say.

Chapter 8

Faith Ivory still hadn't quite recovered from her previous encounter with Holt McClellan when she ran into him again a few nights later, at a glittering fund-raiser in the glorious Crystal Ballroom of the glamorous Brown Hotel. She was decked out in a teeny-tiny black dress that she'd spent hours working up the nerve to put on, and her discomfort was only compounded now by the fact that she was surrounded by high rollers, captains of industry, society matrons, and Junior Leaguers.

All night long, she'd felt as if she were fighting against the undertow in the sea of upward mobility. And now, having spied Holt McClellan dressed in elegant black and white—who, thankfully, hadn't spied her—she felt as if someone had thrown a killer whale into what was already shark-infested waters.

Fortunately, she was on the opposite side of the ballroom, where there was no way he would ever notice her. Not unless he lost interest in what appeared to be a *very* intense discussion with his father, and not unless he looked up from the drink that he clutched brutally in his hand. And she was certain that there was no way he would ever do—

He glanced up then and spied her immediately. —that.

She might as well have just shouted her thoughts at the top of her lungs, so focused was he on the exact spot where she stood. She was about to look away, to search for the nearest hasty retreat, when something very strange happened. Holt McClellan smiled. Not so much *at* her, but as if he suddenly just felt very happy about something.

A warm ripple of excitement shimmied up her spine at his expression, and before she knew it, Faith was smiling, too, the same kind of smile, she was certain. Because suddenly she felt very happy about seeing Holt McClellan again.

In spite of the warm fizzy sensations popping inside her, however, her instincts urged her to hurry home and hide under the blankets, lest the big, bad wolf blow her down. But even when Holt excused himself from his father without looking at him, even when he began to make his way slowly across the crowded room, even when he was only a few scant feet away from her, Faith was helpless to do anything but stand fixed in place and stare at him.

If she had thought him handsome before, she had been badly mistaken. Business attire had made him look too officious, too conservative, too conventional. Tonight, dressed in a black tuxedo, the sapphire studs of his white pleated shirt nearly identical to the color of his eyes, Holt was quite . . .

Oh, my.

"Hi," he said, his voice scarcely audible in the din that surrounded them.

"Hello," she replied automatically.

"So we meet again."

"So we do."

"Three times in one week. This could become habit-forming."

"Oh, no. I don't think so."

Their conversation stalled there, and she wished she were anyone else. Anyone else would know what to say to a man like him. Anyone else would feel comfortable amid all this beauty and wealth and power. Anyone else would be dazzling and witty and charming. Anyone else would be having a good time.

"Can I get you something to drink?" he asked, jerking a thumb toward the bar, surprising her.

She gaped at him. "You're joking, right? Have you forgotten who I work for?"

He expelled an exasperated sound. "Ginger ale, Mrs. Ivory? Club soda? Mineral water? And no, I haven't forgotten who you work for. Believe me—I could never forget that."

She relented some, but couldn't quite banish the reminder that he wasn't someone she should be chatting with, however superficially. If anyone from the Temperance League saw them together . . .

Well, of course they'd think she was lobbying him to shut his business down, she thought. Which wouldn't be a problem, if that were, in fact, what they were discussing. But the goals of the Temperance League were as far from her mind at the moment as the earth was from the sun.

She shook her head in response to his offer. "No, thank you. I'm fine."

Another awkward moment ensued, until Holt rallied the conversation. "What brings you here tonight?"

Oh, good, she thought. Bland small talk. Even

she could handle that. "The Temperance League is a big sponsor for the Boys and Girls Clubs of Kentuckiana."

He nodded. "So is Hensley's."

Well, that was certainly a surprise. "You can't be serious."

He smiled again, this time a bit uncertainly. "Why can't I be serious?"

"A distiller? Sponsoring a juvenile charity? That doesn't make sense."

He seemed honestly mystified by her objection. "Why not? It's a wonderful organization."

"But a distiller? What are you doing? Trying to get kids hooked while they're young? It's not enough that people abuse alcohol as adults?"

He emitted an impatient sound. "Look, contrary to what you think about us, Hensley's isn't some monster intent on turning the world's inhabitants into a bunch of drunks, all right? We're regular contributors to a variety of local charities. Virtually all corporations are. We give money to support the arts, education and the beautification of the city. We even contribute regularly to MADD. Why is that so hard for you to believe?"

"It's just that . . ."

"What?"

She scrunched up her shoulders and let them drop, suddenly feeling silly for speaking. "Well . . . It's just that the Boys and Girls Clubs of Kentuckiana seems an unlikely choice for Hensley's, that's all."

His expression hardened as he spoke. "Mrs. Ivory, if we can't get to at-risk kids when they're young, then they're goners."

His vehemence surprised her. "You sound like you know what you're talking about."

He dropped his gaze back into his drink, but only swirled the liquor around in the glass. "Let's just say I've seen one or two people get into trouble in their lives, trouble they could have avoided if someone had just taken half an interest in them when they were kids."

Faith couldn't imagine how someone like Holt McClellan would understand about such things. He'd grown up wealthy and wanted, privileged and pampered. What could he possibly know about the lives of troubled kids?

"Well . . ." she tried again. But she had no idea what to say.

He seemed to detect her uneasiness, because he glanced up at her again, smiling reassuringly. "I'm sorry. I didn't mean for that to sound the way it did. This is just something I feel rather strongly about. Obviously. Let me make it up to you."

"How?"

"Let me take you to dinner tomorrow night."

Immediately, she shook her head. "Thank you, but I have plans," she replied, the lie rolling effortlessly off her lips. It was her stock-in-trade answer, after all, one she invariably invoked whenever anyone asked her out.

"Later in the week, then," he said. "Friday maybe?"

"I can't. Truly. Thank you, anyway."

He met her gaze pointedly. "Is it that you can't, or that you won't?"

She shook her head more adamantly. "I can't," she repeated.

He nodded, but seemed no more convinced of the veracity of her response than she was herself. For a moment, she almost backpedaled, almost told him she'd be more than happy to alter her plans, change her schedule, rearrange her entire life, anything to spend a little time with him. Fortunately, she wasn't so far gone that she would do something as foolish as that. Not yet, anyway. A few more minutes in his presence, however, and she wasn't sure she could be held responsible for much of anything she did.

"I have to go," she said suddenly.

He didn't seem surprised by her admission, but he asked, "So soon? The evening just started. I think the mayor's going to make a presentation of some kind."

She nodded quickly. "I know, but . . . um . . ."

"But what?"

She scrambled for an excuse. "I forgot to feed my cat." Some excuse, she chastised herself. She didn't even *have* a cat.

"Okay, Mrs. Ivory," Holt McClellan said softly. "I get the message."

"What message?" she asked, feigning ignorance.

But he only inhaled a deep breath and released it slowly. "Where are you parked? If I've managed to chase you off, then the least I can do is walk you to your car."

Ignoring the part about him chasing her off, she replied, "Thank you, but that won't be necessary. I'll be fine on my own." She had, after all, been fine on her own for six months now, right? Well, except for that big gaping wound inside her that nothing seemed capable of healing. Oh, but, hey, other than that . . .

He shook his head. "Absolutely not. I won't let you leave here alone. It's not safe this time of night. Did you check your coat?"

He obviously wasn't going to be put off by her objections, and a quick glance around told her there was no one else available for her to draft as an escort. So she opened her little black cocktail purse and extracted her coat check, handing it to him without comment.

"I'll just be a minute," he said.

Would but that were true. Unfortunately, Faith was pretty certain that even if she never saw him again, it would be quite some time before Holt McClellan left her completely.

As she watched him go, she tried not to linger too long on the broad shoulders that strained against his tuxedo jacket, or on the long legs that cut a swath easily through the packed room, or the blond head that passed well above the crowd. Thank heavens his jacket covered his fanny, she thought wryly. The last thing she needed was to be caught ogling that part of him.

"Faith, darling, there you are."

Especially by Miriam Dodd, the director of the Louisville Temperance League, who emerged from the crowd nearby.

"Miriam, how nice to see you. I was wondering where you were."

The plump redhead smiled, her green eyes sparkling brightly enough to vie with the emerald sequins of her gown. "We just now arrived. George was held up at work. I hope we haven't missed anything."

Oh, only me making a complete fool of myself by telling lame lies to a gorgeous man I have absolutely no business speaking to anyway, Faith thought. "No, not a thing," she assured her companion. "Though I understand the mayor's going to be speaking."

"Wonderful. I was hoping I hadn't missed that."

"Mrs. Ivory?"

The summons startled her, and she scrambled for

an excuse as to why Holt McClellan, of Hensley's Distilleries, Inc., would be standing behind her, holding her black velvet coat open for her to step into. Fortunately, she was spared trying to come up with something plausible, because Holt took it upon himself to greet Miriam.

"Mrs. Dodd," he said, dipping his head toward the other woman in acknowledgment. "Nice to see you again."

Miriam roused herself to her full five-feet-zero inches and snorted. Actually snorted. How rude.

"I doubt that," the other woman said haughtily. "I can't imagine that you or your kind would ever find it nice to see someone of my kind."

Faith turned to Holt to see how he would react. But he only smiled mildly. "It's not like we're matter and antimatter, Mrs. Dodd. We can both occupy the same room without the world coming to a fiery Armageddon."

"That's a matter of opinion," Miriam replied coolly.

But Holt only turned his attention to Faith once again. "If you're ready?" he said, holding up her coat.

Sheepishly, Faith smiled at Miriam as she moved the few steps necessary to don the garment he held with far too much familiarity. Holt settled it around her, brushing his hands over her shoulders momentarily before releasing her. The simple touch was harmless, meaningless. But for some reason, Faith's heart began to hammer hard in her chest.

"Thank you," she managed to whisper.

"You're welcome," he told her, his gaze never leaving hers. "Shall we go?"

"Faith?"

She turned to her boss, having known she

wouldn't get off easily. "Yes, Miriam?"

The other woman inclined her head toward Holt. "Is everything all right?"

Faith nodded. "Mr. McClellan just offered to see me to my car. He didn't think I should go alone."

Miriam pulled her head back to eye Holt, not bothering to hide her contempt. "Are you so sure you wouldn't be safer alone?"

Until recently, Faith would have assured anyone who asked that question that, yes, by all means, she would undoubtedly be safer alone. But suddenly, she was hesitant to feel so certain.

And of course, she wasn't *with* Holt McClellan, not really. A brief walk to the car did not a relationship make. Nevertheless, she couldn't help but feel as if each step she took with him was leading to something. What exactly, she couldn't quite say.

"I'll be fine," she assured Miriam.

"I could ask George—"

"It won't be necessary," she interrupted her employer. "I'll be fine."

Beside her, Holt chuckled, but there wasn't an ounce of merriment in the sound. "Don't worry, Mrs. Dodd," he said. "I never bite until the *third* date."

And before Miriam had a chance to respond with anything other than an open mouth, Holt spread his fingers lightly over the small of Faith's back and steered her toward the exit. Maybe it wasn't their third date, she thought as she allowed herself to be led, but it *was* their third encounter.

Oh, dear.

Holt honestly hadn't expected to see Faith Ivory again for the rest of his life, and he'd been cranky as hell all weekend as a result. Then, as if by magic, she'd materialized like the proverbial stranger across a crowded room, dressed in a skimpy little black dress that had roused him faster and more fiercely than he'd ever been roused before. But as quickly as he'd found her again, she was leaving. And that, he decided, was a fact he was going to have to change. Immediately.

They strode in silence through the Brown's elegant lobby, then Holt held the door for Faith, inhaling deeply of her sweet perfume as she passed through. When he followed her out into the crisp night air, he couldn't resist drawing near her, hooking her hand lightly through his arm, covering her fingers harmlessly with his.

"Where are you parked?" he asked her again, unable to tolerate the silence any longer.

"Not far," she replied, her words emerging from her mouth amid a wisp of white fog. "I found a place on the street near Ninth and Broadway."

"That's five blocks away."

She nodded, but didn't look at him. "Like I said. Not far."

"Maybe not during the day, but at night—"

"I made it to the hotel just fine, didn't I?" she snapped. "And it was dark when I arrived."

"You were lucky," he told her.

"I'm fully equipped to take care of myself, Mr. McClellan." Her tentative tone of voice, however, belied her certainty, as did the tremor that shook her when she slid her fingers from his arm and shoved both hands into her coat pockets.

"Gee, keep saying it like that and you might believe it yourself someday."

She glared at him. "What makes you think I don't believe it?"

"Could be the way you glanced down at the

ground when you said it," he told her as they continued walking. "Or it could be the way you didn't sound anywhere at all convinced. Or maybe it's the simple fact that I just don't believe you."

She hastened her step as they approached Fifth Street, crossing quickly just as the light changed and an LG&E van lurched forward. It was as if she wanted to be free of his company as quickly as possible, even if it meant getting plowed over by a utility truck. "I see," she murmured when they'd made it to the other side. "And, of course, whatever you believe about a person must by all means be the way of the world, mustn't it?"

"No," he responded, matching her stride effortlessly. "But I'm a pretty good judge of people."

"I find that hard to believe."

"Why?"

In direct contrast to her haste to be rid of him, she stopped dead in the center of the sidewalk and spun around to face him. "Because you're completely removed from the masses, that's why. You don't even know any normal people, so how could you begin to be a judge of them?"

She strode quickly forward once more, so Holt hurried alongside to keep up. "Who says I don't know any normal people?"

"How could you? You come from one of the state's most prominent families," she reminded him. "You've had nothing but privilege, nothing but advantage, since day one. And you've worked for none of it. You've *earned* none of it."

This time Holt was the one who stopped dead in his tracks. Faith kept walking for a half-dozen paces before she realized she had proceeded alone, then she, too, stopped and turned, her expression a silent question mark.

"I haven't earned it?" he asked. "Says who?"

She blinked at him, but said nothing in response. So slowly, Holt began to walk again, covering the distance between them with measured, deliberate strides.

"There are a lot of different ways to earn things, Mrs. Ivory," he said as he approached her. "There's starting at the bottom and working your way to the top. There's paying your dues in less tangible ways, through life experience. And there's simple day-to-day survival."

When he stood face to face with her again, he halted, gazing down into her eyes, nearly drowning in the eddy of emotions he saw there.

"Yes, well I'm familiar with all of those," she said, her tone colder than the wintry air that surrounded them. "But I find it hard to believe that *you've* experienced any of them."

"You might be surprised what I've experienced," he told her.

In response, she turned and began to walk away, this time with a less hurried pace. Holt followed, staying even with her. Yet neither said another word until they slowed to a halt at the corner of Ninth and Broadway.

When Faith spoke again, it was after pointing to an older model sedan parked alone across the street. "There's where I'm parked."

The traffic on Broadway was surprisingly heavy for a Monday night, so they waited at the corner for the light to change before crossing. And as they did, Holt realized his last chance with Faith was quickly slipping away. He didn't know why it was so essential that he see her again. He only knew that it was. So while he had her captive on the corner, he turned to her again.

"Have dinner with me this week," he said softly. "Tomorrow night. Please."

He could see that she wanted to decline, but she said nothing right away. Instead, she only watched the signal opposite them, a red flashing hand that seemed to be urging her, *Don't do it . . . don't do it . . . don't do it . . .*

For several moments, she remained silent. And then the signal changed. "Okay," she said softly. "I'll have dinner with you tomorrow night. Call me at work in the morning."

Chapter 9

Absolutely *nothing* in life brought Pendleton greater joy than rolling his car to a stop on the cobbled court in front of Cherrywood with Kit Mc-Clellan at his side. Not even that interlude on the dance floor that the two of them had shared in Veranda Bay, which, at the time, he'd found more enjoyable than he liked to admit. But it had taken them four days to get from there to here, and the sparkle of that moment had tarnished a *looooong* time ago.

Kit McClellan, he had learned the hard way, was *not* a trustworthy woman.

For some reason, after dropping her back at her bungalow at the Veranda Bay Resort, he'd felt compelled to hang around, just to be sure she didn't try anything funny. Like, oh, say . . . escaping, for instance. And imagine his lack of surprise when, less than thirty minutes later, she had slipped out the door with suitcase in hand.

What had ensued was a bout of island-hopping unlike anything Pendleton had ever experienced, culminating in a rather unforgettable—as much as he wished he *could* forget it—incident at the airport

143

in San Juan, where Kit had almost managed to give him the slip. Looking back, he supposed it really hadn't been anything *too* major. She'd just kind of, oh . . . shoved him from behind, yelled to a gaggle of security guards that he had a bomb, and then taken off running at breakneck speed in the opposite direction.

At the time, however, Pendleton had been a bit miffed. But once he'd explained the situation to the guards—no easy feat, considering the fact that he barely knew what was going on himself—and once he'd been strip-searched and interrogated for more than an hour by the Puerto Rican authorities, everything had been fine. Well, sort of fine. There had been that compulsive need for a shower, however, that he still hadn't quite shaken.

Luckily for him, he'd noted the terminal toward which Kit had been running before they'd slapped the handcuffs on him. Unluckily for him, however, it had emptied out into a half-dozen gates, any of which could have been her final destination. He'd had to resort to his dubious masculine wiles and his questionable good looks to cajole a terminal operator to search the manifests for a name. And, thanks to the warning he'd received from the other Hensley's VPs, not for the name Katherine Atherton McClellan, either.

Ultimately, Pendleton and the employee performing the search—a charming young woman named Rafaela, to whom he owed a night of dinner and dancing the next time he found himself in San Juan—had decided that the person traveling first class under the moniker Anne O'Cleves was, more than likely, the object of his pursuit. And how fortuitous that the plane had had a three-hour layover before flying off to St. Maarten, so it was still on the ground.

It hadn't been pretty removing Kit from that plane. And now here he sat with the queen herself, in front of her palace, wanting to chop off Her Majesty's head.

"We're home, Your Highness," he stated unnecessarily. "Now get out of my car."

She uttered a soft sigh. "Gee, Pendleton. Keep being so nice to me, and you're going to turn my head."

"Get out of my car," he repeated, surprised at how even he managed to keep his voice.

She eyed him thoughtfully for a moment. "You're still steamed about the San Juan thing, aren't you?"

Somehow, he refrained from comment.

"How many times do I have to tell you? I'm really sorry. It was just a joke. I had no idea they'd actually strip-search you."

"Get out. Now."

"Aren't you going to walk me to the door?"

"No."

"Daddy's going to be disappointed if you don't carry me in thrown over your shoulder, kicking and screaming."

"No."

"Oh, come on, Pendleton. It'll be fun."

"No."

"Novak carried me in that way."

"No."

She sighed heavily again and settled back into her seat, clearly not going anywhere.

"Miss McClellan, I have better things to do with my time than be a plaything for you and your father. You'll excuse me if I reiterate: Get . . . out . . . of . . . my . . . car.''

She folded her arms over her midsection. ''Daddy won't be pleased. And you won't have a car for me to get out of if you lose your job. The repo guys will come and take it back to Status Symbols-R-Us. Then where will you be?''

He studied her intently, inhaled a deep breath, and counted to ten. Then, when he realized he was still furious, he went on to twenty. Then thirty. Then fifty. Ultimately, he decided he would pass out from oxygen deprivation before he would *ever* be able to feel anything but outrage at Kit. Right now, he only wanted to be rid of her. Whatever it took to achieve that, Pendleton would do.

''I'll take you in,'' he said through gritted teeth. ''But I'm *not* hauling you over my shoulder.''

''Party pooper.''

He unbuckled his seat belt with a vicious snap, then opened his door and unfolded himself from inside the tiny roadster. Cautiously, he strode around the front of the car, his eyes never straying from Kit McClellan. Still playing the role of entitled heiress—as if she were entitled to anything more than a swift kick in the pants—she waited patiently for him to complete his circuit and halt by the passenger-side door. Then she gazed through the window with a smile befitting the most despotic royalty, clearly expecting him to do her the honor of opening the door.

Rolling his eyes, Pendleton reached for the handle, only to find the door locked. In response to his inability to open the door, Kit's smile only grew broader. Then she leaned over his seat and pushed down the lock on the driver's side door, as well.

Okay. That did it. No more.

Pendleton didn't know how he was going to explain it to the insurance company—and frankly, at the moment, he didn't care—but he curled his fingers closed tight above the canvas roof of the convertible, and, with one clean effort, drove his fist right through the fabric. The expression on Kit's face when he did was more than worth whatever rate hike he would have to endure in his premiums as a result. Then he gripped the canvas with rigid fingers and rent a Kit-sized hole right through it.

"N-now h-how are you going to f-fix that?" she asked, masking her fear very nicely. Well, except for that nasty stammer and the terror gleaming in her eyes.

He inhaled deeply, feeling his chest swell with manly ability. "I'll do what any other man in my situation would do."

"Which is?"

"Duct it."

"Oh."

"Now then," he continued, proud of his ability to maintain a thin veneer of civility. "Either you can get out of my car the traditional way . . ." He gazed down at her through the gaping tear. "Or I can reach in and drag you out. Your choice, Miss McClellan. Which will it be?"

She lifted a hand to her neck, then reluctantly unlocked the door. Pendleton jerked it open before she could change her mind, and stood aside for her to exit. The moment she had cleared the door, however, he roped his arm around her waist, lifted her from the cobbled driveway, and tossed her, kicking and screaming, over his shoulder. Fine. They'd do it her way. For some reason, he suddenly liked the idea.

He carried her up the walkway and lifted the

door knocker for three quick raps, then waited with one arm looped around her legs and the other hand cupped over her fanny, until Mrs. Mason answered the door. To her credit, the housekeeper only arched one snowy eyebrow in response to the scene that greeted her. Then she stepped aside to allow them entry, with the quietly offered announcement that Mr. McClellan, Sr. wasn't home, but that Mr. McClellan, Jr. was entertaining a guest in the dining room.

With Kit still howling and pounding on his back with both fists, Pendleton made his way to the dining room. He found McClellan, Jr. seated at the head of the big table, a delicate-looking blonde to his right. Without ceremony, he proceeded forward, dumped Kit into the chair she had occupied that ill-fated night at dinner, and turned to his host.

"McClellan," he greeted the other man with a brief nod.

His host stood, buttoned his jacket, and nodded back. "Pendleton."

"You'll forgive me if I tell you that I can't stay."

"No problem. Thanks for bringing Kit home."

"My pleasure."

"Oh, I sincerely doubt that."

Since the observation required no further comment, Pendleton turned to Kit and bowed with all the chivalry of an evil overlord. "Miss McClellan," he said. "It was a memorable occasion."

Kit had slumped into her chair, but now turned her attention to the table, obviously looking for something in particular. "What? No wine?" she finally asked her brother. "What kind of host are you, Holt? Sheesh."

"Good night, Miss McClellan," Pendleton concluded before turning his back on the lot of them.

A quick reminder spun him back around again, however, this time to focus on Kit's brother.

"McClellan," he said, "do you have any duct tape?"

The other man shrugged. "Of course."

"Mind if borrow a couple of feet?"

"Not at all."

McClellan, Jr. summoned Mrs. Mason to retrieve a roll of duct tape from the kitchen, then, when she returned, he tossed it to Pendleton. Pendleton muttered his thanks and, still ignoring Kit, began to make his exit once again.

" 'Night, Pendleton!" she called after him cheerfully. "Thanks for saving the last dance for me!"

He stiffened at the reminder, but didn't acknowledge her farewell. This time, he remembered quite well how to leave the McClellan house. He only wished he could rid himself of the household as easily.

He dreamed that night about Kit. About riotous music, squawking birds, palm trees, oceans, and marimbas. And hurricanes. Lots and lots of hurricanes. And amid the swirling scenes of turmoil pounding at his unconscious brain, there erupted a single oasis of serenity: He dreamed about lying naked on the beach with Kit McClellan, limbs entwined, mouths joined, bodies slick with salt water.

Pendleton rolled over in bed with a groan. He was still half-asleep, and caught up in the strangeness of the dream, when something halted his progress. Something warm. Something soft. Something that, when he reached over to drape an arm around it for further investigation, murmured a quiet, satisfied sound. His eyes still closed, he moved his hand leisurely down the length of the thing, only to have it stretch languidly and twine its bare legs with his.

Curves. That was what registered first. The revelation was quickly followed by another, however, the realization that those curves were moving closer. Slowly, it dawned on him that he wasn't alone in his bed. So he opened one eye experimentally, and, in the scarce morning light that filtered through the curtains, he saw a rather pronounced lump beneath the covers beside him. A lump with dark blond curls that peeked out from beneath the blanket. A lump that mumbled something incoherently before turning its back to him again.

Ignoring for a moment the fact that he slept in the buff, Pendleton pushed himself up on one elbow to get a closer look at his companion. Of course, he knew who it was without seeing her face, but something inside him was still clinging steadfastly enough to denial that he reached a hand out toward her. He had meant to touch the blanket, to tug it and the sheet back just enough to see if it really was Kit McClellan and not some other blond, madcap heiress who had invaded his bed. But instead of the blanket, his fingers wandered to her hair, skimming lightly over the silky tresses before winding a single dark gold ringlet around his thumb.

And that was when Kit began to stir with more purpose, rolling back to face him again. It was she, not he, who pushed the blanket down past her shoulders, and when she did, Pendleton saw that he wasn't the only one who slept in the buff.

"Miss McClellan," he said, his voice a rough whisper. "What are you doing in my bed?"

She shoved a fistful of hair out of her eyes and smiled sleepily. "Well, good morning to you, too,

Pendleton. Brrr," she added with a shiver. "It's freezing in here. You need to get yourself a couple of cats. Or a woman. Whatever."

"Thank you, but I feel the need for neither. What are you doing in my bed?" he repeated. "How did you get here?"

"I drove, silly," she murmured sleepily. "Your address is in Daddy's Rolodex. I had a little trouble finding a parking place out front, though, so I had to double park. I didn't realize one of your neighbors was a Louisville police officer."

Pendleton sighed. "That would be my next door neighbor. Captain Nichols."

"Oooh. Do you think he'll get mad when he realizes he's boxed in by a Mercedes S-class?"

"Gee, I have no idea. Those guys that hang out across the street in Central Park might notice, though. The Gang o' Car Thieves, I think is what they call themselves."

Kit sighed dramatically. "My car keys are in my purse by the back door. Would you mind terribly moving it for me? There's a good boy."

He ignored her question and posed one of his own instead. "What I meant by 'How did you get here?' wasn't an inquiry into what manner of transportation brought you to my doorstep. What I want to know is how you got past that doorstep and into my house. My bed."

She yawned like a bored cat. "Oh, that. Funny thing about old houses. The locks are generally *soooo* easy to pick."

"You broke into my house?" he asked, surprised at how calm he managed to keep his voice, not to mention himself.

She wrinkled her nose a bit. "Mmm . . . I prefer to think of it as illegal entry."

"Interesting distinction. And exactly where did you learn this particular trade?" he asked further. "Glenview doesn't seem the kind of environment where such skills are passed down from one generation to the next."

"You might be surprised," she murmured. She yawned again, lustily this time, and scrubbed her hands through her hair. "All right. If you must know, when I was seventeen, I dated a guy who was something of a lovable rogue. Until Holt and Mick had him arrested. He was still a lovable rogue after that," she hastened to clarify, "but his presence behind bars did put something of a damper on our relationship." She shrugged her—quite naked—shoulders philosophically. "I guess I should be grateful he was nailed for something he actually did, and not because they trumped up some charge of armed robbery against him."

Pendleton only gazed at her in silence for a moment. "You dated a guy who committed armed robbery?"

She made a face. "Of course not. I said that would have been the charge my brothers had trumped up against him. Actually, Turk—"

"Turk? His name was really Turk?"

"—just ran numbers. He only served six months." She shrugged again, less philosophically this time. "But he didn't want to see me anymore after he got out. Go figure. In spite of that, our short time together was one of my more productive relationships. It lasted four whole weeks."

Pendleton told himself that the only reason his righteous outrage toward her seemed to be fading some this morning was because he was half-asleep and she was totally naked. Surely once they were up and at 'em, he'd be offended to full capacity once again.

"All right," he conceded softly, "now that we have established *how* you got in here, I suppose the next item on our agenda would be *why* you got in here."

She smiled sweetly. "I thought I might move in with you for a while."

She thought she might move in with him for a while. That was a good one. Pendleton almost laughed.

She sighed with much contentment, then continued, "Cherrywood is just so . . . I don't know . . . overdone. And it's so big, you can get lost in that place. I could really use a change of scenery. And since you and I hit it off so well down in the Caribbean, I thought it might be fun for us to be roomies."

She thought it might be fun for them to be roomies. That was another good one. Gosh, if he wasn't careful, he was going to break a rib laughing so hard.

"Miss McClellan," he began.

"Gee, Pendleton. You might as well call me Kit. After all, we have slept together."

"We have *not*—"

"Yes, we have. And Daddy's absolutely delighted about it, let me tell you."

Oh, now *that* brought him wide awake in no time at all. "Excuse me?"

"I said Daddy's absolutely delighted about us sleeping together. He came home last night just as I was leaving with my bags, and I told him all about us."

He chuckled anxiously. "Oh, no, no, no, no, no."

Kit giggled contentedly. "Oh, yes, yes, yes, yes, yes."

"Miss McClellan—"

"Kit."

"Miss McClellan, I don't think you realize what you're saying."

"Actually, Pendleton, it's you who doesn't realize what I'm saying. There's so much more underlying this conversation than meets the ear. You can't possibly imagine."

"Try me."

"Nah. If you knew what I was talking about, all the fun would go right out of it."

"Miss McClellan—"

"*Kit*," she insisted. "Come on, Pendleton. You said my name out loud once already without any trouble at all. What's the problem?"

What's the problem? he echoed to himself. The problem was that he'd said her name out loud once already without any trouble at all. But instead of explaining that to her, he replied, "There's a little something we need to address here. Immediately, in fact."

"Only one little something? That's a surprise."

"I, um," he continued, "I sleep naked."

She smiled sweetly again. Uh-oh. "I know."

"How do you know?"

"I peeked."

"When did you peek?"

"Last night, when I crawled into bed beside you."

"So, uh, so it was dark?"

"I had a flashlight."

"Ah."

"Well, I'd never been in your house before," she said, "so I had no idea where the furniture was, and I didn't want to trip over anything. Imagine my surprise to discover that there *is* no furniture. You're going to have to ask Daddy for a raise."

"Miss McClellan—"

"Kit."

"The reason there's no furniture *isn't* because I don't have the funds to buy it, but because I haven't had the time to shop for it and . . ." He hesitated, wondering just how one went about dealing with this sort of thing. "I'm naked," he finally reiterated.

"So? I'm naked, too."

That was a fact of which he really wished she hadn't reminded him. "Which is something else we need to talk about," he said.

"Okay," she agreed, way too easily. "Let's talk about it. In fact, let's go ahead and talk about *all* the things we need to talk about." She extracted her hands from beneath the covers and ticked off the facts on her fingers as she enumerated them. "Let's see now . . . You're naked—that's one thing. I'm naked—that's two things. We're in bed together, we've slept together, and I can't wait to see what happens when Daddy tells the boys all about it—that's three more things. Oh, wait, another thing—you're going to make my family so happy, Pendleton. And you can't possibly know how important that is to me. I don't know how I'm ever going to be able to properly thank you."

Thinking he should probably just roll belly-up and surrender, he continued heedlessly, "You could start by getting out of my bed."

"Okay." She gripped the covers again, clearly ready to throw them back and reveal herself in all her naked glory.

"Wait!" he cried, squeezing his eyes shut. "Not yet."

"Hey, Pendleton, no time like the present."

"Stop," he commanded her. "Just . . . stop."

He opened one eye experimentally and was delighted to see that she had done as he'd requested for a change. She was still in his bed, and still covered up. But she was also still naked. As was he. Wasn't this just a wonderful way to wake up in the morning.

"What time do you have to be at work?" she asked.

"Not until eight. What time is it?"

Kit reached over to the nightstand on her side of the bed and retrieved her watch, then squinted at it in the dimly lit room. "It's . . . seven forty-five."

It took a moment for that to register. *"What?"*

She tossed her watch back onto the nightstand and reached her arms high above her head with a contented groan. As she relaxed the stretch, she told him, "I guess I forgot to tell you that I turned off your alarm when I came to bed last night. Frankly, those things annoy the heck out of me. I like to wake up gradually, by my own internal alarm clock. And it never goes off until after ten. Not unless some guy running his fingers through my hair wakes me up first."

"I was *not* running my fingers through your hair," he said, more to beat back the panic threatening to overtake him at being so late for work than to actually deny what even he had to admit was a valid argument.

"Well, at any rate, you'd better hurry if you have any hope of getting to work before nine," Kit pointed out as she snuggled back down into the covers and closed her eyes. "Boy," she added in a sleepy murmur, "it must be a drag to be a working stiff."

In spite of running inexcusably late for work, Pendleton could only lie there for a moment on his side and watch Kit McClellan in utter disbelief as she slipped effortlessly back into a nice, steady slumber. Only a person with no conscience could possibly fall asleep that quickly. Of course, his realization of that only compounded his discomfort.

He shook his head slowly, silently. What on earth was he supposed to do with her?

Unfortunately, way too many ideas popped into his head in response to that question, few of them in any way polite. Or legal. For now, he was just going to have to worry about it later. Because he had only fifteen minutes to shave, shower, dress, and make the seven-minute drive to work. So, keeping an eye trained carefully on the woman sleeping in his bed, he threw back the covers and swung his feet to the floor. Then, because he knew better than to trust her, he picked up his pillow and, as he stood, placed it strategically over his lower torso before he began backing toward the bedroom door.

He was as quiet as he could possibly be as he eased shut the door behind him. In spite of that, he wasn't sure, but he thought he heard Kit mumble something in her sleep just before the latch clicked. And although he tried to tell himself her remark must have been some incoherent observation about a half-forgotten dream, he couldn't help but think instead that it sounded a whole lot like, "Nice tushie, Pendleton."

And that, even more than being egregiously late for work, was what made him dash for the bathroom posthaste.

* * *

"You've made me a very happy man, Pendleton."

Pendleton clenched his hands into fists behind his back and silently willed his employer to spontaneously combust. Holt McClellan, Sr. sat on the business side of a massive mahogany desk, the worn leather chair beneath him creaking under his weight as he leaned back with *much* satisfaction. On the dark-paneled wall behind him, stuffed in various poses of literally glassy-eyed terror, was a disturbingly large collection of hunting trophies. But what really bothered Pendleton the most— aside from the obvious fact that his boss enjoyed killing things—was that each of the prizes had been wrested from completely passive animals like deer, raccoons and large-mouth bass.

Boy, you'd think the least McClellan, Sr. could do was go after something that had big, pointy teeth and razor-sharp claws. Even things out a bit, for God's sake.

"Yepper," the CEO continued happily, scattering Pendleton's thoughts. "Very, *very* happy."

"I assume, sir, that would be because of my report on priority enhancement to promote productivity," Pendleton stated, feigning ignorance. "I'm glad you approve. I—"

"Screw the report," McClellan, Sr. interrupted with a smile. "You're sleeping with my daughter. I see great things in your future, Pendleton. Great things indeed."

Pendleton swallowed hard, torn between denying the allegation, even though it was technically true, and ruining his boss's good mood, or conceding that he had, in fact, shared more than just a mattress with his employer's daughter, and thereby perpetuating a lie, to keep the man very, *very* happy.

Ultimately, the decision was taken out of his hands when McClellan, Sr. asked, "So, when are you going to marry her?"

That, at least, was a question to which Pendleton *definitely* knew the answer. With all the vigor and insistence he could muster, he stated quite forcibly, "Sir?"

"Marry her," his employer repeated. "When's the wedding? She's quite a catch, you know."

Pendleton swallowed hard. "A . . . catch, sir?"

The CEO waved a hand impatiently through the air. "Well, all right. Maybe not a catch. But you do have to admit that she's one of a kind."

Finally, an observation with which Pendleton could unequivocally agree. "Oh, yes, sir. I will admit that. Your daughter is nothing if not . . . unique."

The moment Pendleton had arrived at work, Beatrice had told him Mr. McClellan, Sr. was demanding his presence in his office. Naturally, he'd assumed his employer had commanded this performance because he wanted a rundown of Pendleton's Pirates of the Caribbean adventure with the old man's daughter. The last thing he had expected upon walking into his boss's office was for McClellan, Sr. to slap him soundly on the back and say with heartfelt delight, "Welcome back, son!"

But that was precisely what his boss had done. And nothing in Pendleton's entire life had terrified him more than those words. Or at least, that one word. That last word. *Son.* Because the way McClellan, Sr. had voiced that word . . .

All Pendleton could do was remember Kit's assertion at dinner that night in Veranda Bay, that he was currently at the top of the McClellan men's *sap du jour* list. That list of eligible bachelors who might be gullible enough, greedy enough or misguided enough to marry the madcap McClellan heiress, thereby securing the family fortune for the family.

When it appeared that his employer was going to say nothing more, Pendleton ventured, "May I speak frankly, sir?"

"By all means."

With some trepidation, he began, "Although your daughter is certainly a lovely person . . ."

McClellan's eyebrows arrowed downward in concern. "I'm not sure I like the sound of that, Pendleton."

"Uh . . ." he tried again. "It's just that, um . . ."

"Ye-es?" his boss asked, stringing the single syllable out over several time zones.

"Well, sir, although I think Miss McClellan is, um . . ."

"Is what?"

"Is a, uh . . ."

With his free hand, McClellan, Sr. made a slow, gyrating motion, a silent indication that Pendleton should just please, for the love of God, get on with it.

"Well, she has a great personality, sir," he said lamely.

McClellan, Sr. frowned. "Uh-oh."

The softly uttered observation halted Pendleton's thoughts faster than an electrode to the groin would have. "Uh-oh, sir?"

But instead of elaborating, McClellan, Sr. eyed Pendleton malignantly and asked, "Pendleton, how badly do you need this job?"

Oooh, low blow. "Um, pretty badly, sir."

"And can you think of any other corporation in

the country that will pay you the salary you're currently earning in the position you hold?"

Oooh, another one below the belt. McClellan, Sr. sure did fight dirty. "Um, no, sir, I can't think of another corporation in the country that will pay me what Hensley's does. And if I haven't said so already, sir, it's a very generous package, one that—"

"That's what I thought." McClellan, Sr. nodded, triumphantly if Pendleton wasn't mistaken. "Now then. You were saying? About my lovely daughter and her great personality?"

Pendleton sighed. He was really beginning to hate his new job, despite its generous benefits and pay. "I was saying, sir, that your daughter is um, lovely."

"And?"

"And she has a great personality."

"And?"

"And I find her company to be very . . ."

"Yes?"

Demoralizing. Uncomfortable. Maddening. Icky. "Delightful," he muttered, and somehow he managed not to choke on the word.

McClellan, Sr. couldn't contain his glee. "I knew the two of you would hit it off. The minute I laid eyes on you, Pendleton, I knew you were the man for Kit."

Oh, God. "Sir?"

"Yes, son?"

Oh, please, no. Not *son*. Anything but that. "About my report? On priority enhancement to promote productivity?"

"We'll talk about it at tomorrow's meeting. Anything else?"

Well, except for that small matter of your daughter having infested my home and, aside from spraying her

*with some nasty pesticide that might potentially harm
the environment, I have no idea how to remove her . . .*

"Nothing, sir."

"Excellent."

He prepared to leave, thinking his boss would
dismiss him with his usual, cursory "Now get out,"
but instead, McClellan, Sr. rose from his chair and
moved to the front of his desk.

And then, out of nowhere, he said, "Did you
know that I once paid a man a quarter of a million
dollars *not* to marry my daughter?"

Pendleton blinked three times, as if a too-bright
flash had gone off right in front of his eyes. This
really wasn't a conversation he wanted to have
with his boss. It had been bad enough having it
with the boss's daughter. In spite of that, he was
helpless to say anything but, "Now that you mention it, I believe that Miss McClellan did say something about that over dinner in Veranda Bay."

McClellan, Sr. nodded. "Then I assume she also
told you why it's essential that she be married
within two months' time, too, didn't she? Something about one hundred million dollars?"

Pendleton pretended to search his memory for
the recollection. "Seems to me she said it was
ninety-nine-point-four million," he said.

His employer growled impatiently. "Whatever."

"Yes, she did mention that, as well."

McClellan, Sr. nodded. "The man I paid to not
marry Kit was a prick, Pendleton. She deserved
better. She deserved someone like you."

Oh, he *really* didn't like the sound of that.

"And now," his employer continued, "here you
are." For a long time, McClellan, Sr. only studied
him in silence, as if he were trying to gauge the full
measure of the man. Then, evidently having ar-

rived at a decision, he went on, "Seeing as how I once paid a man that much money to *leave* my daughter, when my family's fortune *wasn't* at stake, can you imagine how *grateful* I'd be to the man who *married* Kit now, thereby keeping the family fortune where it belongs—in the hands of the family?"

Pendleton swallowed hard in an effort to dispel the bitter taste that rose from the back of his throat at hearing his employer's offer. The fingers he had curled behind his back fisted tighter as he realized he'd never wanted to hit anyone as badly as he wanted to slug McClellan, Sr. at that moment. The man didn't deserve ninety-nine-point-four cents, let alone millions. To barter one's daughter like so much furniture made the man, to Pendleton's way of thinking, worse than a common pimp.

As if he hadn't already said far too much, McClellan, Sr. added, "I can be a very generous man, Pendleton. Think about it."

Oh, as if he'd be able to do anything *but* think about it. Naturally, Pendleton had no intention of lowering himself to McClellan, Sr.'s distasteful pandering. But he was too outraged at the moment to trust anything he might say aloud, so he only nodded dispassionately and said nothing. Hey, what was there to say? His employer was a slimy, heartless creep, and Pendleton was too much of a gentleman to call him on it. Either that, or Pendleton was too much of a spineless, simpering suckup to call him on it. Whatever.

"I'm glad we understand each other," McClellan, Sr. said with a slimy, heartless smile.

Pendleton responded with a spineless, simpering one of his own. "Yes, sir. We do indeed understand each other." *You creep.*

"Fine. Now remember what I said. And get out."

Unable to follow that last order fast enough, Pendleton pivoted on his heel and hurried out of his employer's office. As he went, he tried not to panic in the knowledge that it was barely nine A.M., and already his house had been overtaken by Kit McClellan, his morals compromised by her father. Call him an alarmist, but it seemed to him that the day wasn't starting off well at all.

He could handle the McClellans, he assured himself as he made his way back to his office. There was no way McClellan, Sr. could expect him to marry Kit and save the family fortune, with or without a bonus for his trouble. This wasn't medieval England, where fathers did that kind of thing, in spite of McClellan, Sr.'s obviously antiquated thinking on the matter.

And Kit couldn't possibly be serious about being his "roomie," Pendleton told himself further. Surely, it was just her . . . unique . . . sense of humor and simple boredom with her life—and *not* a chemical imbalance in her brain—that made her do the things she did. Surely, she would tire of wreaking havoc in his life soon, and then she'd move on. Surely everything would come to rights soon.

Unfortunately, Pendleton felt sure about none of those things. Except for maybe one. He *could* handle Kit McClellan.

Surely.

Chapter 10

It was with some trepidation that Pendleton pulled up behind his big Victorian house in Old Louisville shortly after six that evening. He told himself that the only reason he was shivering like a jackhammer was because of the constant rush of icy air that had blown in through the tear in the roof of his car that even duct tape hadn't been able to mend effectively, and not because he was terrified of a slim, blond woman who couldn't even make a sarong burgeon on her best day. Unfortunately, thoughts of Kit McClellan had left him shuddering every time they'd braved entry into his muddled brain.

Just what the hell was he supposed to do about her?

He folded closed the doors on the dilapidated shed that his real estate agent had called a garage, then made his way halfheartedly up the crumbling creekstones that bisected his small backyard. Once the weather turned warm, he had plans to rip out the stepping stones and replace them with a cobbled walkway that led from the back porch to the new garage he planned to build. Of course, that was going to necessitate building a back porch, too, one to replace the boxy wooden, uh . . . thing with screens . . . that was currently affixed to his house.

For now, however, his yard, porch, and garage were much like his house. In need of major renovation. Kind of like his life, too, he thought further as he approached.

He heard her long before he saw her and knew that Kit McClellan was still very much resident in his home. As he carefully negotiated the slick, mossy steps of his alleged back porch, a sound assaulted his ears unlike anything he had ever heard before. And only when he'd opened the back door and stepped inside did he finally realize what was causing the din.

To say she sang badly would have been like saying Josef Stalin had lacked people skills. And the song . . .

"Oh, don't you remember sweet Betsy from Pike . . ." was what it sounded like she was attacking. Then something about green mountains and a brother named Ike. Then egg yolks? He couldn't really say. But the big yeller dog part was fairly clear, as was the spotted hog part. The rest, however . . . Well, he supposed he should be grateful he hadn't understood it all. Because that would have meant he had some working knowledge of Kit McClellan's repertoire. And the thought of such a possibility really didn't set well with him at all.

"Hi, honey, I'm home," he muttered as he entered his kitchen.

Immediately, he sensed that something was wrong. Well, something besides the fact that his house was currently the migratory receptacle for the rare, but unfortunately not quite extinct, yellow-headed, gravel-voiced hobnobber. And it wasn't just because of the tasteful arrangement of table and chairs situated at the center of the room that hadn't been there this morning when he'd left for work. It was also because of the smell emanating from one of the numerous copper pots cooking ... stuff ... on the stove. A smell that was quite ... extraordinary. Not unpleasant, mind you ... Well, not *too* unpleasant. Just ... um ...

"Kit?" he called out to the house at large.

"Pendleton! Darling! You're home!"

Darling?

"I'll be right there! As soon as I fix your martini!"

Martini?

He told himself it was simple curiosity—and *not* crippling fear—that kept him rooted in place, gripping his briefcase as if it were the only thing that linked him to reality. Which was good, because when Kit entered the kitchen less than a minute later, he was sure reality was fast slipping away. In fact, he had to close his eyes for a moment, then open them again, to be sure he wasn't hallucinating.

Nope. He wasn't. Dammit.

Because that was definitely Kit McClellan gliding through the swinging door that connected kitchen to dining room. And she really was dressed like June Cleaver, right down to the high heels, the poufy skirt, the matching sweater set, and the pearl necklace. She strode toward him with a sweet smile, kissed his cheek, and extended a glass toward him.

And then she asked, "How was your day, dear?"

Okay, now this was just plain bizarre. It was one thing to have your house overrun, but when the woman overrunning it starting acting like this, well ... In a word, *ew*. A shudder wound through him, and he snatched the martini out of her hand, down-ing it in one quick swallow.

Kit patted his arm. "I'm glad to see you, too, honey. Here, let me take your coat and briefcase. Your slippers and the newspaper are in your chair by the fireplace."

Before he even realized what she was doing, Kit had his briefcase on the kitchen table, his coat draped over her arm, and she was refilling his glass from the cocktail shaker she'd been carrying in her other hand. It occurred to him then that not only did he not own a pair of slippers, but there was also no chair by his fireplace. Of course, until a moment ago, he would have sworn there was no table and chairs in his kitchen, either, and look how that had turned out.

"Kit?"

"Yes, dear?"

"What have you done?"

She arched her eyebrows in a way that, judg-ing by the golden age of television still broadcast regularly on Nick at Nite, was endemic to all Eisenhower-era women. "What do you mean, dear?"

He opened his mouth to put voice to the thoughts that had just jelled—more or less—in his head, but all that came out was, "Ummm . . ."

And then he was crossing the kitchen toward the door that connected with the dining room, shoving it open with far more intensity than was necessary. He knew that, because it immediately banged into something on the other side and came hurling back again, smashing right against his nose.

"Ouch."

The commentary came not from Pendleton, but

from Kit, who stood behind him. "That had to hurt," she added.

Without comment, he carefully pushed open the door, peeking around it into the other room to see what had caused its halt the first time. And imagine his surprise to discover a lovely dining room suite on the other side, complete with table, chairs, buffet, and china cabinet. A china cabinet that was half-stocked with what appeared, even to Pendleton's untrained eye, to be pretty primo china.

"Wedgwood," Kit clarified from behind him when she saw where his gaze had settled. "I got Louisville Stoneware for our everyday. Natch. I hope you don't mind me picking out our patterns without consulting you. But the fact is, you men simply do not have an eye for that kind of thing."

He turned to look at her. "My, but haven't you been a busy little bee today."

She grinned. "Yes, I have, haven't I?"

He said nothing in response, only gazed at the new furnishings that were nothing at all like what he had planned to buy for himself. Kit's tastes obviously ran along the lines of English antiques, where his own were far more contemporary and far less excessive. Maybe, he thought, if he was really nice to her, she'd let him pick the interior paint colors when the time came.

"I wasn't sure who to call about the renovation work," she added, almost as if she'd read his mind. She swept her hand toward one of numerous spots of crumbling plaster near the ceiling. "Call me old-fashioned, but I think that's more a job for someone who has at least one Y chromosome, so I thought you could handle it."

"I'll handle it," he said, feeling just so damned

grateful that she allowed him some small say in the destiny of his own home.

Pushing past him, she strode alongside a half-dozen empty cartons filled with bubble-wrapped items Pendleton felt certain he was better off not knowing about. Then she made her way into the living room, where, by golly, there was an oxblood leather chair sitting by the fireplace—where, incidentally, burned a lovely little fire—complete with a pair of plaid wool slippers and a copy of *The Courier-Journal*, all folded nice and neat for his enjoyment.

"What? No golden retriever?" he asked.

"It's being delivered tomorrow," she announced as she spun around to face him.

He nodded.

"As is the sofa-loveseat combination, the club chair, and the chaise."

"I see."

"Unfortunately, our new bedroom suite won't be here until the day after."

He sighed heavily. "Does this mean you're planning to stay for some length of time?"

She waggled her head back and forth, then wrinkled her nose in thought. "Yeah."

"And, may I ask what I did to deserve such a, um . . . such a distinction?"

She shrugged. "You were nice to me, Pendleton."

He hesitated before saying anything more, wondering just how serious she was about this. Then, when he realized she was, more than likely, pretty dead set on it, he asked, "Will your father really fire me if I throw you out?"

He could have sworn that, for just the briefest of moments, she looked as if he'd hurt her feelings by asking what he had. Then he decided that he must have been mistaken, because she immediately appeared to be as cool, calm, and collected as always.

"Yeah, he probably would," she said. "He's done some pretty wacky things since Mama passed away. He used to only have four vice-presidents besides Holt, but he created all those new positions with huge, obscene salaries just so he could hire more potential life mates for me. And even at that, he's fired and hired a whole mess of people over the last two years. He always has what sounds like legitimate reasons for letting people go, but he's fired an awful lot of them when they didn't, oh, hit it off with the boss's daughter."

"So everyone there now is a fairly recent hire?" Pendleton asked.

She nodded. "I don't think any of the VPs have worked for Hensley's for more than a year. That's about how long Daddy gives them to make me marriage-minded. If you throw me out now, he'll probably decide pretty quickly that you're not vying for my affection and replace you with someone who will."

"What about Carmichael?" Pendleton asked as a new thought struck him. "If your father only hires potential husbands for you, then why did he hire Carmichael, who is quite obviously a woman?"

"He hired Carmichael in one of his more desperate periods, when he thought maybe I just wasn't, shall we say, interested in men. It was back when Hawaii was entertaining the idea of legalizing same-sex marriages."

"Ah."

"Carmichael has since met a very nice osteopathic surgeon named Debbie, and the two of them are very happy together."

Pendleton felt triumphant. "Then there's a good chance your father *won't* fire me if I throw you out, if he's kept Carmichael on in spite of her not being a potential life mate for you."

"Oh, please, Pendleton. Carmichael is positively *incredible* heading up advertising. Daddy would have to be crazy—in the medical sense, I mean—to let her go. You, on the other hand, are a new hire who hasn't even proven himself," she pointed out. "You are by no means irreplaceable."

Pendleton naturally took exception to that, but he supposed Kit had a point. Certainly he could fight his dismissal, but such a battle would be time-consuming. He absolutely, positively, without question had to hang onto his job. At least until the last week of April. He had something very important to prove, after all.

"How long are you staying?" he asked halfheartedly.

She smiled brightly, but once again, he got the impression that she was forcing all this cheerfulness. "I haven't decided yet. It'll be fun, Pendleton. You'll see. Just wait. Someday, we'll look back on this, and we'll laugh and laugh and laugh."

He nibbled his lip as he gazed at her, telling himself to hold back the maniacal laughter he felt threatening until that day dawned. And he wondered for a moment if she really was crazy, or if she just had a very sophisticated sense of humor that people from South Jersey couldn't possibly begin to understand. Ultimately, what he decided on was, "You're sick, Kit. You realize that, don't you?"

Slowly, she retraced her steps, her high heels skimming softly across the hardwood floor, her smile thinning as she approached. In one fluid gesture, she plucked from his hand the martini refill that he had yet to taste, then lifted it to her lips for a dainty sip.

"Now, now," she said after she swallowed. "Anyone will tell you that when you have as much money as my family has, my condition is what's known as 'eccentric.'"

He shook his head. "'Eccentric' suggests a certain, oh . . . disorganization. And you don't strike me as being particularly disorganized."

She held his gaze for a long time, and he detected something in her eyes that was almost . . . yearning. "Then think of me as someone who has nowhere else to go," she said softly. "Because in a lot of ways, Pendleton, that's exactly what I am."

He inhaled deeply and released the breath slowly as he pondered his choices. Either he could toss Kit out on her keester and risk losing his job and any potential chance he had to show a certain someone exactly what kind of stuff he was made of, or he could let her stay and allow his employer to think that the two of them were shacking up. For some reason, he discovered he rather liked that latter option. It would serve the bastard right.

And he heard himself ask, "What's your real reason for doing this?"

She sipped casually from the martini again, her gaze never leaving his. "If my father thinks the two of us are romantically involved, he'll leave me alone and stop flinging undesirable men at me."

Sidestepping the matter of his being undesirable—for now, at least—Pendleton asked, "And?"

"And I'll have bought myself a little time to decide what I want to do."

He eyed her thoughtfully for a moment. "I thought you said you had to be married within two months or your family would forfeit everything."

"That's true."

"Then it sounds to me like you don't have a lot of time left to buy."

"Two months is more than enough time," she assured him, though he detected something in her voice that told him she was in no way sure.

"So if you, wise as Solomon as you are," he said, "conclude that your family should go broke for paying your fiancé to dump you, then you'll just string them along for a couple of months, letting them think the two of us will be married before the deadline. And then you'll back out at the last minute, thereby causing them to lose their inheritance."

She dropped her gaze to the floor, nodding slowly. Her voice was a quiet monotone that revealed nothing of her thoughts when she replied, "Yes, that's right."

"And if, at the end of this two months, you decide they—and you—should *keep* the money?" he asked. "What will you do then?"

She snapped her head back up, her eyes clouded with confusion when she looked at him. "What do you mean?"

"Well, if you want to keep the money, then you'll need to be married," he pointed out. "And what will you do then?"

Her eyebrows arrowed downward in consideration, as if she hadn't quite thought that far ahead. "Well," she began slowly, "I suppose . . . I mean if I do decide to do get married—which I'm not saying I will," she hastened to qualify, "I guess . . ." She sighed fitfully. "Well, I guess Novak would do in a pinch."

"Novak?" Pendleton exclaimed. She had to be kidding.

She shrugged. "Well, he's made it clear more

than once that he'd do anything for me," she said.

This time Pendleton was the one whose eyebrows arrowed downward in consideration. Then, immediately, he stopped himself. The last thing he wanted to do was consider Novak doing anything for—or with—Kit.

"Besides," she continued, crossing her arms anxiously over her midsection, injecting a bit more vigor into her voice than he suspected she felt, "I might still decide to stay single. It would serve my family right."

"And you?" he asked. "You'll gladly surrender your share of the millions?"

Her shoulders rose and fell so quickly, Pendleton wasn't sure the gesture qualified for a shrug. "Of course I would," she said hastily. "It would be going to a good cause."

She'd responded too quickly, he thought. She really hadn't given much consideration to the prospect of being broke herself. And he wondered for a moment if he should try to nudge her toward thinking along those lines.

Ultimately, he decided it was none of his business. The McClellans had dug this pit for themselves a *loooong* time before he'd entered the picture, and there was absolutely no reason for him to involve himself in the mess any more than he'd already been pulled into it. Still, that didn't answer his question about what to do with Kit, did it? Should he let her stay or make her go?

"You know," he said, "I don't think I'd be talking out of turn here if I said that I really don't think much of your father."

She smiled sadly. "Yeah, well, you wouldn't be talking alone, either. Not many people *do* think much of my father."

Pendleton studied her for a long time, noting the slump of her shoulders, the downward tilt of her head, and the way she seemed to be holding herself up—as if no one else would do it for her. And little by little, the cool feelings he'd harbored for her began to warm some.

"Kit, what you do about your family fortune is between you and your family," he said. "I really wish you wouldn't involve me."

She met his gaze levelly, beseechingly, for a long time without speaking. Then finally, timidly, she said, "Dinner will be ready in about fifteen minutes. It's something special. I know you're going to like it."

Kit held her breath as she waited to see what Pendleton would say about her continued presence in his home. Any other man would have been dialing the police—or Our Lady of Peace Hospital—by now. But Pendleton was looking at her as if he might honestly allow her to stay. She moved a hand behind her back and crossed her fingers hopefully. *Please*, she thought, *oh, pretty please . . .*

For a long moment, he said nothing, and with every passing moment of his prolonged silence, her heart began to sink, her limbs grew heavy, and she resolved herself to being dumped. Oh, well, she thought. It's not like such a thing came as any surprise. What man in his right mind would allow his house, his very life, to be overrun by some crazy— or rather, eccentric—woman, just because she'd asked pretty please?

She was about to open her mouth and concede defeat, to return Pendleton's house—and his life— to his own capable hands, when he opened his own mouth and cut her off.

"All right, you can stay," he said, hurrying on

before she could comment, "and I'm probably going to be sorry I asked, but . . . define 'special.' "

Kit smiled as a bubble of relief burst in her belly, even allowed herself to surrender to a ripple of laughter as she crossed the room to link her arm with his. "Fried catfish," she told him. "Two words, Pendleton. Yum-mee."

She sensed immediately by the look on his face that he wasn't nearly as excited about the menu as she was. "Oh, boy," he said blandly. "Bottom-feeders soaked in fat and served up for dinner. I don't guess life gets any better than that."

"Well, there's no reason to be sarcastic."

"No?"

She enjoyed another sip from the martini glass she had taken from him, then extended it toward him again. Some Stepford Wife she was turning out to be. She wasn't even making sure her man had his nightly cocktail refill after a long, hard day at work. Surprisingly, Pendleton took the drink from her, but instead of tasting it, he continued to study her face.

And damn him for that. It was just too friggin' cold in this house to wear skimpy little outfits orchestrated to keep his eyes elsewhere on her body. But he'd only given her June Cleaver get-up a perfunctory glance before settling his attention back on her face. Now she was going to have to try something else. Maybe if she dressed up as a nun. Or a dominatrix. Or both at the same time. Hmmm . . .

"What else are we having?" he asked suddenly, dragging her mind back to the matters at hand. "For dinner, I mean."

She lifted her nose indignantly into the air. "Well, after your joyous outburst over the catfish, I think maybe I shouldn't tell you about the side dishes. Or dessert, either, for that matter."

"Oh, I think maybe you should."

She shook her head. "Nah. It'd be more fun to watch your expression when you sample genuine Kentucky cuisine for the first time. Especially the—"

She halted when she saw his eyebrows shoot up expectantly. "Well, you'll find out," she concluded easily.

Pendleton nodded slowly, fatalistically. "That's what I'm afraid of."

Kit had little trouble keeping herself busy in Pendleton's house during the week that followed. She furnished his home from top to bottom with furniture that *she*, at least, adored—how fortunate that his arrival in Louisville had coincided perfectly with Bacon's department store's semiannual home sale (and that twelve-months-no-interest plan had just been *too* irresistible to pass up). She cleared his fridge and cupboards of all that trendy bachelor fare and replaced it with the basic four of her home state—cholesterol, cholesterol, cholesterol, and greens. And she played her Earl Scruggs CDs over and over and over again—only to learn that Pendleton, go figure, did *not* like bluegrass music. Oh, yes. And she'd named their new golden retriever puppy Maury.

All in all, it had been time well spent. And not just because she'd been so successful in organizing her new life with Pendleton. But because while she'd been redoing his home, hearth, and life from top to bottom, she'd also learned some *very* interesting things about him. Like the fact that he had every book ever written by F. Scott Fitzgerald *and* Ernest Hemingway. Like the fact that he owned not one, not two, but *three* pairs of Levi's 501s that had definitely seen better days. Like the fact that he preferred boxers over briefs. And like the fact that R&B and blues ruled in his CD collection. Funny, but he wasn't turning out to be anything at all like she had expected.

Now her second Saturday with him was upon them, a full day with just her and Pendleton, and she was looking forward to learning even more. Especially since he'd steadfastly avoided her last weekend by driving to Paducah, claiming that visiting Paducah, Kentucky had been a lifelong goal, and no, if Kit didn't mind, he'd just as soon go alone. So clearly, she intended to take advantage of his presence at home for a change to try and figure the man out.

Not surprisingly, upon opening her eyes that morning, Kit had found herself alone in the bed. She'd awakened alone every morning since that first one, now that Pendleton was sleeping downstairs on their new sofa every night. At any rate, a metallic rapping from the backyard had been what woke her. She'd moved to the bedroom window to find the door open on the shed-thing outside, and Pendleton's roadster—its roof now mended— parked out in the alley. Even after she'd made her way downstairs to pour herself a cup of coffee and let Maury out for his morning uproar, the pounding had continued.

Now, gazing out the kitchen window, Kit saw Maury yapping happily about the backyard, but Pendleton was nowhere to be seen. Heard, certainly, but not seen. Much as he'd been for the entire length of her invasion. She'd heard him come in from work every night, had heard him shaving and showering every morning. But she hadn't seen much of him at all.

Nor had he spoken to her. Although, all things reconsidered, she couldn't exactly blame him. After all, the only reason he tolerated her occupation of his home was that it meant he kept his job. As reasons went, Kit supposed his was as good as any that men had used over the years to hang around with her. She sighed as that *clink-clink-clink* started up again, and she wondered what on earth he was up to out there.

"Probably building a guillotine," she muttered to herself. Ah, well. Only one way to find out.

It took her almost no time to take a bath and change clothes. She opted for black velvet leggings and a bright purple chenille turtleneck that fell to mid-thigh, accessorizing the ensemble with purple socks and black ankle boots. Maury began to bark incessantly the moment she hit the bottom step outside, and the clamor in the shed-thing abruptly halted.

"Pendleton?" she called out experimentally as she approached, thinking that, if this were a Wes Craven movie, the spooky ax-murderer music would start kicking in right about now. "Everything okay in there?"

Not much to her surprise, she received no reply. Except for the constant *Awr-awr! . . . Awr-awr-awr!* from Maury as he ran in maddening circles around her feet.

"Down, boy," she instructed the dog, wondering why she bothered. He was about as obedient as Pendleton was. Sure enough, Maury only increased his frenzied movements in response. Kit rolled her eyes and drew cautiously closer to the shed-thing.

"Pendleton?" she tried again. "Sweetie? Is that you in there?"

"Go away."

Yep, it was Pendleton in there, all right. "What are you doing?"

"Go . . . away."

Not one to be dissuaded by a surly attitude, nor the potential for becoming a homicide victim, Kit continued valiantly, "When I woke up alone this morning, I was worried about you."

He still hadn't emerged from the shed-thing, and Kit still wasn't quite brave enough to chance a look inside. "Why would you be worried?" his voice came from the other side of the open door. "Unless maybe you thought I might have hanged myself in the stairwell during the night. Which, as we both know, is a definite possibility."

"Would that be that you were hanged or you were hung?" she asked. "I never did know the difference between the two."

That, at last, roused him from inside. And when he poked his head through the door, Kit had to catch her breath at the sight of him, because he was really . . . very . . . quite, well . . . breathtaking.

His dark hair was tousled all over his head, though whether blown there by the cold wind or because he hadn't bothered to comb it since rising, she had no idea. Nor did it matter. Because even tousled, Pendleton was way too handsome. Worse, he had on a chocolate-brown sweater almost the same color as his eyes, one that did absolutely nothing to hide what she knew were a phenomenal chest and spectacular shoulders. Worse still, he was wearing a pair of those faded 501s, and she realized that they were worn and snug in *all* the right places.

His breath left his mouth in a rush of white steam, as if he were breathing very hard in an effort to contain himself. "Go. Away."

"I just wanted to make sure you were okay."

He dipped his head in defeat. "No, you didn't. You wanted to do something to bother me. Admit it."

She gasped at him. "That's not true."

And much to her surprise, Kit discovered that it really *wasn't* true.

What an interesting development.

She tucked her hands into her armpits. Man, it was cold out here. And not just because of Pendleton's reception, either. "What are you doing in there?" she asked him again.

For a moment, she didn't think he was going to answer. Then, out of nowhere, he smiled, the way a man would smile if he were doing something he really enjoyed. So Kit felt pretty certain the smile wasn't for her, but for whatever he'd been doing before she intruded.

"Building the perfect beast," he told her.

She smiled back. "Oooh, sounds neato. Can I help?"

He glanced over his shoulder, then back at Kit. "There are those who might argue that you're the design for the perfect beast, you know."

Her smile fell. How nice of him to remind her. "And you, naturally, would be one of them," she said, not quite able to keep the hurt from her voice.

He seemed to give the suggestion weighty consideration before replying, "Mmm . . . not necessarily."

"Look, can I come in or not?"

"Why would you want to?"

She shrugged. "Just to visit. I've missed you,

Pendleton. You haven't been home much." She told herself she did *not* sound petulant when she said that.

"I've been home every night," he objected.

"Oh, sure, your body has."

Now his smile turned into something else, something that was decidedly—uh-oh—playful. "Been noticing my body have you?" he asked.

"Only its absence."

"You just said it was here."

"You know what I meant."

"No, I don't. Enlighten me."

Yeah, she'd enlighten him, all right. She'd enlighten him all the way back to New Jersey if he didn't knock off the boyish flirtation bit. Like she was dumb enough to fall for *that*.

"Look, can I come in or not?" she repeated.

He actually seemed disappointed that she'd put a stop to their repartee. Like he was really the type of man to go for repartee. But he jerked his head back toward the interior in silent invitation, then disappeared inside himself. Before he had a chance to rescind the offer, Kit followed, only to find the dirt-packed floor of the shed-thing covered with lots of car part-things. Or rather, she decided upon closer inspection, what appeared to be . . . bike part-things?

"What on earth are you doing?"

"I'm working on my bike," he replied, verifying her suspicions.

"Like a Schwinn bike?" she asked.

He shook his head and thrust a thumb over his shoulder. "Like a Harley-Davidson bike."

She looked in the direction he'd indicated and, sure enough, saw a big ol' Harley hog—well, most of a big ol' Harley hog, anyway—leaning against the side of the shed-thing. One wheel was off, and the chain was drooping, but all in all, the big black monstrosity looked very scary.

"Oh," she said.

He glanced over at her with a curious gaze. "Oh?"

She scrunched up her shoulders. "Well, it's just that you don't much seem like the Harley-Davidson type."

"But I do seem like the Schwinn type?"

"Well, no . . ."

"Then why the look of disbelief?"

Good question, she thought. Too bad she didn't have a good answer to go with. "I don't know. It's just unexpected, that's all. Does it run?"

He laughed as he stooped beside the collection of oily, greasy guy things scattered on the dirt floor, and she realized then that his hands were streaked and smudged black in places with the remnants of his labor. For some reason, the sight of his dirty hands skimming so carefully over the odds and ends sent a thrill of heat crashing right through her body. With no small effort, she shook the sensation off.

"Usually it runs," he said as he picked through the assortment of bits and pieces, his mind obviously focused more on those than on the conversation at hand. "But it's a pretty old bike, so I have to keep it in shape. The weather should be turning warm before long, and I want it to be ready to take out on the first good day."

"I bet it's fun," she said.

He smiled as he retrieved a big, round metal thing from the assortment of parts and began to wind it around a long, cylindrical metal thing. "Yeah. It is."

She watched the motion of his grease-spattered hands, the gentle back-and-forth of thumb and forefinger as he slowly, leisurely . . . oh God, so rhythmically . . . spun the round part down lower and lower over the cylindrical part. And for some strange reason, her heart began to pound like mad, sending her blood zinging through her veins with the speed of a locomotive.

She swallowed hard. "So . . . do you usually ride alone?"

"Uh-huh."

"You don't take any passengers?"

"Nuh-uh. Not anymore."

Not anymore? she wondered. "Who did you used to take?"

He glanced up quickly, his eyes cool and distant. Somehow she got the feeling that he wished he hadn't made his last statement, and that he wanted very badly to change the subject. But when he spoke, it was in fact in answer to her question. Unfortunately.

"Sherry," he said as he dropped his gaze back to the floor.

Kit wasn't sure she wanted to know, but asked, "Sherry?"

He sighed heavily and tossed the two pieces he had joined together back down amid the other clutter. Then, restless, he picked up a wrench and moved closer to his motorcycle, where he hunkered down to unscrew a bolt on the wheel that was still attached. For a long time, Kit didn't think he was going to answer her. Then, in one swift motion, he suddenly hurled the wrench hard enough to send it crashing through the window on the other side of the shed.

He must have seen her flinch from the corner of

his eye, because he dipped his head in what resembled an apology. When he looked back up at Kit again, his eyes were turbulent and weary.

"Yeah, Sherry," he finally said, his voice low and gravelly. "Sherry Pendleton."

Something cold settled in Kit's midsection, a sensation she'd felt often enough in her life to recognize as profound disappointment. Even though she knew what he was going to say, she asked halfheartedly, "Sherry Pendleton, your sister?"

He shook his head. "No. Sherry Pendleton, my wife."

Chapter 11

"Your *wife*?" Kit exclaimed. "You're married?"

It took a moment for Pendleton to realize how badly he'd misspoken. "My *ex*-wife," he quickly corrected himself. "Sherry and I have been divorced for almost three years."

Kit looked absolutely stunned by the news. "In Veranda Bay," she said, her voice as quiet as the breeze blowing into the shed, "when you said you were in love once, but that she left you . . . that's who you were talking about, wasn't it? Your wife?"

"*Ex*-wife," he corrected her, stalling instead of answering her question.

"But that's who you were talking about, wasn't it?" she persisted.

"Yes." He uttered the single word through teeth clenched so hard, his jaw hurt.

"But you said then that you didn't know if she loved you."

He sighed, amazed that Kit McClellan, of all people, would try to defend Sherry. Of course, she'd never met Sherry. She didn't know her the way Pendleton did. "I'm not sure Sherry loved *me* so much as she loved what I could do for her," he said.

The look that filled her eyes, so dark, so lonely, so obviously in sync with his own feelings, was simply too much for him to bear. So he dropped his gaze back down to the disassembled parts of his motorcycle and tried to focus on those instead.

Suddenly, however, the last thing he wanted to do was work on his bike. Not surprisingly, his focus was elsewhere, on a time in his life that was as broken up and scattered as the remnants of his motorcycle.

Although he told himself he didn't want to discuss that time with Kit, he heard himself saying softly, "Sherry and I grew up together in the same neighborhood in New Jersey. According to our moms, we started talking about getting married when we were six years old."

"Oh, that's so sweet."

When he glanced up, he saw that Kit hadn't moved an inch from the spot where she'd been standing. Yet somehow, suddenly, she seemed much closer. Slowly, unmindful of the dirt, she dropped down to sit on the floor, crossing her legs before her, pretzel-fashion.

"Not really," he said. "By fifth grade, we weren't speaking to each other. In fact, we had kind of an on-again, off-again relationship until I graduated from college. But when I came home from Harvard with my MBA and a half-dozen job offers from some of the best corporations in the country, Sherry dumped Marv Polanski, who owned three *very* successful Chevron stations, and she took up with me again. We married about six months later."

"So what makes you think she didn't love you?" Kit asked, her voice sounding desperate somehow.

Pendleton reached into his back pocket for a rag to wipe the grease from his hands. He took his time to perform the action, but his words were quick when he spoke. "As soon as I graduated from college, I entered the fast lane, way above the speed limit. I was twenty-four and found myself with a high-stakes job, a high-powered position, a high-stress lifestyle, and a wife with high-priced tastes. Are you getting the picture here?"

He braved a quick look at Kit again, only to find her still sitting transfixed. She did, however, nod in response to his question, so he figured she was keeping up with him.

"To be fair to Sherry," he continued, "I knew that about her when we got married. In fact, we both spent a lot of our time as kids making plans on rising above the old neighborhood. We were both equally guilty in wanting the finer things in life, and I spent money as fast as she did."

"So what went wrong?"

"Nothing, for about four years. We were very happy. At least, Sherry was. She was living the life of a corporate wife—lunching, shopping, and partying to her heart's content." He paused long enough to emit a derisive chuckle. "Oh, yeah. Sherry's life was *great*. But after four years, I started to realize that I had no life at all. My job consumed nearly every waking hour. I was pretty much the big-wheeling corporate type you described at dinner that first night at your house," he said. "My life was just a big, fat zero when it came to leisurely enjoyment. I was a complete loser in the game of life."

She had the decency to look chagrined at that. "I'm sorry about that," she said. "I had no right to—"

"You had every right," he said with a shrug. "You were totally on the mark, at least where my old life was concerned." But Pendleton wasn't that man anymore, and he wouldn't make the same mistakes twice.

"So what turned you into a winner?" Kit asked with a smile.

He forced a smile in response. "Well, I wouldn't go so far as to call myself that," he said. "But one day, right in the middle of an executive meeting, during a presentation about luring the middle-class family consumer, I realized I wanted to have kids. Not just that, but I wanted to spend time with my kids. Hell, I wanted to spend time with my wife. I wanted to have weekends at the shore, and backyard barbecues, and carpools and recitals. But the only way I was going to be able to manage that was with a job that demanded a lot less from me. So, after giving it some thought, I quit my megabucks job."

Kit gasped at the announcement. "Just like that?"

He nodded. "Just like that."

"You just turned your back on all that money and power? All that prestige?"

He shrugged. "Well, it wasn't exactly enriching my life. I wasn't happy."

Kit only gazed at him in silence for a moment, as if she simply could not understand his motivation. Then she asked, "And what did Sherry do?"

He chuckled morosely. "Oh, Sherry wasn't too happy about the new development at all. Especially when I told her I'd done it because I wanted a family. Turns out, she wasn't so hot to have kids."

"Um, color me presumptuous," Kit said, "but

wasn't that something the two of you should have discussed before you got married?"

"Hey, we *did* discuss it," Pendleton told her, indignant that she would suggest such a thing. "At some length, as a matter of fact." Then he conceded reluctantly, "Of course, we were only thirteen at the time, but . . . I just assumed that having kids was a foregone conclusion, you know? That's what people in our neighborhood did. They got married. They had kids. Granted, most of them weren't working seventy or eighty hours a week like I was, but still . . ." He shrugged again. "I just thought Sherry would want what I did. Turns out, she didn't. So she left."

"And what did you do?"

Pendleton glanced back down at his hands, rubbing hard at one particularly stubborn smear of grease on his thumb that refused to budge. "I took a job with a small, nonprofit organization that was trying to raise awareness about inner-city kids at risk. Where before I'd just been making, as you yourself said, some rich, greedy corporation richer and greedier, my new job made me feel like I was actually doing something worthwhile. But it left me without that family I had taken it for. Sherry never came back. The divorce was final a year later."

"How come you didn't just ask for your other job back?" she asked. "If that would have made Sherry stay?"

He stared at her incredulously. "Because by then, the damage was done. I mean, would you have taken Michael Derringer back if your father had changed his mind and offered him *more* money to come back and marry you?"

For a moment, she said nothing. Then, very quietly, she told him, "Yes."

"Why?" he asked.

"Because then, at least I wouldn't have been alone."

He expelled a single, humorless chuckle. "Yes, you would. You would have known he didn't really love you."

"But he would have pretended to."

"And that would be okay with you?"

She shrugged, a gesture so nonchalant, so unconcerned, it gave Pendleton goosebumps. As if she truly didn't care whether or not someone loved her, as long as he at least pretended to.

"Oh, come on, Pendleton," she said. "Do you honestly think I ever believed Michael really loved me?"

"You don't think he did?"

"Of course not."

"Then why the hell did you agree to marry him?"

That careless shrug again, then, "Beats being alone."

"If you're going to go to all the trouble to marry a man, to spend the rest of your life with him, don't you think that man ought to honestly love you?" His words were more forceful than he intended, his feelings more intense than he'd realized.

Kit threw him a look of utter disbelief. "Pendleton, no man is ever going to honestly love me."

The way she tossed off the pronouncement, so casually, so matter-of-fact, as if it were something she'd said every day of her life, chilled him to the bone. She genuinely believed that, he thought. She was as convinced of the truth in that statement as she was convinced of her own name. She wasn't fishing for a contradiction or reassurance from him.

She really didn't believe any man could fall in love with her.

"You really believe that, don't you?" he asked, speaking his thoughts aloud. "You really don't think a man could love you."

But she only gazed at him in bemusement, as if she couldn't understand why he would even ask her such a thing.

"What would it take to make you believe a man was in love with you?" he asked, wondering why he was even bothering to continue with a conversation that had degenerated so badly.

His question obviously stumped her, because her eyes widened, and her lips parted slightly in surprise. "What do you mean?"

"I mean . . . what would a man have to do to convince you that he was in love with you?"

"Silly question, Pendleton," she said. "I just told you no man is ever going to—"

"Just answer me," he insisted. "What would it take to convince you that someone loved you?"

For a moment, he thought she would try to change the subject, but instead, she seemed to give his question some serious thought. Then, finally, her expression lightened, as if she'd come to a conclusion.

"A tattoo," she said simply.

He frowned. He should have known she wouldn't take him seriously. In spite of that he echoed, "A tattoo?"

She nodded. "If a man really loved a woman, he'd get a tattoo with her name." As if further inspired, she opened her right hand over the upper swell of her left breast. "Right here. Where kids put their hands when they say the Pledge of Allegiance to the flag.

"Some guy gets a tattoo with my name on it, I know he's serious about me. Especially if it's a really big one with hearts and flowers and a big ol' nasty cupid playing a harp. And my name," she added. "Not 'Kit,' but 'Katherine.' The pain level would be significantly greater, and therefore the proof more positive."

For a long moment, he only stared at her. She couldn't possibly be serious. "I can't believe that's what would prove a man's love to you," he said.

She shrugged. "Hey, love hurts."

He shook his head. "Love doesn't hurt. And you should be able to take it on faith that a man loves you."

"Yeah, well . . . I never promised anybody a rose garden, Pendleton."

"Not without the thorns anyway."

She narrowed her eyes at him. "What's that supposed to mean?"

"Just that every time I start thinking maybe you and I could—" Thankfully, he stopped himself before he said something he knew he'd regret later.

"Could what?" she asked.

"Nothing. Never mind. I just don't understand why you have to strike out like some wounded animal every time we—"

"Every time we what?"

But Pendleton only shook his head and refused to answer. Hell, he wasn't even sure what he had been about to say. Something stupid, no doubt. Something that Kit would have totally misconstrued and turned around later to mess with his head. What had gotten them on to this line of conversation anyway? he wondered. Oh, yeah. Sherry. Man, even after being divorced for years, his ex-wife was still messing up his life.

"Well, if you were so happy with your last job," Kit said, interrupting his thoughts and reading his mind—boy, he hated it when she did that—"then why did you come to work for Hensley's?"

He didn't want to tell her. Hell, he didn't like to admit it to himself. In spite of that, he found himself saying, "Because the last thing Sherry told me when she walked out the door was that I couldn't cut it, that's why."

God, he wished he hadn't said that.

"What?" Kit asked.

"Just before she left me, Sherry accused me of quitting my job because I couldn't handle the pressure. She told me I wasn't man enough to hack it."

Kit stared at him so intently that he could almost see the little wheels in her brain turning. Then, finally, she said, "You took the job at Hensley's just to prove to your ex-wife, after all these years, that you can still big wheel with the best of them?"

He nodded silently.

"And she knows about your new life change, does she?"

"She may have heard through the grapevine," he said.

For a moment, Kit said nothing. Then, very softly, she asked, "And has she come running back to you, Pendleton?"

This time he shook his head. "No. As a matter of fact, she's getting married again at the end of April. To one of my former colleagues. One of my former coworkers. One of my former best friends."

Kit nodded slowly, knowingly, as if she now understood everything. Which was a lot more than Pendleton could say for himself.

"And I assume," she said, "that this former colleague, this former coworker, this former best friend, is still right there in the thick of the corporate game, hacking it in a manly manner?''

''You assume correctly.''

''You're still in love with her, aren't you?''

As with every other question about Sherry, Pendleton simply was not sure how to answer. So he replied honestly, ''I don't know.''

''What are you planning to do?'' Kit asked. ''Run up to New Jersey to crash the wedding? Walk in at the last minute with a few manly paycheck stubs and try to win her back?''

He dropped his gaze back down to the floor. ''Can we talk about something else?'' he asked.

He saw that Kit was about to say something else, but Maury tumbled into the shed and proceeded to attack her fingers. Smiling, she pushed the puppy away, only to have him crouch comically with his entire back hemisphere wagging like a live wire before assaulting her right ankle.

''You crazy mutt,'' she said, chuckling halfheartedly as she scooped him up into her arms.

Pendleton couldn't help but smile at the scene, relieved that the glacier floating around in his chest was beginning to melt away at the sight of Kit McClellan going all gooey over an inept, overzealous puppy. The only thing weirder than that was the way *he* was suddenly going all gooey over Kit McClellan. But there it was, all the same, and for some reason, the realization wasn't quite so scary as he would have thought it would be.

She nuzzled the dog's nose with hers, and when Maury nipped her playfully, she squealed with feigned outrage. ''Maury! You big doofus! You don't bite the nose that feeds you. How many times do I have to tell you that?''

But the dog only licked her nose this time, with much affection, and somehow, Pendleton found himself wanting to repeat the gesture himself.

"Why did you name him Maury?" he asked.

She set the puppy on the ground, and he scampered happily over to the deconstructed motorcycle, sniffing each and every part as if they were delectable bits of kibble. Kit smiled, a gesture that softened all the sharp angles of her face.

"He reminds me of an old boyfriend," she said.

"Maury? Turk? Michael? You sure have had a lot of boyfriends." Pendleton told himself he did *not* sound jealous.

Kit switched her attention from the puppy to him, but her smile turned sad, and the light fled from her eyes. "I've had a lot of dates, Pendleton, not a lot of boyfriends."

"What's the difference?"

Still reeling from the news of Pendleton's marital state—not to mention the fact that he was still *very* preoccupied by his ex-wife's comings and goings—Kit expelled an errant breath and tried not to think about it.

"Boyfriend," she finally said, "suggests a relationship of some length of time. Date, on the other hand, indicates a solitary event that *may* lead to another, but maybe won't. In my life, there were many dates, many solitary events. Boyfriends, well . . . you've heard about all of my boyfriends now. All three of them."

His surprise was evident. "Only three?"

She nodded. "Maury actually only made it through four dates," she confessed, "but I let myself consider him as a boyfriend. Turk lasted nearly a month, and Michael . . ." She sighed as her voice trailed off, leaving unfinished a discussion of whatever feelings she still had for her ex-fiancé. It wasn't important, she thought. Not anymore.

"Why so few boyfriends after having so many dates?" he asked, scattering her thoughts.

He plucked Maury up from the floor, then moved to sit down beside Kit and settled the puppy in his lap. She watched as the little golden furball made mincemeat out of his boot laces, feeling a bit unsettled by Pendleton's nearness. So she scooted away from him, ostensibly to make more room, but really because she just didn't want him to get too close.

"Because Daddy always sent a watchdog along for the ride," she said. "He wouldn't let me go out with anyone unless one of my brothers went, too. And they tended to put a bit of a damper on any romantic developments. Either their presence frightened my dates so badly that they didn't even speak to me, or else my dates wound up talking Cardinal basketball with my brothers all night. So, obviously, there was little chance for a relationship to blossom."

Pendleton scratched Maury behind his ears, and the puppy yawned with much gusto. "Why would your father send your brothers on your dates?"

"Simple," she said. "Because he knew the guys who asked me out were only after one thing."

Pendleton nodded knowingly. "Sex."

Kit shook her head. "Money."

He arched his eyebrows in astonishment, but said nothing in response to her assertion.

So Kit took it upon herself to state the obvious. "Well, why else would any of them want to go out with me?"

Strangely, he still seemed startled by her train of thought, because he replied, "Um, just a shot in the dark, here, but . . . maybe because they were attracted to you and wanted to get to know you better?"

She almost laughed at that. Almost. "Oh, right. Attracted to me. That's a good one."

"Well, why wouldn't they be?"

"Look, I'm not stupid," she said. "I know I'm not beautiful."

When he opened his mouth to comment, Kit stifled him with a quick wave of her hand. "You've never lied to me, Pendleton. And you're about the only person I know who hasn't. It's one of the things I admire about you. Don't start now."

Without uttering a sound, he closed his mouth.

Saddened by his honesty, Kit continued, "And I know I don't have the most tolerable personality, either. The only reason anyone asked me out was because of the Hensley millions. Hey, Daddy got Mama pregnant on purpose, just to get his hands on her money. There was no reason for him to think some guy wouldn't try the same thing with me."

For a long time, Pendleton gazed at her without speaking, studying her face, her eyes, her mouth. His scrutiny became so maddening, in fact, that Kit finally dropped her head to stare at the fingers she had tangled together in her lap. Why did he keep looking at her that way? He acted as if she were something worth looking at.

"If your father never gave you a chance to have a relationship with anyone," he finally began again, "then how did you get so far as a rehearsal dinner with the notorious Michael?"

Kit was surprised to discover that she didn't feel

nearly as angry about the Michael Derringer incident now as she had before. Before her mother had put the fate of her family in her hands. Before she'd been offered the opportunity to extract a little revenge on her father. Before Pendleton had come along and made all kinds of funny things go jumping around inside her.

"I met Michael when I went away to Vanderbilt for my master's," she told him. "Daddy sent Dirk with me to do his doctoral studies, but I was old enough by then to have developed a few evasive maneuvers. Plus, Dirk was totally consumed by his studies and extremely easy to elude."

"You snuck out to meet with your beau."

She nodded. "Usually under cover of darkness. But there would be the few stolen moments in the library, and once or twice, I managed to make a frat party. Michael even scaled the side of my sorority house once when my roommate was out of town, just to be with me. It was all very romantic."

"Sounds like." For some reason, Pendleton's voice had gone a little rough around the edges. But before Kit could comment, he added, "And by 'be with me,' you mean . . ."

She laughed quietly. "Yes, Michael and I were lovers. I was twenty-three when I finally lost my virginity. Long overdue by some standards, don't you think?"

"Depends on your standards."

"Oh, really?" she retorted. "And how old were you when you lost *your* virginity, Mr. High Standards?"

He began to fidget, then leaped up from the floor and moved back toward his motorcycle. But he never answered her question.

"Well?" she demanded.

He glanced back over his shoulder sheepishly. "Um, I was, uh . . ." He emitted a restless sound. "Fourteen."

"*Fourteen*?" she asked incredulously. "You were having sex when you were *fourteen*? Pendleton! Are you crazy? You could have been arrested for statutory!"

"Um, no I couldn't," he assured her. "Because she was, uh . . . she was eighteen."

"*Eighteen*?" Kit sputtered. "*Eighteen*? Then *she* could have been arrested for statutory. Jeez, Pendleton, what were you? The Casanova of South Jersey? *Don* Pendlet*Juan*?"

"No," he said, obviously feeling defensive. "I was just an early beginner. Don't get so bent out of shape. It didn't happen again until I was sixteen."

"Oh, really? And how old was that one? Thirty-two?"

He arched a dark brow and threw her a salacious smile. "No, only twenty-one. Why? You jealous?"

"Oh, please. Spare me the details. But then," she hurried on, "we were talking about me, weren't we?"

"We always are."

She narrowed her eyes at that, then continued hastily, "When Michael proposed to me, I told him we should elope, because my father would only cause trouble. But Michael said I was entitled to a big, fancy white wedding, and he was going to see to it that I got one. At the time, I thought he was being terribly romantic and showing some real initiative. Later, I couldn't help but wonder if by making our relationship known to my family, he wasn't hoping for exactly the outcome he got."

"Kit, surely you don't think that he—"

"What I think," she interrupted him, her voice quiet, contemplative, and controlled, "is that I'll never be able to trust a man again." She unclenched her fingers only long enough to curl them tighter. "And that's why I can't forgive my father, Pendleton. Not because he paid Michael off. Hey, I knew all he wanted was my money. I knew he didn't love me. Like I said—I'm not stupid."

"Kit—"

"But I could at least *pretend* that he loved me, no matter who my family was or how much money they had. I could *dream* that it was me, not the Hensley millions, that he really cared about. Once Michael took that check and left the restaurant, though, that fantasy was gone forever."

"Kit—"

"So see, it isn't the fact that my father bribed and banished my fiancé that I can't forgive," she interrupted him again. "What I can't forgive is that by doing it, he robbed me of my dream. And *that* is why I will *not* get married before my mother's deadline. So that my father and brothers will know what it feels like to lose what's most important to them, just like I lost what was most important to me." She met his gaze levelly. "They stole my fantasy, Pendleton. They stole my dreams."

Tears were beginning to well up in her eyes, and suddenly, she didn't want to talk to Pendleton anymore. So she pushed herself up from the floor, ignored Maury when he began to yip and bounce playfully around her feet, and stepped carefully over the puppy. Once she cleared that barrier, however, she realized another. Because Pendleton, too, had stood, and he'd placed himself between her and the door.

"Kit, listen to me. I—"

She held up her hands, chest-high, palm out. "Don't," she said simply, tilting her head back in an effort to keep the tears from spilling. "Just . . . don't."

Then she surged forward, shouldering him out of the way as she hurried past. And as she made tracks over the frosty grass in a bee-line back to the house, she congratulated herself on making an escape that was, if not particularly clean, at least complete.

Chapter 12

What ensued after that was a truce—of sorts—that lasted two full weeks. Well, not a truce exactly, because that suggested there were no displays of tension or pique, and that wasn't quite true. So it was really more like a status quo that lasted two weeks. Then again, it wasn't a status quo, either, because that smacked of politics, and although one might consider what went on between them to be political in a bizarre kind of way, wasn't really. So maybe what ensued was more like a sense of peace and quiet—that lasted two full weeks. Actually, that wasn't quite right, either, because with Kit being the kind of person she was— namely, disagreeable and loud—Pendleton's house was in no way peaceful, nor was it particularly quiet.

The two of them did, however, manage to maintain their sleeping habits, for what that was worth. Pendleton continued to sleep on the couch while Kit slumbered in the bedroom, and Maury divided his time between the two, a bond that afforded them some kind of connection. Sort of, at any rate. In a way. At least, they were linked in spirit. Or maybe thought. Or perhaps awareness.

Yes, awareness. That was it. Because whatever else was going on the house, however indefinable, Pendleton and Kit were certainly *aware* of each other's presence there.

As he soaped up in his shower, Pendleton congratulated himself on finally pinning down a definition—however vague—of his relationship with Kit since that mutual baring of souls two weeks earlier. Yep, by golly, that was it. Awareness. Deep, abiding awareness.

In fact, he was aware of her the moment he woke up every morning, because she had adopted the rather unfortunate habit of rising early to cook him breakfast before he went to work. And not his usual Wheaties with skim milk and bananas, either. No, Kit had insisted that since he was living in Kentucky now, Pendleton should start eating like a Kentuckian. And to her, that meant sausage, eggs, and biscuits dripping with butter.

He fared little better upon his return home in the evening, because she cooked dinner for him, too, usually something with pork. Or pork fat. Or pork rinds. Or pork bones. She even prepared vegetables by throwing them into a pot with a big ol' hamhock and boiling them within an inch of their lives. Just like her mama had done, and her mama's mama had done before that. Kit's mother had been a country girl at heart, and had made sure her daughter knew how to please a man in the kitchen. A man who liked pork, at any rate. Pendleton, however, preferred poultry.

He still hadn't quite figured out what Kit did during the day while he was at work. Aside from prowling the city in her celebrated Mercedes S-class in a quest to find things that would really annoy him. Things like, oh . . . a concrete garden gnome for the front yard—which he had *immediately* exiled to the back—or lace curtains for the front windows—which he simply tried his best to ignore—or more of those intolerable Bill Monroe CDs—which he refused to admit were starting to grow on him in spite of the proliferation of banjos.

Just as Pendleton was rinsing his hair, the steamy stream of hot water spurting from the faucet suddenly went arctic cold, and he yelped at the shock of it. "Dammit," he hissed as he leaped away from the icy cascade.

Blindly, because he still had soap in his eyes, he fumbled to turn the water off, then snatched a towel from the rack, and stepped out into the quickly dissipating steam. As he jerked his robe from the back of the bathroom door, he heard the unmistakable sound of water running elsewhere in the house, and he realized that it was Kit who was the culprit behind his sabotaged shower.

He had told her and told her and *told* her about the temperamental plumbing in the old building, had warned her and warned her and *warned* her that when someone was running the shower, the slightest trickle of water elsewhere in the house could potentially cause frostbite for the showerer. Of course, that was why she invariably chose *his* shower time to take *her* baths, he reminded himself. So that he would freeze his—

Assembling what little control he could, Pendleton scooped his wet hair from his forehead and made a decision, right there on the spot: *No more*. Kit had interrupted his leisurely Sunday morning shower for the last time. With a resolute cinching of his bathrobe belt, he exited the second-floor bathroom and proceeded to the one downstairs.

He was still dripping water and shivering enough to qualify for the puree setting on a blender when he rapped hard on the bathroom door. "Kit!" he called out over the rush of water on the other side, envisioning the steam that must be curling up from all the hot water running into the tub.

"What?" she called back.

"Are you decent?"

She didn't respond for a moment, then sang out, "Maybe. Maybe not. Do you feel lucky?"

Not for the last few weeks, he thought. "We need to talk," he told her through the door.

"Can't it wait?"

"No."

A heartfelt sigh, then, "Hang on a minute."

The water shut off, and he heard two quick splashes followed by the rattle of the shower curtain rings along the metal rod. "Okay," she called out sweetly. "You can come in now."

Pendleton grasped the doorknob, clipped it to the right, and entered the fray. Unfortunately, the fray wasn't quite what he had expected it to be, and he was already surrounded by the spicy scent of sandalwood before he realized he'd been set up. And by then it was too late, because he was frozen in place, completely unable to move.

What he had thought was the sound of the shower curtain being thrown closed had in fact been the sound of it being thrown *open*. And now he found himself staring at Kit, who was pink and dewy and humming what sounded like "That Man of Mine" as she nestled beneath a veritable mountain of Hollywood bubbles, one slender calf extended elegantly toward the ceiling as she loofahed her big toe.

"You bellowed?" she asked, not looking at him.

"Uh . . ."

He got no further than that single, ineffectual sound, because his gaze suddenly lit on one particular set of bubbles. The ones snuggling against her right breast. The ones that seemed to be popping at an alarmingly fast rate.

"Pendleton?" she added when he didn't respond.

He sensed, more than saw, her glance up, but he had no idea what kind of expression she had on her face, because, simply put, he wasn't looking at her face.

"Yes?" he asked absently.

"You said we needed to talk," she reminded him.

He nodded.

"So talk."

He opened his mouth to do just that, but a good two or three hundred bubbles that had been *very* strategically placed chose that moment to burst, and he found that he simply could not say a word. Not until Kit shifted in the tub, folding her arms over the side, thereby taking her torso temporarily out of the public eye, and making moot any more bubble evaporation that might or might not occur.

"Pendleton?" she tried again.

He nodded, but said nothing.

"You want to talk or what?"

"Or what. I mean, talk," he quickly corrected himself. He gave his head a good shake to clear it, sending droplets of water—droplets of *cold* water—onto his face and neck. "Talk," he reiterated, the shock of the cold reenergizing him some. "Us. Yes. Talk."

"Oooh, that's a good start. Want to go for

subject-verb now, throw in a predicate here and there, or would that be pushing it?''

He inhaled deeply, ignored the fact that she was naked and covered with skin—covered with soft, wet, glistening, rosy, luscious, hot, uh . . . where was he? Oh, yeah. He *wasn't* looking at her skin. And he tried to remember what had been so important that they needed to discuss.

But all he could think was . . . skin. Hot. Wet. Then he remembered. Water. Oh, yeah. That was what it was.

''Water,'' he said aloud, proud of himself for articulating even that much.

Kit glanced down at the bubbles that were effervescing way too fast for his comfort. ''Yes. Water,'' she echoed, splashing the surface a bit. ''Very good.'' She felt around until she located her sponge, which she then held aloft. ''Loofah,'' she continued. ''Loo-fah. Loofah. Now you try it.''

He bit back a growl. ''You used up all the hot water,'' he finally got out. ''Again.''

She dropped the sponge and rested her chin on her forearm. ''Well, of course I used up all the hot water. What fun is a cold bath?''

''No, I mean *you* used up all the hot water while *I* was in the shower. Again.''

''Bummer. I hate it when that happens.''

Pendleton gazed at her helplessly. Well, what had he expected? An apology? From Kit McClellan? Not bloody likely. In spite of that, he continued, ''I've asked you not to run the water when I'm in the shower. Remember?''

She smacked a palm soundly against her forehead, a gesture, Pendleton noticed helplessly, that popped even more bubbles. ''Oh, wow, I *totally* forgot," she said. "I can't believe I did that. Imagine my embarrassment."

He supposed he *would* have to imagine it, because he was quite sure she wasn't feeling one iota of embarrassment in reality.

"Never mind," he relented, pivoting on his heel to leave. "I don't know why I bothered."

"Wait, Pendleton, don't go."

He heard her moving around in the tub, so he didn't dare turn to look at her again. Instead he shifted his gaze to the side a bit and said, "Why not?"

"It's Sunday," she reminded him.

"And?"

"And . . . it's Sunday," she repeated, as if he should understand implicitly why that was relevant.

"Which would mean . . . ?" he asked.

She uttered an exasperated sound, as if he were the densest person she'd ever had the misfortune to meet. "Sunday is the day when people do stuff together."

Oh, he didn't like the sound of that at all. "And by 'do stuff' you would mean . . . ?"

"You know . . . *do* stuff."

That's what he'd been afraid of. "As in?"

More splashing followed, so he squeezed his eyes shut tight, because he really, really, *really* wanted to turn around to see how many bubbles were left.

"As in going out," she said. "To do things together. Like go to the park. Or shopping. Or to brunch. Or a movie. What do you say? You want to do stuff today?"

"Not really," he replied honestly.

"Oh, come on. It'll be fun."

He expelled a derisive chuckle. "That's what you said about me carrying you in kicking and screaming that night we got back from the Caribbean."

"But that *was* fun," she said.

"No it wasn't. It was humiliating."

She uttered a sound of clear disappointment. "You have a very funny definition of humiliating, Pendleton."

"And *you* have a very twisted definition of fun."

"So what do you say?" she insisted, ignoring his jab. "Let's do stuff. Let's go to KT's for brunch, and then to the Vogue for a matinee, and then we can do some shopping. We need some flannel sheets."

"*We* need some flannel sheets?" he asked.

"Yeah. In case you didn't notice, we don't have any. And this house is just too daggone cold at night."

For some reason, he knew it would be pointless for him to argue. No matter what he said or did, by day's end, he was bound to find himself the proud new owner of flannel sheets whether he liked it or not.

"What's showing at the Vogue?" he asked.

"I don't know," she replied. "But you can bet it's either foreign, controversial, or completely beyond normal human comprehension."

"Sounds perfect," he muttered as he made his way back out the bathroom door.

By the time they returned from their Sunday excursion, Kit felt the oddest sense of well-being wandering through her system. She couldn't remember the last time she'd had such a good time with anyone. Oh, wait. Yes, she could. It had been that night in Veranda Bay, when she and Pendleton had—

But that incident, she interrupted herself before

her memories overran her, hadn't lasted very long at all, where this one had lasted *a whole day*. So this one was infinitely more significant than that one had been. Even without the kiss.

Daggone it. She'd almost managed not to think about that. Then again, not a day had gone by since that kiss that she *hadn't* recalled in glowing, vivid detail every last second.

And as she did every day when the memory came over her, Kit tried to tell herself that the only reason Pendleton's kiss stood out in her memory was because, well, she just didn't kiss that many men these days. In fact, she hadn't kissed one since Michael Derringer. Nor had she really kissed one before Michael. Not like that, anyway.

She shook her head as she watched Pendleton hang up his leather jacket. What a sorry excuse for a woman she was. Almost twenty-eight years old, single, healthy, wealthy, reasonably attractive— and she'd only had one lover in her entire life. Only one man to want her. And only for her current market value, too.

Pushing away thoughts of Michael Derringer— she was surprised at how easy it was to do that these days—Kit shed her own coat and followed Pendleton into the kitchen, trying not to notice what a great tushie he had under those faded 501s, or what spectacular shoulders lurked beneath his charcoal-colored sweater. But as was usually the case when she tried to ignore those things, Kit failed miserably. Which was just as well, because when she joined him in the kitchen, where she found him opening the back door to let Maury out for his evening uproar, Pendleton seemed to be noticing more than his fair share of her anatomy, too.

Unfortunately, as always, the part of her anatomy that seemed to interest him the most was her face, and not the body parts below her neck that were currently decked out in sung jeans and her favorite scarlet velvet shirt. As always, when she realized where his scrutiny lay, Kit turned her face away. And when she did, her gaze fell on the answering machine that sat on the kitchen counter, and she noticed that the little red light was flashing.

"Oh, look, we had a call," she said, brightening some at the prospect.

"You mean *I* had a call," he corrected her as he closed the door behind the puppy. "This is still *my* house, even if I have allowed you to be a squatter."

She lifted her nose indignantly into the air. "Excuse me, but I prefer to think of myself as visiting royalty."

He uttered a derisive sound as he moved to the kitchen counter and pushed the button on the machine. Over the whir of the rewinding tape, he muttered just loudly enough for her to hear, "What a coincidence. Here I've been thinking of you as a royal pain."

Oh, hardy har har har. She was about to open her mouth to comment aloud when a woman's voice interrupted her.

"Hi, it's me, Carny," the recorded voice chirped. Actually chirped, Kit marveled. How very annoying. "Just wanted to say hi," the perky little thing continued. "We haven't talked for a while, and I wondered how you were doing. Give me a call when you get a chance. I love you and I miss you. Bye."

I love you? Kit echoed to herself. Something hot and bitter pooled in her belly like a shot of belladonna. *I love you*? Some woman actually loved Pendleton? And he had neglected to mention this? Worse than that, however, was the fact that he was staring at his answering machine with *much* affection, as if he might potentially love the chirper, too.

"Who was that?" she demanded before she could stop herself, appalled at the rancor she heard in her own voice.

Pendleton's head snapped up. "That was my sister," he told her, his own voice none too sweet-sounding in response.

The word *foolish* didn't quite cover the feeling that came over Kit at the knowledge that the woman who loved Pendleton was a woman who was completely entitled to do so. And the word *oh* didn't quite cover an apology for her outburst.

Nevertheless, her response to his explanation was, "Oh."

"Is it all right with you, Your Majesty, if I give my sister a call back?"

Strange, Kit thought, how she'd never noticed before that slight accent, redolent of the northeast, that colored Pendleton's speech whenever his patience was pushed to the absolute limit. At the mention of his sister, he sounded just a tad like Sylvester Stallone.

"Why would I mind?" she asked.

Instead of answering, he picked up the phone and dialed a series of numbers, enough to total long distance. Not that Kit counted, mind you, just to make sure he wasn't misleading her about keeping some hot little tootsie under wraps here in town, but . . . He did dial eleven numbers. Then he glared at her as he waited for someone to answer at the other end, and for a moment, Kit couldn't figure out why he was staring darts at her that way.

Finally, he bit out an exasperated sigh and said, "Do you think I could have a little privacy while I—Hi, Carny?"

He spun around after the greeting, but not before Kit saw his face go warm and wistful all over. No, that wasn't some hot little tootsie he was talking to, she realized as she turned to make her way out of the kitchen. No man would ever look that affectionate unless he was talking to someone he genuinely loved.

Family. It just now occurred to her that somewhere up in New Jersey, there was an entire Pendleton clan. Funny, how she hadn't considered the fact that he would have loved ones elsewhere in the world. Then again, when one's own family wasn't exactly as loving and close-knit as the Waltons, she supposed it was only normal for one to assume that other families weren't, either. She wondered if Pendleton had fared any better with his folks than she had with hers.

A soft chuckle of delight emanated from behind the closed kitchen door, a sound of happiness, familiarity, and love. Obviously, Pendleton had a much better relationship with his family than she had with hers. He could laugh with his sister. Not sarcastically, not ironically. But warmly. Lovingly. Genuinely.

Kit wanted to eavesdrop on the conversation in the worst way, but she feared hearing his laughter again, so she moved away from the door and into the living room. The Sunday *Courier-Journal* lay scattered where they'd left it that morning, half on the flowered chintz sofa, half on the hooked rug below, and she scooped up a few errant advertisements to skim through them. Value City had just received a massive shipment of Cobbies priced half-off, she noted, fleece wear was on sale at Target, and at Jacobson's, it was Clinique Bonus Time.

But what had once been her favorite time of the week—Sunday evening spent hunting and gathering amid the sales circulars—suddenly held absolutely no appeal. Instead, she found herself focused on the man's voice that was barely detectable in the kitchen behind her, and the way he spoke low and laughed often with his sister.

Forty-five minutes later, when Pendleton finally hung up the phone, Kit was staring clueless at clue number one in the *Across* column of the crossword puzzle. She heard the creak of the kitchen door as he exited, and the soft scuff of his hiking boots accompanied by the clatter of Maury's toenails as they both crossed the dining room. But she didn't turn around. Instead, as she watched the puppy settle himself in front of the hearth, Kit pretended she didn't notice the man, in spite of the way her skin grew warm, her breathing went shallow, and her heart began to hammer hard in her chest.

And she kept not noticing him until he leaned over the sofa from behind, resting his weight on the forearms he braced against the back. But still, she didn't look at him, not even when he turned to look at her. For a long moment, they only remained so, neither speaking nor acknowledging each other. Finally, Pendleton broke the silence with a single, quiet word that almost shattered her fragile composure.

"Honey," he said.

Unable to keep from looking at him any longer, she turned her head, narrowing her eyes at his odd sentiment. Hesitantly, she asked, "Yes . . . dear?"

A flash of confusion tinted his face for a moment, then he smiled. "No, I mean, *honey*. The word. One across," he said, gesturing toward the crossword puzzle. " 'Bee creation.' Five letters. Honey."

"Oh." Pretending that she hadn't just humiliated herself beyond words, Kit clicked her ball-point pen and quickly recorded the word in even, block letters. Then, in a desperate maneuver to drive his attention elsewhere, she feigned indifference and asked, "All quiet on the home front?"

He nodded. "Yeah. Carny just wanted to talk about some guy she met, that's all. She likes him, but Joey doesn't, and she thinks it's going to cause problems."

"Joey?"

"My nephew. Carny's son. He's thirteen going on thirty-five, and naturally, he knows everything. He's a good kid, but he's way too overprotective of his mother."

Pendleton had a nephew, too? Kit thought, oddly envious for some reason. She'd always liked the idea of having nieces and nephews, and had been strangely sad when Holt and his wife had split without having kids.

"Is your sister divorced?" she asked, telling herself she posed the question only because she wanted to make idle conversation, and *not* because she craved knowledge about every single aspect of Pendleton's life.

He shook his head. "She never married. She got pregnant when she was a teenager, but the sonofabitch stupid idiot jerk moron sonofabitch that knocked her up skipped out on her."

"You said 'sonofabitch' twice. Wasn't that redundant?"

"No."

His expression bordered on savage, she noted, so all she said in response was, "Oh."

"Hey, she's done just fine without Joey's father," he added immediately, rising with no hesitation to defend his sister's honor.

"I'm not surprised," Kit told him. "If the rest of the Pendletons are like you, then they must be a resourceful bunch."

He grinned, a happy, easy grin that nearly stole her heart. "Yeah, we are," he agreed softly. But he didn't elaborate.

"And are your mother and father doing well, too?" she asked, wanting—needing—to hear more about this happy family who rose so quickly to help and shelter and protect one another.

"According to Carny, they're fine. I really should call them, too, though. I haven't touched base with Mom for almost a week. She always calls me at work. She and my dad are hard to get at night."

"What do they do?"

"Bowl, mostly."

She chuckled. "No, I meant what do they do for a living?"

"Oh. Well, my mom never worked, and as of last year, my dad is retired. He used to work construction." He smiled, one of those warm, heartfelt smiles, as if he were remembering something very, very important. "In fact, he gave me my first job when I was fifteen. Pouring cement."

"You know," she said, "it's very strange that I know so little about you and your family, when you know so much about me and mine."

"Yeah, a little *too* much," he said derisively.

She made a face at him, but it was impossible to feel irritated when he was gazing at her like that. As if he were happy to be here with her, sharing the kind of innocuous, getting-to-know-you conversation they were sharing. Before she realized his intention, he launched himself over the back of the sofa and landed deftly beside her. Close beside her. Uncomfortably close. She started to stand, but he seemed to sense her unease and scooted over to put a more acceptable distance between them.

"I'm sorry," he apologized. "But if you know nothing about my family, it isn't because I don't want to talk about them."

She dropped her gaze back down to the newspaper folded on her lap. "No, I'm the one who should apologize. You're right. If I'm unaware of the particulars of your family, it's because I've been too wrapped up in the particulars of my own to ask."

He dipped his head in acknowledgment of her apology.

"So," she said. "You have a family in New Jersey."

He nodded.

"Mom and Pop Pendleton, a sister named Carny, and—" She halted abruptly when something extremely important occurred to her.

"What?" he asked. "What's wrong?"

"Pendleton," she said softly, "I just realized that I don't know your first name."

"Well, you never asked me my first name."

"So?"

"So what?"

"So what is it?"

"My first name?"

"Yes."

"You really want to know?"

"Yes." She gave his shoulder a soft smack, a gesture she hoped would make him hurry up and get on with it. "Come on, Pendleton. Tell me your first name."

He smiled at her. "What's it worth to you?"

"I beg your pardon?"

"You heard me. What's it worth to you?"

She narrowed her eyes at him. "What do you mean?"

"If I tell you my first name, what do I get in return?"

She was stumped for an answer. "I don't know. I'll spin you some gold out of straw? What do you want in return?"

Immediately, she wished she hadn't asked, because she knew what his answer would be. He was going to ask her to leave. Something cold and unpleasant settled in her stomach, and suddenly, she wasn't having fun anymore.

"If I tell you my first name," he said, "you have to promise me you'll—"

She held up a hand to stop him. "Don't say it. I already know. You want me to move out of your house."

Her response obviously surprised him, as if it honestly hadn't occurred to him to ask her to do such a thing.

"Don't you?" she asked.

"Actually," he said, "I was thinking more along the lines of if I tell you my first name, you have to promise me you'll start letting me cook dinner sometimes."

"Oh," she said, feeling even more confused. "Okay. If you must."

"Oh, I must."

"Fine. So . . . what's your first name?"

He hesitated, smiling that devastating smile for a moment. Then, plainly and succinctly, he told her, "Rocky."

Oh, now *that* definitely came as a surprise.

"Rocky?" she echoed, unable to prevent the bubble of laughter that punctuated the word. "Your name is *Rocky*? Are you serious?"

"What's so funny about Rocky?" he asked.

"Rocky Pendleton? That's your name?"

"Hey, I'm from New Jersey. What were you expecting? Nigel?"

She laughed harder. "No, but . . . Rocky? Who decided to name you Rocky?"

"My father. Axel."

"*Axel* Pendleton?" She covered her mouth in a fruitless effort to hide her glee, laughing at this newly discovered aspect of Pendleton's persona.

"Yeah. Axel Pendleton. You got a problem with that?"

He must really be getting irritated, she thought, because suddenly, his New Jersey accent was extremely pronounced.

"No, I don't have a problem with that," she said, still chuckling. "You just don't seem like a Rocky, that's all." With no small effort, she managed to squelch her giggles some. Not much. But some.

He tossed his hand into the air. "Fine. You think my name is hysterical."

"No, honestly," she objected. "It was just surprising, that's all. Rocky Pendleton." Another bout of giggles erupted before she could stop them. "No, wait," she urged him when he opened his mouth to say more. "I can say it without laughing. I can. Watch. Rocky . . ." She began to titter, so she bit her lip to stop it. "Rocky Pen . . ." she tried again, still not quite able to contain herself. "Rocky Pendle—" Unfortunately, she never finished, because she began to giggle again. "I'm sorry. I guess I *can't* say it without laughing."

And then she broke down completely.

Pendleton glared at her. "Actually," he said, injecting more volume into his voice to lift it above her outburst, "Rocky is a nickname my father gave me when I was a baby. It's a shortened form of my given name."

Kit inhaled a deep breath in an effort to contain her merriment, then swiped at her watering eyes as she expelled it. Finally, she managed to ask, "And what would your given name be, pray tell?"

He glanced away, and she could have sworn she saw a faint stain of pink riding high on his cheeks. "It's short for, uh, Rockefeller."

"*Rockefeller*?" she said, not even bothering to hide her amusement now as she let her laughter run loose. "You have *got* to be kidding."

"Will you please try to contain yourself?" he asked. "You're making a spectacle."

With a great deal of effort, Kit managed to rein herself in. A little.

"My parents both came from blue-collar backgrounds, all right?" he said. "And my mother, whose name, incidentally is Irene—want to make something of that?" he demanded.

Kit only shook her head in silence.

"My mom," he continued, "wanted something a little better for her kids," he continued. "So she gave us names she thought might . . . you know . . . win us cachet into a higher social circle."

Sounded logical, Kit thought. Still . . . "Yeah, but Rockefeller?" she asked, speaking her thoughts aloud, battling a new fit of chuckles.

He ignored her. "Hey, it could have been worse. Carny's real name is Carnegie."

Kit shook her head. "Unbelievable," she said. "Well, if you don't mind, I think I'll keep calling you Pendleton. Frankly, I'm not sure I could call you Rocky without breaking into a fit of—" As if to prove the point, she burst into another animated round of giggles.

"Do you mind?" he said, clearly striving for an outraged tone of voice. Unfortunately, the smile that curled his lips completely blew the effort.

It also made Kit start laughing harder.

"Show some respect, will ya?" he asked. Then, contrary to his request, and with obvious reluctance, he, too, began to chuckle.

And once he showed that small sign of weakness, all Kit could do was laugh harder. And harder. And harder still. In fact, she began laughing so hard, she had to hug herself tight to keep herself from falling right off the couch. Unfortunately, even that didn't help, because by then, the giggles had irreversibly seized her, and she simply lost control, tumbling right off the sofa and down to the floor. Belatedly, Pendleton reached out to grab her, and for his efforts, he wound up right on the rug beside her. They landed in a heap, arms tangled, laughter joined, the fall having only increased their levity.

Their merriment ceased abruptly, however, when, as one, they realized the precariousness of their position. Kit lay on her back beneath Pendleton, his big body sprawled over hers in a manner that was *most* familiar. His thigh was settled between her legs, and his arm was nestled against her breast. Yet he didn't press his advantage. Nor did he retreat. He only gazed down at her, a lock of dark hair falling over his forehead, his eyes more than a little inquisitive.

Game's over, Kit told herself. *Call for a time-out. Now.*

But instead of shoving him off, as reason commanded, she found herself hooking her arms loosely around his waist, splaying her hands open tentatively over his back. And instead of vaulting off of her to flee, as she had been sure Pendleton would, he nestled more snugly, more intimately against her. For a moment, Kit felt as if she had fallen into the deep end of a swimming pool and couldn't quite touch bottom. Then, oh-so-slowly, he began to dip his head toward hers, and she found that she couldn't quite break the surface to catch her breath, either.

His kiss was quite extraordinary. One minute, he was hovering over her, staring at her face, her eyes, her mouth, and the next, he was consuming her. There was a fierceness and demand in his kiss that went beyond passion, beyond hunger, beyond need. He kissed her as if he drew sustenance from her, as if she were essential to his very survival. So what could she do, but kiss him back in exactly the same way?

When she did, he went limp atop her, uttering a soft sound of surrender. He crowded his body into hers, tangled his fingers in her hair, curved his hand into her hip. She gasped at the quickness and intensity of his possession, and he took advantage of the opportunity to taste her more deeply still. He mated his tongue with hers before sucking it into his own mouth, then he slanted his head for a more thorough invasion. The hand at her hip tugged her shirt free from her jeans, and his fingers danced along the bare skin beneath. Unable to stop herself, Kit drove her own hands under his sweater, gasping at the heat and strength she encountered there.

The warm flesh of his back came alive under her touch, the muscles bunching and writhing beneath her fingertips. She opened her hands wider, to propel him closer, heedless of the fact that they were already as close as two people could be. In response, he groaned and broke away from her lips, then he dragged his open mouth along her jaw and neck, tasting the hollow at the base of her throat before skimming his lips over her collarbone.

Kit scooted one hand higher as the other scooted lower, and she cupped his taut buttocks through the faded fabric of his jeans. A shudder of heat rocked her, pooling in her belly and between her legs, staggering her heart rate, blinding her to anything but the feel of Pendleton as he touched her *everywhere*. His hand skipped briefly over her breast, then, restless, he smoothed his palm down over her ribs, lingering at her waist, her hip, her thigh, where he finally curled his fingers over the denim covering her legs. Instinctively, she hooked her calf over his, fearful that he would be coming to his senses any time now, and would try to pull away.

But he didn't pull away.

Instead he rolled onto his back, tugging Kit along for the ride until she was sprawled over him. With their positions reversed, she tunneled the fingers of one hand through the silk of his hair, and curled the others around his nape. Pendleton raked his rough jaw along the sensitive skin of her throat before fastening his mouth to hers once again. She felt his hands running down the length of her backside, from her shoulders to her back to her bottom to her thighs, before they retraced the journey in a more leisurely fashion. Then he roped his arms around her waist and held her fast against him, so that he could wreak havoc on her mouth some more.

More. That was all Kit wanted after that. More of his mouth, more of his hands, more of his touch, more of the man. Somehow, suddenly, she simply could not get enough of him. There was an emptiness inside her she'd never noticed before—or perhaps she had noticed and had simply refused to acknowledge. And now it was as if the only thing that would fill it, the only thing that would satisfy it, the only thing that would make it whole again, was Pendleton. So, with touch instead of words, she demanded more. And more was what he gave her.

All the while, a fire blazed hot and wild inside her, like nothing she had ever felt before. Where had this come from? she wondered vaguely. This fever, this longing, this unquenchable need? No experience in her life had prepared her for what Pendleton made her feel. Whatever paltry emotion she had thought she felt for Michael was little more than a shadow of what she felt now. Michael had been nothing. And Pendleton . . .

Pendleton was *everything*.

The sudden realization of that shocked Kit to her very core, rousing what little coherent thought she had left. Her response to Pendleton came from every single cell, every single feeling, every single thought she claimed as a part of herself. And that totality of her response terrified her. Terrified her enough to make her pull away from him. Immediately. Completely.

When she jerked her mouth from his, it was only to find that she was clinging to him as desperately as he was holding her, and for one panicked second, she honestly didn't think she would be able to let him go. But somewhere, she found the power, the resolution, the strength to release him. Unfortunately, he didn't seem as willing to release her. When she tried to push herself away from him, he only tightened his hold on her, evidently as determined to keep her close as she was to escape.

"Don't," he said softly, his voice a bare rasp of sound in the otherwise silent room. "Don't go. Please, Kit."

She swallowed hard, knowing better than to try to put voice to the muddled jumble of her thoughts. So she only shook her head slowly, silently, adamantly. And with one final burst of intention, she tried again to break free.

And this time, damn him, Pendleton let her go.

Chapter 13

Faith Ivory was stuffing the last of her Temperance League homework into her briefcase and anticipating a nice long weekend snowed in at her apartment when she heard a man's voice in the outer office. And not just any man's voice. Holt McClellan's voice. Wonderful. Just what she needed. She'd been *that* close to making a clean break of it.

Her gaze skittered to the window, through which she briefly considered hurling herself, but she changed her mind when she realized what a mess that would make on all the pretty snow that had fallen since mid-afternoon. Nuts. These unexpected spring snowstorms were *so* inconvenient. She sighed heavily, snapped her briefcase shut, and sat down and waited for Holt's knock on her door.

She didn't have to wait long.

"Yes?" she called out halfheartedly in response to the three quick raps, almost identical to the ones that had jolted her out of her peaceful existence at her apartment.

With the creak of a hinge, he filled her doorway. And as had happened on every other occasion when she'd found herself in the same room with him, her heart rate tripled. They hadn't parted well that night at Cherrywood almost a month ago. After the appearance of his sister and her . . . her . . .

Well, Faith was still at a loss as to who exactly his sister's companion had been that night. Nor had she ever quite figured out just what that whole Me-Tarzan-You-Jane tableau had been about. All that had been important had been that she exit as gracefully—and as quickly—as possible, to avoid further embarrassing both the McClellan family and herself. So she had fled. In a taxi. After making it clear to Holt that she had no desire to see him again. Ever.

At least, she thought she had made herself clear. But now, here he stood, looking more handsome and overwhelming than ever, and all she could do was feel strangely glad to see him again.

"Faith," he greeted her.

"Holt," she replied, congratulating herself for maintaining such a steady tone of voice. "What are you doing out in this weather? According to WFPK, we're supposed to have eight inches of snow by dark."

He chuckled morosely. "Yeah, and then it'll probably hit seventy degrees tomorrow and make a mess of things. These spring snowstorms can be so obnoxious."

Pushing aside the realization that she had just been thinking the same thing herself, she asked, "What can I do for you?"

"You can give me a second chance."

Well, gee, nothing like getting right to the heart of the matter, she thought. "Please come in," she invited him, seating herself behind her desk. "And close the door behind you."

He did as she requested, and as he shed his coat and sat down in the chair opposite her, it occurred to her that their positions were now reversed from that first encounter in his office. But where Holt's turf was some of the most expensive real estate in town, Faith's digs were decidedly more modest.

The Louisville Temperance League operated on a shoestring—a baby bootie shoestring at that—and could barely afford the aged, nondescript building where they had located two years ago. Faith's office was one of the larger ones in the suite, but even at that, was no more than one-quarter the size of Holt's. And where his had been bright with trendy pastels and furnished with expensively tailored pieces, hers was dark and cluttered with cast-offs that even the most generous observer would be hard-pressed to call "antique."

She steepled her fingers on the scarred blotter atop her desk, then opened her mouth to say something along the lines of, "I never want to see you or your family again for as long as I live, now go away." But he held up a hand to stop her.

"I haven't been able to stop thinking about you for a month," he said without preamble.

Something warm and liquid oozed into her belly, but she refused to succumb to the warm, fuzzy way it made her feel. Really, she did. Honest. She did.

"And I owe you an apology for what happened that night at Cherrywood," he added.

Actually, that wasn't true. It wasn't up to Holt to apologize for a scene someone else had created, even if it was a member of his own family. Nor was he responsible for Faith's reaction to what had happened. How could he have known she would react the way she had that night?

But when Kit McClellan had entered the dining

room so obviously intoxicated, Faith had become immediately uncomfortable. Not because of the potential embarrassment factor for Holt, but because of the very definite fear factor for herself. Kit's drunken state had reminded Faith far too much of the drunken state of another person whose memory was still far too fresh in her mind. Stephen Ivory. Even in death, he ruled her life.

"You don't owe me an apology," she said.

"Yes, I do."

"For what?"

He smiled sadly. "For subjecting you to my family before our relationship was fully cemented."

"You seem to be a few steps ahead of me. I wasn't aware that we had a relationship to cement."

"I beg to differ."

"And I beg your pardon."

He leaned forward, resting his elbows on his knees, hooking his fingers loosely together between his legs. And he met her gaze steadily, intently, unequivocally. But instead of addressing the matter of their alleged relationship, he returned to the subject of his apology instead.

"Faith, I'm sorry you had to witness the scene you witnessed that night," he said softly.

"So am I."

"I tried to explain it to you then, but you wouldn't let me. You were too busy bolting for the front door."

She laughed, the sound an anxious ripple of uncertainty. "The last thing I wanted to do was get caught up in what was obviously a private family matter."

Holt laughed, too, but his was a genuine sound of merriment. "Trust me, Faith, when I tell you that there was nothing private about what happened that night. Everyone who's ever met Kit knows what kind of behavior she's capable of indulging in."

"So then it's no secret to anyone in Louisville that your sister is a lush?"

Faith squeezed her eyes shut and covered them with her hands, appalled that she had said such a thing out loud. She waited to see what Holt would say in response to her inexcusable, unforgivable gaffe. But when she finally corralled the nerve to open her eyes again, she found him smiling at her.

"You thought Kit was drunk that night?" he asked, barely containing his laughter. "Really?"

Faith nodded, growing more and more miserable with every passing moment. "And I . . . I'm just not, um, comfortable around people who over-imbibe. In fact, anyone who shows signs of drunkenness tends to terrify me."

But Holt wasn't listening to her explanation, because he was too busy being doubled over in laughter.

"What?" she said, smiling tentatively, his good humor infectious, even if she had just humiliated herself beyond words. "What's so funny?"

He reined himself in, but a huge grin split his face, and all Faith could think was that she'd never seen him looking more handsome. "It just never occurred to me that anyone would think Kit is a drunk, that's all. She's certainly a unique individual, but I've never seen her drunk in my life."

"Well, what else would cause her to act the way she was acting? Why did her companion bring her in over his shoulder, kicking and screaming that way?"

Holt shook his head and chuckled some more.

"That's going to take a long time to explain, something I sincerely hope will make for an appropriate segue when I ask you out again at the end of this conversation. As for Kit's behavior, well . . . That's just the way she is. She was perfectly sober that night. So was Pendleton, for that matter."

Faith began to smile, too. "So then there's no deep dark secret in the McClellan household?" she asked. "No out-of-control, drunken family member doing something to embarrass the entire clan?"

Holt sobered at her jest. "Actually," he said, "that's not exactly true. We, uh, we do have a lush in the family, someone who has in fact embarrassed the McClellan clan on a number of occasions in the past."

Her embarrassment rose to the fore again, and she wondered how many more times she was going to say the wrong thing around this man before she finally learned her lesson. "You do?"

He nodded.

"Who?"

He hesitated for a moment, before revealing quietly, "Me."

"You?"

He nodded again, and suddenly he looked older than Faith had first thought him. "I'm a recovering alcoholic," he stated evenly, having no trouble whatever putting voice to the words. "No one knows that outside my family, except for a counselor. No one but you. And no one else ever *can* know."

A clump of something cold and unpleasant landed in the pit of Faith's stomach. "You obviously aren't struggling with it. Why keep it such a secret, especially when others could benefit from your experiences?"

He met her gaze again. "Can't you imagine what people would do with that bit of news? The second-in-command at Hensley's Distilleries nearly killed himself with his own product? The Louisville Temperance League, for example, would have a field day if they knew."

Faith blinked at him. "They do know." She wasn't sure what motivated her to say that, but once the words were uttered, she had no way to take them back.

Holt shook his head. "No, they don't know. You know. I'm trusting you not to exploit the information or make it public knowledge."

"How can you trust me to do that?"

"Because I know you."

"You know nothing of me," she countered.

"Maybe I know more than you think."

Oh, how Faith wished that were true. And how she wished that Holt hadn't revealed what he'd just revealed. Not just because of the compromising position it put her in, but because his admission of his weakness—his illness—simply hit too close to home.

"Faith?" he asked.

"Yes?"

"I can trust you, can't I?"

She swallowed hard. "I don't know. If no one outside your family is aware of this, why did you tell me?"

"Because I think it's something you should know. Because I think it will be important in our future."

She shook her head. "We don't have a future, Holt. How many times do I have to say that?"

He stared at her for a long time in silence, and all she could do was stare back. Around Faith, the world seemed to stop spinning for a few moments. Then Holt leaned back in his chair, and the enchantment was broken.

"I can trust you," he said, resolute.

"Then the problem now," she replied just as resolutely, "would be that *I* can't trust *you*."

His eyebrows arrowed downward in confusion. "What do you mean? Why can't you trust me?"

"Because you're an alcoholic."

"Recovered," he hastened to correct her.

"Recover*ing*," she corrected him in turn. "You guys never do fully recover, do you? There's always that chance . . ."

She didn't finish her sentence, but his entire body went rigid in response at her implication.

"My husband was an alcoholic," she said suddenly, uncertain just when she had decided to reveal that particular bit of news. "That was what killed him. He drove off the road one night on his way home from work, and hit a tree at eighty miles an hour. I can only thank God that he didn't take anyone else out with him."

Holt didn't react—didn't move, didn't speak, didn't breathe. So Faith continued.

"On his good days, Stephen was a charming liar," she said softly. "And on his bad days, he was a mean drunk."

Holt nodded, as if he understood completely. "I was never a mean drunk," he told her. "But . . . I was a charming liar. My wife divorced me because of that. I lied to her about everything." He dropped his gaze back down to the hands that lay still in his lap. "On a couple of occasions, I was unfaithful to her. And I was stupid enough to think that she wouldn't find out." He glanced back up and met Faith's gaze with steely determination. "I won't sit here and make excuses for my behavior back then. But I can tell you that, had I been sober, none of it would have happened."

"And how long now have you been sober?"

"For almost two years."

Faith nodded. "That's commendable, Holt. And I'm glad you're doing so well. But you have to understand that, having put up with that kind of behavior from one man, for a lot longer than I should have, I'm not willing to risk having it happen again."

"It won't happen again," he vowed. "Not with me."

She smiled sadly. "I wish I could believe that. But I can't. I'm sorry."

Before he had a chance to say anything more, she stood and circled her desk, amazed that her legs were actually able to carry her. As gracefully as she could, she jerked open the door, then turned to Holt again.

"Thank you, Mr. McClellan, for clearing up the matter of your sister," she said, striving for a formality she was nowhere near feeling. "I think that concludes our business together."

Clearly with much reluctance, he stood and shrugged back into his coat, then began to make his way out. He got as far as the door without speaking, but something made him halt before he passed through it. And when he did, his scent surrounded her, warm and earthy and masculine, reminding her of so many things she wished she could forget. He gazed down at her face for a long time without speaking, then, as if he couldn't resist the impulse, he lifted his hand and stroked her cheek with bent knuckles.

Faith squeezed her eyes shut tight to keep in the

tears she felt welling. Her already jumpy heart leaped at the soft caress, but she neither spoke nor moved in response.

When she opened her eyes, Holt threw her a half-smile. "I'll be seeing you," he murmured. Then he left, crossing the tiny outer office to exit through the other door. He didn't look back once.

"Mrs. Ivory?"

Only then did Faith realize that her secretary had witnessed the entire scene. "It's okay," she told the other woman. "He didn't mean it."

Then she stepped back into her office and closed the door, leaning back against it, as if doing so might keep her demons on the other side. And she saw that outside her office window, in a swirl of white that hid the rest of the world from her view, the snow began to fall in earnest.

Holt guided his big, black BMW back to Cherrywood with little incident before the storm reached full capacity. All the way home, he thought about Faith Ivory. And all the way home, he cursed his life, his family, and his circumstances. But mostly, he cursed himself. Not just because of the things he'd done in the past to mess up his present, but because he simply could not surrender his hope of a future with Faith Ivory.

Why couldn't he stop thinking about her? he wondered. She'd made it clear that she had no desire to pursue whatever attraction had blossomed between them. She'd made it clear that she couldn't trust him. So why couldn't he just let it—let her—go?

As he exited the four-car garage behind Cherrywood, his gaze fell on the battered basketball hoop fastened to the side. He hesitated, oblivious to the fat flakes of wet snow that clung to his hair and snuck down his collar, trying to remember the last time anyone had used it. Years. Maybe more than a decade. He couldn't recall the last time the hollow *thump . . . thump . . . thump* of seemingly careless dribbling had pounded the walkway from the back door to the garage.

There had been seasons when that hoop was never idle, though, when he and his brothers—and frequently Kit—had spent the entire weekend battling it out on the concrete court below. Their mother would lounge with a book by the pool, watching, egging on whoever happened to be her favorite that day, until suppertime rolled around. Then she'd go in the house and fry a couple of chickens, and they'd all have supper at the umbrella tables outside.

For all their wealth and prominence, Lena Hensley McClellan had made sure her children led normal, wonderful lives when they were little. She'd loved to cook, and she'd made sure they were all home for supper every night. And once a week, she'd dressed them all in nondescript jeans and T-shirts, piled them into their grandfather's pickup truck, as if they were any middle-class family in the world, and scuttled them off to all the best places in town.

To the Louisville Zoo, where she'd let them ride the train as many times as they wanted through the green hills pungent with animal smells. Or to Huber Farms in Starlight, Indiana, right when they started pressing the apples for cider, when the air was cold and brisk and redolent of autumn. Or to the Frito-Lay factory for one of those kiddie tours, where they sent everyone home with a free bag of Fritos, and you felt as if you'd been given the most wonderful gift in the world. Or to Showcase Cinemas, back before they'd chopped it to pieces, when the screens were vast and enormous and the picture virtually surrounded you, and from the fabulous fourth row, you felt like you were a part of the film.

Holt closed his eyes and inhaled deeply of the snowy evening, the scent of the cold air assaulting him with too many memories for his brain to process, too many emotions for his heart to hold. God, he missed being a kid. Almost as much as he missed his mother. And he wished he could rewind the years and relive them all in slow motion. Not just to experience the joy all over again, but to make amends for some of the things he'd said and done.

As always, when such feelings came over him, his first impulse was to pour himself a drink. And, as always, when such impulses came over him, he immediately shoved them aside. Instead, he turned his back on the basketball hoop and trudged through the back door, then made his way immediately to the library, where his father kept the best stocked bar. He opened the liquor cabinet, reached past the bottles of Hensley's and found a club soda at the very back.

A soft sound from behind had him spinning around, and he was surprised to see Kit standing at the library entrance. Immediately, he held the bottle in his hand aloft for her inspection. "Club soda," he said. "Really."

She smiled. "You don't have to prove it to me, Holt. I have faith in you."

He smiled back at her choice of words. "Yeah, well, that makes one of us." He twisted the cap off the bottle as he turned to fill a glass with ice. "What are you doing home? Did you and Pendleton have a lovers' spat?''

A chuckle erupted from behind him. ''Not hardly,'' she said. ''We'd have to be lovers for us to have a lovers' spat, wouldn't we?''

Holt turned to face her, drink in hand, and feigned surprise. ''What? You mean all that stuff you told Dad about the two of you sleeping together isn't true? Why, Kit. I'm shocked, simply shocked, that you would lie to our father that way.''

She strode easily into the room and dropped down onto the loveseat. But she said nothing in response to his assertion.

He sipped his soda, then set it on the side table as he shrugged out of his coat and tossed it into a chair. ''So what brings you home?'' he asked again as he joined her on the loveseat.

She tipped her head back and stared at the ceiling. ''I needed a little break. And, just for the record, I didn't lie to Daddy. Pendleton and I really did sleep together that first night. He just didn't find out about it until he woke up the next morning.''

''So it really was sleeping, and nothing else?''
She nodded.
''And the status quo has remained unchanged?''
''Oh, no, it's certainly changed,'' she said. ''Pendleton has been sleeping on the couch since then.''

Holt chuckled. ''I knew Dad had underestimated him. I can't see Pendleton buckling under to either one of you, in fact, even if he did let you move in with him.''

Kit turned her head to gaze at him, her expression inscrutable. ''Are you suggesting that *I* underestimated him? How do you know I don't have him right where I want him?''

''And just where is it that you want him, Kit? Do you even know? Besides spread-eagle, belly-up, food for the buzzards, I mean.''

She seemed to give his question great thought before finally replying, ''I never wanted to make him food for the buzzards. He is kind of cute, after all. I'm sure I could find *some* use for him.''

''Other than as a revenge tool against Dad, you mean.''

She made a face. ''Please, Holt. You make me sound so conniving.''

''Hey, if the shoe fits . . .''

She sighed **heavily**, an empty, defeated sound, but she said **nothing to** contradict his allegation.

So Holt told **her**, ''Dad might not know what you're up to, little sister, but I do. And I don't like it.''

She glanced away, but not before he saw the flicker of anguish that skittered across her features. ''I have no idea what you're talking about,'' she said softly.

''Oh, yes you do. You're letting Dad think that you and Pendleton are building a little love nest together, just to lull him into a false sense of security and make him think you'll be getting married soon. That way, he'll leave you alone, and you can jerk the rug right out from under him at the last minute.''

''I am *not* building a love nest with Pendleton,'' she denied. But he found curious the two bright spots of pink that stained her cheeks.

''No, what you're building is a house of cards,'' he told her. ''And it's going to come down on you eventually. You might be able to fool Dad for a little while, but not for long. He only has a little over a month left to get you married. And once he finds out what you're up to . . ." Holt deliberately left the statement unfinished, knowing that Kit would draw far worse conclusions if left to her own devices.

When she glanced back over at him, her expression divulged nothing of what she was thinking. "Are you going to tell him?"

Holt shook his head. "I ought to, but I won't."

"Why not?"

"Because I think it's important that you come to your senses on your own. Not because someone jerked you there against your will."

She eyed him in silence for a moment, but he had no way of knowing whether she would heed his suggestion.

"Did you know he's originally from New Jersey?" she asked instead.

Holt arched his eyebrows at the quick change of subject. "Pendleton?"

She nodded. "And did you know he has a big ol' Harley hog? *And* he likes R&B? *And* he used to be married? *And* before he came to work for Hensley's, he was working for a nonprofit organization that helped underprivileged kids?"

"Pendleton?"

She nodded. "Yeah, boy, you think you know a corporate drone and then, *bam*. He pulls a stunt like this."

"Like what?"

"Like turning into a human being."

Holt laughed. "So you like him then?"

"No," she said too quickly. "Yes," she then amended just as rapidly. She sighed as she tangled her fingers nervously together in her lap. "Oh, I don't know."

Holt chuckled. "Maybe Dad was right. Maybe Pendleton is the man for you."

"Don't get cocky," she muttered. But her heart clearly wasn't in the admonition.

Holt sipped his soda and loosened his tie and tried to pinpoint when, exactly, his little sister had stopped being such a doormat. He didn't have to think long. Because he recalled the exact moment with crystal clarity, even though he'd been three sheets to the wind at the time. The reading of their mother's will. Scarcely two seconds after Abernathy had apprised them of the conditions surrounding their mother's final wishes, Kit had scooped up the McClellan scepter and run like the wind. And none of them had come close to catching up with her.

Once the shock of their mother's last will and testament had worn off, the McClellan men at first hadn't felt particularly concerned about the problem. Marrying off Kit wasn't such a big deal. She'd been trying to have a relationship with one kind of loser or another since she was fifteen. Just because the McClellan men had chased—or paid—them all off didn't mean there wouldn't be others.

Hey, Kit wasn't half-bad-looking, Bart had reminded them. As long as the lights weren't too bright. And despite her abrasiveness, Dirk had added, she could be fun. Sometimes. And she was smart, too, Mick had thrown in. Maybe a little too smart on occasion. But surely a man could overlook those things in light of millions of dollars, couldn't he? Why worry about some silly little condition of the trust, right?

Yeah, right.

They should have known better, Holt thought now. And they should have given Kit a little more credit, long before Mama died.

"So how are things going with your new girl-friend?" she asked suddenly, pulling him out of his reverie.

Although he knew perfectly well who Kit was talking about, he feigned confusion. "Girlfriend? What girlfriend?"

She clearly wasn't buying any of it. "Oh, come on. You remember," she said, "that sweet blond creature you were entertaining in the dining room the night Pendleton brought me home from the Caribbean. Faith Ivory of the Louisville Temperance League, I believe you introduced her as?"

"Oh, her."

"Yeah, her. How are things going?"

"They're not."

"Oh."

Neither of them said anything further for a moment, and just as Holt opened his mouth to change the subject, Kit opened hers to keep it right where it was.

"You really like her, don't you?" she asked.

It would be pointless to lie, Holt thought. Kit wasn't stupid, after all. Hadn't they all learned that the hard way? "Yes," he said, staring down into his glass, if not at his sister. "I like her very much."

"Why?"

He shrugged. "I honestly don't know." Now he glanced up at Kit, searching her face as if she might somehow give him the answer he was searching for. "But I can't stop thinking about her. There's something there between us. I just can't . . . I just don't . . ." He sighed restlessly, unable to complete the thought.

"So call her," Kit told him, as if that were the solution to all the varied and numerous obstacles facing him and Faith.

"I did better than that. I went to see her in person."

"And?"

"And she made it clear that she doesn't want to see me."

"Why not?"

"Her late husband was an alcoholic," he said. "He treated her badly. She has a small problem with trust." There, he thought. Succinct and to the point. All done.

Not quite, he then realized when he looked over to find Kit gaping at him. "You told her about your drinking?" she asked.

He nodded.

"Boy, you must *really* like her."

Yeah, you could say that, he thought. But aloud, he only said, "And although she thinks my overcoming my problem is admirable, she's by no means convinced that I won't, in a moment of weakness, do something stupid like, oh . . . fall off the wagon and turn mean."

"That's ridiculous," Kit said. "You'll never fall off the wagon. And you couldn't be mean if your life depended on it."

"Yeah, well tell her that."

"Maybe I will."

He eyed her warningly. "Don't you dare. Stay out of this, Kit. This is between me and Faith. And it's over now. She's not going to come around."

Kit said nothing in response, something that troubled him greatly. So in an effort to change the subject and dispel any crazy schemes she might be cooking up in that wily head of hers, he hurried on, "I still can't believe Pendleton hasn't tossed you out by now. Not unless there's more to this arrangement, in spite of the sleeping assignments, than you're letting on."

Kit sighed, obviously disappointed by the lob back into her own court. "Well, he doesn't have much choice, does he? If I come crying back to Daddy that Pendleton doesn't love me anymore, Daddy will fire him."

"Pendleton's a savvy guy," Holt said. "He could find work anywhere he wants."

"Not at the stud rate Daddy's paying him."

"There are some things in life that are more important than money," Holt said, surprised at how easily the words rolled off his tongue.

Kit burst into laughter. "Oh, right. Listen to you. You'd shrivel up and die without Mama's millions."

"And you wouldn't?"

She sobered, but dropped her gaze instead of meeting his. "I couldn't care less about Mama's money. Ninety-nine-point-four million bucks could go a long, long way in the right hands. And Mama picked out some fine, fine charities."

Holt nodded. "Have you really thought about what your life would be like if all our money were taken away from us? Even with Abernathy handling the funds for the last two years, your life hasn't changed one bit since Mama's death. You still get your more than generous allowance. You're still free to do whatever you want. But if all that money were jerked out of your hands, what do you think your life would be like?"

"It would probably be ninety-nine-point-four million times better," she told him.

He shook his head. "You're used to living this

way, Kit. Deny its importance all you want, but if you suddenly couldn't walk into Cherrywood whenever it suited you, if you couldn't use your charge card on whatever struck your fancy, if you had to go out and get a job—"

"A *job*?" she interrupted him, her expression troubled, as if she hadn't considered that aspect of the real world.

He chuckled. "Well, honey, ain't nobody else out there who's going to support you. You'd have to support yourself. And what kind of salary do you think you'll draw with your résumé?"

She fidgeted. "Well. I do have a college degree. Two college degrees, as a matter of fact."

"A BA in liberal arts and an MA in philosophy," Holt reminded her. "Oh, yeah. Those and all that professional experience you have—your most recent position was as a bartender, I believe, and lasted all of twenty-four hours—well, hey, your résumé ought to catch anyone's eye."

She lifted a shoulder and let it drop. "So I'll work as a bartender to support myself."

This time Holt was the one to laugh. "It would almost be worth sacrificing a hundred million dollars to see that. But maybe you should stop thinking about yourself for a minute, and start thinking about everyone else you're going to affect with this adolescent attitude you have."

She gaped at him. "Adolescent? Excuse me?"

Holt dropped his gaze down into his glass, watching as the tiny, crystalline bubbles snapped and fizzed. "Do you remember what you did the day after Mama's will was read?"

Kit kept silent, but he knew she was remembering that day as well as he did.

"You came into my bedroom when the sun was

at its peak," he continued, "and you threw open all the curtains so that I was blinded by the light."

"I remember," she said softly.

"Then you dragged me out of bed and poured me a cup of coffee. And as I sat there sipping it, you pulled out a notebook and enumerated for me, in stark, colorful detail, each and every incident in which I had embarrassed myself or my family or my coworkers with my drinking."

"It had gone on long enough, Holt. I just wish I had done it while Mama was still alive."

He nodded. "Do you remember how long it took for you to list all of those incidents that you had so thoughtfully recorded for so many years?"

"All day," she said. "And all night."

He nodded, too. "All damned day. And all damned night."

"But you haven't had a drink since then," she reminded him.

He dipped his head forward in acknowledgment. "No. I haven't. And I don't think I ever thanked you."

She smiled at him. "Yes, you did. You haven't had a drink since then."

Holt considered her for a moment in silence, then he roped his arm around her neck, pulled her close and placed a loud, smacking kiss at the crown of her head. Kit laughed, but shoved him away, then rose and went to retrieve a club soda for herself. That was the McClellan way, he thought. Reach out impulsively, touch briefly, pull back quickly. No harm done. Mama had been the only one who was able to hug for any length of time.

Holt sighed. "Now, I have the chance to pay you back, Kit."

She had remained on the other side of the room,

clearly needing some space after that overwhelming display of emotion they had just shared. Now she strode slowly back toward him, but dropped into a chair opposite the loveseat.

"No payback necessary," she assured him.

"You're going to get it anyway." He made himself comfortable and watched her closely as he spoke. "These days, it's you who's trying to self-destruct," he said. Immediately, she opened her mouth to object, so he sliced his hand through the air to cut her off. "Your behavior over the last two years has been selfish, juvenile, and unfeeling."

"Must be in the genes," she managed to fire off while he was taking a breath.

"I understand why you're doing what you're doing," he conceded. "I know that what Dad did to you the night before your wedding was unforgivable, and I know that Mick and Dirk and Bart and I had no right to be so overprotective. For my part, at least, I apologize. But I think you've made your point. And I think it's about time you did something to rectify the situation."

"Rectify the situation," she echoed. "And by that you would mean . . ."

"Get married," he stated bluntly. "Even if it's only some phony arrangement that lasts a few months, just do it. Save the family fortune. Return our lives to all of us, so that we can get on with our lives."

She nibbled her lower lip thoughtfully for a full minute before responding, and for a moment, Holt honestly thought she was going to agree to his suggestion. But when she replied, all she said was, "I'll think about it."

And that, he supposed, was as good as he was going to get.

"You know, it was snowing pretty hard when I came in," he said, recalling the fat, furious flakes that had pelted him as he'd crossed the backyard. "And it's probably full dark by now. You're going to have trouble getting home tonight."

She sighed as she gazed wistfully toward the library entrance. "Yeah, I guess I should just spend the night here. It'll give Pendleton a break. He can have the bed for a change."

Holt tipped his head toward the telephone that sat on the end table within her reach. "You going to give him a call? Let him know you won't be home tonight?"

She started to reach for the receiver, stroked her fingers over it lightly a few times, then finally shook her head. "No, I don't think it's necessary. It's not like he's going to worry about me. He probably won't even notice I'm gone."

Chapter 14

Where the hell was she?

Pendleton paced the length of his living room, then hastened to the front windows *again*, shoved aside the lace—God, lace—curtains *again*, and stared out into the white eddies of snow dancing in the darkness beyond *again*. He could barely distinguish the anemic glow of the lamp at the end of his front walk, and he certainly saw no sign of a Mercedes S-class, double-parked or not. It was past midnight, and he was worried about Kit.

Worried about Kit, he marveled again. How could this be happening? He was honestly concerned about the safety and well-being of a woman who had turned his life inside-out and his house into a Speigel catalog. Worried in the truest, most clichéd sense of the word, that she was out there lying dead in a ditch somewhere. Hell, he ought to be celebrating the fact that his house—his *life*—was finally his own again.

As he had done ever since that ill-fated, albeit unbelievably enjoyable, embrace in front of the fireplace less than a week ago, he forced himself to stop thinking about it. He was no closer now to understanding what that particular incident had been about than he had been the night it happened. Surely there was some psychologically sound, socially acceptable explanation for what had occurred that night. He'd been all warm and rosy and missing his family, and Kit had been handy. Likewise, she'd probably only responded to him out of some intense physical needs that had been too long neglected.

Simple stuff. Basic chemistry. They'd both been feeling lonely, and they'd both turned to each other in a fit of handiness. Period. Fortunately, Kit had come to her senses before anything very important had happened.

Well, nothing more important than a soul-shattering, reality-bending, mind-scrambling explosion of libido, anyway. Oh, but, hey, other than that . . . Still, no reason to dwell on it, right? He should simply continue to pretend it hadn't happened, just as the two of them had been pretending—however lamely—all week long.

So Pendleton only gazed out at the white-on-black night, as if in doing so, he might somehow conjure Kit up from the darkness, safe and sound. Behind him, from a cowering position on the rug before the fireplace, Maury whined his distress, as if he, too, were worried. Pendleton turned and offered the dog a halfhearted smile.

"It's okay, boy," he said. "She's fine. She'll be home any minute now."

But he knew Maury didn't believe him any more than he believed himself. So he shoved a restive hand through his hair, bit back the panic that threatened to overtake him, and wondered if he should call the police. Hell, there must be almost a foot of snow on the ground by now.

The storm had come out of nowhere, had caught everyone by surprise. The weather guy on channel three had said not to worry, though, that these spring blizzards were notorious for appearing quickly, only to be followed by balmy, springlike conditions that erased the results just as rapidly. By dark tomorrow night, the meteorologist had promised, the temperatures would be pushing seventy, and the snow would be melting faster than the Wicked Witch of the West.

But right now, the temperatures were hovering around thirty, and right now, the snow wasn't going anywhere except higher. Normally, Pendleton liked snow. But not when it was wet and heavy like this. Not when it trapped people in their houses so they couldn't get out and find people they were worried about. Not when it could be potentially lethal to people who happened to get caught out in it in their Mercedes S-class.

Dammit, where was she?

He released the curtain, somehow not minding anymore that it was lace. Kit was fine, he told himself adamantly. More than likely, she had ventured out to do something that would wreak more havoc in his life, only to realize, too late, that she wouldn't make it home. For all he knew, she was snuggled safe in her bed at Cherrywood, blissfully asleep, dreaming about the kinds of things that only the incredibly rich dreamed about.

Still, it would have been nice if she had phoned to let him know she wouldn't make it back tonight. To tell him that she was safe and sound, and not lying dead in a ditch somewhere. To reassure him that she would be home soon.

Home. Oh, now that was a good one. He really was worried beyond sense if he were thinking that his house was her home. Obviously, he needed some rest.

He should just go to bed, he told himself. Even if there was no way he'd be going in to work in the morning, it wasn't going to help matters to stay up worrying about Kit. Surely she was all right. Yeah, he ought to just use this opportunity to sleep in his own bed for a change, instead of on the couch.

But as Pendleton turned toward the stairs, a section of loose, crumbling plaster on the wall near the stairwell caught his attention. Really, it wouldn't take long at all to patch that, he thought. He had the materials in the basement. It would be a snap.

And he could take care of that one by the fireplace, too, he thought further, turning back toward the exposed area by the chimney. And while he was at it, he might as well patch those places on the dining room wall and ceiling. And the ones in the kitchen.

Hey, it wasn't like he was going anywhere anytime soon.

He'd finished patching up all the places on the first floor and was taking care of the ones on the second when Kit finally came home. And her arrival made Pendleton feel very, very good inside.

For about three seconds.

Then that very, very good feeling was immediately eclipsed by one that was decidedly much less good, because all of the worry, concern, anxiety and yes, dammit, fear, that he had managed to keep at bay for too many hours than he cared to think about suddenly roared up inside him in one huge, angry rush of emotion.

At the sound of the front door closing downstairs, he leaped down from the ladder in his bedroom, nearly toppling it and the tub of wet plaster beneath it. Then he stomped with great gusto out the door, down the hallway, to the top of the stairs. Kit gazed back up at him from her position just inside the door, appearing to be only mildly surprised to see him.

Dammit, she was standing there looking at him as if nothing in the world were wrong. As if she hadn't been missing from his life for almost thirty-six hours without explanation. As if he hadn't been terrified of losing her.

As if she didn't care for him nearly as much as he had begun to care for her.

And that, he decided, was the scariest thing of all. That he had actually started to care for Kit McClellan. When that had happened exactly, or how, he had no idea. But there it was just the same, submitted for his approval, as Rod Serling used to say on *The Twilight Zone*. The comparison was way too appropriate. Because as bizarre as those feelings of affection were, Pendleton did approve of them. Still, there was no reason Kit had to find out about them, was there? God only knew what she would do with the knowledge that he actually liked her.

He expelled a ragged breath of air and knifed his fingers through his hair, discovering, too late, that his hands were still covered with plaster. He glanced down at his clothes to see that they, too, were decorated with clumps of white, dusted with bits of ceiling and wall. In spite of the inclement weather outside, his labor had made him overly warm during the night, and he'd shed his sweatshirt some time ago. Now his overalls were buckled on one side—the other had broken some time ago—over his naked, and likewise plaster-spattered, chest.

When he glanced at Kit again, he realized that her gaze, too, seemed to be lingering on his upper regions, and a thrill of something hot and urgent ripped through him at the speed of light.

"Where the hell have you been?" he bellowed at the top of his lungs before he could stop himself.

Her eyes widened at the vehemence of his delivery, but she offered no other sign that she found his behavior at all out of the ordinary. "I . . . I . . . I spent the night a-at . . . at Cherrywood."

Okay, so maybe there was that little stammer that he might take as a sign that she found his behavior to be a bit peculiar.

"I . . . I went over for a visit," she continued, "and I . . . I got caught by the storm." She scrunched up her shoulders and let them drop. "Once it cleared up, I came home," she pointed out, her tone of voice indicating that even she found the explanation to be tad lame. "It's like sixty degrees out there now. The roads are pretty much clear."

He nodded, clenching his jaw tight. "What, and you couldn't pick up the phone and call me last night?" he demanded further. "Just to let me know you were okay?"

Her lips—those lips that had cost him hours of sleep over the last few weeks, so profound was his preoccupation with thoughts of them—parted fractionally. "Frankly, Pendleton, I . . . I didn't think you'd notice I was gone."

She was serious, he realized, amazed. She honestly hadn't thought he would notice she was gone, he echoed to himself, shaking his head in disbelief.

Now what on earth would have given her a *stupid* idea like that?

Slowly, very slowly, he made his way down the stairs, hoping that his leisurely pace might somehow disguise the turmoil that was tearing him up inside. And little by little, as he moved nearer to Kit, he found that instead of calming down, his feelings only grew more turbulent. She was dressed in another one of those soft, clingy, velvety outfits she seemed to favor, this one leggings and an oversized shirt in a soft lavender that made her eyes appear even bluer than usual. When he finally cleared the last step and stood before her, face to face, he was helpless not to reach out and touch her.

Lifting a hand carefully, so as not to dirty her with the remnants of the decay he'd spent the night repairing, he brushed a finger softly over her cheek. "Oh, I noticed," he said, his voice gentling. "I definitely noticed."

Her lips parted a bit more, as if she had intended to say something, but she suddenly snapped them shut and jerked her head away. Pendleton was left touching nothing but air, so he quickly dropped his hand down to his side.

"I'm sorry," she said. "I should have called you. I just didn't think . . ."

"What?"

"I didn't think you'd be worried about me, that's all." And before he had a chance to comment on that, she took a hurried step away from him. "What on earth have you been up to?" she asked as she went, her voice sounding more than a little shaky.

For a moment, he almost refused her the luxury of changing the subject. Then he decided maybe she was right. Maybe they should just ignore, for now anyway, whatever was going on between them. It wasn't a good idea to go off half-cocked. He really should explore this strange new development a little closer before he did that.

So he jutted a thumb over his shoulder, toward the living room. "I knew I wasn't going to be able to get in to work this morning, so I used the time to get some things done around the house. I've been at it since about one."

She nodded, obviously impressed. "It's only six o'clock now. You did a lot in five hours."

"Not one P.M.," he corrected her, only now realizing the extent of his work. "One A.M."

She gaped at him. "You've been up all night working?"

He forced a chuckle, trying to make light of the situation, but the sound came out thin and weak. "Yeah, well, you get me started on a project like this . . ."

"But all night?" she asked again, clearly incredulous.

This time Pendleton was the one to shrug. "I wasn't sleepy."

"Why not?

He waited until she turned to look at him again, then he told her, "Because I was worried about you."

She stared back at him in silence for a moment, but instead of commenting on his declaration, she only asked, in a very small voice, "Are you hungry? I could cook us some supper."

He hadn't eaten in nearly twenty-four hours, he suddenly realized. Since collecting his tools and materials from the basement in the wee hours of the morning, he'd been so focused on working on the house—anything to keep from worrying about Kit—that he hadn't taken a break. Then again, he'd hadn't been hungry all night, anyway, thanks to that full feeling of unmitigated terror filling his belly. Now, with that gone, however, he suddenly became ravenous.

"Yeah, I could eat," he said. "But let's order a pizza or something, all right? And let me fix a salad. No offense, but I think I've had enough country ham and black-eye gravy to last me a life-time or two."

She smiled. "That's red-eye gravy, Pendleton. You big, dumb Yankee."

He smiled back. "Whatever. I can't remember the last time I ate a meal without pork fat in it."

She breezed past him into the living room, toss-ing over her shoulder, "I want sausage and pep-peroni."

He rolled his eyes. "You can have it on your half. My half is going to be vegetarian."

"You keep eating like that," Kit told him, "and you're never going to fit in down here."

He rocked back on his heels. "Yeah, well, we'll see." And out of nowhere, for the first time, he found himself actually wanting to fit in down here. "*You* keep eating like that," he countered, "and *you're* going to wind up a Christmas ham with clogged arteries yourself."

She smiled. "Not a chance. I have an incredibly fast metabolism. Not to mention a standing date with Richard Simmons every weekday afternoon."

For a long time, neither of them said anything more. Kit only stood there in the middle of the room staring at him, and all Pendleton could do was stare back. Something had changed. He wasn't quite sure what, but there was something there between them that hadn't been present before, not even after that raging hormonal embrace earlier in the week. Comfort, he finally realized. He suddenly felt comfortable with Kit in his house.

"So . . ." he began again, before the awkwardness and uncertainty of his newly discovered feelings for her turned into a stark, raving terror that stampeded out of his control. "If you want to call for the pizza, I could run upstairs to take a shower and change." He tucked a hand idly under the bib of his overalls and scraped his fingers casually over his chest. "I'm not much fit for human consumption right now."

She shrugged, but somehow the gesture was in no way nonchalant. "Okay. Impellizzeri's all right with you?"

"Sure."

She nodded, but again, Pendleton got the feeling that there was nothing smooth or unconcerned about her reaction. She seemed to be completely preoccupied with something other than dinner, because she wasn't meeting his gaze at all, nor did she make any move toward the telephone. Instead, her attention seemed to be focused entirely on . . . entirely on his . . . um . . .

. . . on his chest.

He glanced down to see if something had happened to his person that he should be aware of—like if maybe a slime-dripping alien with retractable teeth had suddenly burst from his chest cavity or something like that. But he saw nothing out of the ordinary, just his half-naked, completely dirty chest fully intact, and he grew more puzzled. Why would Kit be staring at his body like that? he wondered. As if she wanted to have something other than pizza for dinner? Unless . . .

He smiled as understanding dawned on him like a good, solid blow to the back of the head. Deliberately, he rubbed his hand over his chest one more time, then drove both arms up above his head and launched into a lengthy, lusty stretch. Her eyes widened, going as round and as large as silver dollars. Oh, yeah. *Now* he knew what was going on.

"Well," he began again. He completed the stretch, then reached up to unhook the buckle that was fastened on his bib, letting the bit of faded denim fall down to completely expose his bare torso. See if she could resist *that*. "You go ahead and call, and I'll clean up. Give me about fifteen minutes, and I'll be down."

Her face had gone pale by now—except for the two bright spots of pink riding high on her cheeks—and she'd lifted a hand to her forehead, as if she were trying to ward off a sudden fever. "O-okay," she said, stumbling over the word.

"You want wine to go with?" he asked, now reaching for the metal stud at the side of his overalls. "There's some in the basement."

She nodded quickly. "Fine. I'll run down for a bottle as soon as I call. You go on upstairs."

He unfastened the first stud at his side and reached for the second. "You sure?"

"Yes. Go. Now."

He took a step forward. "I don't mind getting it for you now. You kind of look like you could use a drink."

She held up a hand to ward him off. "I'm fine. Really. Fine. You. Go."

"Well, okay . . ."

Before he could comment further, she spun around and fled for the kitchen, little more than a lavender blur. Pendleton smiled as he turned to go back up the steps. Oh, yeah. Dinner was definitely going to be interesting. And it went without saying what they were going to be having for dessert . . .

Kit was still feeling rattled when she submerged the last of the supper dishes into the soapy water in the sink, and she told herself to *puh-leeze* get a grip. Okay, so Pendleton had just looked *too* yummy in his plaster-covered overalls without a shirt underneath. She'd seen him naked, she reminded herself, that first night she climbed into bed with him, and the sight hadn't had any kind of effect on her at all. Well, not a *big* effect, she amended reluctantly.

Then again, all she'd seen was his bare back and tushie that night, and even then, only in the spastic beam of a flashlight. She hadn't much glimpsed the rich scattering of dark hair that decorated his chest from one side to the other. Nor had she much taken note of the hard, sculpted muscle beneath. Or the ruddy glow of his skin that looked like satin over steel. Tonight, however . . .

She inhaled deeply as she rinsed a plate beneath a stream of tepid water and handed it to Pendleton, who readily dried it and stacked it in the cupboard near his head. He had changed into a pair of blue jeans and an exhausted gray sweatshirt emblazoned with the words *Property Colonial High School Athletic Department, Deptford, New Jersey, XXL,* and somehow the baggy shirt only enhanced the solid build of his torso. He leaned an indolent hip on the counter beside him as he waited for her to wash another plate, and she could feel his gaze pinned to her face, just as she'd felt it lingering there all evening.

So, naturally, she kept her face in profile and

didn't look back at him. She couldn't look back at him. Because every time she did, she saw a fire burning in his brown eyes that she told herself she couldn't possibly be seeing.

"Are you ever going to speak again?"

She started at his softly uttered question. Speak? she wondered. About what? About the way he had her all tied in knots all of a sudden? About how the only thing she'd been able to think about last night as she'd lain in her bed at Cherrywood was how alien and unwelcome had become the bedroom that had been hers since she'd outgrown the nursery? About how all she'd wanted to do was pick up the phone in the middle of the night and call Pendleton, just so she could hear the exasperated "Good *night*, Kit" that he bit off every evening before she turned in with her cocoa? How could she speak to him about that?

So what she settled on was, "Speak? Who? Me?"

He chuckled low. "Speak. Yeah. You. Who else would I be talking to? Maury never shuts up."

As if to punctuate the point, the puppy beneath the kitchen table sounded off with a few perfunctory yaps, then went back to gnawing on his rawhide chewy with a growl of satisfaction whose rumble never seemed to end.

Kit scrunched up her shoulders uncertainly. "Well, what am I supposed to say?"

Pendleton tossed the dish towel over his shoulder and crossed his arms—those incredibly sexy arms—over his chest—that incredibly sexy chest. "I don't know," he said. "But it's not like you to keep quiet. In fact, this lack of a running monologue on your part is making me nervous."

She arched her eyebrows in question. "Oh?"

"Well, God only knows what you're plotting

over there," he said. "At least when you're talking nonstop, I know you can't be preoccupied with plans for my downfall."

She met his gaze levelly. "Says who?"

He narrowed his eyes at her, but didn't comment. Instead, he only retrieved the dish towel from his shoulder and folded it neatly in half lengthwise, then hung it on a rack between the counter and stove, a silent indication that he was through being domestic for the day, thank you.

"Hey, you left a cup," she said, pointing to the solitary dish sitting in the drainer.

"Doesn't matter," he tossed off casually.

Doesn't matter? she echoed to herself. *Whoa, whoa, whoa*. This wasn't like Pendleton at all. He never left anything unfinished. He was annoyingly anal about stuff like that.

"You know, you never paid me that dollar you owe me," he said out of the blue.

"What dollar?" she asked.

"That dollar you promised me for dancing with you down in Veranda Bay. You never gave it to me."

She settled a damp fist on her hip. "What, are you running short already? Boy, this is what happens to you executive types. The minute you hit that six-figure salary, you start living beyond your means. When's payday?"

In response to her question, he only smiled. And Kit decided right away that she didn't like that smile at all, nor, she suspected, was she going to like what was sure to come after it.

"Tonight," he said. "Payday's tonight."

Yeah, she'd known she wasn't going to like what came after it. "Sorry," she said, "but I'm busted,

too. I didn't get a chance to go to the money machine."

His smile didn't falter at all. Uh-oh. "That's
okay," he said. "I know another way you can pay
me back. Dance with me."

"Dance with you?"

"Yeah, then we'll be even."

Before she could object, he spun on his heel and
headed through the swinging door into the dining
room, and Kit took advantage of his disappearance
to debate the pros and cons of fleeing through the
back door.

Pro, she would be saved from whatever weird
. . . stuff . . . was currently possessing Pendleton.
Pro, she would avoid having to come within touching distance of him, thereby maintaining what little
composure she had managed to collect since he'd
begun undressing himself in the living room a
short while ago. Pro, she wouldn't have to tolerate
any longer the racing of her pulse, the frazzling of
her brain, the heating of her blood, and the zinging
of the strings of her heart. Pro, she'd stay sane.

Con, she'd get her feet wet, because she'd taken
off her shoes some time ago and left them under
the dining room table, and the ground outside was
still pretty mushy from all the melted snow.

Well, that was it, then, wasn't it? No contest. No
way was she going outside in her stocking feet
with it all muddy and icky and everything. Hey,
those were new socks.

So she wrung out the dish rag, hung it up on the
rack by the towel, and tiptoed cautiously toward
the kitchen door. She was about to push it open
when she heard the sound of music coming from
the other side. And not just any music, but the slow
slide of fingers along the strings of an electric gui-

tar, the melancholy wail of a saxophone, the soft, leisurely scuff of brushes over the surface of a drum.

Uh-oh. Blues. Touchy music. Feely music. Sexy music. No chance they'd be marimba-ing to that.

"Oh, Kiiiiit," he called out, his voice a gentle cajole. "I'm waaaiiitiiinnng."

When, precisely, the earth had shifted on its axis, she supposed she would never be able to say. She only knew that one minute, everything in her life was neat and orderly and well within her control, and the next minute, a whipcord of delicious possibility was slapping at the very edge of her soul. And in spite of its sting, there was something very appealing about the pull.

As she pushed open the door and passed through it, Kit reminded herself that there was still time to scoop her shoes off the floor and hie herself out the back door, safely into the night, regardless of its mushiness. But she ignored the three-inch heels as she passed them, and focused instead on the man who stood center stage in the living room beyond.

It was just a dance, she told herself. Hey, she could handle that. She'd been dancing since she was eight years old, and had put all the instructors she'd ever had to shame. Kit McClellan was nothing in this life, if not an absolute expert at dancing.

Unfortunately for her, though, Pendleton had pulled her well into his arms before she realized that *dancing* was the *last* thing he had on his mind.

Chapter 15

She discovered that the minute he tugged her forward and crowded her body into his, roping his arms around her waist and back with *way* too much familiarity. Hey, just what kind of girl did he think she was?

Okay, so once she'd offered him money to marimba with her. *Lots* of women offered men money to marimba, didn't they? And okay, so she'd broken into his house and climbed naked into bed with him. Like that didn't happen every night of the week to guys in some countries. And okay, so she'd kind of been cohabitating with him against his will for more than a month now. What man didn't experience something like that at least once in his life?

Did those things give Pendleton the right to question her moral steadfastness? No, they most certainly did not. Hadn't he been watching Lifetime Television? Hadn't he seen any of those Nike commercials? Didn't he know that a woman could do things like that these days if she wanted to, without fear of being labeled loose and immoral and up for hanky-panky?

The righteous indignation she was trying so desperately to corral evaporated completely when Kit felt one of his hands venturing in a decidedly southern direction. So she reached behind herself to halt his progress, curling her fingers softly around his wrist before scooting his hand back up to the small of her back. But Pendleton, clearly not one to be put off so easily, only retraced the journey with his other hand. So she reached *her* other hand back, as well, and repeated the service.

Unfortunately, putting both hands behind her back that way left her arching her front toward Pendleton. Too late, she realized how intimately her breasts skimmed against his chest. Too late, she noted how salaciously her torso pressed into those hard-as-rock abs of his. Too late, she saw how cordially her libido jumped up to greet his with a heartfelt howdy-do.

"Just what do you think you're doing?" she asked, trying not to notice the way her heart was jumping around in her chest.

"Oh, I'm sorry, didn't I make that obvious?" he murmured. He twined his fingers easily with hers at the small of her back and, with a single, gentle nudge, pushed her closer still, so that she felt his heart galloping erratically against her own.

"Um, no," she lied. "I'm afraid you didn't make it obvious at all."

"Gee, just goes to show you how long it's been since I found myself in this position," he said softly, dipping his head ever so slightly toward hers.

"Wh-what position?" she asked.

His lips curved into an oh-so-suggestive smile as he lifted one shoulder and let it drop. "Trying to show a woman how much I want to make love to her."

"Eh-eh-excuse me?" she stammered.

In response, he moved his head a little bit closer to hers, then began to sway their bodies in time to the leisure rhythm of the music. And as he brought Kit along for the ride, she was helpless to do anything but follow him, so addled had she become by the closeness of him, the scent of him, the heat of him. He backed himself slowly, slowly, oh-so-slowly toward the solitary lamp lit in the room, then released one of her hands to switch it off.

Before she had a chance to protest, he immediately settled his hand at her waist again. He raked his fingers down along her hip to her thigh before cupping her leg with much affection, then he skimmed his hand back up, to curve it gently over her fanny. And as she opened her free hand lightly over his chest, whatever objection Kit had been about to utter got completely stuck in her throat.

The softly flickering fire in the hearth sent a pale glow dancing over them, as if the flames, too, were caught up in the subtle to-and-fro of the music. The changing yellow glimmer threw Pendleton's face first into stark clarity and then into deep shade, a play of light and dark that kept her from ever knowing for sure what he was thinking about. His eyes were fixed on her face, but for some reason, she suddenly didn't mind so much his scrutiny. The darkness, she knew, hid the shortcomings of Mother Nature. And besides, she really wanted to look at his face, too.

Gradually, she forgot about everything, except for the way his fingers tripped lightly over her fanny, her hip, her back. Except for the warm breath that caressed her forehead. Except for the stampeding of his heart against hers.

"You are so beautiful."

His words erupted like a barrage of artillery between them, exploding in Kit's belly with all the heat and force of a cannon shot. For one brief, lunatic second, she actually believed what he said. Then she came to her senses, and with a forced and difficult humor, she laughed off his comment.

"Spoken like a man dancing in the dark," she said softly, uncertainly, striving for a levity she was nowhere close to feeling. "Light a candle, Pendleton. You'll get over it."

"I mean it, Kit. I don't know why I'm just now noticing it, but you really are very beautiful."

She swallowed hard. "Yeah, well, so is a big chunk of coal to a man who's been freezing to death for a while," she told him quietly.

He said nothing, only hooked his hands loosely at the small of her back and continued to gaze down at her face in the darkness. And as he did, something inside Kit kindled and caught fire, the flames flickering and licking at her belly until she wasn't sure she could stand the heat. And, God help her, as hard as she tried not to, she found herself wanting desperately to believe what he'd said.

"Don't do this to me, Pendleton," she petitioned softly.

He gazed at her in silence for a taut moment before asking very quietly, "Do what?"

She wanted to look away, but was helpless to do anything but meet his gaze. "I made a vow a long time ago that I'd never make love to a man again unless I was in love with him, and he was in love with me."

"And your point would be?"

The fire in her belly leaped higher, burned hotter. Surely he wasn't suggesting what he seemed to be suggesting. Surely he wasn't saying that they were . . . that the two of them had . . .

"My point would be that I don't love you and you don't love me," she stated emphatically.

There. She'd said it out loud. And it hadn't been nearly as painful as she'd thought it would be.

"You're pretty quick to make that assumption," Pendleton said. "Why can't we be in love?"

She bit back a hopeful sigh. "Get serious."

"I am serious. Why can't we?"

"Okay, I agree that you may be a man in love," she said, proud of the detachment in her tone that she faked very nicely. "A man in love with his ex-wife."

He opened his mouth in what she was sure would be an objection, so she quickly cut him off. "Hey, I've seen the look on your face when you talk about her, Pendleton. I know you're indulging in some fantasy about going up to New Jersey with every intention of stopping her wedding. You want to try to seduce me, fine. Try to seduce me. But don't do it by lying to me. Have a little more respect for my intelligence than that, will you?"

In response, he only pulled her closer and began to move their bodies in slow time once again. And as she felt her IQ plummeting, Kit nestled against him, wishing hard that he wasn't such a liar, wishing harder still that she wasn't such a coward.

For a long time, they remained so entwined, through song after song about mistrust and betrayal, until she wasn't sure she could listen to any more. So she piped up impulsively, "How about a little Tito Puente instead? We never did get in that merengue down in Veranda Bay. I brought a few of his CDs with me. They're up in the bedroom. I'll just be a sec."

She tried to extricate herself from Pendleton's embrace as unobtrusively as she could, but for every attempt she made to free herself, he deftly pulled her close again. And then, before she had a chance to utter a single further objection, he began nuzzling her throat and nibbling the curve where her neck joined her shoulder.

"Oh," she cried softly at the unexpected intimacy. "Oh, Pendleton."

"I like this music better," he said, his words a quiet murmur against her bare skin. "It suits my mood."

She was about to suggest another musical alternative—like maybe something along the lines of *Barney Sings the Best of Stephen Sondheim*, anything to completely crush the romantic mood—but Pendleton moved a hand from her back to her rib cage, strumming his fingers slowly and methodically along each one. He didn't stop until he cradled the lower curve of her breast in the ample L-shape of his thumb and forefinger. Then, in one swift, easy motion, he covered her breast completely and palmed the ripening peak.

And then all Kit could do was echo, "Oh, *Pendleton*."

It was all the encouragement he needed, evidently. Because with that single, softly uttered sentiment, he took full control of the situation. He skimmed his lips along the line of her jaw, then brushed them once, twice, three times across her open mouth. Kit told herself to *do* something, quickly, before the two of them ended up in a position that her hastily fleeing reason told her would be a very big mistake.

So she did something. She slid her hands up over his chest, curled her fingers over his shoulders, cupped one hand at his nape, and pulled his head down to hers for a more thorough kiss. He was an eager student, falling right into the rhythm she set with the first brush of her mouth over his.

Score one for the heart, she thought. Boy, it looked like reason was going to take a real beating tonight.

"Then again," Pendleton murmured as he ended the kiss and brushed his lips up over her cheek, "maybe it wouldn't be such a bad idea to go upstairs to the bedroom, after all."

Oh, yeah, Kit thought. At this point, reason was pretty much a goner.

In spite of her conviction, she managed to attempt one final stab at rationality. "I'm not sure this is a very good idea," she said. Then she completely negated the objection by trailing the tip of her tongue along the line of his rough jaw, savoring the fine, salty flavor of him.

"Oh, I think it's an *excellent* idea," he countered, turning his head to catch her tongue in his mouth again.

Somehow, Kit found the strength to pull away one final time. She gazed up into his eyes, wishing, wanting, wavering. And she said, "But I'm not sure I—"

"*I'm* sure," he interrupted her. "Just trust me, okay?"

Trust him? she echoed to herself. No, she couldn't do that. What she could do, though, was allow herself the temporary and unwise luxury of pretending to. She'd always been good at pretending where her emotions were concerned. Right after dancing, that was the thing she did best.

Silently, slowly, she nodded her assent. But she almost changed her mind when she saw the feral smile that spread over Pendleton's features.

"I'm not using any birth control," she told him. And she honestly didn't know if the remark was meant as a last-ditch effort to stop what was happening, or as a prelude to something else entirely. She couldn't think about that right now.

"I've got it covered," he assured her.

Involuntarily, she dropped her gaze downward, to a part of him that even now, she felt ripening against her.

"Well not at this exact moment," he said with a soft chuckle. "But I'll have it covered when the time comes."

He lowered his mouth to hers again. Then Kit forgot about everything in the world except Pendleton, and how he made her feel. She was totally unprepared when he bent and hooked one elbow behind her knees, then hauled her up into his arms and against his chest. Instinctively, she wrapped her own arms around his neck, and a little chuckle of sheer pleasure bubbled up from inside her.

"You're not really going to carry me up the stairs, are you?" she asked.

He smiled. "Oh, yeah."

"Just like Rhett?"

He cocked his head to the side. "What, you don't think I could pull it off?"

She eyed him playfully. "Well, fiddle-dee-dee, Pendleton. Rhett only had Scarlett to deal with. You, on the other hand . . ."

"I have the notorious Katherine Atherton Mc-

Clellan," he finished for her. "Clearly, I'm the lucky one."

She chose not to respond to that. It would only mess with the fantasy. Instead, she tipped her forehead to rest it against his and closed her eyes. She didn't open them again until he'd crested the top step, and then only because she couldn't tolerate any longer not being able to look at him. So she looked her fill, noted the seductive curve of his smile, the unruly lock of hair that fell rebelliously over his brow, and the dark spark of passion that glittered in his eyes.

My man Pendleton, she thought. *At least for tonight.*

His gaze never left hers as he carried her effortlessly over the bedroom threshold, where the faint light of a bedside lamp gilded and gentled his features even more. He didn't stop moving until he stood beside the bed, and when Kit glanced down at it, she uttered a soft, derisive sound. She really should have made it the day before, she thought as she took in the pile of rumpled bedclothes. Ah, well. Just saved them that much trouble now, didn't it?

Silently, Pendleton released her legs so that they swung parallel to his own, but he didn't quite let go of her completely. Her toes only skimmed the floor as he wound his arms tightly around her waist, pulled her to him again, and touched his lips to hers.

There was a lot to be said for being tall enough to see almost eye to eye with a man, Kit thought just before letting hers flutter closed. Funny how she'd never noticed that before. Then Pendleton slanted his mouth more fully over hers, and she ceased to think at all.

With agonizing, exhilarating slowness, he lowered her body to the floor, pressing her against him from head to toe, so that she felt him everywhere—against her legs, her belly, her breasts, her mouth. She reached behind him to bunch his sweatshirt in both fists at the same time he lifted his hand to the top button of her shirt. They each chuckled at their single-mindedness, but neither halted the actions. Pendleton did pause to let Kit pull his sweatshirt over his head, but the garment remained caught around his forearms until he'd freed the last of her buttons. Only then did he step away long enough to toss his shirt to the floor.

And then, Kit could only stare at him, at the rich scattering of dark hair that decorated his entire torso, narrowing as it arrowed down to the waistband of his blue jeans, but never diminishing. Muscles roped and banded his shoulders and arms, bunching poetically as he settled his hands on his hips to observe her in return.

What on earth had she gotten herself into? She'd been with a total of one man in her entire life. And Michael hadn't come anywhere near Pendleton on the *hombre* scale. She strove for a deep breath, to steady her nerves and gather her thoughts, but all she managed was a thin little hiccup of air. At the tiny, defenseless sound, Pendleton's smile grew broader, more intent, more predatory. And she realized then that she was in for the night of her life.

For a moment, she thought he was going to tell her she was beautiful again, something that would totally destroy the mood, but he remained thankfully silent. Instead, he took a single step forward and reached for her, dipping a hand beneath each side of her shirt. Then he moved them slowly outward, until the garment skimmed over her shoulders and fell to the floor.

Instinctively, she crossed her arms over the wisp of lavender lace beneath, suddenly feeling modest for some reason. She'd crawled into bed naked with the man, she reminded herself. She'd invited him to witness her bath. But the stakes were so much higher now, the odds so much more uncertain.

"Don't," he said softly, curling his fingers around each of her wrists. "I want to see you."

She shook her head, but he ignored the gesture, tugging gently on her wrists until she unfolded her arms again. The moment she did, he released one of her hands and cupped his fingers possessively over her breast. Just like that. No preparation, no warning, no preliminaries. He simply reached out and made her his own.

And Kit discovered quickly that she wanted him to possess the rest of her body as completely. As if reading her mind, he lifted his other hand to her other breast, and covered it just as masterfully.

A shock of heat erupted where he touched her, pooling in her heart, where it gathered strength before shooting out to warm every other part of her body. For a long moment, Pendleton only filled his hands with her, palming her sensitive flesh. Then, with the softest of touches, he skimmed his hands upward, under the straps of her bra. With a quick turn of his wrists, her straps fell down over her shoulders, and he hooked his fingers beneath them to push them down the rest of the way. Kit found herself bared for his perusal, her arms effectively trapped at her sides. Before she could voice a protest, he leaned forward and pressed his lips to her breast.

He kissed her softly before drawing her deep into his mouth, laving her with the flat of his tongue, teasing her with the tip. She shuddered at the quickness in his change of pace. Then she took some initiative, reaching behind herself to unhook her bra and free her arms, so that she could bury her fingers in the silk of his hair and push him closer still. Eagerly, he followed her lead, curling the fingers of one hand beneath the lower curve of her breast, lifting it higher, for a more thorough maneuver.

Kit wasn't sure how it happened, but she vaguely registered the cool crush of flannel under her back, and she knew that they had somehow managed to find their way to the bed. She buried her heels against the mattress and pushed herself higher, an action that left Pendleton's mouth caressing her belly. To facilitate his endeavors, he gripped the waistband of her leggings in both hands and tugged downward, taking those, and her panties, and her socks in one easy motion.

And then she lay beneath him, naked, exposed, vulnerable. Strangely, though, she felt none of those things. She was, after all, covered by Pendleton, by his warmth, by his strength, by his tender, loving care.

When he tossed the last of her clothes to the floor, she expected him to return to his original position, and it took a moment for her to register the fact that he hadn't. When she glanced down to see where he was, she found him standing by the bed, one hand unhooking the top button of his jeans.

Oh, yes, she thought. He definitely needed to do that. It was no fun at all if only one of them was naked. Well, not nearly as *much* fun, at any rate.

"Hurry up," she whispered, surprised at the vehemence of her edict.

He smiled. "Now, now. We have plenty of time."

"Do we?" Somehow, she wasn't quite convinced.

But Pendleton seemed to be, because he nodded with much certainty. "Oh, yeah."

As if to illustrate his patience, he opened his jeans *verrrry* slowly, button by button by button, so that she heard the whisper of each as it pulled away from its fastening. When he completed the action, he spread the fabric open with another leisurely motion, then pushed the garment down slowly, slowly, slowly over his hips. Beneath, he wore a pair of gray flannel boxers, deceptively conservative, and in no way modest, seeing as how they did nothing to hide the extent of his arousal.

Kit chuckled low, the sound of a woman who was utterly and irrievably turned on. "Are you going to take all night?" she asked.

He nodded. "Count on it."

But he seemed to become as impatient as she then, because he hastily shed both his blue jeans and boxers. When he stood, she caught her breath at the sight of him, a quick little intake of air whose hiss was unmistakable in the otherwise silent room.

Pendleton smiled. "You know," he said softly, "I don't think there's anything that turns a man on more than hearing his lover gasp when she sees the size of him. I'll try not to worry about the fact that you have almost nothing to compare me to, and just take it as a compliment, shall I?"

She nodded. "Most definitely." She didn't need to be an expert on the male anatomy to know that Pendleton was a man of measure. She only hoped she was enough woman to accommodate him.

"Come back to bed," she said simply. "Please."

He smiled again, and for the first time that she could recall, Pendleton did as she asked. He settled first one knee, and then the other, on the mattress, then bent down on all fours to make his way to the head of the bed, where she lay on her side, watching him. Somehow, she thought she knew how a small animal must feel just before a wolf trotted in to effortlessly carry it off, intent on enjoying it at his leisure.

The image stayed with her as Pendleton circled her ankle with strong fingers and tugged her down a bit. Then he curled his other hand around her knee and pushed her legs open wide. It took a moment for Kit to realize his intention, and when she did, she tried to clamp her legs together again. But Pendleton had already insinuated his hands and himself between her thighs, and he deftly opened her for his clearly growing appetite. Before she could utter a word in protest, he lowered his mouth to her, drawing an idle circle with his tongue before tasting her more deeply.

Kit went limp at the mind-numbing sensation that shot through her like a heat-seeking missile. She tangled her fingers in Pendleton's hair, ostensibly to urge him away, but she found that she only held his head fast in place, silently commanding him for more. And more. And more.

So he gave her more, over and over, laving her, loving her, teasing her, tasting her. And just when she thought she couldn't tolerate another moment, he moved back up her body, dragging his open mouth over her flat belly, dipping his tongue into her navel, treating each of her breasts to another slow perusal. He paused on his journey only long enough to fulfill his promise of protecting her, donning a condom he pulled from the nightstand.

Then he rolled her over to her side and aligned his body behind hers. He splayed one hand open over her belly, the other across her breasts. Then he lowered his head until his mouth hovered right beside her ear.

"Are you ready for me?" he whispered. "Because I don't think I can wait any longer. I want to be inside you, Kit. Deep inside you. In every way either one of us can possibly imagine."

Somehow, she found the strength to nod, then she turned her head to kiss him. And as he consumed her mouth with his, Pendleton eased himself inside her.

"Oh," she murmured. "Oh, that's so good."

She thought he uttered a sound of agreement, but she couldn't be sure. Deeper and deeper he entered her from behind, his movements slow, steady, certain. Kit had never felt so full, so satisfied, so complete. Until Pendleton began to move inside her. Then she realized just how empty she'd been all this time. And she knew, too, that the void was one she would never be able to fill again without him.

He moved his body up and down against hers, in and out of hers, alongside hers, until she thought she would burst with the fullness. Then, just when she felt herself approaching that elusive edge, he shifted their bodies so that she lay beneath him.

"I want to see your face when it happens," he said softly. "And I want you to see mine."

Then deftly, swiftly, he entered her again, even more resolutely than before, doubling his rhythm. Over and over, faster and faster, deeper and deeper, he moved inside her, until both of them were nearly insensate with the wanting, the longing, the needing. At exactly the same time that Kit felt the coil of heat inside her explode, Pendleton pelted her with one final thrust. Then both of them arched against each other, stilling as ripples of absolute pleasure wound through them.

For one long, silent moment, they only clung to each other, as if doing so would preserve their union forever. Then Kit drove her fingers into Pendleton's hair and pulled his head down to hers for an almost brutal kiss.

I love you, she thought, and by some wild miracle, she kept the words locked deep inside. *I love you.*

When he pulled away from her to speak aloud whatever he was feeling, she quickly, gently, covered his mouth with her fingers and shook her head. "Don't," she whispered. "Don't say anything."

"But—"

"Don't."

He searched her face in silence, cupping a hand over her jaw before dipping his head to kiss her cheek. Then he rolled away from her and rose from the bed, to tend to that little matter of sexual convenience that had prevented the mingling of their physical essences.

Would that it had been as effective dividing their emotional ones, Kit thought sadly.

At the sound of water running in the bathroom, she closed her eyes. And when Pendleton returned to bed, drawing his hand slowly, gently along the length of her spine, she pretended to be asleep. Doubtless, she didn't fool him for a minute. But, thankfully, he had the decency to simply lie down beside her, draw her close, and shut his eyes, too.

Always the gentleman, Pendleton, she thought.

And she wasn't sure whether to be happy about that or not.

As had become his habit of late, Pendleton awoke slowly, clinging to the edge of a dream about Kit. This one, however, had been different from the others. Normally, right about the time he got Kit naked in his dreams, the scenario went a little surreal. Like she was suddenly dressed as Carmen Miranda, and she shook a couple of maracas as she marimba-ed out the door.

But this time in his dream, she'd stayed Kit. A naked Kit—a warm and wonderful naked Kit who had made love with him in the most warm and wonderful—not to mention naked—ways.

It had been some dream.

As he rolled over in bed, he threw an arm across his eyes, as if by denying himself a view of his room, he might somehow make real the erotic images parading through the forefront of his brain. Amazingly, the gesture succeeded. Because, just as he had in his dream, he heard the soft sigh of Kit's breathing, tasted the lingering flavor of her on his tongue, smelled the musky fragrance of their coupling, felt the heat of her body as it pressed into his.

In fact, so realistically did four of his five senses recreate the events of his dream, that Pendleton removed his arm from over his eyes to see if there might be an equally genuine vision to greet him. But all he saw was the ceiling overhead, noting with some disappointment a patch of flaking plaster that he had missed the day before.

"Damn," he muttered under his breath.

A languid, muffled murmur was his reply, and he turned his head on the pillow to find that—lo and behold—Kit had indeed emerged from his dream in warm, wonderful, naked reality.

And that was when it finally hit him, like a bag of wet plaster upside his head. That dream he'd had about Kit last night? It hadn't been a dream at all. They really had made love. More than once. After all the sniping and snipping, after all the fighting and flirting, after all the denial of feelings, finally, finally, the two of them had come to their senses and submitted to what should have been obvious from the beginning. They'd wanted each other all along.

As if she'd read his thoughts, Kit stirred, turning onto her side to face him. One arm was shoved beneath her pillow, and the other was folded over her bare breasts. Her eyes were closed, but her mouth was open, curled into the hint of a smile that was very, very naughty.

"Sleep well, dear?" he asked, returning her smile with an equally naughty one of his own.

"Mmm," was all she said in reply. Her eyes remained closed, but she extended one long leg into a graceful stretch that rocketed Pendleton's blood to the boiling point.

"Did you have nice dreams?" he asked further.

"Mmm-hmm," she replied with a stretch of her other leg. Oh, God.

"Was *I* in any of your dreams?" At this point, Pendleton was really only half paying attention to his side of the conversation, as the comings and goings of Kit's legs were really much more interesting.

She opened her eyes to half-mast and smiled some more. "No."

Well, that, finally, brought his attention back around. A little. "No?" he echoed. "I wasn't in

your dreams?" He probably would have felt indignant if it hadn't been for the fact that the sheet
chose that moment to fall away from her legs, exposing them from thigh to calf.

"No, you weren't," she repeated sleepily. "But
Keanu Reeves was."

Pendleton's smile fell. "Keanu Reeves? I thought
I was the man of your dreams."

She chuckled low, a profoundly erotic sound.
"Oh, come on, Pendleton. Why should you be the
man of my dreams when I can have Keanu Reeves
in them?"

He scooted over to close what few inches of
space separated them, then rolled to cover the top
half of her body with the top half of his. Man, he
loved the feel of Kit McClellan naked beneath him.

"Why should I be the man of your dreams?" he
repeated.

She looped her arms loosely around his neck and
nodded.

"Because I'm the one who knows where to touch
you so you make that extremely erotic little sound
that drives us both wild."

He reached down between their bodies to touch
her in that very spot, and her eyes fluttered shut
as she emitted a quiet murmur of delight.

"Yeah, that's the sound I was looking for," he
said with a smile, his body tightening at hearing it
again.

She bent one knee to facilitate a more thorough
exploration, and Pendleton took advantage of her
offer. Gently, he nudged her thighs further apart,
palming the heated core of her, noting the immediacy of her dewy response to his touch. Her eyes
closed more tightly, and she bit her lip, but the
gesture did nothing to quiet the ripple of pleasure

that escaped her lips on a sigh. Wanting to hear more, he dipped a finger deep inside her, reveling in the shudder that wound through her entire body.

"Oh," she murmured. "Oh, what a wonderful way to wake up in the morning."

This time, Pendleton was the one to respond, "Mmm."

He parted her soft folds and plowed her more deeply, furrowing his fingers back and forth and around and around, until she bucked her hips up to meet his petting.

She curled her fingers around his nape and pulled his head down to hers for a voracious kiss. "More," she commanded him.

He rolled on a condom and tumbled his body over hers, then entered her swiftly and deeply, setting a rhythm that was at once leisurely and demanding. Over and over he buried himself inside her, until their entire bodies rocked with their reactions. Then, at precisely the moment she arched herself against him, crying out in her completion, he, too, went utterly rigid.

For a moment, they remained as if frozen in space and time, neither moving, neither speaking, neither breathing. Then, gradually, Pendleton relaxed, blanketing Kit as her body eased beneath his. He threaded his fingers through her hair, kissed her forehead, her temple, her cheek, her jaw. Then he pulled back far enough to gaze upon her face.

And what he saw there nearly stopped his heart.

Nothing. He saw absolutely nothing in her expression. Kit had pulled a shutter closed over her face that made it impossible for him to tell what she was thinking or feeling about the intimacy that had just passed between them.

"Kit?" he said softly. "Are you all right?"

She nodded in silence, then lifted her hand to feather her fingers through his hair. It was a simple, affectionate gesture, but for some reason, it felt like neither of those things.

"I'm okay," she said softly. "I just—"

She never finished the statement, because the alarm clock erupted on the nightstand beside her, and she jerked at the shrillness of the sound. Pendleton slapped a hand down over the intrusion, but the moment of her revelation—whatever it might have been—was gone, and there was little chance of recapturing it this morning. So he dipped his head to hers again and kissed her tenderly on the lips.

"I have to get ready for work," he said. "But there's no reason you need to get up. Unless you want to, oh, I don't know . . . shower with me?"

He wasn't sure, but he thought she smiled at that. "I better not. You'd never get to work."

"And the problem with that would be . . . ?"

"Daddy would fire you if you missed two days in a row."

"Not if I missed because I'm making wild, jungle love to his daughter, he wouldn't. He'd probably give me a nice, big raise."

He'd meant it as a joke, but something clouded her expression when he said it. And then he remembered that it wasn't a joke at all. Hadn't McClellan, Sr. done just that? Promised Pendleton a great, fat bonus if he married Kit and secured the family fortune? Of course, she had no way of knowing about that. But it made sense for her to conclude that if her old man had paid good money to chase a guy off once in an effort to save millions, then he'd certainly be amenable to offering cold, hard cash to another one, if it meant saving a bundle in the long run.

"Oh, come on," she said, clearly striving for a levity she was nowhere close to feeling. He could tell that, because instead of sounding happy, she sounded wounded. "Daddy has a business to run," she went on, her voice hollow. "Sure, he'll be delighted to find out that you really are boffing his daughter, but—and I know this will come as something of a shock to you, Pendleton—my father's not much of a romantic at heart."

"Boffing his daughter?" he echoed, finding the suggestion more than a little distasteful. "I beg your pardon. What I've been doing to the boss's daughter goes way beyond boffing."

She arched her eyebrows in query. "Oh?"

He smiled and pressed another kiss to her forehead. "I've been making love to her, sweetheart. Big difference."

She eyed him with an expression that was at once hopeful and disappointed. "You don't expect me to believe that there was any more to last night than a good time."

"Why don't I?"

"Because there was nothing more to last night than a good time, that's why."

Oh, sure, he thought. Like she expected him to believe *that*.

He threaded his fingers gently through her hair, framing her face with his open hands. For a long time, he only looked at her, silently willing her to please, just this once, open herself up to the possibility that there was more to what went on between a man and a woman than a financial arrangement.

Yes, she'd grown up with the knowledge that her father had only married her mother for her money. And yes, she'd been forced to acknowledge that the one relationship she'd been allowed to have with a man had ended with a check for six figures. And yes, her father had only ever looked at her in terms of her monetary value when it came to keeping the family fiscally sound.

Money and the worth for being loved were irreversibly linked in Kit McClellan's mind—she'd never quite been taught to separate one from the other. But surely, Pendleton thought, the suggestion that she couldn't be loved without money wasn't so deeply ingrained in her that she couldn't at least give their budding relationship a chance.

"We have lots of time to talk about this," he said. "But right now I have to get ready for work." He dipped his head to hers and kissed her tenderly, first on one cheek, then the other, before brushing her lips softly with his.

Reluctantly, he pushed himself off the bed and padded naked across the bedroom, but he couldn't resist turning around for one more glimpse of her warm, rosy body. "Get some sleep, because you're going to need it," he told her. Then, rousing the most libidinous smile he could muster, he added, "I have plans for you, tonight, Kit. Big, *big* plans."

Chapter 16

"**B**ut I told you this morning that I already made plans for tonight."

Pendleton hooked his hands on his hips and glared at Kit, silently demanding an explanation. She was dressed for an evening out, wearing an elegant little sapphire dress that hugged her in much the same way he wanted to be hugging her himself. Her long, long legs—which he'd frankly planned on having wrapped around his waist right about now—looked absolutely decadent in black hose, and her black high heels defined quite nicely the calves he'd rather be gripping in his fists.

Briefly, he wondered if maybe she had on stockings instead of pantyhose, wondered, too, just how long it would take to skim her panties down around her ankles, hike up her skirt, lift her onto the dining room table behind her and—

"Well, what was I supposed to say?" she asked, interrupting what had become a *very* nice daydream. "I can't remember the last time my father invited me to dinner."

"That's because until about a month ago, you

were living with him. An invitation hardly seems necessary under those conditions.''

''Well, it still would have been rude to turn him down. He invited you, too, you know.''

''Gee, how thoughtful of him.''

Pendleton shook his head morosely. Damn. All day long, he'd been looking forward to coming home to Kit and picking up where they'd left off this morning. Now, here he was, barely in the door, not even close to being undressed, and she was telling him they had to turn around and head out again. Out into public. To her father's house, no less.

Like they were going to have any chance to strip down and do the naked boogaloo there.

''Do we have to?'' he asked, telling himself that was *not* a petulant little whine that colored his voice.

She reached out and patted his hand soothingly. ''There, there,'' she cooed. ''We don't have to stay late. I promise when we get home, we can do all the naughty things you've been planning all day.''

''I'll hold you to that.'' And then he'd hold her to himself. For hours and hours and hours.

''By the way,'' she added offhandedly, her voice going way too perky all of a sudden. ''Something interesting came in the mail for you this morning.''

With a quick, jerky motion, she spun around to the dining room table and lifted a creamy vellum envelope from the assortment of scattered mail. When she turned again to hand it to Pendleton, her smile was way too bright, way too sweet, way too kind.

''It's an invitation to your ex-wife's wedding in two weeks,'' she told him before he even had a chance to look at the envelope.

"Two weeks?" he said. "I thought it was still a month away."

"Well, I guess that grapevine of yours has a short circuit or two."

"But two weeks," he said softly, knowing the objection was pointless, because Sherry had already set the date. And how did Kit know about that date, by the way, he wondered, unless she'd been—

"Not that I was snooping or anything," she said hastily, reading his mind in that damnably annoying way she had of doing. "I just accidentally glimpsed the return address and saw that it was from an S. Pendleton in Mount Holly, New Jersey. Then I accidentally held the envelope over a steaming teakettle until it opened. And then I accidentally turned it upside down and shook it real hard until the invitation fell out. That actually accidentally happened twice, because it had one of those inside envelopes, as well. It, by the way, I noticed accidentally, was addressed to R. Pendleton and guest, so in a sense, I suppose it was addressed to me, too, because, hey, who else would you take to your ex-wife's wedding but a new flame, right? So really, when you get right down it, I didn't accidentally break any postal laws at all, did I? You ready to go?"

Pendleton's head was spinning by the time Kit concluded her story. Only now did he notice that the exterior envelope was indeed open, the flap still neat and tidy and the return address smeared by steam. When he glanced back up at Kit, she was looking at him as if she had nothing more on her mind at the moment than what was on tonight's dinner menu.

"Sherry invited me to her wedding?" he asked.

Kit nodded quickly. "Looks like."

"Doesn't Miss Manners frown on that sort of thing?"

Kit threw her arms open wide in what was quite clearly a very nervous gesture meant to look very nonchalant. "Hey, etiquette has changed so much in the past few years, who can keep up, huh?"

"But still . . ." Pendleton's voice trailed off before he completed the thought.

"I'll tell you one thing," she said, her voice still annoyingly happy as she crossed her arms over her abdomen in what looked, for some reason, like a gesture of self-preservation. "A woman inviting her ex-husband to her wedding? Sounds to me like she's still thinking about him. A lot."

He snapped his head up at that. "What do you mean?"

Her too-bright smile nearly blinded him. "Just that you must still be on Sherry's mind in a big way if she wants you to come up for the wedding, that's all. Maybe she's having second thoughts about taking a powder on your marriage."

Pendleton eyed her carefully. She was way too cheerful for his comfort. Kit McClellan that happy could only mean trouble.

"And hey, now you won't have to crash it, will you?" she asked. "Because you've been invited. That's just so convenient, don't you think? So . . . are you going?"

A weighted question if ever there was one, Pendleton thought. But because it involved his ex-wife, he knew exactly how to answer it. "I don't know."

Kit nodded, but instead of commenting, she only asked again, "Ready to go? We don't want to keep Daddy waiting, do we?"

Instead of pointing out to her that she'd been

keeping Daddy on pins and needles for nearly two years now, he only nodded. "Yeah, I'm ready," he lied. He only wished he knew for what.

Pendleton was nearly overcome with dread as he turned off River Road into Glenview and approached the majestic McClellan home. Again. So far, he was zero for two in having a good time at Cherrywood. And even when Kit directed him to pull his car around to the back of the house this time, thereby providing him with at least one small change, he was more than a little uncomfortable at the prospect of another evening spent cozily curled up at home with those crazy—oops, he meant *eccentric*, of course—McClellans.

It helped little when he rolled his roadster to a stop near the four-car garage, only to see Holt McClellan, Jr. not ten feet away, wearing one of his two-thousand-dollar power suits and dribbling a basketball on the pavement. Evidently, he'd been at it for some time, because he'd worked up a sweat, despite the cool evening.

"Oh, goody," Kit said when she noted her brother's activities. "It's been a long time since I went one-on-one with Holt."

Before Pendleton could say a word, she leaped out of the car and made a mad dash for her brother. So he climbed out, too, eager to see just what kind of chance she thought she had at roundball when pitted against an adversary who was four inches taller, seventy-five pounds heavier, *not* wearing spike heels, and, well . . . a guy.

"Kit!" Holt shouted in greeting when he saw her, clearly delighted by his sister's arrival.

He laughed when she made a grab for the ball, and deftly ducked aside. Kit laughed, too, then feinted to the right, her maneuver successful in psyching him out enough for her to steal the ball. With a few easy dribbles and a couple of swift, elegant moves—and in no way hindered by the handicap of her high heels—she spun and executed a beautiful jump, tossing the ball toward the goal. Then she landed easily, poised like a pro, watching as it arced through the air and descended cleanly through the net with a soft, but unmistakable, *swish*.

"In your face, Holt!" she shouted with another laugh. "Just like old times!"

Okay, so maybe she had a pretty decent chance, Pendleton conceded. He made a mental note to brush up on his own moves a bit before taking her on himself. Then he smiled when he realized that he should have followed that advice a long time ago.

Her brother grinned at her before he moved to retrieve the ball from where it bounced below the goal. Pendleton wasn't sure he'd ever witnessed a stranger scene than two people dressed like a photo shoot for *Vogue* behaving like a spread for *Sports Illustrated*. But this was clearly an activity that the two siblings had played out for a long time, and he wasn't about to do anything to interrupt it. Especially since Kit looked so happy. Really, genuinely happy, and not the phony happiness she'd adopted when she'd presented the invitation to Sherry's wedding.

Man, she was beautiful, he thought. Whether she would ever believe it or not herself, he didn't know. But Pendleton was sure that he'd never encountered a woman in his life who looked better than Kit McClellan. Funny, how he hadn't noticed that long before now.

The sister and brother completed another half-dozen baskets before Kit looked up and saw Pendleton watching. She blushed a bit when she did, as if she'd completely forgotten he was there and only now remembered. He wasn't prepared for it when she shot the ball out quickly toward him, and he only barely caught it with a muffled *oof* as it slammed into his belly.

"You and Holt shoot a few," she told him. "I'll go see if Mrs. Mason needs any help in the kitchen."

Although he much preferred to follow Kit, something in her suggestion and demeanor made him think that she wanted to go in by herself for now. So he let her go, watching until she had passed completely through the back door. Then he spun around to find McClellan, Jr. posed for action.

"Give it your best shot, Pendleton," he said.

Somehow, he seemed to be talking about something other than basketball, but Pendleton shrugged the impression off. He tipped his hand over and let the ball drop, then dribbled it a few times before taking a shot from where he was. The ball missed the hoop by a mile, but for some reason, he didn't really care.

"Jeez, Pendleton," McClellan said as he moved easily to retrieve the ball. "How long has it been since you played?"

"A long time," he confessed. "Too long, really."

"How about a game of twenty-one?" the other man goaded. "Dinner won't be ready for an hour."

Pendleton nodded. "Yeah, okay. Why not?"

For the better part of that hour, he and McClellan went at it like two adolescents. Well, almost like two adolescents. There was that small matter of a rapid-fire pulse rate barely a few minutes into the game that Pendleton simply did not remember from his youth. Nor did he remember his muscles pulling so painfully tight so terribly easily back then as they seemed to now. Nor had even the simple act of dribbling caused him to feel just so damned exhausted.

Two discarded suit jackets, two loosened neckties, and four rolled cuffs later, the two men were tied at eighteen points and two cardiac arrests each.

"McClellan," Pendleton panted as he scooped up the ball after the latest of his foe's aborted attempts at a basket. "What say we pick this up where we left off later, hmm?"

The other man nodded, but declined comment, probably because he was too busy gasping for breath himself. With no small effort, he made his way over to Pendleton, then the two of them, obviously of the same mind, sank down against the side of the garage for a session of deep breathing. As the sun sank low, staining the sky with the pinks and oranges of another spectacular Kentucky sunset, the only sound to be heard in the McClellan backyard was the warble of two feuding cardinals and gasps of two dying men.

McClellan leaned his head back against the garage wall and swiped a damp sleeve over his forehead. "I don't remember basketball being nearly that taxing."

Pendleton knifed a hand awkwardly through the air. "It's the suits. You can't possibly play good ball when you're wearing a suit."

McClellan nodded, as if he were sure that was the only reason for his state of total exhaustion.

For another few moments, they sat in silence, until McClellan broke it by asking, "So things with you and Kit aren't going too well, huh?"

Pendleton arched his eyebrows in surprise and turned his head to look at the other man. "They're not?"

McClellan, on the other hand, arrowed his eyebrows down. "Are they?"

Not that it was any of his business, Pendleton thought, but . . . "Yeah. They are. At least, I thought they were. You heard something I haven't?"

His companion eyed him warily. "Are you sleeping with my sister or not?"

Pendleton gaped at him. "What the hell is it with you McClellan men?" he demanded before he could stop himself. "Did it ever occur to any of you that it's none of your damned business who's doing what to Kit?"

"Hey, there's a hundred million dollars at stake, and my mother put it all in Kit's hands," McClellan said. "I'd say we all have a stake in Kit's activities right now."

"Ninety-nine-point-four million," Pendleton corrected him, mainly because he knew it bugged the hell out of the McClellans to hear that.

"Whatever," McClellan said. "Are you and Kit being intimate or what?"

"Maybe you should ask Kit."

"Maybe I already did."

Oh. Well. That sort of changed things. And it sort of stumped him for a response, too. So he asked, "And what did Kit say about it?"

McClellan eyed him thoughtfully. "She told me the two of you were sleeping in separate rooms."

"When did she say that?"

"Two days ago. When she spent the night here during the blizzard."

Pendleton fidgeted a bit nervously. "Yeah, well, um . . . Maybe you should ask her again."

He braced himself for the fist of an outraged older brother that was certain to land in his face, but when he braved a quick glimpse at McClellan, he found a broad, white smile splitting the other man's face.

"Pendleton!" he fairly shouted. "My man! That's what I want to hear!"

Actually, Pendleton thought, he was Kit's man, not McClellan's. No need to dwell on that, though, he supposed. "Boy, whatever happened to the days when a guy beat the hell out of anyone who compromised his sister's virtue?" he asked.

McClellan shrugged. "We've been trying to compromise Kit's virtue for almost two years now, Pendleton. Forgive me if I find the news of your conquest to be . . ." His smile broadened. "Incredibly good," he finished.

"Man, I can't figure you people out to save my life," Pendleton muttered, biting back some of the choicer words he wanted to use. "I have a kid sister, too, you know."

McClellan looked surprised, as if he'd never considered the possibility that there might be more to Pendleton than a corporate title. "Do you?"

"Yeah, I do."

McClellan sobered suddenly, his smile falling, his eyes darkening, as if an entirely new subject were at issue. "And did you spend the better part of your youth, as my brothers and I did, making sure no guy ever got close enough to hurt her?"

Pendleton shook his head. "No, I didn't. I let her live her own life. Make her own mistakes."

"And how did that turn out?"

Pendleton fidgeted a bit more. "Well, she sort of got knocked up when she was sixteen by some sonofabitch stupid idiot jerk moron sonofabitch."

"You said sonofabitch twice."

"Yeah, I know."

"Oh."

Pendleton waited to see vast disappointment and a total lack of respect on McClellan's face at hearing that a big brother had failed so egregiously in keeping his little sister safe from harm. But the other man only gazed at him speculatively in silence, as if he weren't quite sure what to make of him.

"Carny's done all right, though," he said by way of defending his sister. "The mistake she made when she was a teenager, she took responsibility for it, even if the sonofabitch stupid idiot jerk moron sonofabitch didn't. And her son has been the bright spot in her life ever since. She owns her own business now, and Joey is a straight-A student and major hockey fiend. The two of them have their share of problems with curfews and adolescent outrage, the usual stuff, but they do okay."

McClellan only continued to look at him in silence, then, slowly, he nodded. "You're saying we all should have left Kit alone to make her own mistakes instead of sheltering her from life. That she never had a chance to experience the good with the bad, so she has no way of knowing now exactly which is which. She hasn't really grown up, because she simply never had a chance to. If she's behaving like a child now, we have no one to blame but ourselves."

Pendleton nodded. "Yeah. That's what I'm saying."

"That ultimately, she would have done all right if we hadn't interfered."

"Yeah."

"That none of us would be in this mess right

now if Kit had been left to her own devices."

"Exactly."

"Of course, that means she'd be married to that little prick Michael Derringer right now," McClellan pointed out, "and not sleeping in *your* bed."

Pendleton furrowed his brow at that. "I guess it would."

"Or maybe not," the other man conceded. "She probably would have come to her senses eventually when she realized how unhappy she was. Then again, I guess we'll never know for sure, will we? Since she never had a chance to fall on her ass like the rest of us."

"I don't know if I'd go that far," Pendleton said. "I think Kit's fallen on her ass more times than anybody wants to admit. She just hasn't had the opportunity to pick herself up and brush herself off, and lie and say, 'I meant to do that,' like the rest of us have. Someone else has always done that for her. I'm just saying maybe right now you guys should back off and see what happens."

Again, McClellan only gazed at him in silence for a moment, as if he were weighing some matter of great import. Then he said, "Look around you, Pendleton. What do you see?"

The question was unexpected, but Pendleton did as he'd been asked and scanned his surroundings. "I see a big, beautiful house. Some primo real estate. A couple of expensive cars." He turned to meet McClellan's gaze levelly. "But I also see a beautiful sunset. A basketball hoop. A couple of birds who warble a mean tune. And inside that house, there's a woman who'd really like to be closer to her family than she is."

"Meaning?"

Pendleton met the other man's gaze levelly.

"Meaning maybe you and your father and brothers are worried about losing the wrong thing."

For a long time, McClellan said nothing, as if he were letting that little suggestion settle in. Then he replied, "So if Kit blows the entire fortune, loses every nickel that generations of my family have worked most of their lives to earn, then I shouldn't worry, because I'll still be able to watch the sunset every night, is that it?"

Pendleton nodded, but knew the suggestion sounded lame when phrased like that. In spite of that, he said, "It's my understanding that your great-great grandfather started off with nothing but a recipe and an illegal still way up in the mountains."

McClellan nodded. "Yes. That's true."

"So who do you think enjoyed his work more? You, or him?"

The other man inhaled deeply, then released the breath in a slow, steady steam. "I'm not a simple man, Pendleton. Neither is my father. Neither are any of us. We've grown up with a certain lifestyle, and I, for one, don't want to lose it. Especially when it's such an easy matter to preserve it."

"And I'm saying that maybe if you stepped back and looked at the big picture, you and your old man might have more success in preserving the family fortune than you've had messing around with Kit's life. There's more to that fortune than money. A lot more."

McClellan narrowed his eyes at him. "I don't follow you."

Pendleton nodded angrily. "Yeah, I know. That's the problem."

Concerned that saying anything more might further confuse the matter, he pushed himself up from the pavement and began to make his way to the house. Almost as an afterthought, he spun around and lobbed the basketball carelessly toward the goal. It bounced on the rim before hitting the backboard, then it spun on the hoop a few times before finally falling through the net. When it did, McClellan caught it deftly in both hands, then looked up at Pendleton with a frown.

And all Pendleton could do was shake his head, and wonder how a smart guy like McClellan, Jr. could be so damned dumb.

Kit fought off the ripple of déjà vu that threatened to swamp her when the dinner party retired to the living room with coffee. It was hard to believe that a month had passed since that first night at Cherrywood. Pendleton had been a complete stranger to her then, and she'd suspected he was nothing more than a corporate drone dancing at the end of her father's leash. She had so looked forward to taking him down a peg that evening. But things hadn't turned out quite the way she'd planned.

And since that night, everything, like clockwork, had blown up in her face. Because she, like an idiot, had gone and fallen in love.

Oh, but hey, no biggie. It was love, not brain surgery. She'd get over it. Eventually. Certainly by the end of the twentieth millennium or so. And by then, if what all those post-nuclear-holocaust movies said was true, the world would just be a big ol' ball of dried-up, burned-out carbon anyway. And where was the fun in pining for someone when you had to wear a gas mask all the time?

She sensed Pendleton's approach long before she felt him move up behind her, and a shudder of anticipation mixed with apprehension skittered through her. Before she could even acknowledge him, he leaned in close, his mouth hovering right at her ear. His breath, his entire body, was warm, welcome, intoxicating. And she found that she simply could not wait to go home and get naked with him.

"You ready to go?" he asked, his voice low and seductive, murmuring exactly her thoughts just loud enough for each of them to hear. "We could get an early start on all those things we planned on doing."

A sad, salacious smile curled her lips as she nodded. "Most definitely." She turned to her father and brother and added, more loudly, "Pendleton and I have to be going. It's getting late."

Her father's eyebrows shot up in surprise, but the smile that curled his lips was absolutely . . . Victorious, Kit noted dispiritedly. Strange, that he'd been acting so triumphant all evening, when not once had he mentioned her relationship with Pendleton. Not once had he demanded to know how things with the two of them were going. Not once had he asked if they'd made any wedding plans.

It almost felt as if he knew something they didn't. And she really hated feeling that way.

"So soon?" he asked. Then, before either of them could offer to stay longer—not that either of them was going to offer to stay longer—he rushed on, "Well, if you must. Good night. Drive safely. Holt? You up for a nightcap?"

And without further notice, he spun on his heel and departed for the library. Holt shook his head at her, smiled, and shrugged, then, after a quietly uttered good night, departed in the same direction as their father.

"My family," Kit said wistfully as she watched them go. "I suppose I have no choice but to keep them. They're just smart enough to leave a trail of bread crumbs if I tried to abandon them in an enchanted forest."

Pendleton smiled. "At least we have each other."

For now, at any rate, she thought.

They had made it all the way to the car before Kit realized she'd left her purse behind. And seeing as how it was one of those evening bags roughly the size of an electron, she knew it could be hiding almost anywhere.

"It's probably in the kitchen," she told Pendleton as he opened the passenger side door for her. "I put it down to set the table for Mrs. Mason. Go ahead and start the car. I'll only be a minute."

But it wasn't in the kitchen, she noted fairly quickly. So she must have left it in the dining room. That room, too, however, provided her with no clue as to her purse's whereabouts. So she mentally retraced her steps of the evening, and finally concluded that she must have left the accessory in the library.

Where her father and Holt had retired for a nightcap, she recalled. Gee, just like old times. They were doubtless having one of those major father-son conversations right about now, and there was always that outside chance that her name might crop up . . .

She slipped her shoes from her feet and dangled them from her fingers as she tiptoed quietly toward the library, remembering idly that this was exactly how that first, fateful evening with Pendleton had concluded. How terribly ironic, she thought. Sure enough, the moment she entered the main hallway, she heard the soft murmur of masculine voices, and silently, she made her way to just outside the door. Then she hugged the wall and cocked an ear, and eavesdropped shamelessly on the conversation coming from within.

". . . about wedding plans?" Holt was asking.

"It wasn't necessary to ask them about any wedding plans," her father answered.

Holt chuckled anxiously. "We have a month before the deadline expires, and you don't think it's necessary to ask when Kit's getting married?"

Her father, chuckled, too, though the sound of his laughter was far more menacing. "Didn't you see the way she was looking at him? Kit is completely smitten. And you know how she is when she finds something she really likes. She wouldn't give up Pendleton now if her life—or one hundred million dollars—depended on it."

Holt uttered an exasperated sound. "Don't be so sure. Even if she's fallen in love with him—which is still open to debate, if you ask me—that doesn't necessarily mean she'll be *marrying* him before the deadline. It would be just like her to tie the knot the day *after* Mama's deadline, just to piss us all off."

Maybe, Kit responded silently. Then she pushed the thought away. It was immaterial. Marriage, regardless of the timing, was out of the question, at least where Pendleton was concerned. Because it wasn't like he wanted to marry *her*. The only wedding he'd be showing up at in the future would be his ex-wife's.

"Trust me," her father continued in a confident tone of voice that snapped her attention back around right quick. "Pendleton will make damned sure they're married before the deadline."

"Oh?" Holt replied mildly, echoing the very

word circling in Kit's head. "He doesn't seem to me to care one way or another. And even if he did, he's the type of man who would respect Kit's wishes in the matter. If she wanted to wait, he'd wait, too. He doesn't even have a stake in this thing."

"Oh, yes, he does."

"He does?"

Kit realized she whispered the words out loud herself at exactly the same time her brother uttered them to her father. She covered her mouth with one hand, lest she slip up like that again. Still, she couldn't deny the sick feeling that settled in the pit of her stomach at the unmistakable certainty in her father's voice.

"Damn right he has a stake in this," he stated further, too adamantly for her comfort. "I made it clear to Pendleton the day after Kit moved in with him that there would be a nice, fat reward for any man who took her on as his lawful wedded wife, thereby saving the family a bundle."

"Oh, Dad. No. Please. Tell me you didn't do that."

For a moment, Kit thought she had said those words aloud, too. Then she realized that it had been Holt who had echoed the plea that had erupted in her own head.

"Of course I did that," her father said, his voice colored with impatience. "I told Pendleton that I'd paid that little prick Michael Derringer a quarter-million to abandon Kit before, then I assured him that I could be even *more* generous to any man who would marry her now."

The dinner she had consumed less than an hour ago rolled over in Kit's belly like a dead, bloated fish, threatening to replay itself on the foyer carpet in glorious Technicolor and SurroundSound. It was with no small effort that she kept herself from spilling her guts all over her mother's favorite Aubusson. And it was with an even greater effort that she kept herself from sobbing out loud.

Well, what had she expected? she asked herself. She should have known her father would do something like this. She should have realized that the only reason Pendleton had been tolerating her presence in his life was that he'd been promised a substantial reward for his trouble. She should be in no way surprised to find out that his motivation all along had been financial, not emotional.

But Kit *was* surprised. And that frankly surprised her. Because if she was surprised to find out that Pendleton had only been wooing her for her monetary value, then that meant that somewhere deep inside herself, she had started to believe—to really, truly, honestly *believe*—that he liked her. Perhaps even loved her. Loved *her*. Katherine Atherton Mc-Clellan. And *not* the Hensley millions.

She should have known better. Any logical human being would have realized what was going on from the beginning. Any logical human being would have been able to see exactly what was what. Unfortunately, it was kind of hard to be logical when your heart was calling all the shots. And then, when your heart starting breaking into a million pieces . . . Well, forget about it.

Although her father and brother continued to talk, Holt's voice, she noted vaguely, becoming remarkably angry about something, Kit knew she'd heard enough. No longer caring where her purse was—no longer caring about much of anything, in fact—she made her way silently back through the house. When she got to the kitchen, she only stood for a moment, gazing out the window at the sleek little sports car idling in the darkness, its parking lights glowing in anticipation of her return.

Pendleton had made it clear that he wanted to make love the minute they arrived home. Until a few moments ago, that was what she had wanted, too. But now, that was going to be something of a problem. Because Kit suddenly realized that what she'd told him the night before had been absolutely true. Although, at the time, she'd only made it up in an effort to put him off, she realized now that she really didn't intend ever to make love with a man again unless she loved him and he loved her.

Last night, subconsciously anyway, she had thought Pendleton loved her. Tonight, however, she knew the truth. And knowing what she did, there was no way she could tumble into bed with him when they got home. Or ever again, for that matter.

This one-sided stuff, she thought as she made her way slowly and without enthusiasm toward the back door, was really for the birds. Not only that, but it sure could make a person powerful sick to her stomach.

Chapter 17

"Are you sure you're feeling okay?"

Pendleton cupped one hand over Kit's forehead, the other behind her nape, but she barely acknowledged either gesture. Instead, she only lay in bed looking pale and fragile, little changed from how she had appeared before he'd prepared for work, which had in turn been little changed from her condition of the night before.

She didn't feel feverish, he noted, taking some heart in that, but man ... Did she look like ten miles of bad road. The Jersey Turnpike, as a matter of fact. Right around Exit 7, if he wasn't mistaken. Trenton.

She'd become ill just as they were leaving her father's house the night before, and the closer they'd gotten to home, the sicker she had felt. By the time they'd walked in the back door, she'd barely had the strength to walk across the kitchen. He'd ended up scooping her into his arms to carry her up to bed, and then being caught completely off-guard when she suddenly—and with surprising strength for one so sick—fought hard enough to make him put her right back down again. He'd only watched in utter mystification as she feebly made her way up the stairs and into the bathroom, unaided in spite of her obvious need for someone.

She hadn't come out again until he'd turned in himself. Certainly, he'd had no intention of trying to make love with her, but when he'd scooted his body next to hers, just to be close to her, draping an arm carefully over her waist, she'd asked him to move away. She'd told him the feel of his skin against hers was painful. And although he'd heard that high fevers could do that—make a person's skin hurt—Kit hadn't felt feverish then, either. Still, she'd clearly been sick with something.

"I'm not going in to work today," he said, removing his hands from her face.

"Of course you're going to work," she said, her voice lacking all the sparkle it normally held.

"Not with you sick like this, I'm not."

"I'll be fine," she said softly. "It's nothing I haven't had before. I'll get over it."

"You look terrible."

She closed her eyes, then folded her forearm across them. "Oooh, Pendleton, you sweet-talker, you. You sure know all the right things to say to a woman when she's feeling down."

"You know what I mean."

"I'll be fine," she assured him again. "Go to work. I need some rest, and you'll just be in the way if you stay home. I'll feel obligated to spend time with you."

He smiled. "Now who's sweet-talking?"

She inhaled feebly, but kept her arm over her eyes. "Go," she said. "I'll be fine."

Although he didn't believe that for a moment, he figured he probably ought to do as she said. She did need to rest, and he probably would just be a hindrance if he stayed with her.

"I'll come home on my lunch hour to check on you," he said.

She nodded. "Oh, I don't doubt that for a moment. Got to keep an eye on those investments, after all."

Great. Now she was becoming delirious. What next? Hallucinations? "What investments?" he asked mildly.

But she only shook her head slowly in response and repeated, "Go."

He bent forward to press a kiss to her forehead, and was surprised when she turned away before he had the chance to complete it. He reminded himself that she was sick, that he shouldn't take her withdrawal personally. But it stung him that she wouldn't even allow him that small gesture of affection. He lifted a hand to stroke it over her hair, thought better of the action, and dropped it back down to his lap.

"Call me if you need anything, okay?"

She nodded.

"And I'll be home in a few hours for lunch."

Another nod, then she rolled over to her side, effectively turning her back on him.

Hoo-kay, he thought. Message received loud and clear. He pushed himself up off the bed, strode across the room, and closed the door behind himself as quietly as he could. But somehow, he had a very bad feeling that whatever was ailing Kit went way beyond the physical. And he wished for the life of him that he knew what to do.

Lunch, he reminded himself. They could talk more about it then. By then, she'd have gotten a few hours more rest, and maybe she'd be up for a little conversation. Making a mental note to stop by Heitzman's for one of those butter kuchens she liked so much, Pendleton headed off for work.

Unfortunately, he never made it home for lunch. In fact, he didn't make it home for dinner, either. An accident at the distillery in Bardstown had the entire executive staff on the road by ten A.M., and they didn't make it back to Louisville until nearly eight that night. By then, Pendleton was exhausted, overwrought, and dispirited. Not because anything had gone wrong at the distillery that couldn't be fixed with minimal expense and trouble, but because he had called home on a half-dozen occasions that day, only to have the answering machine kick on every time. And although he'd left a brief message each one of those times, asking Kit to call his cell number, she never had.

Worse, now as he passed through the back door, stepping aside to let a *very* anxious Maury out for his evening uproar, he saw the little light on the answering machine flashing six times in quick succession, an indication that Kit had never even replayed any of his messages.

"Kit?" he called out as he headed for the dining room.

Funny, how quiet the house was, he thought as he strode through the dining room and into the living room. There was no eardrum-crushing singing of rural Kentucky folk songs, no equally abrasive a-pickin' and a-grinnin' banjo music shaking the stereo speakers. Nor was there an indistinguishable, alleged foodstuff on the stove spitting and crackling in its deep fat pit. The house was utterly, unhappily, deadly silent.

Actually *funny* wasn't the right word at all to

describe the complete lack of life in the house, Pendleton thought as he topped the last stair. *Scary* was more like it. Real scary.

"Kit?" he tried again.

But again, all he received in reply was a stone-cold silence that made his flesh crawl.

The bedroom door was ajar, he noted, a faint light spilling from within. Carefully, he pushed it open and peeked inside, and saw much to his relief that the bedclothes were rumpled and piled in the middle of the mattress, and *not* covering the lifeless body of a late, lamented, madcap heiress. But as soon as that relief shot through him, it was replaced once again by fear. Because if Kit's *lifeless* body wasn't lying on the bed, then it must be *living* somewhere else.

Don't panic, he told himself. A quick survey of the room told him she wasn't completely gone. Her discarded clothes of the night before were still slung across a chair, and her underwear and stockings were still on the floor, where she had an annoying habit of leaving them. For some reason now, though, Pendleton wasn't annoyed at all, and he found himself wishing she'd hurry home so she could toss as much underwear on the floor as she wanted.

Too, the nightstand on her side of the bed was still accessorized by a crossword book and a romance novel she'd just finished reading, and the photograph of herself and her brothers that had been taken at her high school graduation still sat on the dresser. Nevertheless, a sick sensation settled in Pendleton's gut as he crossed to the closet. Immediately after opening the door, he realized something was missing. Most of Kit's clothes, to be exact, along with two of the suitcases she'd brought with her the day she'd invaded his house.

Yeah, she'd been sick that morning when he left for work, all right. But evidently not sick enough to keep her from bailing out on him.

"Dammit," he hissed under his breath.

What the hell had gone wrong? he wondered. What could he have possibly done or said that would make her take a powder this way? Okay, granted, men tended to be a trifle more clueless than women did when it came to the whole relationship thing—and, hey, throw a woman like Kit into the mix, and that cluelessness was magnified a good five-, six-hundred percent—but still . . .

"Dammit," he muttered again, a bit louder this time.

Where could she have gone? He tried to tell himself that she'd simply packed up a few things and returned to her father's house. That she would be coming back to his place to gather the rest of her stuff—like every stick of furniture and every pot and pan—later, when she had more time, not to mention a moving van at her disposal. Maybe, he thought, her recent visits to Cherrywood had stirred up her need for luxurious surroundings and finer things, and now his fixer-upper in Old Louisville—even if it was coming along nicely, thanks, if he did say so himself—just wasn't good enough for her anymore.

Somehow, though, he couldn't quite bring himself to believe that Cherrywood was where she would hole up. She'd seemed far happier in Pendleton's house than she ever had in her father's. Something—namely a cold, dark feeling in the pit of his stomach—told him that Kit had gone a whole lot farther than Glenview. Somehow he was certain that she'd taken off for parts unknown, more than likely some destination south. Way south. Somewhere amid thousands of miles of ocean, and thousands of acres of islands.

"Dammit," he repeated. Then he punctuated the sentiment by kicking the baseboard. Hard.

The sound of Maury's mad yipping at the kitchen door stirred Pendleton enough to make him find his way back downstairs to let the puppy inside. And on his way through the dining room, his gaze inadvertently fell to the table, where the scattered mail from the day before still lay unopened. Except for one piece that *was* open, he noted. The invitation to Sherry's wedding.

Oh, man.

Pendleton gave his forehead a good, mental smack, then, because he deserved it, he opened his hand and gave his forehead a good, physical smack, as well. Only two days ago, Kit had accused him of still being in love with his ex-wife. And only two days ago, he hadn't been able to contradict her. But now, two days—and two nights—later, he knew better.

He wasn't in love with Sherry.

It was that simple. And in many ways, he was beginning to wonder if he'd ever really loved her at all.

Cared for Sherry? Yes, much as he cared for all the friends he'd made in childhood. Lusted after Sherry? Oh, most definitely. He absolutely lusted after her. Much as he lusted after Michelle Pfeiffer, Anais Nin, and Miss January 1979.

But the thing about all those women was . . . they weren't Kit. And what he felt for Kit—the caring, the affection, the lust—went *waaaaay* beyond the tepid reactions he'd had to other women. Too, Kit commanded *more* from him than other women had.

Admiration, for one thing. Respect, for another. And fear. And worry. Exasperation. Confusion.

And, of course, love.

His gaze fell once again to the wedding invitation that had been addressed to R. Pendleton and guest. He smiled as he picked it up and read the words engraved so elegantly upon the creamy card. Then, without one whit of emotion, he tore the card in two, casting one half to the left, the other to the right.

Gee, that had been easy. Would that all things in life were dealt with as effortlessly. Of course, Pendleton was in love now. That meant ease and effortlessness went right out the window.

The first thing on his agenda, he knew, was finding the woman who had kidnapped his heart and was holding it for ransom. He'd pay whatever price Kit demanded, as long as he got her back. Safe and sound, and in one piece. Oh, and in love with him, too, something he was fairly certain wasn't going to be a problem at all. No one could have made love the way he and Kit had without being utterly, irrevocably in love. So the only problem he could see for the short term was that he had absolutely no idea where to look for her.

Only one thing to do now, he thought. Wait for a postcard. And just hope like hell that one came soon.

Kit stood outside the surprisingly inoffensive offices of the Louisville Temperance League, realizing that she had expected a temperance group to house themselves in something a little more dramatic. Say a bleak, impenetrable castle, sitting atop a craggy, impassable mountain, beneath angry skies rent open by the wrath of God.

But when she reached the office of Faith Ivory, all she saw was your basic working woman's environment. Wall-to-wall beige carpeting, icky eggshell paint, old, fat Venetian blinds on the windows, a handful of framed degrees and awards on the walls. And behind a scarred, battered desk, one slight, impassive woman in a simple, gray flannel suit. A woman who looked very, very tired and very, very unhappy.

Goodness, but Kit was glad she had come.

"What can I do for you, Miss McClellan?" Faith Ivory asked, clearly uncomfortable with her unannounced visitor. "You'll excuse me if I say that it's something of a surprise to see you here."

"I don't know why that would be surprising," Kit said mildly as she brushed a nonexistent piece of lint from her brown tweed trousers and smoothed an invisible wrinkle from her cream-colored shirt. "I'm a social person by nature. And I thought it was about time you and I got to know each other a little better. We didn't have much of a chance to chat that night at Cherrywood." She punctuated the observation with a bland smile.

Faith responded with an equally tepid smile of her own. "Yes, well, although that's certainly true, I didn't expect to see any of the McClellans again, since I told Holt—"

"Now, now," Kit interrupted her, still smiling benignly. "Don't be coy with me. Holt may fall for that kind of thing—he's unbelievably soft-hearted, the big sap—but you're talking to a seasoned professional now, li'l sugar dumplin'. You say you don't want to see Holt again—or any of the rest of us, for that matter—but I ain't buyin' it. So let's chat."

Faith Ivory's expression probably would have

been the same if Kit had just hit her in the face with, well, a li'l sugar dumplin'. "I'm sorry," she said, "but I have no idea what you're talking about."

"Oh, come on," Kit cajoled. "I'd know that wounded martyr role anywhere. I perfected it myself a *looooong* time ago. You're wasting your time playing it with me."

Two bright spots of red colored Faith's cheeks. This was going to be *sooooo* easy. "In the first place, Miss McClellan—"

"Please. Call me Kit," she interrupted. "And I'll call you Faith. Since we're going to be speaking so frankly, I think we might as well put ourselves on a first name basis, 'kay?"

Faith inhaled deeply, held the breath for what Kit could only assume was a count of ten, and then began to speak again. Her voice was low, calm, and monotonous, a clear indication that she was starting to get really, really steamed. Perfect.

"Miss McClellan—"

"Kit."

"Whatever," the other woman bit off crisply. "I have no idea what you're talking about, nor do I think I want to know. Perhaps it would just be best if you left right now."

Kit pretended to think about her suggestion, then shook her head. "Nah. Not until we've cleared the air about something."

Faith didn't even blink as she asked, "And that would be?"

Kit leaned forward in her chair, cupped her hands daintily over her knees, smiled sweetly and said, "About how much it pisses me off when someone hurts somebody I care about."

For one long moment, Faith only gazed at Kit as

if she'd lost her mind. Then her expression softened just the tiniest bit, and she dropped her gaze to the hands she folded stiffly on her desk. "Miss Mc-Clellan—"

"Kit."

"Kit," Faith conceded. She glanced back up and said, more evenly this time, "I appreciate your motives, but whatever happened between your brother and me is really none of your business."

Kit eyed her thoughtfully for a moment in return before requesting, "Just tell me one thing."

Faith dipped her head forward in consideration. "All right. If I can."

"Do you like my brother?"

Faith hesitated before responding. At first, Kit thought she was going to try to lie about it, but surprisingly, the other woman nodded once, almost imperceptibly and said, "Yes. I like him very much."

"Then why do you refuse to see him?"

This time Faith hesitated not at all. "You couldn't begin to understand the reasons that I can't see your brother again."

"Try me."

Faith shook her head adamantly. "Unless you've lived with an alcoholic yourself you can't possibly imagine—"

"I have lived with an alcoholic," Kit interrupted again. "Holt started drinking when he was still in high school, and it went on until just a couple of years ago. I saw the way he acted, heard the things he said. I understand completely what living with an alcoholic is like. It's hell."

Faith shook her head. "You didn't fall in love with one. You weren't married to one. You didn't go one-on-one with him. You weren't in a situation where you had no one but yourself to rely on, no one but yourself to find comfort in. You had your family there to help you cope."

This time Kit was the one to answer crisply. "You obviously don't know my family." When Faith arched her eyebrows in surprise at the statement, Kit chuckled, but there wasn't an ounce of good humor in the sound. "I told you you're not the only one who can play the wounded martyr."

"You don't know what went on in my marriage," Faith pointed out, her voice softer now. "You can't know what it was like. Stephen was . . ." She inhaled a shaky breath, but didn't elaborate. Instead, she said, "There was a time in my life when I was a strong woman. I thought I could handle Stephen. I thought I could help him. I thought I could change him." She met Kit's gaze levelly. "I was wrong. And I paid for that . . . I paid for that with my soul. He took it away from me, piece by piece, a little more every day, until there was just nothing of me left."

Kit didn't flinch. "I wouldn't say there's nothing left. You seem pretty hardy to me."

Faith smiled sadly. "That's because you don't know me. You don't know what I was like before."

"I know enough to see that you're a woman who's trying to come to terms with what happened to her. Who's trying to put her life back together again. You haven't just given up on everything."

"Haven't I?"

Kit shook her head. "No. You haven't. If you'd given up, you wouldn't be working here now, trying to change something you see as wrong. You're fighting, Faith. Can't you see that? That's what this organization does. It fights. And you're a part of that."

The look in Faith's eyes became positively bleak, so dark, so cold, that Kit found herself wanting to physically reach out to her. "But there was a time in my life when I was so much more. When I—"

"That time is gone," Kit interjected. "Whatever went on in your marriage, it affected you. It changed you. Accept that and know that's over now. Now it's time to put that behind you and start new. To do that, you *have* to take chances. You *have* to have trust." She smiled. "You have to have faith, Faith."

When Faith said nothing to counter her assertion, Kit continued hopefully, "Look, Holt doesn't make excuses for what he was when he was drinking. He knows what he did to his family, to his wife, to everyone he came into contact with. But he's done his best to make amends. He got help, stopped drinking. He takes chances, has trust, has faith, every single day of his life. That's how he's getting through life. And sober, he's a good man. He deserves a chance to prove that to someone he cares very much about."

"I don't dispute the fact that he's a good man," Faith said. But before Kit could pounce on her concession, she added quickly, adamantly, *"When he's sober.* That's the point. I don't know what he's like when he's drunk. And I don't want to find out."

"You won't ever see that side of him," Kit vowed. "He's not that man anymore, and he never will be again."

"Can you guarantee that he'll never take another drink again, for the rest of his life?"

"Yes," Kit assured her. "I can."

Faith didn't look convinced. "You'll forgive me if I don't believe you."

"No, I won't forgive you."

The other woman gaped at her. "Pardon me?"

"I said I won't forgive you," Kit repeated. "You could have someone in your life right now who genuinely cares for you, who could potentially *love* you, if you'd allow him to. Don't you understand how important, how rare, that is? To be loved? Genuinely, truly loved?"

Faith shook her head. "No. I don't know how important that is. It's never happened to me."

Kit nodded, fully understanding. "But it *could* happen to you, don't you see? The possibility is there for you, if you'll just open yourself up to it and let it happen. Not everyone has that opportunity, to be loved for the simple fact of who they are. But you do. And right now you're just throwing it away without even giving it a chance."

Faith studied Kit for a long time in silence before she finally looked away. "Giving it a chance," she said quietly, "could cost me everything I've gained since Stephen's death. It's not much, but it's all I have to hold on to right now."

"Not giving it a chance could cost you even more. Faith," she added softly, sincerely, "whatever you're holding on to now, it's got to be exhausting doing it by yourself. You don't have to do it alone anymore. I don't know what to say to make you understand how very precious that is—to have someone there to help you. Someone there to cling to. To love. To love you back. Forever."

Kit realized then that she wasn't just talking about Faith's situation with Holt anymore. The advice she found it so easy to offer someone else, the solution that seemed so clear to her, was suddenly far more personal, and therefore far more impossible.

"Look," she said, standing, "maybe you're right.

Maybe this is none of my business. I didn't mean to intrude. I apologize. I just know that my brother cares for you very much. And I wanted to try to talk you into giving him a chance. Into giving yourself a chance. So that both of you might find happiness."

"Your brother has already tried to talk me into giving him a chance," Faith said. "What makes you think that anything you say will change my mind?"

"I don't know," Kit replied honestly. "Maybe because I've been where you are. I know how it feels to have someone you cared for, someone you trusted, turn on you. But I know my brother, too. Holt may have his faults, even in sobriety, but betrayal isn't one of them. You can trust him. Truly you can."

Faith said nothing in response right away, conceding neither victory nor defeat. For several long moments, the two women only stared at each other in silence, the late afternoon sun spilling through the blinds in shafts of pale yellow, gilding into fairy light the dust dancing in the air around them. When it seemed that their impasse would remain just that, Kit turned away and covered the distance to the door in four slow strides. But just as she settled her fingers over the knob, Faith's voice came softly from behind and halted her.

"And you, Kit," she said. "You say you've been where I am. If someone offered you a second chance, would you take it? *Could* you take it? Would you be able to trust that you wouldn't be betrayed again?"

Kit swallowed hard as she turned to meet the other woman's gaze. But she simply did not know how to answer. In a way, she *had* taken a second chance. And, just as before, the person she cared for had betrayed her. But it was Pendleton this time, she reminded herself. Unlike Michael Derringer, she loved Pendleton. And that changed everything. Didn't it?

"If you want to talk for some reason," she told Faith, "I'll be staying at the Seelbach for a few days."

The other woman looked puzzled. "Why are you staying in a hotel?"

Kit shrugged halfheartedly. "I'm in the middle of some traveling right now. It's just easier this way. But I'll be in town for another week." She smiled as she tugged the door open and took a step through it. Over her shoulder, she tossed out, "After that, I'm heading up to New Jersey for a few days. I've been invited to a wedding."

The week following Kit's disappearance passed like a slow boat to China, as far as Pendleton was concerned. No, wait—that wasn't exactly right. That metaphor had far too romantic a connotation, not to mention an appropriateness and possible reality he simply did not want to consider. He could visualize too clearly Kit all wrapped up in a blanket, wearing big sunglasses and a floppy straw hat, lounging in an Adirondack chair on the deck of a tramp steamer, while crew members with names like Sven and Bjorn and Helmut, dressed in little white shorts and knee socks, waited on her hand and foot.

Nuh-uh. No way would he let her get away with that.

So the week following her disappearance actually passed more like a . . . more like a . . . like a . . . hmmm . . . More like a kidney stone. Yeah, that was it. The week passed like a kidney stone. Painfully. Uncomfortably. *Sloooowly*. Always on his mind. And there wasn't a damned thing he could do about it but wait. And wait. And wait. And wait.

But the postcard he had hoped for never materialized. Nor had there been a letter. Nor a brief note, a phone call, a fax. No telegram. No Hallmark card, either. No e-mail. No jungle drums. Nary a smoke signal to be had. Not even a flare. Wherever Kit had gone, she clearly intended to stay gone this time, and for a lot longer than a few days. And all he could do was—

"Pendleton!"

Dammit. Why did McClellan, Sr. always interrupt him right when he got to the depressing, self-pitying part?

Pendleton had yet to tell his employer that his daughter had taken off for parts unknown. Not only was he not sure it was any of the CEO's business, but he was fairly certain his boss was somehow to blame for it. Even with the evidence of Sherry's wedding invitation staring him in the face, thereby making himself a key player in Kit's motivation for bolting, Pendleton had decided that the McClellans had put the *fun* in dys*fun*ctional. Therefore, *they* were the ones who were really to blame in this, and *not* Pendleton. Even if Pendleton could have prevented this whole idiotic mess just by telling Kit how much he loved her.

"Sir?" he responded halfheartedly to his boss's summons.

McClellan, Sr. eyed him warily. "Novak just made an excellent point about diversifying and upgrading proactive criteria. What do *you* think?"

What Pendleton thought, McClellan, Sr. didn't want to know. Frankly, he was getting awfully tired of all the corporate double-speak that had once rolled so fluidly off his tongue. He had some damned important things on his mind right now, for God's sake, and diversifying and upgrading proactive criteria sure the hell wasn't one of them.

So he met his boss's gaze levelly and said, "Sir, I have just one word to say to you."

McClellan, Sr. arched his eyebrows in expectation. "And that word would be?"

Pendleton narrowed his eyes in what he hoped was a convincing show of *je ne sais quois*. And he announced in a bold, where-no-man-has-gone-before voice, "Incentivizing."

His employer gazed back at him without expression for a moment, then began to nod slowly. "I like it. I like it very much. Incentivizing. Yes. That shows real insight."

Pendleton swallowed the gag reflex before it could make itself public. "Thank you, sir."

"Why don't you and Kit come round to the house tonight?"

Oh, great. "Sir?" he asked, stalling.

"You. Kit. My daughter. Come over for dinner tonight. Bart's home on leave, and Mick is supposed to be calling from Yemen."

Pendleton brightened. "Oh, so he's already made it to the countries beginning with a Y, has he?" he asked in an effort to stall some more. "That's got to feel good. Very manly, and all that."

"Pendleton."

"Yes, sir?"

"Are you and Kit coming or not?"

"Uh, no sir, I don't guess we will."

"Why not?"

"Because, sir, Kit's sort of, um . . . Well, she's . . . Actually, sir . . ."

"Spit it out, Pendleton."

Okay. If he insisted. "Kit's run off again."

"WHAT?!"

Atomic wind couldn't be more powerful than that one word was as it erupted from McClellan, Sr.'s mouth. Pendleton imagined himself in an anti-nuke suit and repeated, "Kit's gone, sir."

His employer shot to his feet with his son not far behind. "Gone?" he demanded as he thrust his fists onto the table. "Where the hell did she go?"

Pendleton shrugged, and with that simple gesture, he felt an enormous weight just tumble right off his shoulders. Wow. That felt really, really good. "I don't know," he said with a smile.

McClellan, Sr. glared at him. "You don't know?"

"No sir," he confirmed, his smile growing broader. "I have absolutely no idea. She just took off while I was at work one day, and I haven't heard from her since."

McClellan, Jr. stared at him, his expression, like his father's, one of stark, raving terror. "Well, when did she leave? How much of a head start does she have?"

Pendleton pretended to think about that. "Gee, I guess it's been a little over a week ago. Gosh, she could be *anywhere* by now, couldn't she?"

"And you didn't bother to tell us about this?"

Pendleton shrugged again, and any little pebbles of obligation and responsibility that might have been left just rolled right off. "Well, considering Kit's history of running away, I didn't think you guys would be too concerned about her."

"Not concerned about her?" This time the question came from McClellan, Sr. "Well, of course we're concerned about her! We have less than a month left to get her married!"

"Oh, that," Pendleton said mildly, leaning back in his chair. He cupped both hands behind his head in a gesture that indicated very clearly just how worried he was about the McClellans' financial state. Specifically, not one iota.

"*Oh, that*?" both McClellans echoed in one thunderous voice.

"Her mother's will thing, I mean," Pendleton clarified, though he was quite confident that no clarification was necessary. "You're worried about losing all that money, aren't you? Ninety-nine-point-four million dollars, right?" As blandly as he could, he added, "Wow. Golly. Gee. I completely forgot about that. You're right. I should have called you guys the moment I realized she was gone. Imagine my chagrin."

Out of nowhere, a bubble of something warm and wonderful fizzed up in Pendleton's midsection, effervescing in a tickle of pleasure he hadn't felt in a very long time. Freedom. That was what it was. He felt utterly and completely free, for the first time he could recall since childhood.

He suddenly realized that he didn't have to work for Hensley's anymore if he didn't want to. He no longer cared about whether his ex-wife was impressed by his earning power. He no longer had a point to prove. He didn't have to wheel and deal with the big boys and wear eight-hundred-dollar suits to be of value to anyone. He didn't have to make six figures and drive a bitchin' car to be important.

Though, mind you, he really did like his bitchin' car.

What was far more important than that, however, was the fact that he'd found infinitely more meaning elsewhere in his life. He had Kit. He loved

Kit. And Kit loved him. Nothing else in his life mattered except that.

Nothing.

Once he found her—and naturally, he would find her . . . eventually—they could settle down in their house in Old Louisville with Maury, and he could get a job doing . . . well . . . something. Something he would enjoy. Something where he could feel productive, could feel good about what he was doing. Where he could just be himself. Be appreciated for himself. Be loved for himself.

Yeah. That's the ticket.

"Sir?" he said as he stood and collected his things.

His boss still looked ready to explode. "Yes, Pendleton?" he asked through gritted teeth.

Pendleton smiled. "If you'll excuse me, I have something very important I need to do right now."

McClellan, Sr. fumed, and Pendleton paused for a moment to see if smoke would come out of his ears. Unfortunately, none did. But his boss demanded, "And that would be?"

Pendleton buttoned up his suit jacket and tucked his portfolio under his arm. "I need to find Kit and make her my wife."

Immediately, the storm cloud above the CEO evaporated, to be replaced by a chorus of glorious sunlight. "That's the spirit, Pendleton," McClellan, Sr. said with a victorious smile. "I should have realized you were only joking in that strange way of yours. I knew you were our man all along."

This time Pendleton was the one to glare. At his employer. "I'm *not* your man. The reason I'm going to marry your daughter is because I love her, not to keep you two . . ." Somehow, he managed *not* to say the word *bozos*. "To keep you two rolling in dough. But whether the wedding takes place in six days, or six months, that's entirely up to Kit."

"Pendleton . . ." McClellan, Sr.'s voice trailed off before he completed his sentence, but his warning was unmistakable.

And Pendleton ignored it. "Now, if you'll excuse me," he said again as he made his way around the table full of gaping, incredulous executive vice presidents, "I've got better things to do with my time than sit here and bullshit with you guys all day. Oh, and one more thing, sir."

"Yes, Pendleton?"

He hesitated just before opening the door to the conference room, no longer caring whether he insulted the man who employed him. "I quit. If you sorry sons of bitches want to make more money, you'll have to do it without me."

That said, Pendleton touched a finger to his forehead in salute, then exited gracefully and went to look for his wife.

Chapter 18

"She's out in the backyard with Mom and Dad."

Carny repeated the announcement she'd made over the phone the night before as Pendleton entered his parents' house. Filled with relief, affection, exasperation and so much more, he pulled his sister into a massive bear hug, and dropped his duffel bag onto the floor with a comfortable *thump*. An emotion so strong he dared not try to identify it shuddered through him, and for a moment, he could only cling to his sister and will his taut body to relax. Then he pushed himself to arm's length and cupped his hands over Carny's shoulders, studying the face that looked so much like his own.

Less than two months had passed since he'd last seen his sister, but she suddenly looked so much older than he remembered. Her brown eyes crinkled at the corners with the smile that lit her whole face, and her dark hair, half-in and half-out of a stubby ponytail, was kissed with bits of silver. Jeez, when had Carny started to go gray? he wondered. And if she was starting to show signs of aging herself—however appealing they were on her—how must he, three years older than she was—be faring himself?

He pushed the thought aside. "So Kit's here? She's safe?" he asked.

Only now was he beginning to realize how worried he'd been that Kit might be gone for good. At best, he had thought she'd taken off for the Caribbean again. Over and over, he had imagined her standing behind a bar in her sarong, being hit on by some jerk who wouldn't have a clue how to handle her. Or worse, who would have *more* than a clue how to handle her. The week and a half that had passed since she'd left felt more like a decade and a half to Pendleton, and even now, he couldn't quite believe he had her back.

Of course, he reminded himself, he didn't have her back. Not completely. Not yet. But once they talked, once he explained everything, once he told her how he felt about her, he was certain everything would be all right. And somehow, it was just so appropriate that she had turned up here, at his parents' house. Kit being with his family somehow made perfect sense, felt totally right.

Besides, he recalled with some distaste, Sherry's wedding was only three days away. And, hey, Kit had been invited, after all. Social creature that she was, he was sure she was planning on making an appearance. Or a spectacle. Whatever.

Carny chuckled, jerking him out of his ruminations. "Kit's safe enough for the time being," she said. "But if she keeps telling Dad how to cook ribs, he's gonna send her straight to the moon."

Pendleton laughed, too. His father was generally a good-natured, easygoing man, the kind of person who made immediate friends with everyone he encountered. Unless you tried to come between him

and his barbecue. Do that, and Axel Pendleton of
Deptford, New Jersey became more temperamental
than a Paris-dwelling, cordon bleu chef.

"She's actually a very good cook," he told his
sister. "She could probably teach him a thing or
two."

Carny chuckled some more. "Yeah, I know.
Mom says Kit hasn't let her cook a meal since she
arrived."

For some reason, that didn't surprise him at all.
For all Kit's wealthy, upwardly mobile upbringing,
there was an earthiness, a down-home quality
about her that was completely inborn. Her
mother's doing, he supposed. As well as Kit performed in high-brow social settings, she was still
too real a human being to ever be too good for
something like a blue-collar, South Jersey kitchen.

"I'm sorry no one called you before now," Carny
said. "I just found out about it myself last night.
Evidently, she's been here since Monday, but somehow she talked Mom and Dad into not telling you
she was here. Said she wanted to surprise you."

Pendleton could believe that. Kit could probably
talk Queen Elizabeth into abdicating her throne
and giving it to Izzy the charwoman. "She's been
staying here at the house?" he asked his sister.
Somehow, that didn't surprise him, either. Hey,
he'd seen for himself that she had a propensity for
such things.

"She started off up at the Holiday Inn," Carny
told him, "but Mom talked her into checking out a
couple nights ago and taking your old room instead."

Pendleton paled. "*My* old room?" he demanded.
"Kit's been sleeping in *my* old room? Why not *your*
old room? Those pink ruffled curtains are more ap-

propriate for her than my race car wallpaper."

Carny gaped at him as if his brain had just come oozing out his ears. " 'Cause Mom knows how I am about my Barbie collection, you big jerk."

Oh, yeah. He'd forgotten. Anybody who came between Carny and her Barbies, even now, wound up with a little plastic high heel sticking out of their nose.

Reluctantly, Pendleton released his sister. "It's good to see you again," he said. "I've missed you and Joey, and Mom and Dad. A lot."

"We've missed you, too. But be warned—Joey's still majorly pissed at you for moving away before the end of hockey season."

"I'll make it up to him. He can come visit in a couple weeks for the Kentucky Derby. Apparently, it's something of a big deal down there."

"So, you liking it all right in your new town?" she asked, the question carrying far more importance than her voice let on.

So Pendleton took a moment to really think about it. South Jersey was in his blood, and Philadelphia was, to his way of thinking, the greatest city ever erected on the planet. Every milestone of significance in his young life had occurred within a few miles of the very spot where he now stood. He'd taken his first step, ridden his first school bus, cracked his first bat, copped his first feel, all within blocks of his parents' house.

Yet somehow, this place didn't quite feel like home anymore. He didn't know exactly why that was. It just felt different now. There was no longer a pull on his soul toward the history he had here. Instead, he felt tugged toward the future, wherever Kit McClellan called home.

"Yeah," he finally told Carny. "I like it just fine."

She nodded. "Maybe I'll come down with Joey and go to that Derby thing. And Mom and Dad, too." She smiled one of those all-knowing sister smiles. "Or maybe we'll all just wait and come down this summer. Like for the wedding, maybe."

He smiled back. "Wedding? What wedding? Whatever could you be talking about, Carny?"

Carny wiggled her brows playfully. "Yours. Kit's. Whatever."

He was about to comment when a cry from the direction of the backyard silenced him. His father was yelling at the top of his lungs, something about . . . cumin?

Carny rolled her eyes. "Not again," she muttered. "Mom says they've been having this argument ever since the night Kit arrived."

Even knowing Kit as well as he did, Pendleton found this news to be a trifle confusing. "They've been arguing about cumin?"

Carny nodded. "Yeah."

But she said nothing more to elaborate, only spun around and made her way through the living room toward the kitchen, with Pendleton following helplessly on her trail.

"Will you just trust me on this, Axel?" Kit's voice rose from the backyard. "For once in your life? Don't be such a Pendleton."

As he followed the sound toward the open back door, some great weight in Pendleton's chest shifted aside. Yeah, he thought, it was definitely good to be home.

Kit studied Pendleton's father in the waning light of a day in the life of New Jersey, and marveled again at how much he looked like his son. A bit softer around the middle, maybe, a little grayer and thinner on top, but all in all, a striking likeness. In twenty-five or thirty years, she thought, this would be Pendleton. Man of the House. Head of the Household. Master of the Suburban Domain.

Keeper of the Holy Barbecue.

Axel stood on the minuscule cement patio, gripping a Rolling Rock beer in his bare hand and a pair of tongs in the one that was covered with a lobster claw oven mitt. The apron protecting his plaid shirt and sans-a-belt trousers read, *Who invited all these tacky people?* And somehow, even having spent only a few days in the man's company, Kit felt closer to him than she'd ever felt to her own father.

"Now, Axel," she said, "don't be so hasty. We've been over this before. I don't know why you refuse to even consider the possibility that just a touch of cumin might improve your special sauce."

"Don't nobody mess with my special sauce, little girl." He shook his tongs at her. "This barbecue sauce took ribbons eight years straight at the Deptford Township Fall Festival."

She adopted her most solicitous smile and tried again. "But a little cumin would go a long way toward—"

"No."

His reply was succinct, to the point, and final. Kit shook her head. Fine. She gave up. No cumin. "How about a little rosemary?" she asked.

"No. No cumin, no rosemary."

She opened her mouth to say something else, but he cut her off with a quick swipe of his tongs.

"And no marjoram, either. Foggiddabbuddit, Kit."

Foggiddabbuddit, she had learned on her first day in New Jersey, was Northeastern for *Forget about it*.

Kind of like *y'all* was Southeastern for *youse guys*.

"But, Axel—"

"No," he said again. "My recipe ain't gonna change in this lifetime." He eyed her warily. "And it better not change after I go to my reward, either, you hear what I'm sayin'?"

"All right, all right," she conceded reluctantly. "Boy, you are so much like your son, you know that?"

That, at least, made Axel smile. "Rocky? Yeah, he's a good kid."

As if conjured by the comment, a familiar voice called from behind, "Yo, Dad!"

A huge grin split Axel's face at the same time Kit's smile fell. They spun around as one to find Pendleton striding casually across the backyard, one arm slung over Carny's shoulder, the hand of the other shoved deep into the pocket of his jeans. The sleeves of his faded blue sweatshirt were shoved up nearly to his elbows, exposing one of those incredibly sexy forearms that even now, in the middle of a family gathering, made Kit go hot and bothered inside.

"Sonny!" Axel cried, throwing his arms up into the air.

He set down his tongs and beer and went to meet his son, intercepting him halfway across the yard. Immediately, fiercely, both men embraced. And not one of those phony, he-man, homophobic embraces, either—the kind where the guys slap each other silly on the back for a few seconds before springing uncomfortably apart. But a truly heartfelt hug, both men gripping each other tightly for a solid minute before letting go.

In the meantime, Irene Pendleton cried out happily and jumped up from the chaise longue where she'd been reading a recent romance, and she thrust herself into what became a three-way, marathon hug. Behind them, Carny shook her head and laughed, before she, too, came forward and threw her arms around the lot of them as best she could. And then the Axel Pendletons of Deptford, New Jersey clung together as if their lives depended on it.

Something stung Kit's eyes suddenly, and she quickly swiped a hand across them. When she looked up again, it was to find Pendleton gazing at her over the top of his mother's head, and somehow she received the distinct impression that he wanted her to join in the fray.

Yeah, right, she thought. She'd probably suffocate in a huddle like that.

So she only picked up Axel's discarded tongs and flipped the ribs over to the other side. Hey, no reason to interfere in a family thing.

She felt, more than saw, the group disperse, and likewise only sensed Pendleton's approach. She told herself to be a man about it, to meet him head-to-head on his own turf. Just because she'd fallen in love with another guy who only wanted her for her money, hey, what was so terrible about that? It wasn't like she hadn't already traveled this road before, right? She ought to be used to it by now. Next stop, heartbreak. She should have seen it coming from a mile away.

Pendleton came to a halt with a good six feet of lawn and patio still separating them, then softly greeted her, "Hi."

She dropped her gaze back down to the grill. "Your folks promised they wouldn't call you until I told them it was okay."

"They didn't call me. Carny did."

Kit nodded. That's right, she recalled. Carny never had stated in so many words that she would abide by Kit's request. Sisters were always such troublemakers. She should know that by now.

"Well," she said softly, still forcing herself not to look at Pendleton. "I suppose I should apologize, but at least this way you get to visit with your family on Daddy's dime, don't you?"

"You think that's the only reason I came?"

Unable to stop herself, Kit glanced up to look at him, and immediately wished she hadn't. He looked tired. Anxious. Sad. Then again, he'd had some dizzy dame turning his life upside-down for a couple of months now, hadn't he? How else was he supposed to look?

"That's right, I almost forgot," she lied, not even bothering to feign good humor. "Your ex-wife is getting married this weekend, isn't she? Wouldn't want to miss that, would you?"

"Why wouldn't I?"

His response stumped her. Hey, if *he* didn't know the answer to that one, she sure wasn't going to try and jog his memory. In spite of that, she heard herself say, "Well, there is that small matter of you still being in love with her. Of you wanting to show her that you've still got what it takes to flex PR and push pencils with the big boys."

He smiled, a wistful kind of smile unlike any Kit had ever seen from him. "Although I have to confess that there was a time not too long ago when I did indeed fantasize a nice little revenge about attending Sherry's wedding with some big, busty, bitchy blond—"

"Oh, and hey," Kit interrupted, "with me, you got three out of four, anyway, didn't you?"

His smile fell some, but his eyes were still warm

and affectionate as he watched her. "I didn't come up here to go to Sherry's wedding, either. Frankly, that's the last place I want to be."

Kit nodded. "Yeah, I bet. So then if you didn't come up here for that," she rushed on, "I guess you wanted to rescue your folks from the crazy McClellan daughter, didn't you? But I promise you, Pendleton, although I might do some crazy stuff, I'd never hurt anyone."

"Oh, sure. That's what you *say*."

Uncertain what he meant by the comment, Kit let it slide. "I just needed to get away from Louisville for a little while, that's all. After hearing you talk about your family, your hometown, I was kind of . . . curious. It sounded . . . nice." She lifted a shoulder and let it drop. "I wanted to see for myself."

"Why did you need to get away from Louisville for a while?" he asked. "Things were just starting to . . . to . . ." He waved a hand restlessly in front of himself, as if he were trying to pull the proper word out of thin air. "To go right. Between us, I mean."

Her eyes began to sting again, so she dropped her gaze back down to the barbecue. Axel seemed to realize where her attention lay, because he suddenly appeared at her side and snatched the tongs out of her hands.

"Why don't you and Rocky go talk?" he said, nudging her aside with an elbow that was in no way subtle. "I can handle things here."

Instead of arguing with Axel's suggestion, Kit dropped her arms to her side and her gaze to the ground, and wandered toward the back stoop. Not surprisingly, Pendleton followed right behind her. And with Carny and Irene having retreated into the house, the two of them were left pretty much alone.

"Mind if I ask what you're doing here at my parents' house?" he asked again.

There was really no easy answer, Kit thought. She was doing a lot of things here. She was taking a little vacation, enjoying a small break from her usual reality. She was visiting a part of the country she'd never seen before, observing a slice of life that she hadn't known existed. She was making friends and having some truly enlightening conversations. She was feeling like a human being, living life instead of struggling with it for a change.

And she was falling in love with Pendleton's family in much the same way that she had fallen in love with Pendleton.

Which was the last thing she had intended to do. Thinking about it now, she wondered if maybe her whole reason for heading north instead of south this time hadn't simply been that she wanted to exorcise Pendleton from her system by witnessing the source of his genesis. With some of his mystique removed, she'd thought, maybe the man himself would cease to be interesting.

Naturally, the maneuver had backfired, just as everything else in her life had backfired since Pendleton had entered it. Instead of disdaining his origins, she found herself charmed by them. Instead of viewing his family as alien life forms with whom she couldn't possibly ever relate, Kit found herself feeling more comfortable with them than she did with her own relatives. Instead of demystifying and commonizing Pendleton, her visit to his hometown only made him that much more intriguing, that much more appealing.

Daggone it, nothing worked the way it was supposed to anymore.

"Kit?"

With an impatient sound, she snapped her head around. "What?" she demanded.

"What'd I do?" he asked. "Just tell me that. What did I do that made you run off without a trace to, of all places, Deptford?"

She expelled a restless sigh, then returned her attention to the backyard. "I can't decide what's made me feel more foolish," she said softly. "The fact that you and Daddy cut a deal, the fact that I didn't even see it coming, or the fact that I let myself fall in love with you."

He said nothing in response to her revelation, so she braved a glimpse in his general direction. His face, she saw, was impassive, completely devoid of any expression. And his voice was nearly silent as he asked, "What did you say?"

For a moment, she only stared at him in silence. Then, corralling what little moxie she had left, she said, "True or false, Pendleton? My father offered to pay you a substantial amount of money if you married me before the deadline stipulated by my mother's will, thereby ensuring that the family would keep the Hensley millions."

A muscle twitched in his jaw, and his eyes darkened dangerously. "Why do you ask that?"

"Just answer the question. True or false?"

For a moment, she didn't think he was going to respond. Then, very, very quietly, he said, "True."

If she'd thought it had hurt to hear her father say that, she'd been way, way off. Because nothing could have prepared her for the slash of pain that twisted in her heart at hearing Pendleton verify it.

"Oh, God," she said, nearly choking on the words.

"Kit, you don't under—"

"True or false?" she interrupted him, before he could say anything to make matters worse. "You flat-out turned the offer down, said you were outraged by such a proposal, and told my father to go to hell."

Her question was met with another unsettling silence, then, even more quietly than before, Pendleton said, "False."

She swallowed hard as a chill wound through her body. "True or false?" she said softly, having no idea where she found the strength to continue. "You never really loved me at all."

"Absolutely false. Kit, I—"

"Oh, Pendleton," she said. "You've never lied to me. Why start now?"

"Kit, I'm not lying to you. I do love you. Don't you see that?"

She chuckled dryly. "No. I don't see that. What I see is a man just like Michael Derringer."

His eyes went flinty cold. "I am *nothing* like Michael Derringer."

She didn't—couldn't—say anything in response to that.

"How did you find out about your father offering me money to marry you?" he asked. "Did he tell you that?"

She folded her denim-clad knees up before her and wound her arms tightly around them, as if doing so might keep her from falling apart. Then, because she suddenly felt restless—and because she wanted to be far away from Pendleton—she scooted her body backward until she felt the cool roughness of the bricks abrading her back through her sweater. Strange that she even noticed the sensation outside her body, seeing as how she'd gone numb inside.

"Although I certainly wouldn't put it past Daddy to throw something like that in my face," she said softly, "no. He didn't tell me that. I overheard him and Holt talking in the library that night at Cherrywood when I went back in to get my purse." She turned to face Pendleton, and somehow managed to meet his gaze without flinching. "I heard Daddy tell Holt that the day after I moved in with you, he offered you a substantial bonus if you married me."

Pendleton nodded. "That's true. He did."

Wow. It hurt even more to hear him say it a second time. She hadn't thought that was possible. "And since my father was so confident that night that you would make an honest woman of me by the deadline, I can only assume that you took him up on his offer."

"That," Pendleton told her, his gaze never faltering, "is *not* true."

She opened her mouth to object, but he quickly cut her off. "Kit, I didn't say *anything* when your father offered me his bribe. I couldn't. Hell, all I wanted to do was pop him in the chops. I couldn't believe he would . . . would *barter* you like that. I was afraid if I opened my mouth, it would be to call him every name I ever learned in a Jersey schoolyard." He lifted one shoulder and let it drop, then offered her a little smile. "So I did like my mother always taught me. Since I couldn't say something nice, I didn't say anything at all. And I let him assume whatever he wanted to.

"Hey, you're the one who wanted to string him along," he added, "make him think things were going his way so he'd leave you alone. What makes what I did any different than what you did?"

Kit smiled sadly in response. "Nice try, Pendleton. But it ain't gonna wash."

"You'd believe what your father said before you'd believe what I said?"

Well, gee, when he put it like that . . .

"Yeah," she said softly. "I think I would."

His eyes iced over at that. "Then you're the one who's a liar, Kit, not me."

She gaped at him. "Me? What did I lie about?"

"A minute ago, you told me you'd fallen in love with me."

She felt her cheeks burn at the reminder. Unable to tolerate the fierceness of his gaze, she dropped hers to the ground. "Yeah, so?" she asked softly.

"So if you'd take your old man's word over mine, if you'd trust him, and not me, then there's no way you could be in love with me."

She still couldn't look at him. But she could say quietly, "Oh, Pendleton. You are so wrong. You have no idea."

"Then have a little faith in me, will ya?"

She wished she could. Truly, she did. But she couldn't quite make herself believe him.

"I want to marry you, Kit."

She chuckled derisively. "Yeah, I bet you do. As soon as possible, too, right?"

"Wrong."

"What?"

She glanced back up to find him studying her with an intensity that made her uncomfortable. He wasn't smiling. He didn't look happy. But he did look dead serious.

"I said, 'Wrong,' " he repeated. "I mean, yeah, I want to marry you, but you're the one who's going to name the date. If you want to get married tomorrow, I'll call my cousin Sal's uncle-in-law, who happens to be a judge, right now, and see how fast we can make it happen. But if you want to wait, for however long, I'll wait.''

She narrowed her eyes at him. ''What are you saying?''

''I'm saying that I want *you*, not your family's money. I want to spend the rest of my life with *you*. I love *you*. Why is that so hard for you to believe?''

''You'd honestly marry me after the deadline?'' she asked, incredulous. ''But I won't have any money then. I'll be broke. I won't even have a job.''

''And your point would be . . . ?''

''I'll have nothing, Pendleton.''

''Hey, you'll have me,'' he said, a genuine smile dawning on his face. ''Then again, I'm not the greatest catch around, myself. I'm kind of unemployed right now.''

She gasped. ''Daddy fired you?''

He shook his head. ''Nah. I quit.''

She gasped again, louder this time. ''You quit?''

''No offense, Kit, but I didn't much like working for your family. I think I'd rather look around for something else.''

''Like what? Where?''

He shrugged again. ''Wherever you want. Although I have to admit that Louisville has kind of grown on me. I like our house there, and—''

''*Our* house?''

''And there's Maury to think about,'' he went on blithely. ''Don't want to disrupt the little guy's life any more than we have to.''

''Hey, who's taking care of Maury, anyway?'' she

asked, sidetracking for a moment, because she suddenly felt way, way off-course.

"Holt. He's not nearly as steamed at me as your father is. Though, mind you, he's none too happy about losing a hundred million bucks."

"Ninety-nine-point-four," Kit corrected him automatically.

"Still, I think he's more worried about you."

That, Kit knew, was open to debate. Still, it was nice to think that maybe her brother was coming around, learning that there really was more to life than money. If only Faith Ivory would give him a chance. That would go light-years toward bringing him around.

"Anyway," Pendleton went on, "the main thing is that you and I are together. You have to believe that, Kit. You said it yourself—I've never lied to you. I will never, ever, lie to you. If you look deep inside yourself, you'll realize you know that's true. I love you. I . . . love . . . you. If you look deep inside yourself, you'll know that's true, too."

She came so close to believing him. So very close. But she just couldn't take that final step that would carry her over to his side. Even looking deep inside herself, she couldn't quite find the faith, the trust, that was necessary for the lifelong commitment he was talking about.

"Pendleton," she said, hardly able to hear her own voice, "I can't do it. I wish I could, but . . . I can't. I'm sorry. I just can't."

His expression told her he wasn't much surprised by her response. He smiled a little sadly, and extended his hand toward her. "Come on," he said. "I want to show you something."

Even feeling the way she did, there was no way she could deny him. Feebly, she started to lift her hand, and Pendleton reached out to meet her more than halfway. He curled his fingers around hers capably, possessively, lovingly. Then he pushed himself to his feet and pulled Kit up with him.

And although his eyes never left hers, he called over his shoulder, "Yo, Dad!"

Axel looked up, clearly surprised by the summons. "Yeah?"

"How're those ribs coming?"

His father glanced down briefly, then back up again. "Just about done."

Pendleton nodded and continued to look at Kit, but his words were still clearly intended for his father. "How long has it been since you and Mom had dinner with the Robys next door?"

" 'Bout a week. Why?"

"Why don't you and mom and Carny treat Mr. and Mrs. Roby to a nice rib dinner tonight?"

Axel smiled knowingly. "You know, Sonny, I was just thinkin' that exact same thing. You remember how much Denise Roby likes her ribs."

Pendleton nodded. "Yeah, I remember."

"And Dick Roby, well . . . foggiddabbuddit."

"Dad?"

"Yeah?"

"Think you could collect Mom and Carny and get lost for a couple hours?"

"Sure thing, Rocky. Just gimme five minutes."

Chapter 19

They were five minutes that Kit and Pendleton spent standing at the foot of the back porch, staring at each other in silence. And as each one of those minutes passed, all he could think was that he'd never seen her looking more beautiful, more lovable. Why Kit couldn't envision herself the same way, Pendleton couldn't imagine. But somehow, some way, he'd make her understand exactly what kind of woman she was. And what he had up his sleeve right now—literally—was going to go a long way toward proving to her just how important she was.

Only when the other Pendletons had waved goodbye and closed the gate behind them did she finally break the silence. "I can't believe your family does what you ask them to do. You have them trained so well."

He shrugged. "They only want what's best for me."

She eyed him thoughtfully. "And what would be best for you, Pendleton?"

Hey, that was an easy one. "You."

Kit started to shake her head, but he tugged on

her arm and led her toward the back door.

"Come on," he repeated.

"Why?" she asked. "What is it you need to show me?"

"Just come on," he said again, weaving his fingers snugly with hers. "You'll see."

He thought she was going to balk, but after only a small hesitation, she swept the hand that wasn't holding his forward, indicating he should precede her through the back door. Then, her footsteps dragging only a little bit, she followed him into the house. Then through the kitchen. Then through the dining room. Then down the hall.

Pendleton didn't stop moving forward until he reached his old bedroom, which his parents had changed not one bit since he'd moved out of it to go to college almost fifteen years before. The walls were still decorated with faded blue race car wallpaper, and the twin bed was still covered with a red chenille bedspread. The windowsill played host to a half-dozen models of World War II tanks, the bookcases were overflowing with Hardy Boys mysteries and back issues of *Road and Track*, and his desk was virtually obscured by an elaborate HO setup.

Man, he'd always loved this room. And having Kit here with him now fulfilled an adolescent dream of his that he'd never thought would be reality. He closed the door behind them, so that fantasy wouldn't be disturbed.

"Sit down," he told her as he released her hand.

She watched him warily for a moment, then began to make her way to the chair by his desk.

"Not there," he said. "On the bed."

She whipped around to face him. "Oh, I don't *think* so."

He held up his hands, chest high, palms out, in a gesture of surrender. "I have no intention of taking advantage of you," he told her. Then, after a meaningful pause, he qualified, "Until you tell me to."

She lifted her chin defiantly. "That's not going to happen."

He smiled indulgently. "We'll see. Sit."

Miraculously, she did as he asked without further argument, perching on the side of his bed near the foot. But instead of sitting still, she lifted the bedspread and reached between the mattress and box springs, feeling around as if searching for something.

"Oh, by the way," she said, "my first night here, while I was searching your room, I found something that belongs to you."

"You searched my room?" he asked, wondering why he was surprised. "You violated my boyhood domain?"

She kept feeling around beneath the mattress, but met his gaze with an expression that clearly stated, *Well, duh.* "Ah-ha," she said before Pendleton could comment. Her hand ceased its movement, then, with one swift gesture, she withdrew a battered, dog-eared glossy magazine, turned to the middle of it, and unfolded the naked woman dwelling within. "In addition to eighty-seven cents in change and a fossilized Milky Way that was stuck behind one of your bookcases, I found this."

Pendleton smiled wistfully. "Miss January 1979."

She arched her eyebrows in surprise. "You remember?"

"Oh, you bet."

"This is your idea of the perfect woman, I suppose."

He shook his head. "Nah. That was my idea of the perfect woman when I was thirteen. I was an idiot then."

"I see."

"But until you came along, she was the only woman I ever brought to this bed."

Kit quickly refolded the centerfold and stuffed the magazine back under the mattress. "I don't want to know."

"Aw, come on. Sure you do. Because you're about to take Miss January's place. In my bed. In my heart. In my life."

"In your dreams."

"Yeah, there too."

She narrowed her eyes at him, but said nothing more. So Pendleton reached behind himself with one hand and bunched his sweatshirt in his fist, pausing only long enough to make his intentions perfectly clear. Evidently, he succeeded, because Kit's eyes widened to the size of silver dollars.

"What do you think you're doing?" she demanded.

He hesitated, but didn't release his shirt, making it obvious that he intended to snatch the garment over his head. Still, just in case she didn't understand, he told her, "I'm taking my shirt off."

"Oh, no, you're not," she said.

He tugged once, hard, and pulled the garment over his head. "Oops," he countered easily. "Guess you were wrong. Guess I am taking my shirt off." He jostled his arms so that the sweatshirt scrunched down, revealing the T-shirt he wore beneath. Then he scooted it down over his hands, wadded it up in a ball, and turned halfway around to toss it toward a basketball hoop that hung on the back of his bedroom door. It fell through easily, scoring a two-pointer quite nicely.

"*Ye-esss*," he murmured as he turned back around to Kit.

"Well, don't you dare take your other shirt off," she commanded.

In response to her edict, Pendleton reached behind himself again, this time bunching his T-shirt in his fist.

"Pendleton . . ." she said, her voice laced with warning. "Don't . . . you . . . dare."

In one smooth move, he removed his T-shirt, too, pausing with it wrapped around his upper arms, obscuring his naked chest. "Oops," he said again, smiling. "Guess you were wrong about that one, too."

Kit stood, both hands clenched into fists at her sides, clearly intending to bolt.

"Sit," Pendleton instructed her.

She shook her head. "If you're not going to do what I tell you to do, then I don't have to do what you tell me to do."

"You're not going anywhere until I've shown you what I need to show you."

Her cheeks suddenly stained with a blush of pink that Pendleton found *very* becoming. "Thanks, but I've already seen it," she said.

He wiggled his eyebrows suggestively. "Not like this, you haven't."

"Pendleton would you just—"

He shed his T-shirt completely then, tossing it aside, and Kit's mouth immediately quit running. It didn't close, but it did stop running. And then she only gaped at him, her gaze fixed intently on his chest. A specific part of his chest, as a matter of fact. The part where kids put their hands when they say the Pledge of Allegiance to the flag.

Right where his new tattoo was.

"Oh, my God," she whispered. "Is that real?"

He rotated his left arm slowly, working out some of the faint achiness he still felt in the muscles beneath the spot where the week-old decoration lay. "Yeah. It's real."

Kit only shook her head in silence as she approached him, her gaze never leaving the illustration of not one, but *two* big ol' nasty cherubs hovering on each side of a heart. As she drew nearer, she lifted her hand toward the tattoo, her fingers curled gingerly in preparation of touching it. At the last minute, though, she halted, turning her gaze up to meet his.

"Is it okay?" she asked. "If I touch it, I mean?"

"Why, Miss McClellan," he said with a smile. "I thought you'd never ask."

With a shaky smile of her own in return, she extended her hand and traced her fingertips gently over the words inscribed within the heart. Not Kit. Not Katherine. What Pendleton had had the tattoo artist inscribe was *Katherine Atherton McClellan Pendleton*.

"Oh, Pendleton," she murmured, her eyes filling up to brimming with tears. "I can't believe you did this."

"The pain factor was *enormous*," he told her. "It hurt like a mother. Not to mention the fact that they had to shave my chest to put it there. Do you know what it's like for a man who's entering the hair-loss phase of his life to watch while someone shaves his chest?"

She shook her head, laughing softly. "No. I have no idea what that's like." A single, fat tear spilled from each of her eyes, tumbling down her face in a slow stream. "But I do know what it's like to have someone fall in love with me. Pendleton . . ." Gingerly, she brushed her fingers over the tattoo again. Then, very, very quietly, she repeated, "I can't believe you did this. I can't believe you . . ."

As her words trailed off, he brushed his thumbs over each of her cheeks, wiping away her tears. Immediately, however, two more took their place. "What can I say?" he asked softly. "Love makes a guy do crazy things."

She smiled. "You really do love me. You love *me*."

The fact that she said the words as a statement, and not a question, indicated that Kit had come a long, long way in her view of things. He cupped her jaw with his hand and dipped his head forward, brushing his lips tenderly over her cheek. "Yeah," he said quietly when he pulled back to gaze upon her face, "I really do love you."

She swallowed hard, her eyes never leaving his. Then, in a soft murmur, she said, "Pendleton?"

"Yeah?"

"Take advantage of me."

He smiled. "Well, okay. If that's what it takes to make you happy."

As if she couldn't wait for him, Kit pushed herself up on tiptoe and covered his mouth with hers, scooping her fingers into his hair, urging his head down for a more complete taste of him. Where their previous joining had been slow, leisurely and tentative, Pendleton found himself wanting a union this time that was fast, intense, and decisive. And considering the demand in Kit's kiss, not to mention the wanting inside him that came with more than a week's separation between them, he felt pretty certain that that was exactly what they were going to have.

Evidently, Kit was pretty certain of that, too, because she removed her hands from his hair long enough to cross her arms over her torso and grab the hem of her sweater. Unfortunately, she seemed less willing to remove her mouth from his, and once her sweater was over her arms, it only made it as far as her neck. No matter, Pendleton thought as he moved his hands behind her back to deftly unhook her brassiere. They could work around this. They could.

She pulled her arms from the straps of her bra, and that, at least, fell to the floor. Then, as she went to work on the buttons of his fly, he lowered the zipper on hers. Awkwardly, they undressed each other as well as they could, then finally, finally, Kit pulled away long enough to drag her sweater over her head and toss it to the floor. Pendleton started to move in for another mating of the mouths, when Kit lifted a hand, index finger extended upward, to stop him.

"Wait," she said.

"Wait?" he repeated incredulously. "But I came all this way just so you and my tattoo could become intimately acquainted."

"Hold that thought."

She smiled as she turned her back on him, and he had to admit that observing her from this new angle had its advantages. Hey, what could he say? Kit had a great tushie.

"I found something else when I was violating your boyhood domain the other night," she told him. "Something that might come in handy now."

He watched as she moved toward the bookcase and briefly scanned the shelves before removing a copy of *Carnal Knowledge*. After opening it, she withdrew a length of condoms and dangled them from thumb and forefinger for his inspection. Oh, man. He'd forgotten all about those. Talk about your wishful adolescent thinking.

"Those have got to be fifteen years old," he told her.

"Yeah, but latex means never having to say you're sorry, doesn't it?"

"I don't know. Does it?"

"Guess we'll find out, won't we?"

She replaced the book and strode naked toward him, and just like that, Pendleton was hard as a rock and ready to roll. Unbelievable. Never had a woman had such an immediate, unequivocal effect on him. And he wondered then if he would ever get enough of Kit McClellan.

Probably not, he decided as she came to a stop in front of him. So it was a good thing they had the rest of their lives to enjoy each other.

She swung the band of condoms in front of his face and said, "You pick."

He closed his fist around them. "What happens if the one I pick turns out to be too old to rock and roll? What if it breaks? What if you wind up pregnant?"

She cocked her head to the side and eyed him with much consideration. "What if I do?"

Something warm and wonderful welled up inside him. "So you want to have kids?"

She cupped a hand over the tattoo, stroking her thumb back and forth across it in a way that made his heart race like the wind. "Yeah, I do," she told him. "If it's all the same to you, I'd just as soon wait a couple of years and have you to myself for a while. But if it happens before then . . ." She shrugged. "I think it would be a lot of fun to have a couple of little Pendletons running around the house."

"Well then," he said, tearing the first packet free from the chain, tossing the others over his shoulder, "say no more."

So she didn't. Instead, she smoothed her hand across his tattoo one final time, then skimmed it over his heart, up along his throat, and into the hair at his nape. And with a gentle nudge, she urged his head down to hers, and as she kissed him deeply, she backed both their bodies toward the bed.

Somehow, between the two of them, they stripped the bedspread, sheet and blanket down, then Pendleton folded his body over Kit's as she leaned back on the mattress. The moment they were prone, however, he rolled to his back, pulling her atop him. He flattened his palms over her shoulder blades, ran his fingertips along her spine, curled his palms over the twin curves of her fanny, dipped his fingers deftly into the crease that separated them.

"Oh," Kit murmured against his mouth. "Oh, Pendleton."

Hastily, he sheathed himself in the condom, then he lifted her hips over his rigid length and guided her down. The moment he was inside her, Kit straightened, arching herself forward as she reached backward to cup him in her fingers. He groaned out loud, filling his hands with her breasts, thumbing the velvety peaks to ripening. And then he moved inside her. Again and again and again. Kit caught his rhythm easily, matching her body's motions to his.

Incandescence. That was what the two of them

created together. And the fire built, higher and higher, until it threatened to consume them both. Just when Pendleton thought he would burst with the extremity of it, Kit cried out above him, stilling as a shudder rocked her body and went crashing through his. And then, he, too, fell silent, as wave after wave of euphoria washed over him. For one interminable moment, their slick bodies felt fused as one. Then Kit slumped forward, burying her face in his neck, and Pendleton wrapped his arms around her waist, fully intending to never let her go.

When they finally found the strength to move, she rolled from atop him and nestled against his side. He curled an arm around her neck, covered her breast with his hand, and pressed his lips to her temple. For long moments, they only lay in silence, catching their breath, collecting their thoughts. And, with one final sigh, Pendleton smiled.

"Do you know," he whispered breathlessly, "how many times I lay in this very bed as a teenager and envisioned some big blond under the covers with me?"

Kit smiled as she cupped her hand over the tattoo on his chest, but she said nothing.

He rubbed his cheek affectionately over the crown of her head, curling his fingers into her hair. "I love you, Katherine Atherton McClellan."

She propped herself up on one elbow and gazed down into his face. "And I love you, Rocky Pendleton."

He grinned. "Hey, you said my name without laughing."

She grinned back. "Yeah, well, I guess I should get used to it. You're going to be my husband after all. Still, you won't mind if I call you Pendleton, will you? I've kind of gotten used to it."

He shook his head. "I don't care what you call me. As long as you promise to have me and hold me till death do us part."

"Oh, I definitely intend to have you and hold you. Over and over again. It's going to take more than a little thing like death to keep me away from you."

He reached up to thread his fingers through her hair, over her cheek, along her jaw, across her mouth. "Then there's just one thing left to settle," he finally said.

She inhaled a shaky breath, then released it slowly. "The wedding date," she said softly.

He nodded. "The wedding date. Your call, Kit. Whatever you decide, I'm behind you all the way."

She ran her fingertip over his lower lip, smiling when he gave it an affectionate nip. "You'd take me even without the Hensley millions?" she asked.

His gaze fixed with hers. "You know I would."

She nodded. "Yeah, I do know that."

"Then it's your choice. You do whatever you have to do."

She continued to study him in silence for a moment, then she nodded again, slowly. "Okay," she said. "I will."

It was a beautiful day for a wedding. Kit stood before the mirror in her bedroom at Cherrywood, turning first to the left, and then to the right, as she observed herself in the cheval mirror one final time. Her bridal gown was a simple, ivory silk, sleeveless sheath, her only accessories a pair of tea-length, ivory silk gloves and the pearl necklace and earrings her mother had given her upon her high school graduation. Her hair was a mass of glimmering dark gold curls, and her face . . .

Kit smiled at the reflection in the mirror. She was, to her way of thinking, very, *very*, beautiful. And she was all set to go downstairs and marry the man she loved. The man who loved her.

Her man. Pendleton.

A quick knock at the door alerted her that the time was nigh. "Kit?" Holt called out from the other side. "The minister's here. You all ready?"

Oh, she'd never been more ready for anything in her life. "You bet," she called back.

When she opened the door, Holt's expression softened. "You look beautiful," he said with a smile.

She smiled back. "Yes, I do, don't I?" Then, with a quick perusal of her brother in his dove-gray morning wear, she added, "You don't look so bad yourself. If it weren't for the fact that Pendleton is such a spectacular specimen of manhood, I'd say there's a chance that the best man was going to outshine the groom today."

Holt thought about that for a moment before saying, "Thanks. I think."

"You're welcome."

"Where's your bouquet?"

"My maid of honor has it."

His expression clouded with confusion. "You have a maid of honor? This is the first I've heard about it. She wasn't at the rehearsal last night."

"No, she wasn't able to make it," Kit said easily as she tucked a stray curl behind her ear. "She had another appointment last night."

"Well, who is she?"

With a delicate tug on her gloves, Kit pushed

past her older brother. "She's downstairs. Come on."

Still gazing at his sister suspiciously, Holt crooked his elbow, and Kit graciously linked her arm with his. Then, together, they descended the stairs. Clearing the kitchen was something of a challenge, seeing as how a bevy of caterers was in there putting the finishing touches on a wedding feast to serve the fifty-odd guests seated outside. But without so much as a misstep, Kit and Holt survived the press, and made their way through the back door.

Beneath a cloudless sky of perfect azure, the backyard glittered like an emerald. And there, in the farthest corner, amid Lena Hensley McClellan's celebrated rose garden, was a wedding party that awaited the appearance of the bride.

Sister and brother strode forward, and Holt nodded at the chamber ensemble as they neared. Immediately, the delicate chords of Pachelbel's Canon lifted into the air.

"Oh, there's my maid of honor now," Kit said, lifting a hand to wiggle her fingers in greeting at the woman who approached.

She saw Holt follow her gaze, noticed how his mouth dropped open in surprise, and watched as his lips slowly curled into a smile. Faith Ivory did look stunning, Kit had to admit. Her lavender tea-length dress, otherwise identical to Kit's gown, suited her well.

"Hi," she said softly when she drew alongside Holt. She dropped and lifted her gaze a few dozen times, then smiled shyly.

"Hello," Holt greeted her back.

But, being the goofy older brother that he was, he said nothing more. Funny, Kit thought, how she'd never noticed that Holt was so prone to blushing.

"You're Kit's maid of honor?" he finally asked, dispelling the awkward silence.

Faith nodded coyly.

His gaze ricocheted from her to Kit and back again. "You'll forgive me if I find this development a little surprising. I didn't realize the two of you were even acquainted, let alone friendly."

This time Faith was the one whose glance flitted from face to face. Ultimately, however, her attention lingered on Holt. "Yes, well, your sister can be very . . . persuasive. About a lot of things."

Sparing a brief glance toward Kit, Holt replied, "Yeah, she sure can be." Then he returned his attention to Faith. "It's good to see you again."

"It's good to see you, too. It sounds crazy, but I've really missed you. Funny, isn't it? Since we hardly spent that much time together. I still missed you."

He shook his head, lifting his hand to skim his fingers lightly over her cheek. "That's not crazy. I missed you, too. Will you stick around for a while this time? Find out how things are going to develop?" He smiled. "Even if it is a conflict of interest for us?"

"It's not a conflict of interest anymore," she said. "I quit my job with the Temperance League. I'd like to start practicing law again."

"You'll have to tell me all about it."

She smiled. "I will. In fact, I think we have a lot to talk about."

He smiled back. "Good thing we have a lot of time to do it."

Kit cleared her throat as unobtrusively as she could. "Yes, well, as enchanting as I find this little reunion—after all, I *am* the one who's responsible for it, something I hope the two of you will remember when it comes time to name your firstborn daughter—you'll have that lot of time you want later. After my wedding. Right now, I'd like to get married if the two of you don't mind."

It was with obvious reluctance that Holt released his sister's arm and dismissed himself from the two women. Then he strode easily up the white satin aisle that spilled over the grass, and took his place beside the groom.

The *groom*, Kit marveled for perhaps the hundredth time since waking that morning. Now *there* was a word she'd never planned on using personally in her lifetime. But there he was all the same. Her groom. Pendleton.

The music swelled and segued into *Pictures at an Exhibition*, Faith's cue to make her own way down the aisle. With a brief smile for Kit, she handed over the modest bouquet of gardenias meant for the bride, then clasped her own smaller version to her abdomen and made her way slowly toward the rest of the wedding party.

And then it was Kit's turn. Once again the music changed, and as the tune blossomed into "That Man of Mine," she inhaled a deep breath and took a slow step forward. Then another. And another. And another.

And she didn't stop moving forward until she stood beside Pendleton, who, she had to admit, looked good enough to eat. Like Holt, he was dressed in formal morning coat and trousers. Unlike Holt, however, he stirred a need deep inside her that she wasn't sure would ever be satisfied. He lifted his hand toward her, and, without hesitation, Kit curled her fingers over his.

The minister inclined his head toward both of them, and then, in a voice full of warmth and promise, he recited the words that would bring Kit and Pendleton together for all eternity. And when he came to the part about speak now or forever hold your peace, only one person spoke up.

Kit.

"Hold on a sec," she said, lifting one gloved hand, index finger extended for emphasis. She turned gracefully to face her father.

"Although you know how much I absolutely *adore* that cheese dome you got us, Daddy, I think there's one more wedding present you promised me. Do you have it?"

Her father's face was impassive as he reached into his jacket and withdrew a slender white envelope from the breast pocket. Without a word, he approached his daughter and handed it to her.

"Thanks, Daddy," she sang out happily as she curled her fingers around it. Then she turned even further, scanning the group of guests seated on the bride's side. "Mr. Abernathy?" she called out to the elegantly dressed man in the second row.

Mr. Abernathy rose, and when he came forward, Kit handed the envelope to him. "Not that I think for a moment that Daddy would try to pull a fast one, but would you mind checking that over real quick, before Pendleton and I get on with the *I do* segment of our program?"

"I'd be delighted," Mr. Abernathy replied as he withdrew the document from inside.

For five full minutes, the wedding paused, while Hatton Abernathy inspected the wedding gift from Kit's father.

Finally, he looked up and nodded. "Everything is in perfect order, Miss McClellan. At the trust's expiration next week, Mrs. McClellan's estate shall revert to the family as she indicated. And over the next twenty years, Hensley's Distilleries, Inc. will donate a total of ninety-nine-point-four million dollars to the six charities of which your mother was so fond, in addition to their usual philanthropy."

Kit smiled. "Thank you, Mr. Abernathy."

Her father grumbled beside her. "Don't you think there's someone else you should be thanking other than Abernathy?"

Kit turned to face her father and smiled. "Yes," she said. "Yes, I do. Thank you, Daddy. Thank you for agreeing to the terms I asked for. And thank you for Pendleton, too."

And then she leaned forward and brushed her lips over her father's cheek. When she pulled back, Holt McClellan, Sr. nodded gruffly once and returned to his seat, with Hatton Abernathy following immediately behind.

After that, nothing in heaven or on earth could have stopped Kit's wedding. And with the announcement that she and Pendleton were husband and wife, the two of them turned and embraced, kissing each other for all they were worth.

A rousing cheer went up from the groom's side, initiated by Axel Pendleton, and quickly chorused by virtually everyone present. Then Pendleton scooped Kit up into his arms and carried her back down the aisle, under the trellis, across the backyard, and through the back door to Cherrywood. And although he was tempted to just keep on going and not stop until he reached their honeymoon destination of Veranda Bay, St. John, U.S. Virgin Islands, he knew his wife would never forgive him if she didn't have the opportunity to say her proper goodbyes.

So Pendleton made his way into the majestic Mc-Clellan dining room and set his bride down near the buffet. And he was surprised when Kit looked upon him with obvious consternation.

"What?" he asked.

"You know," she began slowly, "why don't we just cut the cake and then beat a hasty retreat?"

He arched his eyebrows in surprise. "You don't want to hang around for your own wedding reception?"

She shook her head. "No. I'd rather go to a hotel and make wild monkey love with my husband for the rest of the day and night."

Pendleton pretended to give that some consideration. "Um, yeah, okay. We could do that."

"Kit! Rocky!"

"After I get rid of my family," he amended when he saw the other Pendletons striding toward them. When he noted that Carny was accompanied only by her son, Joey, he asked, "What? You didn't bring your new boyfriend?"

His sister didn't seem too concerned about the man's absence. "We split up. He was such a wimp. Call me a sexist, but I think a man should just be, you know . . . Manly."

"Oh, look," Kit piped up beside him, pointing toward the main entrance to the dining room, where a very tall, very fit, very blond-and-blue-eyed man stood, his face handsomely lined and tanned from obvious exposure to the elements. "My brother Mick made it after all. He must be fresh off the plane from Zaire. And doubtless, by now, he's feeling very, very manly. Perhaps Carny would like to meet him."

Pendleton chuckled. "Perhaps she would."

Before he could move to make the introductions,

however, Kit continued blithely, "And Bart brought Donna. How sweet. They're planning to elope tonight. Did you know that?"

He shook his head. "No, I didn't."

"*And*," Kit continued, "observe my brother, Dirk, over yonder."

She pointed to the other side of the room where Professor McClellan stood with a woman who was even taller and broader than he. She was an acquaintance of Bart's, a woman the youngest McClellan son had introduced as a Marine Corps drill instructor.

"Dirk and Matilda are hitting it off really well," Kit noted. "And I think she's exactly the kind of woman he needs, don't you?"

"Could be," Pendleton agreed. "Could be."

"Well, then," she went on in a rush of words, "I think that takes care of just about everything, don't you?"

He thought about that for a moment. "Don't you want to say hello to your brother, Mick?"

Kit raised herself up on tiptoe, fluttered her gloved hand in the air and yelled, "Hello, Mick! Good to have you home!" Then she lowered herself to Pendleton's side and said, "There. Now can we go?"

"Does this mean we can get on with that wild monkey love thing you mentioned?"

Kit nodded eagerly. "Uh-huh."

"Then cut the cake, sweetheart, and let's get out of here."

Without further comment, Kit picked up the beribboned, sterling silver knife that sat beside the enormous, three-tiered, heart-shaped froth of white that was their wedding cake. Then she lopped off a serving for two, wrapped it in a linen napkin, and spun around to face her husband.

"I'm ready when you are."

"Let's do it."

The couple turned to the guests, the last of whom were making their way into the dining room, and lifted their hands in farewell.

"See y'all later!" Kit called.

"Yeah, we're outta here!" Pendleton added.

As their guests gazed at them in complete befuddlement, Kit snatched her bouquet from where she had laid it on the buffet, and lobbed it into the air. Pausing only long enough to see it descend beautifully into Faith Ivory's hands, she turned to her husband again.

"I love you," she said.

"I love you, too," he told her.

And that, she knew, was all that mattered. So, turning their backs on everything else in the world, Mr. and Mrs. Pendleton beat a hasty retreat. They paused at the front door for another lengthy kiss, then, laughing, made their way out to the little roadster parked in front—the one that was decorated with a slew of tin cans tied to strings, a homemade sign announcing their newly married state, and a bumper sticker that read I LOVE MY TATTOO FROM TATTOO CHARLIE'S. As the motor revved and they lurched away from Cherrywood, Kit turned to gaze upon her husband.

And as she leaned over to brush her lips across his cheek, she murmured, "You're my man, Pendleton. You're my man."

Dear Reader,

If you're looking for a sensuous, utterly romantic historical love story, then look no further than November's Avon Romantic Treasure *So Wild a Kiss* by Nancy Richards-Akers. It's filled with all the unforgettable passion you're looking for! A young woman needs protection and help to keep her family together, so her little brothers and sisters arrange for her to drink a love potion—and it seems to work when a dashing man enters her life...and steals her heart.

There's nothing like a sexy lawman to steal a working woman's heart, and in Cait London's Avon Contemporary romance debut, *Three Kisses*, you'll meet Michael Bearclaw, the strongest man in Lolo, Wyoming. He sweeps Cloe Matthews off her feet...and together they discover the secrets of Lolo. Learn why *New York Times* bestselling author Jayne Ann Krentz calls Cait, "...An exciting, distinctive voice."

Lovers of historical westerns won't want to miss the latest in Rosalyn West's exciting series, *The Men of Pride County: The Rebel.* A former Confederate soldier travels west, and finds love in the arms of a Union colonel's daring daughter.

And Danelle Harmon's delicious de Monteforte brothers make another appearance in *The Beloved One*. An English officer spirits a young American woman to his English home, only to discover he feels much, much more for her than he ever dreamed.

You'll find the very best romance here at Avon Books. Until next month, happy reading!

Lucia Macro

Lucia Macro
Senior Editor

AEL 1098

Discover Contemporary Romances
at Their Sizzling Hot Best
from Avon Books

SIMPLY IRRESISTIBLE *by Rachel Gibson*
79007-6/$5.99 US/$7.99 Can

LETTING LOOSE *by Sue Civil-Brown*
72775-7/$5.99 US/$7.99 Can

IF WISHES WERE HORSES *by Curtiss Ann Matlock*
79344-X/$5.99 US/$7.99 Can

IF I CAN'T HAVE YOU *by Patti Berg*
79554-X/$5.99 US/$7.99 Can

BABY, I'M YOURS *by Susan Andersen*
79511-6/$5.99 US/$7.99 Can

TELL ME I'M DREAMIN' *by Eboni Snoe*
79562-0/$5.99 US/$7.99 Can

BEDROOM EYES *by Hailey North*
79895-6/$5.99 US/$7.99 Can

W'eve got love on our minds at

http://www.AvonBooks.com

Vote for your favorite hero in <u>"He's the One."</u>

Take a romance trivia quiz, or just <u>"Get a Little Love."</u>

Look up today's date in romantic history in <u>"Datebook."</u>

Subscribe to our monthly e-mail <u>newsletter</u> for all the buzz on upcoming romances.

Browse through our list of new and upcoming titles and read <u>chapter excerpts.</u>

Avon Romances—
the best in exceptional authors and unforgettable novels!